Covert-Ops: The Legacy

Steve Barker

Published in 2024 by

GREEN CAT BOOKS

19 St Christopher's Way

Pride Park

Derby DE24 8JY

www.green-cat.shop

ACKNOWLEDGEMENTS

Thank you to
George James
Simon Munnery
Derek Barker
George Holland
Joshua Standen
Ricky Tyson

for their help with this book

Purchase the Covert-Ops box set for a great price.

www.green-cat.shop/steve-barker

Contents

Chapter One – The Message 5

Chapter Two - Contact.. 19

Chapter Three - Arrival at Bonaire 34

Chapter Four - Contact... 49

Chapter Five - Lucas' House.. 63

Chapter Six - Arrival on St Kitts................................... 80

Chapter Seven - Information 91

Chapter Eight – Café Calypso....................................... 106

Chapter Nine - Weapons Collection 123

Chapter Ten - Entrapment 138

Chapter Eleven - Alex Acosta Cartel 152

Chapter Twelve - Unexpected....................................... 164

Chapter Thirteen - Intel 177

Chapter Fourteen - Night Recce................................... 193

Chapter Fifteen - The Plan 210

Chapter Sixteen- The Rescue 223

Chapter Seventeen - Escape And Evasion 242

Chapter Eighteen - The Crossing 258

Chapter Nineteen - Landing On Oranjestad 274

Chapter Twenty – Pursuit... 292

Chapter Twenty-One – Journey Home 306

Glossary 325

Chapter One – The Message

Back home on the Isle of Wight, it's 13:00. Lucy and I have just returned from the local boozer when my phone rings. I'm sitting on the edge of my seat, wondering who wants some part of me today. As Lucy is closer than me to the phone, she reaches over and picks up my mobile.

"Hello?" Lucy's vocal cords quiver with anticipation.

"Lucy," a familiar yet chilling voice says on the other end of the line "It's Simon. I need to talk to Steve. It's a matter of the utmost importance."

She hands me the phone. "It's Simon, and I think something is wrong."

At that moment, the room appears to hang in suspended animation, the atmosphere electric with tension. This one conversation could change our lives forever. It sends shivers running down my spine as I take the receiver from Lucy's trembling hand.

"Steve," Simon begins, "I need you to stay calm. I have some unsettling news, and I don't want you to lose it before I can explain everything." Something about the tone of Simon's voice tells me this is no ordinary call. Simon is not one to panic; whatever he says must be grave. After placing the mobile on speakerphone so Lucy can hear the conversation, my jaw clenches as I struggle to keep my composure, "Alright, Simon. Tell me what the fuck is going on."

Simon's voice wavers as if even he is finding it difficult to control his emotions. "I received a letter this morning. It's handwritten and pushed through my letterbox. It has your name on it, Steve. Because it was delivered to me instead of you, I sensed something must be wrong before reading it."

A wave of dread washes over me, and my mind races to comprehend the gravity of his words. How did I end up on a note given to Simon, and what could it contain that would be so disturbing?

"What does it say, Simon?" I manage to croak out, my throat dry with apprehension.

The few seconds of silence stretches for what appears like an eternity before Simon speaks again; his voice is calm and strained. "The letter... it's a ransom demand from someone called Acosta. It says they have Abbie and Bethanie. Steve, your daughters have been taken."

The world appears to spin out of control, each word Simon utters sending shockwaves and anger through my veins. My grip on the phone tightens, and my knuckles turn white. How did this happen? Who would dare lay their hands on my girls?

"And, Steve," Simon adds with a tremor in his voice, "there's something more. Something that will send chills down your spine. The letter came in a blue-striped envelope, like the ones that kept popping up after our assignment on St Halb a few years back. It's addressed to you."

My mind races, trying to piece together the fragments of this macabre puzzle. Someone from our past is out for retribution and has targeted us, using my daughters as pawns in their game of vengeance.

As Simon's words echo in my ears, I can sense the rage boiling inside me, threatening to consume me. But years of military training say I must be strong and stay composed, so I soon manage to put my emotions away for now. This is something I always tell people we meet on assignments. It's a lot easier to do if you don't have a personal connection.

The time for these people to suffer will come soon enough. For Abbie and Bethanie, I will do whatever it takes to bring them back home, safe and unharmed. I don't care who I hurt or kill on the way; I will find the ones responsible, and I will make them pay. This is a battle I cannot afford to lose.

"Simon, does it say where they are being held?" I say after a few moments, letting the logical part of my brain kick in.

"No, It says they will be in touch again tomorrow by telephone."

"Have you been in contact with George?"

"He's with me now, booking the ferry tickets. We'll arrive in West Cowes in two hours and then take a taxi to the park. Do you want me to contact Derek?" says Simon, regaining his usual composure.

"No, I will call him straight after we finish. Before you come over, call Katie and Cody and give them a list of stuff we will need."

I place the phone on the table and stroll over to the window to join Lucy, who is staring out across the field. The hairs on my neck start to stand up, accompanied by a sensation of numbness, which is now flushing through my body once more, my mind running in all directions.

The voice of reason, Lucy, grabs my hand. "Whoever this is, they will pay with their lives. But before we do anything, you better contact the girls and make sure this isn't someone testing our reactions."

Without saying a word, I walk back to the mobile phone, pick it up, and dial Abbie's number. No answer. I try Bethanie, but nobody answers. After several calls with no answer, I call their brother, Hadley and ask him to check if anyone is home. While I'm doing this, Lucy dials Derek's number.

The telephone rings four times before Derek comes on the line, "Hi, Lucy, what's up? You and the boys are coming over to St Bethanie?"

"Sorry, not this time. We need you to come here. We have a major issue. Some idiots have kidnapped Steve's daughters," says Lucy, her breathing now calm and slow, as though she is preparing to take a distant sniper headshot.

After taking a few seconds for the message to sink in, "What the fuck? Who are they, and why, Lucy?"

"I don't have all the details, apart from a letter that was delivered to Simon in an envelope with a blue stripe down the middle saying something about revenge for the death of someone called Henry. They will call tomorrow at 12:00. Simon and George are on their way over."

"Tell Steve I'm on my way. If everything goes according to plan, I will be with you tomorrow — if I can catch the first flight out of here."

"Thanks, Derek. Should have more elements by the time you arrive."

In the meantime, I call Hadley and ask him to visit Abbie and Bethanie's houses to try to find them and report back to me as soon as he has any information.

By now, my tactical brain is kicking in. Gone are the instant emotions of anger and guilt at putting my kids in this situation, replaced by how we will bring them back. Lucy and I spend the next hour checking and packing our equipment for wherever this mission will take us. It's not long before my mobile rings. The name on the screen is Hadley. I brace myself for the worst.

"Hi, son, what did you find? Please tell me you located them."

"Sorry, I went to Abbie's first. The house had been ransacked, with furniture thrown across the room. It looked like a bomb had gone off. I found her children crouched in the corner of the room, crying and shouting for their mum. So I took them with me to Bethanie's. The same had happened at her house. Luck was in, as James returned from work while I was looking around Bethanie's house, so I left all the kids with him. I'm now on my way to your house. I want to help get my sisters back."

"OK, I'll see you when you arrive. You may spot Simon and George on the ferry," I reply.

Two hours later, George and Simon enter my lodge with rage etched on their faces. Over the years, they have become acquainted with my entire family and treated them as close friends— something I will rely on. This is a mission where lives are at stake, and no money will change hands. They, too, have come prepared for the task at hand and brought their kit with them. After dropping their stuff off in the bedroom, they sit on the vacant sofa.

In an attempt to keep myself busy, I grab several cold beers from the fridge and pass them out before taking the envelope from Simon. Read through the letter, trying to spot any signs or slip-ups from the person who wrote it that might give away their location, such as postmarks, stamps, etc.

The fact there isn't any indicates we are dealing with people who know what they are doing. More important, for now, as it was hand delivered, they must be in the UK. Which, with any luck, our meetings, or the first one, at least, will be local, hopefully in Southampton or close by.

This means that we won't have to travel far to the meeting. Plus, I can take along the 9mm pistols from our last mission, which I have stashed in the hide under the bush close to the front door, without worrying about customs officials at the airport.

The worst thing about the present situation is that we can do nothing but wait until they make contact tomorrow at 12:00. It's this lack of action that is building up within us, and the room is quiet. Everyone is sitting, speechless, their eyes fixed on me, waiting for me to say or do something.

"I take it you didn't see anyone deliver the letter, Simon?" I say, breaking the silence.

"No, sorry, mate. I even asked my neighbours if they saw something or someone unusual approaching my house. As always, we live on a busy street, but nobody spots anything."

After taking a swig of my beer, "Yep, some people are blind to what's happening around them."

Half an hour later, there is a knock on the door. Lucy gets up and opens it. It is Hadley.

"Come in, son, grab a drink and plonk your arse down with the rest of them," I say, pointing towards where Simon and George are sitting.

"Who has them, Dad?" says Hadley, handing me something. "I found this on the floor of Abbie's house. It looked out of place, as Abbie doesn't like driving out of Totton, and they wouldn't deliver that far."

Hadley gives me a torn scrap of cardboard from an Indian restaurant in Northam. This little snippet of information could be helpful if the meeting, which, if the players stick to the normal routine in these situations. It will take place within the next 24 hours. If it is in any part of Southampton, we have an advantage.

"At last, we have something to go on," I say, passing it to George.

After examining it, "It could be, Steve, but we do not have much to go on until they call again tomorrow. As it's now 17:00, how about we go down or, in your case, back to the local boozer for something to eat? If nothing else, it will take everyone's mind off things for a while. "

Once we are ready, I leave via the front door with Lucy. I walk 100 metres away and stop. I turn around and glance back in the direction of the lodge, to check that nobody is watching or about to tail us. Over in the far corner of the car park, a man wearing what appears to be jeans and a blue bomber jacket is leaning at the wooden fence, talking on the phone. Is this just an innocent person, or something different? We will find out in the next few minutes.

As planned, the rest wait a short time before leaving and following me and Lucy. Now, if the man does follow me, which I hope he does, the team will be behind him, watching his every move.

Halfway to Shanklin High Street, my mobile vibrates in my pocket. On the screen is a message from Simon: 'You are being followed'. This must be the man we saw earlier, so there is no need to glance back- I know what he looks like. I tap a reply: 'Roger, monitor him and what he does'.

I take the next right, down the alleyway between the café and W H Hurt, leading to the parking area. Two minutes later, we make a left turn at the end of the alley. Then take up a position concealed by a small concrete wall behind the buildings and wait to find out what the man does.

A few minutes pass before he appears. On most occasions, this is where I would grab the arsehole and beat the crap out of them until they tell me the information I need. But the car park is too open with no secluded corners to take him to. So, for now, I leave him to wander off to try to pick us back up again. Another piece of the puzzle of who has my girls clicks into place.

By the time we catch up with the rest, they are waiting on the patio near the entrance to the boozer.

"Thanks for coming to help us." I say.

"Stop whining, you green numpty. Sure you and Lucy would have dealt with the situation if required. Talking of which, where did he go?" says George, heading for the wooden door leading into the pub.

"We left him to wander off; he will probably stick his head in here looking for us," says Lucy, before following George inside.

The place is quiet, with only a few patrons scattered around. Some are sat at the bar, staring down at their half-filled glasses, trying not to stare at anyone. Another group of five people is sitting at the far end of the room near the back door. I glance over to my right, in the direction of an open fire and our favourite spot, the two brown leather sofas, which are unoccupied.

"You lot take a seat while, Hadley and I grab some beers," I say as the rest, as if on autopilot, are already heading for the sofas.

As I approach the bar, Gary enters from the stockroom, "You back again, Steve?" he says.

"Yep, come for some scran with the riffraff," I point towards the others.

"No problem, I'll bring the menu over in a moment. You want your normal round of drinks?"

"Yes please."

Once back with the beers, I place the tray on the small coffee table that separates the two sofas before plonking my arse down next to Lucy. Soon, Gary appears, detecting by our mood something must be up.

He asks, "You lot appear like someone's killed your granny. What's up?"

I've known Gary for some time now. He helped us several times on our past missions, so he can be trusted. After he pulls up a chair, I explain what is going on. From his appearance, he is as angry as the rest of us.

He met the girls numerous times when they came to the Isle of Wight to see me and Lucy. After telling us that if there is anything we need him to do, we only have to ask, he returns to the kitchen to check on our food.

One thing you can count on in life is that a veteran will always try to break up any awkward silence with sarcasm. With that in mind, Simon says,

"Tell me, you green numpty, have you been living like a hobo and kipping rough in the woods?"

"Yes, Lucy and I went out over the downs last weekend. We found some trees and bashered up. A great sensation of freedom. Something you can't appreciate, you donkey walloper, due to your love of sleeping in a tin can."

"I can't argue with that, more room to store the beer; talking of which, who wants refills?" comes the reply from Simon.

The instance Simon returns with the beers, his phone starts ringing. After a couple of minutes of listening to Simon having a one-way conversation, he hangs up and takes a drink from the half-filled glass in front of him.

"That was Katie. They have primed up their contacts around the Caribbean. I made an educated guess about where the people holding the girls would be located, due to the envelope and its connection with St Bethanie. The best part is, as we are good customers and our mission is personal, they are letting us have what we require for a heavily reduced price, with the remainder to be settled after we have Abbie and Bethanie back home."

"Sounds like everything is starting to come together. Shame we can't go and kick some arse right now," says George, putting down an empty glass.

"We can't do much till after the call tomorrow, when we have more details, and Hadley is out of the way."

"No way am I staying out of this. They are my sisters. Besides, you may need my taekwondo skills in a punch up," says Hadley, annoyed at the suggestion that he monitor from the sidelines.

"OK, you're in until we have to head overseas. But you better stay close to me and do what I tell you. The people we are dealing with will not hesitate to kill you, and no way I'm risking all my kids. Your talents will be needed here, and you can work with someone who has helped us before."

A short time later, Gary appears with the grub. "Here you go, boys, and of course, Lucy. Enjoy."

By the time we finish the meal and several more drinks, it's 22:00, so we decide to leave and head back to my place. Not knowing if the idiot we encountered earlier is still around, Lucy, Hadley, and I exit the building first. Like a good Rifleman, I vary the route.

Instead of the direct way home, I cross over the road, take a left, and follow the footpath. The rest depart five minutes later, taking the route we had discussed prior to leaving. It isn't long before Lucy hands me her phone. It is a text from George. 'Same numpty that followed you earlier is tailing you'.

The man escaped a battering a few hours back when he followed us to the pub, but his luck has now run out. I turn to Lucy and tell her to send the following message: 'At the junction, turn right. I will lead the target to the coastal path. Once we arrive, close in'.

Moments later, we make the turn and head down a narrow alleyway lined with cobblestone-walled buildings. At the end, a faint glow from a street light throws a beam of light onto the tarmac footpath. To our left, a little down the hill, a small alcove juts out facing the English Channel, containing four battered-looking benches. The area is surrounded by high green bushes, making the seats useless for sitting on and looking out to sea, but perfect for what I have in mind.

Our plan is working. Our new friend makes his second fatal mistake this evening. He turns left and heads down towards us. In one swift movement, we turn a charge towards him. Sensing he is in danger, he spins around and tries to sprint back the way he came.

He covers only a short distance before running straight into George and Simon. Acting like a rabbit caught in the glare of headlights beneath the street lamp, the man is confused, not knowing which way to run. The decision is made for him. Simon knocks him hard into the railings.

At the same time, George pins the man's head against the guardrail. Once they have him under control, he's led down to where I'm waiting. I need to ask the arsehole a few polite questions. The cover of the hedgerow and the lack of light in this area should conceal any movement that might attract some nosey bastard to what we are doing. When he arrives, I force him to sit on the front bench facing the sea, with George pinning his arms down and behind the backrest.

For a couple of minutes, we do nothing. The only sound is the waves below lashing the shoreline, and the occasional noise from some sort of nocturnal creature. Not that I didn't know what was coming next, but I want his mind to venture into the dark recesses of his brain, wondering what we were going to do to him.

The eerie silence is broken when I nod to George, who punches the man hard in his face, before we let loose our trained interrogator, Lucy, on him. Lucy moves her face millimetres away from his and blows softly, the cold air condensing her breath as she does. He tries to move his head away, but Simon holds it firm.

"Now, some bad people, who we believe you can tell us who they are, have pissed my friend, here, off," Lucy points at me. "He wants to kill you without you answering any of my questions. Positive that isn't good with you. So talk to me and all will be fine, and you can go on your way." Of course, there is no way this man is leaving here alive, but he doesn't know that yet.

"Don't answer, or try lying to me, you will be swimming face down in the ocean via the cliff behind me. Say yes or grunt if you understand." Lucy moves away to let the message sink in.

The man says nothing. Losing my cool, "This is my daughter's lives on the line, arsehole. And trust me, I'll kill you if you don't give me the information we require."

Simon places his hand over his mouth while George smacks him again, so hard in the stomach that he tries to scream but can't as Simon's hand muffles the sound.

"Shall we try that again? Say yes, so I understand you comprehend what I'm asking you," Lucy asks again.

Once more, there was nothing but silence. "Grab his arms and legs, boys, and let's toss him over the cliff," I say, my patience running out.

With him struggling and fighting for his life, we move him closer to the hedgerow before picking him off the floor.

"Last chance, arsehole," I say, after moving my head towards his left ear.

"OK, put me down and I'll tell you everything, if you promise to release me and allow me to leave here unharmed," comes the plea of a person on the edge of meeting his demise.

"You have my word, scouts honour," I say with some menace.

"Someone called me — I don't know who — and offered to pay me two grand if I watched you and reported back to them if you tried to catch a ferry off the island in the next 36 hours. That's all I have."

"Hand me the number of who you are to contact, or it's flying lessons for you," says Lucy, back in the man's face.

"I don't have it on me. It's back at my house; I can take you or give you the address." His slow, deep breaths and anguish in his voice are now more noticeable than our own.

I move closer to our friend. "This is your fault. You have put me in a position where I have two issues. First, I can't be bothered to search for an address, which I'm sure will be false. Second, I was never in the Boy Scouts. Grab him, boys."

Without saying another word, the man, once more struggling and pleading for his life, is tossed over the hedge down onto the tarmac below. The usual course of action would be to check the person is dead before leaving the scene, but in this case, there would be no way anyone would survive the fall. If he did, for some divine intervention, prevail, then he deserves to live.

"Dad, doesn't that bother you that you've just killed a man?" asks Hadley.

"Hadley, let's put it this way. First, he has connections with the people who have your sisters. If we had let him live, he would be straight on the phone to whoever paid him to let them know we have a lead. Second, due to my PTSD, I have a lack of empathy, so I don't care. Welcome to our world."

By the time we arrive back at the lodge, it's late, so everyone goes straight to bed, to be fresh for whatever tomorrow brings. I can't sleep with the thoughts of my girls alone, kept hostage by some cartel out for revenge on something that happened a long time ago.

The signs were always present if we had thought about it. Something like this would happen. It was only a question of time.

We had all seen them. Envelopes with blue stripes have followed us around the world. This is my fault Abbie and Bethanie are being held and what nightmare they are now going through.

Sensing I can't sleep, Lucy moves closer, wrapping her arm across my chest, her head resting on the pillow beside mine.

"Try to rest. We will bring them back in one piece. Remember, they are your daughters, so it's the captors I feel sorry for," she says in a soothing voice.

Due to my PTSD and the lack of empathy, it's rare for me to show physical emotions, but this changes everything. This time, it is personal; they have my girls.

"You are right, of course, night, honey."

Chapter Two - Contact

It goes to say I had a crap night with not much sleep and laid awake most of the night thinking about today's call. By 04:30, I gave up and headed for the front room to make myself a brew.

The first rays of morning creep through the windows, casting a faint light on the living room of my lodge. Shadows dance across the room, mocking my frantic state. I sit on the sofa facing the window. My eyes are bloodshot, exhaustion etched into every line of my weathered face.

In the semi-darkness, time moves at a snail's pace as I sit, staring at my phone, wishing for it to ring; and it is either Abbie or Bethanie saying they are back home. Every tick of the clock echoes in my ears, each second like an eternity.

My thoughts are a tumultuous whirlwind, an amalgamation of fear, frustration, and determination. I relive every moment leading up to this agonising present, questioning every decision, every choice that has brought us to this point. How has it come to this? How have I failed to protect my own children?

From the back of the lodge, I catch a faint sound, almost imperceptible, of someone stirring from their slumber. It has an unmistakable gait, a rhythm true only to her. I can almost detect the sound of her footsteps drawing nearer. The floorboards creak under her weight. It's Lucy. Lifting the cup I am still holding onto, I swallow the bitter dregs of the forgotten coffee.

I sense the tender touch of two hands resting on my shoulders. "Morning, honey. Would you like a fresh brew?"

"Yes, please, Lucy."

"I take it you didn't sleep well, as you were up at daft o'clock," says Lucy, sitting beside me on the sofa. She passes me a fresh brew before holding her white mug with both hands.

"Yeah, not much, but rest can wait until we have the girls back," I say, taking a sip of coffee.

Thirty minutes later, George and Hadley appear through the door that separates the living room from the bedrooms, followed by Simon. It appears they're all suffering the same lack of sleep as me.

"You receive any calls through the night, Steve?" says George.

"No, wish I had, but there isn't anything we can do until later, at 12:00," comes my reply, getting up and heading for the kitchen, where Lucy is preparing a full English breakfast.

Twenty minutes later, "Right, you lot. I hope it is true that an army fights on a full stomach as I've made enough brekkie to feed one," says Lucy, carrying several plates to the table.

"I'm not sure about an army, but fat boy does," Simon says, pointing at me.

"Do one, you skinny twat," I reply.

With breakfast out of the way, we brainstorm every possible scenario for any physical contact. Who will make contact, and where will any lookouts be located? We break down what we already have from the letter, the man who took a short walk off the cliff, and a scrap of cardboard Hadley found.

The first contact would have to be somewhere on the island or in Southampton. It will have to be busy, with an abundance of people around and with lots of witnesses for the safety of the person making the contact, in case we try to take them out when we have the information we need. The most logical location would be in a shopping centre with plenty of people and quiet areas for such a meeting.

The next strategy would be us being told to go to a drop box again. This would have to be in a public place so they could monitor our movements and ensure not only do we pick up the parcel, but no one else takes it. Our position would be the same with two people, Hadley and me, collecting the package while the rest try to spot anyone paying attention to our movements.

The final method would be just a call telling us to send money via a bank account; if this happens, we are fucked. They will have done their homework, know how much money we can raise, and ask for double. This is the less likely option, as the letter delivered to Simon mentions revenge for Henry. This makes it personal, and they will want to see us suffer and die. To do this, they need to get us to someplace.

As we start to wrap up, there is a knock on the door, and it is flung open. We are not expecting anyone, as Derek will not be here until this afternoon, so we all take up defensive positions. Two bags are thrown through the door. I pull the cushions from the sofa over Hadley and me, waiting for them to explode.

A figure stands in the doorway laughing out loud; it's Derek. "What's up with you idiots? Never seen George move so fast."

"What the fuck, Derek! You scared the crap out of us all," I say, getting up off the floor and replacing the pillows.

"Yep, because terrorist scum always knocks before throwing bombs at people," replies Derek, walking over to the table and sitting down.

"I didn't think you were here until this afternoon," says Lucy, sitting at the table beside him.

"I wasn't, but you said they are calling today at 12:00, so I managed to board an earlier and quicker flight from St Bethanie. Plus, I have some new equipment to help when they contact you again."

I join him and Lucy at the dining table. "I'm glad you're here, mate. What is this kit you brought?"

Derek walks over to his bag, pulls out a computer, lifts the lid, and enters a password before spinning the laptop around to face Lucy and me. By this time, the rest of the team have joined us and is looking at the screen, fascinated. Derek then explains the software can track the position of any incoming calls. All it takes is for them to be on the line for 60 seconds. Plus, if they are close enough to us, within a mile, we can pinpoint their location with a tolerance of only two metres.

By the time Derek finishes his explanation, it is 11:35, and the call from the people holding Abbie and Bethanie is only 25 minutes away. I hand him my mobile, which he connects to the laptop. Now, all the conversations will go through the software and be tracked and recorded, allowing us to listen again once the conversation is over. We might detect something in the background that can tell us where they are calling from, if they are more than a mile from our location.

Only five more minutes to go. We move back to the living area. The countdown from the final minute begins. My heart starts pounding as the laptop on the coffee table comes to life with a shrill ring. I exchange a glance with Lucy, her eyes filled with dread. This is it – the call we've been waiting for – the call from the kidnappers who have my precious daughters, Abbie and Bethanie, holding them hostage.

I take a deep breath, trying to steady my trembling hands, as Derek clicks the accept button. "Remember, you need to keep them talking for at least 60 seconds."

The voice on the other end lacks any human inflexion; its mechanical tone sends a shiver down my spine. It's an artificial intelligence, cold and calculating — perhaps their choice of messenger to distance themselves from the heinous act they're committing and us.

"You are aware, we have your daughters," the robotic voice states matter-of-factly, its chilling melody grating against my senses. "You have until 16:00 today to be at the Marlands shopping centre. Wait by the lifts," the voice instructs, devoid of any emotion. "Another telephone call will come through with further instructions."

"What's the ransom?" I ask in a tone that betrays my anger, the knot in my throat making it hard to speak.

The message repeats itself, so we know it's a recording. I ask another question, and even though I will receive the same answer, I need to keep the call going for Derek to locate where it is coming from.

The screen blinks off, leaving us in a vacuum of silence and anticipation. Time is against us, the seconds ticking away. At least we can now start the mission underway.

"Derek, tell me you got the location."

"The only information we can tell is that the call originated in Southampton. It is too far away to pinpoint the exact location. Let's listen to the message again and see if we can detect anything."

We listen to the recording several times, not hearing anything until Hadley says, "Stop, go back a few seconds. I detected something in the background, but it's faint." Derek then plays back the recording, one section at a time.

"There, I hear this all the time from my house. It's a cruise ship horn," says Hadley.

"Well spotted, son. At least we now have two bits of information that will come in handy. First, the call came from Southampton, which means whoever has my girls has connections in the city. Second, we have our first meeting point.

As we do not have time to spare, everyone collects their equipment and the five 9mms from the stash, and prepares to drive to East Cowes to catch the ferry to Southampton. Going forward, there is no point in wasting time returning to the island. Any further contacts and travel will be away from Southampton.

When we arrive at the Red Funnel kiosk in East Cowes, we are in luck. The Osprey is pulling into port. Within no time, we are sitting on 'A' deck, tucked away in one of the corners, away from the dozens of other people on the same boat. The moment the ship departs, we start making plans for the second contact.

The Marlands has two floors. The top level is reached by an escalator at one end near the CEX electronic and DVD exchange shop, or via the lift close to Savers, a health and beauty establishment. There is also a set of stairs at the entrance to Southampton High Street. The good news for us is that the Marlands only has three entry/exit points, all on the ground floor.

When I'm sure nobody can listen in on our conversation, "Here is the plan. We should arrive by 15:30 at the latest. This will give us plenty of time before the meeting to sweep the centre, looking for anyone or anything that appears out of place. With your years of military training, this shouldn't be a problem. Try to spot any people acting like they are up to no good. They are easy to recognise by the fact they are trying not to look out of place."

"Take it you and Hadley will be the ones waiting by the lifts, Steve?"

"Yes, Simon. If it all goes wrong and we need to fight our way out, we may require Hadley's particular set of skills. As we know, George doesn't like the cold and will wiggle like a big baby if he is put outside. Can you take the High Street exit point? Position yourself where you can see the entrance and the stairs behind the fruit and veg stall…"

I'm interrupted, " That's a fucking lie."

"That's true, George, unless your sorry arse is out in the cold, and we are all inside. Remember New York?" replies Derek with a stupid grin.

"Do one, numpty," comes the reply from George.

"Before you idiots stopped me, Lucy, if you take the entry point by CEX, you will see a small café with tables and chairs in the mall. From here, you will be able to monitor both the exit and the escalators. That leaves George to man the Portland Terrace Road entrance near the pawnbrokers. Derek, find somewhere close to Hadley and me to set up your laptop and ensure it is running. If they are here, you can pinpoint them. You will be the closest to Hadley and me, ready to provide our aid if required. We will be sitting on the brick wall that surrounds the lifts. Any questions?"

By the time we have departed the ferry, parked the vehicle, and arrived in the Marlands, it is 15:30. This gives us 30 minutes to sweep the area and for everyone to be in position. Inside is an array of stores selling everything from greeting cards to perfume. Each shop window is decorated to invite customers in to purchase their goods.

The centre would be quiet if it weren't for the hum of conversations by a few shoppers going about their business. A whiff of the aroma of therapy scents comes from a stall set up in the space between shops. The lights that hang from the ceiling illuminate the place. I check in with the team via the earpiece radios Derek brought from St Bethanie. So far, nobody is sticking out. I glance down at Mickey on my wrist. The time is 15:51, time for Hadley and me to wait close to the lifts.

Everyone is in position at all the exits and waits in tense anticipation. The atmosphere crackles with anxiety, thickened by the knowledge that time is fast running out. I lower myself onto the brick wall surrounding the lifts to the first floor, with the weight of the situation settling on my shoulders. Beside me, Hadley shares my unease; his eyes scan the near-deserted centre.

My training has me scanning every person who walks past, checking their clothing for any bulges that might conceal a weapon. Any sign of coiled wires leading up through the collar of their tops to their ears indicates a radio is in use. Do they have any disabilities or weak spots we can manipulate if they need taking down?

Yet again, I peer at my wristwatch—one minute to go. My hand grips my phone, my fingers clenching so hard around it that my knuckles turn white. I can't help but wonder what fresh horror awaits us. The first call had necessitated this crude game of cat and mouse, and now, we brace ourselves for the second act.

At last, the telephone springs to life, filling the quietness with its jarring ringtone. I answer with a tone that betrays my true feelings. I need to make whoever is on the line believe I will do whatever they say with a sense of panic in my tone. I need to make them think they have me under control and will do anything they say. Of course, I will, but not in the way they are hoping for. My nerves pulse through me like an electric current. On the other end, a distorted, menacing, chilling to the core tone.

"You have my attention. Where are my girls?" I ask, looking around for someone on a mobile phone.

The same robotic voice as earlier says, "I'm glad you're here and sitting on the wall. Listen to what I have to say. Go to the information desk situated between the two sets of escalators. You will find a white envelope on the bottom shelf with a blue stripe running down the middle—you know the type I mean. Inside, you will discover a set of instructions. You have five minutes."

I grab Hadley on the shoulder, "Follow me."

Walking as fast as I can without breaking into a run, I race towards the info desk. As I move, I tap my radio, "Anyone seen anything? If not, stay put. They must be here somewhere; they knew me and Hadley were sitting on the wall. They may try to leave in a rush."

When I arrive at the white wooden information kiosk, my racing heart intensifies its rhythm, urging me to hurry. The blue-striped envelope rests on the bottom shelf, bathed in artificial light. I reach for it, aware that every second counts. I lean against the counter. Printed on the outside are the words, 'Well done, you now have the instructions for your next move. Make sure you are there in the next 56 hours'.

Again, I press the mic, "They are watching us. Anyone seen them?"

There is radio silence until Lucy spots something out of place. "It may be nothing, but why take the chance? The CCTV camera pointing at the escalators appears to be following you."

Thinking as I run, I press the transmit button of the radio, "Derek, make your way to the centre's office. It is on the second floor in the far-left corner near the toy shop. Hurry. The rest stay in location."

When Hadley and I arrive, Derek is running towards us from the direction of the lifts. Without stopping, we barge in. A lone woman dressed in a white shirt is sitting at a grey metal and glass desk, now frightened by our entrance. Behind her is a row of television screens showing scenes from around the centre. Making sure we can't be seen by any camera pointing at the woman for her protection and not giving her time to regain her composure, I yell,

"Who monitors the cameras, and have you been watching us?"

27

She has lost control of her body, which is now starting to shake. In a trembling voice, "No, and they are monitored from a secure location somewhere off-site. Don't hurt me."

My anger and frustration grab hold of me as I slam my fist down on her desk.

"You better not be lying to me, bitch?" The woman still sitting behind the desk shakes her head.

"She knows fuck all, mate. Let's leave before the police turn up," says Derek, heading for the door.

"All call signs meet at the exit to the high street; we have another drop box to go to," I say through my radio.

By the time Derek, Hadley, and I arrive at the meeting point, the rest are already waiting. I take out the envelope from my jacket pocket and open it.

"What does it say?" Hadley asks.

"We need to go to the Amazon collection boxes in West Quay. There is a code to open a particular box, and the code expires in one hour."

Shit, we are not dealing with any normal unorganised group here. They know what they are doing and ensure they cover all their tracks. With any luck, this will be the last one before we find out where they are holding Abbie and Bethanie.

From what we saw at the last drop box, there will be nobody around, so there is no need to use any tactics to try to spot someone. With that in mind, we walk through the busy shopping centre as a group. At the top of the escalators, turn left on the food hall level.

We arrive at the Amazon lockers, tucked away out of the line of sight from most people, with time to spare. I take out the note and enter the code into the control panel. A door to my right springs open.

Once more, inside is another envelope larger than the previous ones, but still with the blue stripe running down the middle.

I rejoin the others, who are now sitting at the long blue wooden table behind me. I pry open the top and pull out the contents. Inside is a map showing some disused buildings and tennis courts. Next to them is a vast lake. On the edge of an inlet from the sea are the words, 'Harbour Village Beach Hotel and Marina, Bonaire. Be here in 56 hours. There you will meet a man called Lucas'.

Also, another note saying, 'If you still haven't got the drift of what is happening, you killed my uncle, Henry in London and disrupted our local business. If you do not come to your final meeting point, your daughters will not only be killed, but they will suffer in the process. No doubt you still don't believe what is happening, so you can speak to them at 19:00 UK time tonight for one minute. Call late, and the number will be disconnected'.

"What the fuck! Better head for the airport," says Simon, taking the letter from me.

Lucy grabs my hand. "We will bring them back. But for the sake of those here who still don't know or cannot remember who Henry is or what business he is in, can you tell us?"

"Sure I've explained this before, but a few years back, Henry paid Simon, George, and I to go to an island called St Halb, which is close to where Derek lives. Our mission was to remove a drug cartel that had taken up residence on his property. To start with, the mission went without too many issues. In the end, we killed everyone on the property, stole his expensive wine, and left. This is where we found out we had been double-crossed."

"What happened?"

"We found out that Henry was the boss of the entire organisation, and he had sent us to the island to get rid of one of his henchmen, who was out of control and trying to take over the business for himself. Back in England, we travelled to London to see Henry, confront him and collect the rest of the money he owed us for the job. This is where things went bad. Instead of giving us the money, he tried to do a runner, resulting in him being shot in an alleyway behind his business."

"Sure did; the bastard got what was coming to him," adds George.

Still holding the map, "Because of this, he has taken the girls in an attempt to make us pay."

"Thanks for reminding us. But what is the connection between this envelope and Henry?" asks Lucy.

"It keeps appearing through every mission we carry out that has any connection with drug cartels—thinking back once, a letter in one envelope did mention something about Henry and one of his relatives taking over the cartel after the killing of Henry. The envelope must be the link between cartels. Like a company trademark. It makes you think there could be an overall boss that links them all. "

"Makes me want to put a bullet in the people who took Abbie and Bethanie," says Lucy, taking the letter from Simon.

Before heading for the airport, we drop Hadley off at his house. "Hadley, we will retrieve your sisters. Here is what I want you to do. Call this number; it is Gary, who you met at the pub yesterday. Whoever did this will still have contacts in Southampton. Find them and extract as much information as you can. You may have to beat some people up to obtain the info. You still want in?"

"Yes, you can count on me, Dad. When we have something, I will contact you."

On the way to the airport, George calls a friend named Billy, who owns his own travel business and manages to purchase tickets and get us on the next flight to Bonaire.

The car is parked in the long-stay parking area before catching the bus to terminal five. As we step into the terminal, we are welcomed by a cacophony of chattering travellers, announcements over the intercom, and the click-clack of rolling suitcases echoing through the expansive terminal.

The scent of cuisine wafts through the air, mingling with the distinct aroma of freshly brewed coffee. The flashing screen provides constant visual stimulation, displaying flight information and destinations to and from every corner of the world. Vivid advertisements projected in vibrant colours bring the terminal to life. Each entices passengers with a promise of luxury, experiences and adventure.

As we navigate the labyrinth of the many airport procedures, my mind is a wave of emotions that I try to keep in check. I owe it to my girls to stay strong and focused if I am to bring them out alive. So, I push them aside.

At last, we reach the business lounge, our oasis away from all the chaos outside. It is a sanctuary of calm where we can eat, drink, and take a breath until the kidnappers make contact at 19:00. After taking drinks from the help-yourself fridges, we find a quiet corner close to the window overlooking the runway. We've been here that many times over the years, the place has a strange, welcoming atmosphere to it.

I glance at the clock at the bottom of the flight information screen. It reads 18:30. I stare at it for a few seconds, trying to urge time to move along with my mind. Each second ticks by with unbearable slowness. I peer down at my phone on the small coffee table in front of me.

Willing the arseholes who are holding Abbie and Bethanie to call, so I can listen to their voices and prove they are still alive and safe in the situation they find themselves in. I'm comforted in the knowledge my girls can give as much as they take.

I recheck the information board. It is 18:58, two minutes to go. I pick up my phone and hold it in both hands.

Turn to Derek, "Is the laptop switched on and recording?"

"Yes, mate. When they ring to answer the phone, the computer will start recording," says Derek, tapping the laptop lid.

Dead at 19:00, the mobile springs into life, vibrating in my hands. I take a deep breath. This is what I've been waiting for.

My mouth says, "Hello, please now let me speak to my girls," which is the tactical approach, but my mind is saying, 'I want to speak to them, and if they have been injured in any way, you're a dead man walking'.

The voice on the other end echoes through the receiver, cold and calculated. "You have one minute."

With that, I can detect the sound of the phone hitting a metal object. "Hi, Daddy. We are OK. We do not know where we are, but it's hot here, and the sound of parrots and monkeys is a welcome relief."

'That's my girl'. Beth is sending me clues to their location — at least some of the training I gave them growing up sunk in.

A voice in the background shouts out, "Get a move on, bitch, you have 30 seconds."

Then I detect a familiar voice in the background, "Fuck off, idiot. We are talking to our dad, and when he finds you and your family, you will die." It's Abbie.

"OK, Beth, let me talk to Abbie," I say with pride. The girls are giving their captures as much shit as they are receiving.

"Hi, Dad, I'm fine, unlike the idiot over there if I get my hands on him."

"Leave him for me, Abbie. We are on our way and will see you both soon. I love you both."

Before I can say more, the phone clicks off. "Did you record all of that, Derek?"

"Yep, they are your daughters for sure. Can tell by the attitude."

At least they are alive and safe. Now, all we need to do is go and fetch them. The next hour goes a little faster than before I talked to the girls, and it isn't long before the flight information board tells us to go to our boarding gate.

Chapter Three - Arrival at Bonaire

Derek's oversight about our upgraded seats on KLM adds an unexpected twist to our journey, filling me with anticipation and unease. The luxurious surroundings of the business-class cabin appear almost too good, a stark contrast to the dangers that await us at our destination.

Upon stepping onboard, I am instantly surrounded by an aura of sophistication and luxury. The gentle, cosy lighting that fills the cabin induces a sense of comfort, but deep down, I am unable to overcome the premonition of imminent danger.

Seated in my plush leather chair, I take in every detail of my surroundings, my senses on high alert for any sign of trouble. The flight attendant's offer of sparkling wine sounds like a tempting distraction, but I decline, preferring to remain vigilant.

With a quick glance around the cabin, I see the rest of the team settling in, their relaxed demeanour belying the tension that simmers just beneath the surface. I take a moment to pull a photo of the girls from my wallet, a silent reminder of why we're embarking on this perilous journey.

As the cabin crew begins their pre-flight routines and the captain's voice fills the air, detailing our flight plan and the weather forecast, I can't help but feel a sense of foreboding. The reassurance of the welcome message is overshadowed by the knowledge of the dangers that lie ahead.

As the plane taxis down the runway and accelerates towards takeoff, the gentle vibration beneath me is a stark reminder of the gravity of our mission. We may be on our way to Bonaire, but with each passing moment, the stakes grow, and the risks become more intense.

The last two days have caught up with me. I'm soon asleep, only to be woken up by a young lady passing me a menu for an evening meal. I glance down at Mickey on my wrist. I'd been asleep for at least an hour.

With scran out of the way, I walk over to Lucy, who is wearing headphones and busy watching a movie about a group of veterans taking on a group of thugs.

Tapping her on the shoulder, "You, OK, honey?"

Lucy removes her headphones and smiles back at me, "Yes, no problem, watching this to pass the time. How are you holding up?"

"I'm fine, gone past the 'what the fuck' phase and buried my emotion and can now concentrate on the tactical element of getting the girls back. And, of course, killing anyone who gets in my way."

"I'm glad you're back in the right mind for the mission. Now go away. I'm watching the film."

The rest of the flight and the change of planes in Amsterdam go without any issues, and we are soon on the final approach to Bonaire Flamingo Airport.

Stepping off the aircraft, the warm, tropical breeze envelopes me. At the top of the covered walkway, I wait for the others to join me before stepping out onto the pristine floor of the terminal bathed in a golden glow, which casts elongated shadows that dance across the marbled floor.

The terminal is bustling with people eager to explore Bonaire's wonders. The sound of laughter and chatter from locals and tourists fills the air, blending with the melody of steel drums played by a band at one end of the terminal.

As we make our way to passport control and customs, we are welcomed by a sea of smiling faces as we approach the customs counter. The officers' uniforms are spotless and authoritative.

Although I've been through these passport and customs checks more times than I can remember, I'm still overcome with the sense that I'm guilty of something and about to be taken away and forgotten.

Like most people who are close to the control point, waiting their turn, I stand in silence. As I wait, I monitor the officials and can't help but admire their dedication to ensuring a smooth entry process for visitors, so they can enjoy all that Bonaire has to offer.

As we are together, I walk up to the counter with Lucy. The official smiles and welcomes us to Bonaire and takes our passports. Next, there is the reassuring sound of our passports being stamped and the words, "Have a nice stay."

The moment the rest are through, we head for a position at a small café on one side of the terminal, taking up seats at small round metal tables outside, close to a huge glass window to the right of the open doorway. At the same time, Simon goes inside to purchase a round of drinks. I scan the area, looking for anyone or anything that stands out to the trained eye, like a spare prick at a wedding.

Over to my right, the person behind me in the line for customs is standing talking to another man in long blue trousers and a matching t-shirt. He appears to be looking over the man's shoulder in our direction. Over to my left, close to the exit from the terminal, three men are scrutinising everyone who leaves. By the way they are dressed, they are not undercover police. Even these people dress smartly when wearing plain clothes. These people are something else. Could they be here for us? Are they connected to the cartel?

There is only one way to find out. We head for the terminal's exit before making a detour. To ensure we are not being followed, we head up to the second-level departures before coming back down.

The man from the line appears to be following us. In an attempt to confirm, we take the next three lefts in a row. We lose him.

We find another exit point and leave the terminal, entering an oasis of tropical foliage and lush greenery. Several palm trees are swaying in the light breeze. Two parakeets fly past and land in the tree to my right. The unmistakable scent of frangipani teases my senses, infusing the air with an enchanting fragrance.

We head for the taxi rank rather than a car hire establishment. Not only would a taxi get us to the hotel quicker, but also because I don't want an official document showing where we are going on the island, never mind the hire company's vehicle trackers. When we arrive, the vibrant colours of the taxis stand out against the azure sky. Each one is a canvas, giving away the driver's personality. Alongside each vehicle, the driver exchanges friendly banter with the tourists, welcoming them to the island and hoping for their business.

With five of us, we manage to grab a minibus taxi. Its doors are adorned with intricate paintings of the local marine life. Like the other drivers we witness, our driver is no different and welcomes us with a huge smile. He opens the door and invites us to clamber aboard. Once we are all in, he reminds us of the law about wearing seatbelts in Bonaire.

I lean forward, toward the driver and ask, "Can you please take us to the Harbour Beach Hotel?"

"No problem, man. Hold tight, and I'll have you there in no time," the happy reply came.

As we depart, Derek turns around and glances out the rear window before saying. "Someone dressed similar to the people we have just been evading in the terminal has clambered in a taxi a few cars back which has pulled out. They are now a car behind us."

I tap the driver on the shoulder and say, "There is an extra 50 dollars in it if you take the long scenic route and lose the car now two cars back." I want to find out if the cab behind us is tailing us or is just a coincidence.

The new route takes us through the small town centre past the cruise port before we rejoin the busy road. A glance behind confirms that the other vehicle isn't following. We must have lost them in the traffic; either that, or I'm not giving them enough credit. Throughout the journey, Colin, our driver, treats us to a delightful description of his home and Bonaire, accompanied by reggae music blaring from the radio.

The midday sun beats down on us as we step out of the taxi in front of the Village Beach Hotel. A quick scan of the area confirms that the cab that followed us out of the airport wasn't nearby, going on the pictures that adorned every cab. The air is thick with the scent of tropical flowers and the inviting sound of waves crashing against the shoreline.

The reception area is a bustling hub of activity, a microcosm of the vibrant island life. The walls are painted a brilliant shade of turquoise, echoing the sparkling waters just beyond the glass doors. The ceiling fans rotate at a lazy rate, casting a gentle breeze that stirs the air and provides relief from the heat. The floor is tiled in a mosaic of intricate patterns, each tile telling its own story of the island's rich history.

Behind the reception desk stands a smiling young lady, her ebony curls cascading over her shoulders. Her light blue uniform blends seamlessly with the hotel's decor. Her name tag reads 'Jane'.

"Good afternoon!" Jane greets us, her voice a harmonious symphony. "Welcome to the Village Beach Hotel Bonaire. How can I assist you today?"

"Yes, good afternoon. We have two rooms booked for the next two nights," says Derek, showing her the confirmation on his phone.

While Derek and Lucy are checking in, I gaze around the room. To my right is a young couple cuddling on a nearby sofa, their laughter blending in with the melody of the music playing in the background. Several murals depict vibrant underwater scenes, with brightly coloured fish swimming around the corals painted on the walls. Sitting at the bar at the far end are two young men in jeans and t-shirts. I could be paranoid due to the situation, but they seem to be watching us. If they are, we will deal with them later.

At the reception desk, Jane hands Lucy the room keycards with another warm, inviting smile. "Enjoy your stay. Let me know if I can help you with anything."

I grab one of the luggage trollies near the door and throw everyone's bag on it before heading for the two rooms.

Stopping outside the first room, "Dump your kit and meet back in the car park in 10 minutes. The meeting point is across the road. We need to recce the place before the meeting so might as well do it now."

Inside Lucy's and my room is a large double bed covered in a crisp white quilt. Against one wall is a brown wooden wicker open wardrobe. Next to that is a small desk on which stands a telephone and hotel leaflets. By the side of the bed are bedside tables, each with a bedside lamp. There is a separate seating area that overlooks the beach. But we don't have time to explore the room and its comforts, we have more pressing matters to attend to.

We are the first ones to arrive outside. While waiting for the others to show up, I take out the map from the envelope we obtained from the kidnappers' locker at West Quay. I do my best to orient it to the ground.

The meeting place should be straight in front of us, across the road. At my 11 o'clock, as I look over the road, an enormous blue lagoon stretches out into the distance. Its calmness belies secrets lurking beneath the surface. Several flocks of flamingos are feeding in the water.

To the right, a group of thick green bushes adorn the periphery of a disused street running away from the road. Their verdant foliage conceals secrets as much as it shields them from prying eyes. Palm trees, their fronds swaying in the warm breeze, emerge from the centre of the bushes.

So far on this mission, it appears people must have been watching our every move. Somehow, they knew when we reached every drop box. So why would now be any different?

Once the boys have joined Lucy and me, I say, "To be safe, I'll go first with Lucy. Once we are across the road and out of your line of sight, you three come over." I show them the map. "Make your way here," I say, pointing to the buildings on the map.

On the opposite side, we follow the broken roadway to the right, past three tennis courts, all needing repair. Beyond them are the two buildings where the meeting will take place tomorrow. There is something unsettling about the scene. Behind the near impenetrable curtain of greenery, the decrepit and overgrown buildings stand as forgotten ruins. Shrouded in lush vegetation, the rotting structures possess their own dark secret history as if they are silent observers of a past that refuses to be forgotten.

We need to ensure that there isn't a place an attacker could hide during the meeting. While Lucy stays out waiting for Simon, George, and Derek to join us, I venture inside the first of the two.

The interior is open and dark, with light coming through small holes in the torn metal sheets covering the roof. The place smells of rotting foliage. Scattered across the floor are a multitude of broken bottles. It would appear that the local youths use the place to conceal their drinking habits. The good news is there is only one way in, the way I entered.

A wire fence about 10 feet high is at the far end of the four-metre gap separating the two buildings. Like the buildings, vegetation has overgrown the fence, its vines intertwining through the gaps in the mesh. I pull back the leaves to discover a gate. It's locked. I make my way to the next building, which is the same as the first one.

Back outside, Lucy is standing with Derek. "Where are the other two idiots?" I ask, looking around.

"They crossed that small concrete bridge over there, spanning the inlet to check for an escape route, if we need one," Derek replies.

I wander over to take a look for myself. The fragile bridge is only about two metres by one metre, with no room underneath for anyone to hide. Across the other side, the ground is covered with short prickly bushes no more than knee high. A small dirt track only just visible meanders off to one side, on which, a short distance away, George and Simon are inching their way back.

"Wouldn't recommend that as an escape route, unless it is our only option. There are too many sharp spikes. Almost got one stuck in my bollocks," says Simon, as he reaches my present location.

"The same goes for the buildings. They are empty, so there is no place for someone to hide. But apart from a locked gate at the rear, there is only one way in and out. Better check around the back to see if we can find an alternative route," I say, pointing behind me.

"The lagoon is a no-go as well. It isn't deep but has a soft, muddy bottom. I poked through the water with a stick, which sunk too easily for my liking. We would be stuck in no time. It must be deeper on the far back, as a small jetty-like structure is jutting out. Two men are sitting on chairs at the end. They are too far away to glimpse what they are wearing, " Derek adds.

"While Derek and I try to find a way around the back, you three go back to the road and scan the area, looking for places someone could be waiting in a vehicle to collect the contact after the meeting. We'll meet back at the hotel in half an hour."

"Roger that, Steve," replies Simon.

A worn track winds around the building's back, passing bushes and the occasional palm tree. Follow the path for a short distance, ending at the same inlet covered by the bridge. This time, there is no crossing, and it is only a couple of metres wide.

On the other side, the track curves off over the brow of a small hill. Take a look around for something that can span the gap. Spot a half-buried red and white section of a plastic barrier used by road working companies for cordoning off areas while they work.

"Derek, help me to pull this out. If we throw it in the middle of the creek, we can use it as a stepping stone to reach the other side," I say, stamping on the ground. You never know, a silver snake could be inside and might get pissed off with us for waking it.

Once free, Derek grabs one end while I take the other and launch it into the water. It lands almost halfway. Now, we need to find out where the path leads.

"Ladies first," says Derek.

Step back a few feet, run and jump. One leg lands on the barrier before leaping to the far bank. Once I'm over, Derek does the same. Leading off, we once more follow the track until it comes to the road. Perfect, we have an escape route if it all goes wrong tomorrow. The road we came out on is the one that goes past the hotel, so we make our way back to meet up with the others.

The rest were already waiting when we returned to the hotel lobby. After agreeing to meet in one hour at the hotel restaurant on the seafront, we all went to our retrospective rooms to carry out personal admin. Back in my and Lucy's room, I remove the brew-making equipment from the wardrobe, fill the kettle with water and switch it on.

Turn to Lucy, who is opening the patio doors, "You want a brew, honey?"

"Not yet. The first thing I need is a shower. You can join me if you like."

"Sorry, Lucy, my mind is in the wrong place," I reply.

While she is in the shower, I take off a sheet of hotel paper from its pad. The last thing I need is some clever twat checking the imprint of a pen on the page below and deciphering what I wrote. I will burn this page once we have discussed everything later. First, and the most important point, we do not have any weapons yet. Simon is keeping Katie and Cody in the loop, but we can't arrange a weapon pickup until we know where Abbie and Bethanie are being held.

Second point, the meeting will be at 11:59 across the road from the two buildings where we carried out the recce earlier. From the information collected and seen, the routes in and out are limited. Due to this, I'm sure the person meeting us will come from the direction of the road. The big question is, will they be alone, or will an accomplice be waiting in a vehicle somewhere?

Third point, where can the rest of the team be located? During the meeting with the contact, I will need our trained interrogator, Lucy, with me to interpret any questions and actions that I miss.

Fourth point, if the contact doesn't give us the location of where the girls are being held, what actions will follow? Do we risk the kidnappers not contacting us again, or, worse, take retribution on Abbie and Bethanie if we kill the contact?

By the time I look up from the paper, Lucy is out of the shower and standing naked in front of me, her slim, perfect body glistening from the water dripping down from her body onto the floor. It does not matter how many I've seen her naked, it still sends shivers through me like it is the first time.

"Stop staring. You missed your chance, " says Lucy, catching me looking at her.

After my brew, I clamber into the shower, letting the water and soap flush away some of the tension from the last couple of days. By the time I finish showering, it is time to go to the restaurant to meet up with the boys.

As we walk through the lobby, a sense of anticipation hangs heavy in the air, heightened by the elegant surroundings of the hotel restaurant. Perched on a wooden veranda overlooking the ocean, it offers a breathtaking view of the sparkling blue waters below. The sandy beaches and lush tropical greenery paint a picturesque scene, but beneath the surface lies an undercurrent of tension.

A soft ocean breeze drifts through the open terrace, carrying the rhythmic sounds of waves crashing on the shore. The sun dips below the horizon, casting a golden hue over the marina and the island of Bonaire. The restaurant's wooden beams frame the scene, creating a captivating play of light and shadow.

As we push open the mahogany doors, a stark contrast unfolds. The opulent decor, a feast for the eyes, stands in sharp contradiction to the tranquil beauty outside. Modern and traditional elements blend without a glitch, yet there's an unsettling undercurrent in the atmosphere, a mystery waiting to be unravelled.

The clinking of fine china and the hushed murmurs of conversation add to the tension, creating an undercurrent of apprehension. Soft music fills the air, its soothing melodies masking the underlying sense of foreboding.

But it's the aroma that truly sets my nerves on edge. The smoky scent of slow-roasted pork, the warm fragrance of fresh bread, and the exotic spices mingling in the air create a tantalising symphony. It's a scent that promises pleasure, yet beneath its alluring surface, a hidden danger lurks, adding a thrilling sense of anticipation mixed with fear.

Our waitress, a young lady in her early 20s, is called Mary, from her name tag. She takes us to a table at the far end of the veranda, overlooking the ocean. After ensuring we were seated, she hands us a menu and explains the special offer of the day is the local dorado fish. She leaves, promising to return with our drinks and take our order in a few minutes. I explain three other people will be joining us, so she leaves extra menus.

Six minutes later, Simon, George, and Derek walk through the door, spot us, and sit at the table. "Has anyone ordered the beers?" asks Simon.

"Yes, mate," I reply.

At that moment, our waitress reappears, carrying a tray loaded with drinks. "Here you go. Are you ready to order?" she asks with a welcoming smile.

I glance around the table. Everyone nods to indicate they are ready, "Yes, please, Lucy and I will have the fish special."

"I'll have the same," says Derek, passing her the menu.

"And me, you want a kid's meal, Simon, you skinny runt?" says George, grinning.

"Fuck off, fat boy, and yes, please," comes the reply from Simon.

Once Mary has disappeared with the order, "OK folks, down to business. The next contact with the arseholes who have my girls is tomorrow at 11:59 outside the two ruined buildings we recced earlier. From what we can see, the contact will come from the direction of the road. We don't know if they will walk here or come by transport. With no vehicular access, it must be left on the road. This is where you come in as our transport expert, Simon. Position yourself somewhere on the road close to the hotel so you can see our contact approaching and if he has any accomplices waiting in a car. Be prepared to make contact with the driver and seize the vehicle, we may need it."

"No problem, Steve," replies Simon.

"Next, Derek and I confirmed there is no escape route on the other side of the bridge for either of us, or the contact. However, we have prepared a crossing behind the building, which we will use for the way out. In case Simon spots someone watching the route we go on, the lagoon is out of the question for any entry or exit. I need you, Derek, to go to the crossing we made and ensure the route stays open."

"Roger that," says Derek.

"As for you, George, I need you to provide close protection for Lucy and me during the meeting. I checked inside the buildings. You can conceal yourself there via the hole in the wall..."

"Will the fat bastard fit?" I am interrupted by Simon, who is getting his own back from the comment about the size of his meal.

"Might be a squeeze for him, but he'll fit," thinking revenge is a bitch.

"Lucy and I will conduct the actual meeting. I need her skills to ask the right questions if the situation asks for it. Speaking of which, do you have any questions so far?"

"One at the moment. Where is the emergency RV?" asks Lucy.

"Will get to that bit. If everything goes to plan once the meeting is over, and we have the details of where they are keeping the girls, we will allow the contact to leave first. So, everyone, stay in your assigned positions until I give the message over the radios to depart. Remember, for everyone except Simon, it will be via the back of the buildings. We will then meet up and enter the hotel via the rear exit. From there, we will plan our next move; for example, contacting Katie for weapons and getting transport to get around the island. If nobody has any questions, let's move on to emergency procedures in case things don't go as planned."

At that moment, Mary returns with our food. "Here you go, five fish dinners. Enjoy. Can I fetch you another round of drinks?"

"Thank you, and yes, five more beers, please," says Lucy.

Again, wait for Mary to disappear. "Contingency plans. The foremost point here is we have no weapons at this point, so if you have to kill anyone, it will have to be done with your bare hands. If our contact tries anything stupid and does not give me the information I need, he may have to die. I'll make the snap decision at the time. I will send 'bug out' over the radio if it happens. Simon, if you have spotted a vehicle and a person waiting, dispatch them and take it, but only if you hear from me. We may need the contact and the people with him to depart unharmed. The rest of us will then leave the area via the rear route and meet up at the emergency RV, which will be at Karels Beach Bar." I point to it on a map collected from the hotel lobby.

"Sounds like some sort of a plan, Steve," Derek says, after taking a swig of beer.

"If all goes right tomorrow, we will be on the road to getting your daughters back," Lucy says, grasping my hand.

I am about to stand up when Mary comes back over, "This was hand-delivered for you a few moments ago," she says, handing me an envelope with the recognisable blue stripe.

I open it and pull out the paper with the words printed on it, which I read out loud: "Glad you could make it. Remember the meeting is at 11:59 tomorrow; do not be late."

Fuck, we have not given these people enough credit. They must have paid someone at the hotel to contact them if we showed up. But who? Was it the two men at the bar, or even the receptionist? Nothing we can do now. They will not make a move until tomorrow, so it will be safe to stay here tonight. It's agreed that one person in each room will always be awake until we meet up tomorrow morning for breakfast.

Chapter Four - Contact

I glance down at my wristwatch in the faint moonlight coming into the room. It's 02:00. I'd taken over from Lucy an hour ago, who is now sleeping under the quilt. I walk over to the window, sit on the small ledge, and peer out onto the car park below. All appears quiet for now.

I have one doubt running through my mind: 'Did I make the right decision to stay in the hotel tonight? Or have I left the team open to a possible danger while they sleep?' Has my desire to get my daughters back clouded my judgment? I comfort myself with the fact that whoever has them wants us to continue their dance, which means my girls are still alive.

Another hour passes without incident. But something tells me I need to check the hotel for signs of anyone who might belong to the cartel and be waiting for us in the morning. I pull the door a few inches. The hinges groan as if setting off an alarm in the silence. I turn to check Lucy is still in the land of nod. I pull the door further before exiting into the corridor and making my way to the room next door where the boys are sleeping.

Not wanting to be hurled to the floor when I enter, I tap on the door just hard enough that whoever is on stag inside knows it's me.

I say, "It's Steve."

Derek peers through the eyeglass peephole before opening the door a few inches. "What's up?"

"Going to check the hotel for bad guys. Can you stand in the corridor so you can monitor both rooms?"

"No problem. Call me if you find any issues."

I leave Derek and walk down the emergency escape stairs, stopping at the lobby level. I peek through the glass panel in the door. I can't see much in the dim lights of the room. The hotel must be trying to be green or save energy, and half the lights are off, leaving just enough for any wanderers to see where they are going. I pull the door with one swift moment; better one noise than several.

The lobby area is void of people. Through the open door behind the reception desk, I detect a man sitting at a desk, staring at a computer screen. I would guess he is watching a film or video due to the lack of hand movements. My training tells me that just because I can't see something doesn't mean it isn't there, so I walk over to check the restaurant. The place is in darkness, apart from the occasional glint from the glasses on the tables as the rays of moonlight strike them.

My next stop is the bar, where I spotted the two men earlier who had me questioning why they were there. Again, the area is clear. I am beginning to think my decision to stay here the night rather than out in the derelict buildings was right after all.

I am about to turn to return to my room when something attracts my attention, through the glass in the double doors leading out to the car park. Tucked away in the corner, a door light comes on as someone opens the driver's door. Are they late arrivals hoping to find a room for the night?

What happens next changes my mind. By the faint glow of the light, I see three men sitting in the vehicle — one in the front and two in the back. Rather than climb out, the door is shut, and they continue to sit in the twilight. They could be local youths smoking drugs or drinking, but in the current situation we find ourselves in, I would guess they are to here monitor our movements. Our druggy friends have made their first mistake in this dangerous game they are playing.

I better check the rear, not only for people but also for a way out. Following the same procedure I used to enter the lobby, I peer into the rear garden towards the restaurant we used last night. Several lampposts cast bright beams of light downwards, illuminating a wooden footpath leading to the beach.

The silence is broken by the chirping of some type of nocturnal creatures in the bushes and the sound of the waves crashing onto the beach. A quick scan confirms nobody is around. This will be our way out later if the area stays clear. To ensure it is, we will slip out before breakfast and head for the locations for the contact we located earlier.

After completing the hotel recce, I head back upstairs. As I round the corner in the corridor, Derek is leaning against the wall to the left of the door. To any layman, his choice of sides would be at random. But that would be far from the truth. Derek chose this spot because the door handle is on the right. This means all he has to do is reach down with his right hand, push down the lever and alert the others of any danger.

When I reach a spot a couple of feet from his position, Derek whispers, "You spot anything we need to worry about?"

"The interior of the hotel is clear. The only issue we may have is three men are sitting in a car in the front car park."

"Shit, Steve, what's the plan?"

"Wake the others up at 05:00, ready to move at 05:30. We will slip out the back way before breakfast. Then head along the beach for a few hundred metres before cutting back to the road and heading for the contact point."

"Fat boy isn't going to like the idea of skipping brekkie," comes the reply from Derek.

"Knowing George, he will have food stashed in his Bergen."

I glance down at my watch; the time is now 04:00. The recce took longer than anticipated. When I enter the room, Lucy is still fast asleep. I walk back to the window and check if the people I saw in the vehicle are still there. They are.

My Bergen, like the rest, is already packed and ready to depart. The army always taught you the importance of keeping your kit prepared to move. If you take anything out, you must repack it once you are finished with it. So, with time to spare until I need to wake Lucy, I wander over to the drinks station on the cupboard, doing my best not to make a sound. Fill the kettle with water and empty the sachets of coffee into two cups, along with the milk ready for our morning brew.

I forgot Lucy is like the rest of us. When on a mission, the slightest sound will wake her.

A voice calls out from under the quilt, "What time is it?"

"04:30, you still have 30 minutes."

"I'm awake now, so I might as well get up. Yes, please, to that coffee."

Lucy clambers out of bed, one body part at a time, and heads for the bathroom. A few minutes later, I detect the sound of running water. At first, the patter is gentle and almost musical in rhythm. Then it swells, cascading into a symphony of droplets as Lucy takes her morning shower. 'Good idea', I think to myself, as we don't know when we will have the chance again.

Once out, Lucy sits on the bed, and I pass her a cup filled with coffee. We sit in the dark, not wanting to switch on the bedroom light in case it silhouettes us every time we pass the window, giving anyone outside with a rifle a perfect target.

Lucy takes a sip from her drink and asks, "Any changes in the plan from last night I need to know about?"

I spend the next few minutes outlining my recce of the hotel and the three men in the vehicle. To make sure, I wander over to the window and peer through the netting to confirm if they are still there. They are. One man is now standing outside the car and leaning against the roof, the light from a nearby lamppost illuminating him. He appears to be a young man wearing a T-shirt, the rest of him concealed behind the vehicle's body.

"We will leave here at 05:30 via the rear entrance, moving along the beach before going to the meeting point."

"You have been a busy boy," says Lucy, now getting dressed.

It is soon time to leave. We pick up our Bergens and head into the corridor to meet the boys. Once everyone is ready, I lead the way down the emergency stairwell to the lobby level. A quick check confirms there are still no signs of life. We exit and make our way to the rear entrance. Again, I stop and check. The place appears void of people, so we leave, keeping in the shadows and away from the wooden walkway bathed in a yellow glow from the lampposts.

A few minutes later, we reach the end of the garden. To the front, a small wall separates the hotel from the sandy beach five feet below. Simon is the first to jump down and take a defensive posture, facing along the sand towards the restaurant veranda. The rest of us follow and do the same. Once we are sure nobody witnesses us jumping, we continue along the water's edge.

We keep the ocean to our right. We pass several large houses with immaculate gardens that back up to the water. A couple of fishing boats stand with thick ropes anchored to the sea wall, their nets swaying in the gentle breeze, casting shadows from the moonlight.

We continue for 200 metres until we come across a concrete slipway. This should lead us back to the road. From there, we can cross over and make our way to our positions for the contact later in the day.

I place my left hand on my head and signal the team to close up. Take out the map.

"According to this, we are not far from where we need to be. We will cross the road one at a time. That way, if we are spotted by a motorist driving along the street, they will only ever see one person. I'll go first, then the rest of you tag along, leaving a two-minute gap between you. On the other side, I will wait for you a little way inside the bush. From there, we make our way along the creek until we reach the crossing Derek and I made yesterday. From there, we will go and RV in the disused building. If everyone is ready, let's go."

I stop at the edge of the road and look both ways. I'm in luck, there are no vehicles. I have no time to waste, as the next person will be along soon, so I cross over and head towards a dirt track visible in the morning light and heading in the right direction.

After a couple of hundred metres, I come to a small clearing and lie beside a dead bush facing in the opposite direction than the way I came, to wait for the others. Two minutes later, Simon appears and takes up a position facing the way he came. Within minutes, we are all across the road and spreading out.

About to move when George says, "As we don't have any weapons, if I shout bang, will the bad guys play the game and lay down?"

"Fucking idiot, but I know what you mean. As soon as we know the location of Abbie and Bethanie, we'll contact Katie. No point doing it yet as we don't even know if they are on this island, going on the way we have been sent to this point." replies Simon.

It reminds me of a time in the army during an exercise when we and the people playing the enemy both ran out of blank ammunition. We assaulted the trenches, shouting, 'bang!' as we ran. The funny thing was they were shouting 'bang' back, followed by the words 'you're dead. I fired first'. It still makes me chuckle.

Wait a few minutes before moving off towards the creek crossing. When we arrive, I leap over, using the plastic barrier as a stepping stone. Then, take position behind the first building. The rest follow. There is a strange near-silence as we lay in the undergrowth.

The only sounds are the chorus of nocturnal creatures chirping away, communicating our presence, the wind blowing across the tops of the two-foot-high bushes, and the rattling of torn corrugated iron sheets on the roof of the buildings.

We do not have much time, as first light is arriving fast. Whispering, "Things could have changed since yesterday, so Derek and I will peek inside to ensure nobody has taken up residence during our absence. If we have any problems, Derek will let you know by radio."

While the rest stay put, I lead off by trying not to snap any twigs underfoot that might announce our approach. At the corner of the first building, I bend down behind a shaggy green bush and peer through a gap in the wall. I can't see anybody, so I turn to Derek, who is crouching down next to me.

"I'll check this one if you check the other."

"Roger that, " replies Derek, as he moves into the gap between the two buildings, ready to enter the building on his right.

I give Derek the thumbs-up, and we enter our respective buildings at the same time. Inside, it is still in the same state as yesterday, apart from a few extra empty beer cans scattered across the floor. I am about to leave when something moves in the room's darkest corner.

In the shadows, the figure of a person sits on the concrete, their knees drawn up to their chest. Instinct kicks in, and I launch towards them. Startled, they try to stand up. I knock them to the ground. The withdrawn eyes of a man stare back at me.

His withdrawn cheeks, frail frame, and rags he is dressed in indicate this is a homeless man.

In a quiet, trembling voice, he says, "Please don't hurt me."

By this time, Derek has heard the commotion and joins me, radioing the team to join us.

"Who have you got there, Steve?" enquires Lucy.

"A problem. Some old geezer I found sleeping in the corner," I point to the end of the room.

"You're right; you can't have him anywhere near here for the meeting. He might put off the contact approaching, thinking the site has been compromised. But what to do with him?" replies Simon.

The majority of the brain, with the lack of empathy due to PTSD, is saying break his neck to kill him, then throw him in the lagoon, accompanied by a few concrete blocks. The tiny other bit says this is an innocent homeless man with nothing. Let him leave in one piece. Before I can make the decision, it is made for me.

"We can't afford to let him wander off and tell someone, like the wrong person in the hotel, after what just happened. Suggest we gag and tie him up and leave him in the other building until after the meet, then let him go." says Lucy.

I peer around the room, and the others agree with Lucy.

"OK, as killing him is out of the question, help me move him next door, George."

Once there, he's made to sit on the floor, his back leaning at one of the metal pillars holding the structure up. Grabbing his arms, force them behind the man's back, and use a black cable tie to secure them together. A tear starts to roll down the man's cheek.

I bend down and whisper in his ear, "Don't worry, mate. This will be over in a few hours, and I promise I will let you go unharmed." To ensure he understands his situation, I add, "If you keep quiet... that is."

With a few hours before we need to be in position, after collecting bits of old tin and wood, Simon sets himself up in the back corner. He erects a small barricade to conceal the flame from his gas stove and boils water to make everyone a brew.

This would be the time we prepare our weapons, but since we have just arrived on the island, we don't have any yet apart from the knives we brought through in our hand luggage. Up against a wall, George has removed the knife he brought from the UK from his jacket pocket is sharpening a stick he picked up outside into a point to use as a makeshift harpoon.

"OK, numpties, bring your mugs over if you want a brew," says Simon, standing up with a pot of boiling water.

I grab my mug from my backpack and walk over to Simon. "Cheers, mate. But where did you get the gas? You couldn't have brought it with you, or the nosey bastards at the airport would have stopped you."

"Magic, Steve. OK, remember when I was checking the road yesterday for a possible place for the contact to park? Well, along the road there is a dive shop selling camping stuff, and stuff to make you act like a fish. Those diving types must like to go wild sometimes, I suppose. Well I went in and picked it up then. Also, I grabbed some packet food stuff."

While Simon is filling my black mug, "Genius!" I thought I was being smart when I stole all the biscuits and coffee sachets from the hotel room.

After everyone is finished drinking and eating, Lucy stands up and walks over to Simon. " Do you have any of that food and brew left?"

"A little, why?" asked Simon.

"We need to find out what information our friend next door has for us. He might have information on the area and the possible location of the girls," replies Lucy.

She grabs a cup of coffee and a small amount of food and heads over to where the homeless man is tied up. As Lucy enters, the man is startled and tenses up. Expecting the worst, he draws his knees closer to his chest to protect it from any beating that might come his way. His dark brown eyes stare at Lucy, watching her every move. Walking through the dim light, she kicks an old rusty can which bounces across the concrete floor, sounding like a drum roll in the silence.

Bending down next to the man, she removes his gag and says, "Don't worry, we don't want to hurt you. I've brought you a drink and something to eat. When was the last time you ate anything?"

The old man, still unsure if he can trust us, "A few days back."

Lucy lifts the mug to his lips, and he takes several long sips. "You want some food?" The man nods.

Lucy feeds the man one spoon at a time, always speaking to him in a non-aggressive way. She needs to build his trust.

After the man has eaten half the food, Lucy asks, "What is your name?"

"Carlos," comes the reply.

"I'm Lucy. Have you lived around this part of the island long?"

"Yes, been in this part for most of my life. I was successful once, owned a small shop before bastards from a local drug gang came to my house and told me I had to pay them protection money or my business would burn. I didn't have the money, so they set light to my shop." Lucy witnesses the clear signs of regret in his swollen eyes.

" I take it then you have no love for them. Do you know a man called Lucas?" Picking up the mug, Lucy gives the man another drink and the remainder of the food.

"Yes, everyone on the island knows him. From a young age, he witnessed the allure of power and wealth that came with a life immersed in organised crime. Some say he was seduced by the possibility of escaping a future of poverty and hopelessness. He was drawn into the clutches of the drug cartel, progressing from petty theft to more substantial and dangerous roles within Alex Acosta's operations. Each step he took, took him deeper into the world of organised crime. He now runs the gang operation on the island. And is well known for his brutality. He lives in a big house on the edge of the next town, surrounded by a five-foot-high cactus fence. His men patrol the grounds 24/7. If you set me free, I will take you there."

With a big smile, Lucy replaces the gag, picks up her stuff, and leaves. She wants to say yes, but we still want him to remain quiet. This is something he would only do if he still thought his life was in danger. When she re-enters the other building, the rest are sitting around in a group — apart from George, who had been sent out to check the area in case our contact turns up a few hours early.

"Take it you have been interrogating the man next door, Lucy," I say, half knowing the answer.

"Nope, just having a conversation," replies Lucy with a wink.

Zulu time is now contact minus one hour. The time we move to our positions for the meeting.

"OK, folks, it is time to go. Remember to contact us via the radio, Simon, the moment you think the vehicle with people or the person who may be our contact turns up. I will leave this up to experience in reconnaissance. Same for you, Derek. Spot anyone approaching from the rear, let us all know," I say, before heading outside to wait for the contact.

With that, everyone moves to their starting location for the meeting. Simon takes the long way back, heading for the road where he can monitor people arriving. At the inlet crossing, Derek is hidden among the bushes. While George relocates to the other building, Lucy is wandering around the location on a roving patrol.

Within the next few hours, we will know the location of where my daughters are being held hostage and, at last, be able to make a plan of how to get them back.

The following 45 minutes tick away second by second, like time itself doesn't want to move forward. Plus, for some reason, the area is quiet, as if it is expecting the situation that is about to unfold. I take up a position across from the buildings close to a clump of bushes, providing me with some concealment.

As I wait inside, anxiety gnaws at me, twisting my stomach into knots. My mind races with thoughts of my daughters; I can almost see their faces before me, their innocent smiles replaced with fear and uncertainty. I clench my fists, my knuckles growing white with the pressure. These people will pay for what they have done.

I glance down at my wristwatch. It's 11:45, 14 minutes more. A sudden rustling to my left brings me back to the present. It's Lucy, who's been wandering around pretending to look at the flamingos on the lake.

She comes over to join me and says, "Someone is approaching. It could be our contact." This confirms Simon's message over the radio a few seconds earlier.

At last, the moment we have been waiting for. A figure emerges, walking like a person on a mission down the disused road toward us. It is a well-dressed, slender man about six feet tall with black hair. Behind him, another man. They move with caution toward the meeting point.

It must be Lucas, a man known for his brutal tactics and ruthless actions. A cold shiver runs down my spine. I've dealt with this type of person many times, not only with the team but on many special operations during my army days. But as they say, a little fear and apprehension keeps you alive.

Within a few seconds, the man is standing in front of me. His companion stops short, his eyes scanning the area for any attack that might come their way.

In a deep, powerful voice lacking compassion, he says, "Are you Steve?"

I reply in the same tone, not letting him know that if he doesn't give me the information I want, he or his friend will never be leaving this site. "Yes, have you the details I want?"

Without saying a word, Lucas reaches into his jacket and pulls out an envelope with a blue stripe. With a gloved hand, he opens the envelope and half-pulls out the contents before pushing them back in. My heart skips a beat, hope surging through me. At last, the information we've been seeking is within reach. As Lucas hands over the envelope, I strain to glimpse its contents, aching for any clue about Abbie and Bethanie's whereabouts.

Handling the envelope over to Lucy, who is standing by my side, "You have five days to make your next meeting, followed by another four days to come up with the money, or your daughters will be shot. In case you try to do something stupid, my boss is waiting for my call on the success of this meeting. If he doesn't get the call at a prearranged time known only by him and myself, your daughters die. So don't try anything foolish."

"In that case, you will not mind if we take a glance at the documents before I allow you to leave?"

"Help yourself, Steve. I'll give you two minutes of my time, and then I'm leaving."

With that, Lucy takes out the envelope's contents and reads the information typed on white sheets of paper. More evidence we are dealing with people who know what they are doing.

After Lucy puts the envelope in her jacket pocket, Lucas glances up and says, "Remember, five days or they are dead."

With that, he turns and walks back towards the road. Everyone stays in position for the next half-hour in case the gang tries something stupid. From this moment on, there is no nice Mr Steve, only the person who will kill anyone who gets in his way.

I send the message over the radio for everyone to return to the road, the one we left the beach earlier after leaving the hotel. While I'm doing this, Lucy, determined to keep her word, goes back into the building, unties the homeless guy and brings him outside. The man's eyes are now squinting in the bright sunshine after being in a dark room for so long.

"He has agreed to take us to Lucas' house if that is the plan," says Lucy, leading the man back towards the road.

"Can't say yet. Let's wait until we join the others and analyse the information. Lucas might have some assets we may need, like money."

Chapter Five - Lucas' House

By the time Lucy, Carlos, and I arrive at the RV, the rest of the team is already on the edge of the shoreline in a casual defensive position, covering all angles of view. I first scan the area to ensure I can't be overheard.

With Carlos out of earshot, Lucy removes the envelope the contact gave us.

"This doesn't tell us much. It just states we need to receive more instructions in five days and then another four to pay the ransom. I, for one, don't fancy sitting around here waiting. Suggest we go and see what Lucas has to say on the matter," I say in a hushed voice.

The team agree with me, so I call Carlos back over. "OK, Carlos, you have agreed to help us because, as you told Lucy, you don't have any love for Lucas because he burned down your business. Before we go any further, let me say this. Cross us, and this will be your last day alive."

"Trust me, I hate Lucas as much as you," comes the uneasy reply from Carlos.

"As long as we understand each other. So, how far from here does Lucas live?"

"It isn't far, only a 40-minute walk from here on the edge of a small remote village called Bona Bista."

I turn to the rest of the team, "Here is the plan. Lucas will know the whereabouts of Abbie and Bethanie, and he will have assets that will come in handy, such as information, money, and maybe weapons. We need to go to his property and ask him a few polite questions. If you all agree, we will head there one hour before last light.

In the meantime, let's regroup and perhaps grab a bite from the kiosk further along the beach. With the team agreeing, Lucy, Lucas, and I move first. The food kiosk, our rendezvous point, stands 200 metres away; a nondescript structure with faded signage and peeling paint. I scan the horizon, noting every potential threat, every movement, with my team by my side.

Lucy, her gaze sharp and unyielding, walks beside Lucas. She's a ghost in the crowd, unseen but ever-present. At the kiosk, we order, blending into the rhythm of the place. We sit, spreading out just enough to cover different vantage points while maintaining cohesion. I bite into a sandwich, the taste barely registering as I watch the ebb and flow of people.

Ten minutes pass. I catch sight of Simon, Derek, and George making their approach. Simon's posture screams nonchalance, but I know his mind is a whirl of calculations. Derek's attention flicks between the crowd and his concealed comms device, always the diligent watchdog. With his sniper's eyes, George dissects every detail, his gaze lingering on potential high ground.

They join the people at the kiosk, and their integration is seamless, a testament to their skill and expertise. We eat, our actions mundane, yet every sense remains on high alert. The minutes drag, each tick of the clock heavy with unspoken tension.

The hours pass, and the sun starts to creep towards the horizon, casting an orange hue across the beach. At last, it's time to head back to our last RV; this time, our groups swap, with Simon, Derek, and George now taking point and moving towards the RV. I signal Lucy and Lucas, and we wait, counting down the minutes.

When our turn comes, we stand, discarding our wrappers and containers, blending back into the few beachgoers still on the beach. The walk back feels longer, the sound of the waves crashing against the shore, the smell of salt in the air, and the sight of the sun starting to set on the horizon all add to the tension.

By the time we reach the RV, Simon, George and Derek have retaken their previous positions and are observing the area while doing their best to blend in with their surroundings.

With only one hour until last light I glance around the team as they shoulder their Bergens. This could get dangerous, and unlike other missions, they are doing this for my girls and not for money.

"Come on then, you ugly bastard," shouts Derek, starting to head down the beach in the opposite direction of the kiosk.

Leading the way, I scan the area ahead, my senses on high alert as we move forward with our local guide, Carlos, by my side. His confidence in the terrain is palpable, a stark reminder of the dangers lurking in this non-tourist area. The beach now appears deserted, except for a few locals scattered along the shore, their presence adding to the ominous atmosphere.

As we traverse the powdery white sand, the crashing waves are a constant reminder of the urgency of our mission, their rhythmic sound a stark contrast to the serenity of the surroundings. Lucy trails just behind me, her presence a reassuring anchor amidst the uncertainty. Derek and Simon engage in a hushed conversation, their voices barely audible over the roar of the ocean. At the same time, George maintains vigilance at our rear, ever watchful for any sign of danger.

We soon leave the beach behind, entering a maze of weathered buildings that lean precariously against each other. The vibrant walls, faded over time, add to the village's nostalgic charm, but there's an underlying tension in the air. The aroma of local cuisine mingles with the salt of the sea, a bittersweet reminder of the risks we face.

Pressing forward through the narrow streets, we quicken our pace, eager to reach the other side of Bona Bista before nightfall. The chatter of locals fades into the distance as we move away from the town centre.

I turn to Carlos, "How far now?"

"Lucas lives on the other side. Follow me," says Carlos, leading off down a damaged tarmac road full of potholes, with grey concrete dwellings on both sides surrounded by broken fences.

Once more, we follow Carlos, hoping he isn't walking us into a trap. The air crackles with anticipation as we continue every step, taking us closer to our objective, Lucas' house. After 10 minutes, the tranquillity is shattered by the sound of approaching footsteps closing in on our location. I motion the team to stop and go to ground. I hide in the shadows cast by a brick wall.

The crunch of gravel becomes louder as a group of local thugs materialise out of the shadows. Their predatory intentions are evident in their glares. They are going to try to rob us.

"Well, well, what do we have here?" sneers the apparent leader, sizing us up.

My mind shifts into tactical mode, weighing our options. "We're just passing through. No need for trouble," I raise a hand, attempting diplomacy.

"Drop the bags. This is our turf," growls the leader, stepping forward.

Laughter echoes in his response. "Trouble found you."

"Tell you what, you fuck off, and we will not hurt you," I say now, getting pissed off with these idiots.

With that, he lunges at me. My reflexes take over, and I sidestep his attack. His off-balance body is trying to steady itself and gain composure. Swing my right arm around his neck, coming to rest on the elbow of my left arm. I squeeze tight as his arms grab mine, trying to stop life from escaping from his body. He drops the pistol he's been holding, the metallic clatter resonating in the night air.

Seconds later, all movement from his body ceases. I let go, and he slumps to the floor.

Another of the thugs shouts, "Wrong move!"

The rest of the team springs into action, engaging with precision and putting all the unarmed combat training to practical use. The night air vibrates with the clash of bodies. Ten minutes later, the remainder of the local gang runs away, disarmed and defeated. The night, once disrupted, settles back into an uneasy calm. The team regroups, silent acknowledgement passing between us as we resume our journey to Lucas' house. Now, at last, the team have weapons taken from our attackers, which will make the questioning of Lucas more fun.

As we disappear into the shadows, the encounter reminds us that every step forward carries the weight of potential conflict in the dangerous world we navigate.

The encounter with the youths had cost us time, but soon, Carlos leads us through the remainder of the village. The air is thick with anticipation as we stand on the outskirts. The village is a mere shadow, shrouded in obscurity. In the darkness, I catch the glint of determination in the team's eyes. I call them onto my position. The mission's objective is clear: find Lucas, the elusive leader of the local drug cartel operating from his massive estate surrounded by a five-foot fortress of cacti standing sentinel, a natural fortress guarding the secrets within.

After thanking Carlos for his help in getting here, we say goodbye, and I turn to the team. "This needs to go like any operation. We will approach and bypass the fence, and from there, we will split up. Derek and I will take the front of the house while Lucy and Simon enter from the rear. George, I need you to patrol the grounds. Take the rifle we liberated from those idiots in the village. Kill anyone you see. Once inside, Lucy searches the upper level with Simon. We will check the ground floor.

Remember, we need to ask Lucas questions, so if you have to shoot him, make it non-lethal. If nobody has any questions, Let's make a move."

Everyone shook their heads, relieved that they had something other than their hands and knives to squash any resistance. At the edge of the 50-metre open ground that separates our present location from the edge of the property, I pause for a few seconds before sprinting and zig zagging across, making it difficult for anyone looking to get a lock on me through their rifle sights. As I approach the cactus fence, its prickly shadows dance across my path. Take cover behind the wall while the team sprints across to join me.

Once there, Lucy peers over the fence between two heads of cacti.

"Are there any signs of activity, Lucy?" I ask.

She nods, her voice quiet. "All appears quiet, but there's an energy in the air. We're not alone."

"Roger that. If everyone is ready, let's go."

Close by, a lower section beckons, and we breach the cactus fence, the thorns clawing at our clothes like desperate fingers. Once over, the estate's grounds unfurl, a labyrinth of darkness and doubt. The night envelops us like a suffocating cloak as we plunge into the hunt for Lucas. The darkness is our ally, and the mission hangs on the precipice of revelation.

Amidst the shadows and uncertainty, the faint glow of lights illuminates the contours of the building across the manicured lawn and raised flowerbeds. Working in tandem, our teams navigate towards the house. I take cover near a raised flower bed, my senses heightened as I scan the surroundings. To my right, Simon disappears into the darkness, trailed by Lucy.

I tap Derek on the shoulder, my voice a whisper. "We've got a problem. One of Lucas' men is patrolling near the front door. We need to dispatch him without alerting anyone. Once he walks towards the far corner and faces away from us, we rush him."

A few agonising minutes pass until we get the chance. At the same time, both Derek and I spring into action, closing the distance in a blur of motion. The impact sends the henchman sprawling onto the slabbed patio, his body limp and vulnerable. Without hesitation, I lunge the knife I've been holding deep into his neck. Moments later, his lifeless body lies on the ground. The metallic tang of blood fills the air as thick blood oozes from a gash, his life ebbing away in a crimson pool.

We can't afford for anyone to detect our presence yet. While I grab his upper body, Derek grabs the legs, and we conceal the body in the undergrowth to the right of the building, before heading for the front door. The sounds of cicadas provide a rhythmic backdrop. As we stand in silence on either side of the door, a subtle click, and the door creaks ajar.

Lucy's voice crackles over the radio from the rear of the property. "Steve, we're in position."

I signal to Derek to send the message to get things underway.

"Go," Derek whispers into the radio.

At the same time, I push the door open the rest of the way, allowing us passage into the cool darkness beyond. At the same time, Lucy and Simon enter from the rear, their movements seamless and silent.

There is a scent of cigar smoke in the air which is getting stronger, and the atmospheric lights reveal plush furnishings. The muted glow of lights reveals a grand staircase leading to the upper floors.

We tread with caution, every footfall a whisper against the polished marble floors. The air carries a faint hint of expensive cologne, a testament to the opulence surrounding us.

I signal to Derek to move to the next room, each step a careful negotiation. The tension tightens with each room. The air is heavy with the weight of our mission. The dimly lit corridor on the lower level beckons, and we press forward, shadows dancing on the walls.

We come across closed doors that guard the secrets within for now. The sprawling house becomes a labyrinth of uncertainty as we scour every corner for the elusive Lucas. Moving with calculated precision, our senses are heightened by the tension in the air. Ambient lights flicker, casting erratic shadows that play tricks on our perception. The next move rests in the delicate balance of our silent dance with shadows.

A single shot echoes through the house from the rear, a signal of a person's demise. The sound of someone moving behind a door attracts my attention.

"Derek, let's check the study," I murmur, my voice hushed.

Derek nods, as we descend the hallway and navigate toward the living room, each step progressing into the unknown, every footfall echoing like a drumbeat of anticipation in the dimly lit corridor. The scent of cigars hangs in the air like a harbinger of danger lingering — a breadcrumb trail leading us closer to our prey. Could Lucas, our elusive target, be lurking within these walls?

We reach the living room and adhere to our standard procedure. Taking our positions on either side of the door, I signal to Derek. Then, with a steady hand, I swing it open, revealing Lucas' inner sanctum — an expansive office adorned with opulent mahogany furniture and walls adorned with trophies of his ego. The desk, a polished mahogany masterpiece and a bastion of power and secrecy becomes our focal point.

The air is heavy with the musty aroma of aged leather and the faint scent of old books. Framed photographs of Lucas adorn the walls, a testament to his vanity and wealth. Each captures Lucas in various poses of opulence. The ornate desk is cluttered with documents and a computer screen.

Derek wastes no time, his fingers dancing across the keyboard, attempting to breach the digital fortress and encrypted files that may guard the secrets of the girls' whereabouts.

"Can you log in and download the files?"

"Sure, give me a minute or two," Derek replies, taking his laptop from his Bergen.

While Derek works, I search the room for anything useful. On the far wall, a massive painting which appears not to be hanging right, jutting out slightly from the wall. I walk over and grab the bottom. It moves. I pull harder to reveal a massive safe with an electric keypad.

I am about to turn to ask Derek if he can get the passcode, when a man in his early 20s appears in the doorway brandishing a pistol. He must be new to this life of crime. He hesitates. I don't. A nanosecond later, there is a crack and a thump as a bullet strikes home, and the back of his head explodes.

"I'm in!" declares Derek, taking out a flash drive and inserting it into the computer.

"You got the code for the safe?" I ask.

"Yep, the man's a fucking idiot. He's only written his passcode in a document labelled 'safe'. It's 0542 8173."

I enter the numbers into the safe and turn the handle. It doesn't open.

"Shout that number out again."

Derek repeats the numbers one by one as I enter them. This time, the door opens. I pull the metal door wide open. Inside, something makes me grin. Inside, there are stacks of dollar bills. I gab one bundle. The notes are wrapped in a strip of paper stating $10,000. I do a rough calculation. There must be at least half a million dollars.

"What you found?" Derek yells from over by the desk.

Opening my Bergen and scooping the money into it, "It would appear we are getting paid for the mission after all."

I press the radio transmitter, "All call signs, sit rep. Over."

"LK. We're searching the upper floor; there's no sign of Lucas yet. Over," Lucy's voice comes through.

"All clear out here, GD. Over," comes the message from George, still keeping a lookout located somewhere in the grounds.

"S3, Roger that. Out," I reply.

At the same time, Lucy and Simon move as shadows in another part of the house. Their synchronised footsteps echo through the dim corridors.

"Simon, look for anything that might give us a clue," Lucy instructs.

Simon nods, his gaze dissecting each room he enters.

After leaving the study with the files and money, Derek and I continue searching the ground floor. It isn't long before we come across a solid wooden cellar door. From behind it, a murmur, a sound that didn't belong to the house's ambient symphony. We exchange glances, a silent confirmation that we may be closing in on our target.

"All call signs, this is S3. Found something, all to my location by the cellar door. Out."

I pull the door open. We pause for a second, listening for footsteps coming our way. There aren't any, so we start descending the stairway into the cellar. The air grows colder, and the scent of dampness is in the atmosphere. The flicker of lights hanging from the wall along the brick tunnel guides us toward another closed door. Behind could be the epicentre of a clandestine operation.

As we approach, the murmur intensifies, voices now audible. The door creaks open, revealing a hidden chamber. Bodyguards, unsuspecting of our presence, are engaged in hushed conversation.

"Looks like we've got company — armed guards," says Derek, stopping short of the door.

I reload the magazine of the pistol so I can enter any firefight with at least a full mag of ammo. Derek does the same.

"You ready, mate?" Derek nods.

I take a moment to steady my breathing and put any fears aside. I take a deep breath, exhale, and repeat several times. With a deep breath, I push aside doubts and focus on the task. Beside me, Derek stands poised and ready, his eyes betraying the same determination as me. One final inhalation and I throw open the door.

The room erupts into a symphony of chaos, as bullets tear through the air in a flurry of controlled violence. Each shot is a calculated strike to eliminate the threats between us and our objective. Each bullet is a step closer to finding Lucas and the answers we seek. Amidst the chaos, the scent of gunpowder lingers in the air. The shadows dance in sync with our movements, a ballet of conflict in the cellar's near darkness. Each action is a calculated risk, bringing us closer to our target.

"Where is he?" Derek mutters, frustration etched on his face.

Lucy and George appear at the doorway, their eyes scanning the room for any hidden passages.

"Over here," Lucy's voice rings out, a beacon of hope amid the swirling chaos.

Her finger points to a hidden doorway camouflaged by a stack of shelves against the far wall. Beyond it, a staircase descends deeper into the bowels of the house.

We must be getting closer. We proceed with caution as we descend into the darkness. Every step we take brings us closer to our target. The air is thick with anticipation, and the unknown lies in the hidden depths below. As we reach the bottom, we hear a hushed murmur of voices.

The room is suffocating as we confront Lucas, the enigmatic cartel leader on the island. The man we came here to find. My eyes lock onto his, searching for any cracks in the façade. This is my arena, and Lucas is about to become the prey in my silent dance. A nod is my only response as I approach Lucas, the atmosphere charged with tension. I circle him like a predator closing in on its prey.

"You know, Lucas, we can do this the easy way or the hard way. Your call."

Lucas chuckles, an annoying sound that reverberates through the room. "You think you can break me? You're just a pawn in a much larger game."

With an air of arrogance, Lucas takes a seat, believing we need him alive if we want to find out where Abbie and Bethanie are being held.

"Boys, help our friend stay seated. I would hate for him to miss the opportunity to talk to Lucy. Tie his hands and feet to the chair with a couple of cable ties," I say, walking towards and stopping a few feet from Lucas. I maintain my composure, masking the unease that his words stir within me.

"Once last thing before you start, Lucy."

I walk over, remove the electric cables from the air conditioning unit, and connect them to the metal frame of the chair Lucas is now sitting in. From a drinks cooler, I remove the water bottle and pour it into a washing-up bowl from over near their coffee-making area. Remove his socks and shoes and place them into the bowl of water.

"Over to you, Lucy, do your thing."

I stand alongside Lucy, our collective focus honed on Lucas, our sole beacon of hope in the desperate quest to locate Abbie and Bethanie. Lucas appears like a cornered animal, his posture tense and defensive, his eyes darting between Lucy and each member of our team.

Lucy initiates the interrogation with soft, measured words, a veneer of kindness masking the steel beneath.

"Lucas, we're here to help," she says, her voice dripping with false warmth, gentle yet firm. "We know you've been working with Acosta. Can you tell us where he's keeping Abbie and Bethanie?"

Lucas squirms in his seat, his agitation palpable, his eyes flitting around the room like a trapped creature seeking escape. Fear gnaws at him, etching lines of desperation into his features. Despite this, Lucy continues her questions growing sharper, more pointed, with each passing moment.

"Don't play games with us. Don't make this harder than it needs to be, Lucas," Lucy snaps, her patience wearing thin. "We know you're lying and hiding something. Tell us where they are, or things will get very unpleasant for you."

I monitor Lucas as he shifts uncomfortably. Beads of sweat appear on his brow as he struggles to find the right words.

"I don't know what you're talking about," he protests, his voice devoid of conviction.

Lucy's interrogation intensifies. Her demeanour is unwavering as she leans forward, her gaze piercing.

"You've been working with Acosta for years," she accuses. "You know where he's keeping Steve's daughters. Tell us, and maybe we can help you."

My frustration boils over, a tempest brewing beneath my calm exterior. I advance, my steps heavy with anger, and with a swift, unyielding motion, I strike Lucas across the head, the crack echoing through the cellar like a gunshot.

"Enough of your games, Lucas," I snarl, my voice thick with fury. "Tell us where they are, or I swear..."

Lucas reels from the blow, his persona crumbling as he recoils, hands rising to shield himself out of instinct. But before he can utter a word, Lucy interjects, her voice cutting through the tension like a blade.

"Steve, calm down," she commands, her tone measured but resolute. "Violence won't solve anything. Let me handle this."

Her planned words offer a glimmer of false comfort to Lucas, a fleeting hope that someone here might have his best interests at heart. But beneath Lucy's calm demeanour lies a relentless determination, a resolve to extract the truth by any means necessary. And in this high-stakes game, there's no room for sentimentality or mercy. As Lucas' breaths come in shallow gasps, he frantically searches for an escape.

"I... I can't," he mutters, fear evident in his eyes, doubt flickering within.

Leaning back in her chair, Lucy crosses her arms, her tone cutting through the silence. "You can't, or you won't? Think about what's at stake here," she urges, her voice intense.

Lucas swallows hard, his fear palpable. "I... I can't," he admits, his voice just above a whisper.

"The longer you wait, the worse it's going to be for you," Lucy presses, her voice quiet yet intense, with a hint of urgency.

Leaning forward again, her eyes boring into his, Lucy implores, "Listen to me, Lucas. Your only chance of getting out of this alive is to cooperate. You can either help us, or you can face the consequences. The longer you wait, the worse it will be for you."

Lucy's persistence pays off. Lucas slumps back in his chair, defeated, his resolve crumbling under her relentless pressure. With a defeated sigh, he finally speaks.

Now pleading for his life, his voice trembling with fear, "First, they're not on the island," he stammers, desperation evident in his tone. "You were brought here to keep you motivated and unable to plan an attack."

His words hang heavy in the air, sending a shiver down my spine. Lucas' eyes dart around the room, betraying his unease as he continues, "Yes, we know about your team's reputation. Your daughters are being kept near the fort called Brimstone Fortress on St Kitts."

His admission sends a chill through the room, the gravity of his revelation sinking in. Lucas' voice falters as he reveals, "As for whom? You're right. I've been working for Alex Acosta, who runs the biggest drug cartel in the Caribbean. He has your daughters. I do not know why."

Fear consumes him, his words a desperate plea for mercy. "Now let me go," he begs, his voice trembling with terror.

As Lucy continues to question Lucas, coaxing out every detail he knows about Acosta's operation, the tension in the room remains palpable. We're walking a tightrope, every word fraught with the potential to tip the scales in our favour or lead to our downfall.

But Lucy's determination remains steadfast, her resolve unshakeable. With each word she pries from Lucas, we edge closer to the truth, armed with the knowledge we need to find Abbie and Bethanie.

"OK, untie him, boys, and let him leave," says Lucy, her voice unnerving yet calm despite the gravity of the situation.

Following Lucy's instructions, Simon and Derek move towards Lucas, their steps deliberate and calculated as they loosen his restraints. With a shaky breath Lucas rises from his chair, his eyes darting around the room in search of hidden threats, fear etched into his trembling frame. Unease fills the room. We all know he won't reach the door alive but we play along. This is a game with a foregone conclusion.

Despite our unexpected act of clemency, he remains on edge, his instincts warning him of impending danger.

As Lucas takes tentative steps towards the door, "One thing before you leave, Lucas," I call out, my voice laced with a chilling edge.

Lucas freezes in his tracks, his body tense with apprehension as he turns to face me, a mixture of confusion and dread clouding his expression.

"She said you could leave. I didn't," I declare, my words heavy with malice.

With a swift and calculated motion, I draw the pistol concealed behind my back, the cold metal chilling my palm as I take aim. The air hangs heavy with anticipation as I squeeze the trigger, the deafening crack of gunfire shattering the silence.

A single round strikes Lucas in the centre of his face, his body convulsing with the force of the impact before crumpling to the floor in a lifeless heap.

"Now we have the information we need," I state, my voice devoid of remorse as I holster the weapon. "Now we have a better understanding of where my girls are, let's get moving towards the airport."

Turning to Simon, "See if you can find the keys to any of his vehicles parked in the underground car park. We'll meet you there once we're ready. Nobody is waiting for us outside."

Chapter Six - Arrival on St Kitts

With Simon at the wheel, we speed away from the village as dawn breaks on the horizon. Silence fills the car as we all come to terms with the gravity of our situation. The events that took place at Lucas' house weigh on all our minds, serving as a haunting reminder of the dangers we face.

As we approach another small town, the clock reads 07:00. Lucas' interrogation took longer than expected, but we've gained control of the situation. No longer are we pawns in their game; we hold the reins now.

I glance at Simon, breaking the silence.

"Find a spot to pull over," I instruct. "We need new clothes, if yours looks anything like mine—stained with someone else's blood. There's a town up ahead. There must be a shop where we can outfit ourselves."

Minutes later, Simon veers onto a dirt track, stopping beside an isolated, grey concrete building. With the engine silenced, he swivels in his seat to face the team.

"What's the plan, going forward?" asks Lucy, from the rear seat.

"I'm still running that through my head. The first thing we need to do is make our way to St Kitts. I've had a quick look on my phone, and it says it is only a four-hour flight, and according to a booking site, there are six flights a day. So I suggest we buy some new clothes and head there. Once we are on the island, set up camp somewhere, then rescue Abbie and Bethanie. I can make a better plan once we are on the island."

"Are you sure they are there, and these idiots haven't fed us another load of bullshit?"

"In my opinion, George, people being interrogated and fearing for their lives tend to tell the truth. They have nothing to lose," says Lucy, shifting in her seat.

"The question is, do we carry out normal operating procedures or go straight in and grab the girls, making a plan as we go?" asks Derek.

"One thing we have learned over the years of doing operations is, always making a plan. This time, it is more important, as the people who have the girls hostage are no fools. They are well prepared and have us on a merry dance the whole time. We will be walking into a major firefight, that's for sure. Without planning, one of us may not come back alive."

"That's all true, Steve. We better have a plan. Once we are on the island and have established a base, I suggest we complete a recce from there, as we do on every mission, and always come back alive without many holes in any body parts."

"I'm with Simon on that point. A recce is important. Not only to ensure we come back intact but also to prevent these people from appearing in some shape on every mission we go on," I say, glancing down at my wristwatch to check the time.

"Yep, now that is one thing we can all agree on. Fucking sick of seeing envelopes with blue stripes," adds George.

We debate the next course of action for the next hour or so. In the end, we decide we can't plan anything in detail or make concrete plans until we gather more intel on St Kitts. With a wary glance around, we agree it's time to hit the town; the shops should be opening soon.

If anyone asks why we have blood stains, we will say we have been hunting, which isn't too far from the truth. The shopkeeper doesn't need to know we were hunting people, not animals.

Once we are ready, Simon fires up the engine and with a nod of agreement, we set off. Simon at the wheel navigating the streets, luck seems to be on our side as we spot the perfect shop on the outskirts of town, inconspicuous yet promising.

It is an unobtrusive beige brick shop with two big windows facing the road. In these windows, mannequins are dressed in jeans and T-shirts in various colours. Parking just outside, we make our way inside.

A bell above the door rings as we enter. The shop's interior is a stark contrast to the chaos swirling outside, bathed in a welcoming glow but does little to ease the tension in the air. Shelves display an assortment of clothes, some hanging from rails. At the rear of the shop, a blue curtain hides a changing room. A young woman in her early 20s emerges from the back.

"Good morning, how can I help you?" she greets us, her voice tinged with innocence.

"Morning. We're in need of some new attire," Lucy chimes in smoothly, her tone light but calculated, diverting attention from our blood-stained clothes. "Lost our bags, you see. Catching a flight later, and I doubt they'd let us on looking like this," she adds with a forced laugh, a façade to ward off unwanted scrutiny.

The shopkeeper's demeanour softens at Lucy's explanation and her suspicions calm.

"Of course, you're free to try anything. They're all priced," she offers, unaware she is falling into our trap.

Fifteen tense minutes later, we emerge from the shop, clad in fresh garments. With a collective intake of air, we pile back into the vehicle, our disguise in place as we brace ourselves for the journey to the airport.

After an hour's drive, we are back at Flamingo International Airport. Due to the fact we purchased the tickets via Billy back in the UK, and already have our boarding passes, there is no need to to go to the check-in desk. So after going through security, we are now waiting at the gate to board. The departure gate is full of locals and tourists alike, ready for the short flight to St Kitts.

The constant hum of chatter of people breaks into near silence as short messages come via the tannoy. Each person is eager for their group number to be called. As this is only a short flight, we have booked ourselves into cattle class at the back of the plane, so we are one of the last people to board the aircraft.

I take up my window seat next to Lucy and Simon. The other two are behind us. After listening to the usual speech from the flight attendants about safety on the plane, I take their advice and sit back and relax. Well, I try to.

The moment the aircraft takes off, my thoughts turn to the team and what I'm asking them to do, not only for me but for my daughters. Yes, we have done plenty of missions in the past and put ourselves in harm's way for different situations and rescues. But this time, it is different. There is no money for the job except what we liberated from Lucas. They are doing this one for free.

I've known George and Simon the longest, going back to the days at the Combat Stress Treatment Centre in Leatherhead. We were all there because of our battle with PTSD in some shape or form. Each of us had individual battles to win, from Simon picking up body parts in Iraq to George watching his friends being killed.

As for my own issues, this goes back to the forgotten war, Northern Ireland, due to the terrorist trying to blow me away by pointing a pistol at my head and pulling the trigger. Lucky for me, it misfired. Or maybe it was due to me working undercover and coming across an IRA vehicle check on my own, driving a plain convert car in the middle of the Irish countryside with no place to hide.

Whatever the case, we all knew the risks. In my case, due to my PTSD, I do not have any empathy, which makes the killing easier. I work on the philosophy: I do not know them, so I don't care.

For Lucy, her story is different. Even though we only met up after the mission on the Isle of Wight, we have been together since. I would be lost without her. Her past goes back to her army days in the intelligence corps. So she is used to working under pressure. She spent some time fighting for whoever paid her the most.

As for Derek, he helped us out on our first mission on the island of St Halb, and from then on, he's been on all the missions. He is a great asset with his skills in radio and communication.

But somehow, even though they have agreed to help and aren't worried about the money, they are doing this because they got to know Bethanie and Abbie. I feel guilty about asking them to risk their lives for the girls and me. This is a strange emotion to me due to my lack of empathy, which usually makes me not care. But these are my small group of friends, so it is different. I do care what happens to them.

My chain of thinking is interrupted when Lucy grabs my arm.

"You want a drink?" she asks, pointing at the air steward standing by Simon with a cart of drinks.

"Yes, please. Do you have any beer?" I ask the hostess. She hands me the can and a plastic glass, and I sit back again.

"You're miles away, honey. You OK?" asks Lucy, also opening a can of beer.

"Fine, thanks, Lucy, I'm just running through a few things in my head."

"Well, don't become lost in there," Lucy smiles and goes back to watching a movie.

I put on the provided headphones and switch on a TV screen in the back of the chair in front of me. The first movie photo on the screen depicts a happy family. My mind starts to focus on Abbie and Bethanie and the fun days we had when I was able to pick them up from their mother's house.

On many occasions, I would drive from Magdeburg in Germany, where I worked, to their mum's house in Southampton on a Friday night. See them for the weekend, making sure we always do something fun. Then, I would drive back to work on a Sunday night, for a total of nine hours driving each way.

Sometimes, I would turn play into essential life lessons and teach them unarmed combat and survival techniques. I always ensured I did it in a way they loved doing it. Now, they are being held hostage for something the team did a long time ago. I push away the thoughts, in the knowledge they will remember what I taught them. With luck, they are giving as much as they are receiving from the people I will kill to get them back.

According to the moving map I'd put on the screen, it is still two hours before we land on St Kitts. I decide I need a coffee, so being too lazy to get up and get one from the hard-working flight attendants, I press the button above my head.

"Anyone want a brew?" I turn to face Derek and George, who are both asleep.

"I'll have one," says Simon.

"And me, honey," comes the reply from Lucy.

Within minutes, a young man named Jason asks if he can get us anything. "Three coffees, please."

"What have you been watching?" I point at Lucy's screen.

"I tried to watch some soppy romantic film, but my mind keeps returning to the name Lucas confirmed to us, Alex Acosta."

"What about him? Do you know of him?" I ask

Before we say any more, the coffees arrive, and Simon takes them from Jason.

"No, it's worse than that. I think I used to work for him indirectly for a while. Well, before I met you and the team. If he is the man, I think it was in Columbia. A group of us were employed and paid a shit load of money via an agency that recruited mercenaries to protect a person, who may have been Alex Acosta.

"We were tasked to escort him back to an island in the Caribbean. I can't remember the name of the place. But I do remember it got fucked up as a rival gang ambushed us. They knew where we were and the route we planned to take. A lot of people got killed. I'm positive I saw him lying face down in a ditch. If he was dead or not, I couldn't tell you. I was lucky to get out of there myself. That is, of course, if this is the same person we are talking about."

"Don't worry. It was a long time ago, and we will not judge for it. Thinking about it, when I tell the rest, they will take the piss out of you for working for the enemy for a very long time." I say, chuckling, trying to lighten the mood.

"You're right there, Steve," says Lucy with a smile, as if a weight had been taken off her shoulders.

"In case you are wondering, yes, I did hear what Lucy just said, and Steve is right, we are going to take the piss," says Simon, after taking a swig of his brew.

The captain's voice crackles over the speakers, announcing our imminent descent towards Robert L Bradshaw Airport in St Kitts — 30 minutes until touchdown. The cabin crew prepares for landing.

I brace myself as the plane descends, my heart pounding in anticipation.

With a jolt, the undercarriage touches down on the runway, and we taxi towards our designated gate. I resist the urge to join the scramble to grab bags from the overhead locker or the rush to be first off the plane. Instead, we wait, watching the passengers surge past us towards the exit. Patience is our ally in this game of stealth.

Stepping into the terminal, the atmosphere crackles with energy. The warm Caribbean breeze caresses my skin. The scent of tropical blooms mingles with the distant tang of sea salt, creating an olfactory welcome that's as comforting as it is invigorating. But danger lurks beneath this serenity, ready to pounce at any moment.

As we weave through the corridor towards passport control, the fluorescent lights cast sinister shadows on the polished floors. The hum of conversations in multiple languages fills the air, blending into a cacophony of international travel. I remind the team to stay vigilant as we're walking into the unknown. Alex's or Lucas' people could be waiting for us to land. Even in this paradise, vigilance could mean the difference between success and failure.

The line at passport control crawls forward, each step a test of patience and nerves, with each person moving through the process at a painstaking pace. The uniformed officers, though professional, emanate an aura of suspicion as they process each traveller with meticulous care. Overhead, announcements echo in a blend of English and local dialects, a constant reminder of the chaos and uncertainty that engulfs us, keeping us on our toes.

As we near the customs area, Lucy and George exchange a wordless glance, a silent acknowledgement of the tension in the air. The rhythmic clatter of luggage wheels echoes against the floor as our bags, brimming with mission-critical supplies, trail behind us.

In impeccable attire, the customs officers inspect bags with a meticulousness that borders on suspicion, their eyes darting from one item to the next. The walls are adorned with vibrant Caribbean artwork, a stark contrast to the serious formality of the security checkpoint. The air crackles with anticipation, each arrival and departure contributing to the airport's electric energy.

As I approach the customs officer, he greets me with a friendly smile. "Welcome to St Kitts. Business or pleasure?"

I respond, "Business, mostly."

The officer nods and scans my passports and documents with a trained eye.

The ambient hum of conversations and the occasional click of a suitcase being opened create a soothing background as we move through customs. The anticipation of a new phase of the mission lingers in the air, blending with the sounds of travel.

"Clear," announces the customs officer, handing back my passport.

Stepping into the arrival hall, the vibrant colours of the Caribbean beckon.

Perhaps it's the gravity of our mission or simply ingrained habit, but we find ourselves in a terminal café, scanning the faces around us with suspicion. Every person lingering near an exit becomes a potential threat. Are they innocently waiting for loved ones, or are they here on orders, watching for us?

To ascertain their intentions, Derek and George volunteer to scout the area, exiting the building through one door while the rest of us remain vigilant from our seats. Minutes stretch into eternity as we wait, our nerves on edge. No movement at the door suggests our presence remains undetected. Minutes later, George and Derek reappear through a different exit, unharmed but no less wary.

"While we're here, it's best to bide our time until the next flight arrives from a location we haven't visited," I suggest, glancing around the bustling terminal. "Once we're clear, we'll head to the hotel I booked online during the flight. It's only a short drive from where Lucas indicated the girls are being held. I've secured accommodations for a week."

"What about transportation on the island?" Lucy interjects, her gaze sharp.

"Renting a vehicle might tip off anyone watching our movements. It may be safer to purchase one in the local area, even if it's an old banger. I can have it up and running in no time."

"Excellent idea, Simon. A chance we might have to take," I reply.

As the crowds from customs swell, our plan is set in motion. I consult the terminal map on my phone, identifying the departure area on the floor above.

"No time to waste. OK, let's move and head for a taxi," I assert, tucking my phone away.

To disorient anyone watching our movements, we weave through the crowd, positioning ourselves near the end of the taxi rank. Memories of our encounter at the Bonaire airport spur us to remain vigilant. Instead of hailing a cab straight away, we backtrack into the terminal, pausing just inside the doorway to assess the situation. Thus far, there's no sign of pursuit. Satisfied, we proceed to the departure level via the lifts and exit the building.

Outside, we spot a cab unloading passengers and their luggage. I approach the driver, who's busy closing the boot, and enquire, "Can you take us to the Ramada Hotel, please?" The team remains silent, understanding my intentions.

The driver hesitates, citing some unwritten cabbie rules, and suggests we head to arrivals for a taxi. I slide a crisp 100-dollar bill under his nose, my voice steady but firm.

"Alright, just this once. Get in," he relents, succumbing to the temptation of easy money.

The contrast between the car's cool interior and the Caribbean heat is stark. The scent of leather and the hum of the engine offers a temporary respite from the sweltering outdoors. As we depart from the airport, I glance at the palm trees swaying in the breeze, their fronds beckoning us to the island.

As we wind through St Kitts' roads, vibrant colours blur past the window. Quaint houses painted in pastel hues, locals engaged in animated conversations by the roadside, and the azure sea stretching to the horizon.

The Ramada emerges like a beacon of modernity amidst the island's natural splendour. We step out into the warmth. I can't shake the unease lingering from our ordeal at the Bonaire hotel. We head inside, taking a seat in the bustling lobby and keeping a watchful eye.

After 10 tense minutes, we emerge back into the open air and slide into another cab. This time, the driver navigates us to the Kittitian Hill Hotel, nestled away from the tourist hubs. It's the perfect hideout for our mission. Yet, a nagging sense of apprehension gnaws at me — what if someone traces our steps from the previous cab ride? We've taken precautions, but there's no room for complacency in our line of work.

Chapter Seven - Information

As the taxi winds its way toward the secluded villa atop the hill, the midday sun casts an oppressive heat over the landscape, intensifying the sense of isolation. The dense foliage shrouding the villa appears to be closing in on us, creating an ominous atmosphere despite the vibrant hues of the tropical flora flashing past.

As we approach, tension crackles in the air, almost tangible beneath the natural beauty that surrounds us. The taxi halts at the entrance, and I exchange a wary glance with my team before paying the driver. The distant crash of waves serves as a stark reminder of our vulnerability in this unfamiliar territory.

A man emerges, immaculately dressed in a tailored suit, the subtle glint of a wristwatch catching the sunlight. His demeanour is polished but inscrutable.

"I'm Victor. I'm here to give you the key and show you around the villa," he announces, extending a hand in a greeting that invites us into the villa's sanctuary.

"Hi Victor, nice to meet you," I respond, accepting the key with caution, as my PTSD makes it hard to trust someone I've just met.

With Victor as our guide, we step into the villa's opulent interior, every luxury belying the potential danger lurking within its shadows. The marble foyer gleams under soft lighting, its polished surface betraying no hint of the shadows that may linger. As he leads us deeper into the villa, my senses remain on high alert, attuned to any sign of threat.

Victor guides us through the expansive space, leading toward a corridor that extends into the villa's depths.

Our senses are attuned to any anomaly in this tranquil setting. The air is thick with the scent of tropical flowers, and a warm breeze carries the distant melody of the Caribbean. But in the world in which we operate, appearances can deceive.

"The meeting room awaits, ladies and gentlemen," Victor gestures. "Feel free to acquaint yourselves with the surroundings. I've left the keys on the kitchen table along with my number. If you have any problems or need a local guide, give me a call."

"Will do, thanks," I reply, watching Victor walk off.

With Victor out of the way, I turn to the team, "First, let's check the place out. George, you and Simon check the perimeter while the rest of us check the interior. Any problems, radio it through."

We disperse, moving with calculated precision. The villa layout is open, but my instincts remind me that every corner could harbour a potential threat. I scrutinise the artwork on the walls – not mere decorations but could be concealing surveillance equipment. I lift each one, checking the rear of any wires or holes that could be hiding cameras.

Lucy, her eyes sharp, leans in and murmurs, "This place is a fortress disguised as a vacation home. Don't let it fool you."

I nod in agreement. I walk over to the window and scan the horizon for potential snipers. Derek removes his laptop and focuses on the villa's technological nerve centre, searching for electronic eyes and ears.

As I approach the meeting room, I notice movement in the corridor and draw my knife, approaching the shadowy corners with caution. The villa's intricate design presents countless paths, and the team uses radio communication to navigate through the interconnected rooms, all decorated with a Caribbean-inspired theme.

Moments later, I detect a stray noise in the secluded courtyard that grabs my attention. I radio George, "Check the courtyard. Something out there is moving."

"On my way."

A few minutes later, George's voice comes over the radio, "Clear," his voice affirms.

After half an hour, we regroup and move towards the meeting room. The villa's luxurious exterior masks its true nature—a battleground where every corner and shadow could conceal danger. Our every move is calculated. The line between opulence and covert operations blurs, and I know that even in this paradise, the shadows may hide more than just secrets.

Once everyone has returned and is standing in the meeting room, "This is it, team. St Kitts may look like paradise, but every shadow will hold a secret, and danger lurks behind the beauty. Let's unearth them. So, let's get our bearings.

"Simon, can you check any alternative routes that leave here, in case we need to leave in a hurry? While you are looking, find the best route from here to where Lucas said the girls are being held."

"No problem, Steve, I picked up a Splashmap at the airport," replies Simon, opening his Bergen.

"Derek, with your equipment and the phone you took from Lucas, see if it contains any local numbers on St Kitts stored in recent calls. Then, see if you can tap into the villa's electronic devices and the phoneline if we need to trace any calls. Also, set up the encoding protocols. Don't want any nosey gits listening in on our communications."

On it, mate," comes the reply from Derek, opening his laptop.

I continue, "George, make your way to the roof and scout sniper positions you and Lucy can use to your advantage. Plus, any position you believe if we come under fire, the possible locations of the shooter. Lucy, can you check the maps with Simon and try to locate street cafés or bars where we might find locals who may provide information? We need to know how deep the Acosta roots go on this island."

"I'll take a look, but it will be hard. Would be better if we take a trip around the local area to find spots of interest," Lucy replies.

As the team disperses to their designated tasks, the villa transforms into a hub of covert operations. At last, we are the ones deciding what we do next, not the arseholes holding my daughters.

The air within the villa is charged with focused determination. I look at each face. Derek hunches over his tech gear, fingers dancing over the keyboard, engaging any encryption protocols we might require.

The Splashmap is unfolded on the small mahogany coffee table, and Simon and Lucy trace the intricate web of St Kitts.

While the rest of the team goes about their assigned tasks, my mind turns to a plan for gathering information and how we will get it. Lucy is right, we need to visit the local village. Think we should visit a café or bar, act like stupid tourists, and ask questions in a manner that appears random to the untrained.

One of the big ones we need to uncover is how far Acosta's influence goes. Does his cartel do more than drugs? What other criminal activities do they carry out? Apart from hostage-taking. Like all criminal gangs, they will be armed and ready to kill anyone who gets in their way.

I walk over to Lucy and Simon, "How are you getting on?"

"It appears there is a track that leads away from the rear of the property, before winding its way through a forest and coming out at a local village. It could be a good alternative route if we need to bug out," Simon replies.

"What about you, Lucy? Do you find anything interesting?"

"Not sure, Steve. A few places on the map are identified as bars and restaurants, but as I said, we need to go there to gain any intel."

At that moment, George enters the room after his visit to the roof to scan for sniper positions. "Only a few issues that I can see for possible firing locations. One by the concrete posts when you turn off the road and enter the property. The other area is the rear. There is a forest about 200 metres from the rear fence. Could conceal a sniper. As for our sniper hides, plenty of scopes up there."

"Cheers, George," I say, my mind starting to plan for defensive positions in case of any attack.

Two hours later, everyone has finished what they were doing and join me in the kitchen, where I am sitting at a table drinking a cold beer I found in the fridge. Victor must know his job.

"Grab yourselves a drink," I point to the cans on the table.

"What's the plan?" asks Simon, downing half a can of beer.

"As Lucy said, we need to go to the local village to gather intelligence once we have set up protection around the villa with our limited resources. This reminds me: can you contact our friends, Katie and Cody, and arrange weapons and explosives, Simon? We are then heading out. With any luck, we will find a 4x4 vehicle for sale, so we will have transport while we are here."

I scour the house for items I can use for IEDs and find a roll of clear tape, a coil of thin wire, a couple of bits of thicker wire, a 12-volt battery, and a Bic pen. 'That will have to do', I think to myself.

I give the tape to George and Simon, who then create tell-tales on each window by taping a hair between the window frame and window. If anyone comes in that way, the connection will be broken, and we will know somebody is in the house.

While they are doing that, "Derek, can you rip the electrical lead out of the toaster? Try to make the cable as long as possible," I say, putting the pen down on the table.

I remove the inner part of the pen and discard it, insert the thicker wire, and check it slides up and down with ease. Next, thread one wire into the hole on the side. After inserting the other a little way into the bottom, attach it to the rear door handle. Ensure the wire inside moves and comes in contact with the other two wires when I push down.

The final piece is to attach the small wires to the one Derek removed from the toaster. With the team busy and away from the door, I put the plug back in the mains. Now, if anyone tries to open the door, they will be electrocuted.

Twenty minutes later, the house is set, and the taxi Simon called a few minutes ago arrives.

As we leave, I try to engage with the driver to find out if Alex Acosta's reach includes taxi firms. "So, is this your cab, or does it belong to a company?"

There is a few seconds of silence before the driver reluctantly answers, "It is my cab, but I have to pay another firm a small amount."

He doesn't have to say more; I suspect he needs to pay someone for the right to use his vehicle without hiccups.

Twenty minutes later, we pull up outside an establishment on the outskirts of town. The night unfolds in a symphony of tropical allure as we step into the dimly lit sanctuary of The Siren's Call—a local bar hidden from the prying eyes of casual tourists.

Inside, the air hangs heavy with the scent of exotic blossoms, masking any hint of danger that may lurk in the shadows. Conversations hum like a sinister undertone beneath the soft melody of reggae music, setting an uneasy atmosphere.

The bar's layout appears innocuous at first glance, with wooden tables and chairs arranged in an intimate setting. But beneath the veneer of tropical charm lies an undercurrent of tension, amplified by the worn stools lining the bar counter and the small stage where a live band plays steel drums in the corner.

Local artwork adorns the walls, and their vibrant colours are a stark contrast to the clandestine nature of our mission. As we blend into the crowd, our attire carefully chosen to blend in with the tourists, I can't shake the feeling of being watched. Each clink of glasses and burst of laughter is like a warning, a reminder of the dangers that lurk in the shadows.

Seated in a corner booth, I run my fingers over the worn wood, its history a silent testament to the secrets it has borne witness to. We order drinks with caution, choosing rum-infused elixirs with names that sound like hollow promises of escape, each sip tinged with the bitter taste of uncertainty.

The clinking glasses echo our silent pact, and Lucy, with an air of casual curiosity, navigates the conversation toward our elusive target.

"So, folks, what's the buzz around here? Any exciting local stories or hidden gems we should explore?" Lucy asks, her tone casual, a perfect mimicry of a curious tourist.

A couple at the adjacent table, emboldened by their shared love for the island, dive into narratives of festivals and secluded beaches. George engages the bartender, a wizened local with tattoos that hint at untold stories.

"Barkeep, what's the secret behind the 'Mystic Sunset'?" George remarks, his genuine grin masking his ulterior motive.

Derek initiates banter with a group at the bar, seamlessly transitioning to the topic at hand. An older gentleman, his face weathered and worn after a life of hard work, sits sipping on whiskey, basking in the camaraderie. He regales us with stories of island life, each anecdote adding depth to the tapestry of St Kitts. Derek, ever the master of conversation, steers the discussion toward our mission, his enquiries cloaked in the guise of curiosity.

"Where does one find the most authentic flavours around here?" Derek's question hangs in the air, drawing the attention of the patrons.

Another man perched on the adjacent stool leans in, his expression guarded yet intrigued. "If you're after the real thing, you'll need to venture beyond the tourist traps," he advises, his words tinged with caution. "Head to the local villages. That's where you'll find the true flavour of the island."

Derek nods, his interest piqued. "That sounds like my kind of adventure. Are there any particular spots you'd recommend?"

The bartender, wiping down the counter with practised ease, chimes in. "There's a little joint down in Basseterre that serves up the best jerk chicken you'll ever taste. And if you're up for it, you can try your luck at one of the village street food stalls."

His words hang in the air, a subtle warning beneath the veneer of hospitality. "Just be careful," he cautions, his tone grave. "The streets can be dangerous, especially for outsiders asking too many questions."

A chill runs down Derek's spine as the implications sink in. The bartender's warning is clear — the local cartel, led by the notorious Alex Acosta, does not take kindly to prying eyes.

As the night progresses, we entwine our questions within the fabric of innocent discourse. The live band, its rhythm a strategic backdrop, provides a symphony for our covert ballet. The team are working well.

Simon is engaging with a group of young men near the stage, their laughter blending with the band's melodic tunes. Amidst the crowd, one figure merges into the background like a shadow in the night: a lone man leaning against the back wall, clad in casual attire that fails to conceal his calculated demeanour. His eyes, hidden in the dark shadows, survey the room with a keenness that sends shivers down my spine.

A glimmer of suspicion flickers in my mind. Could this be the man we've been searching for? The one with knowledge of the cartel's inner workings? Or perhaps he's just another tourist, oblivious to the dangers that lurk beneath the surface of this island paradise.

My doubts linger as a man in his early 20s wearing jeans and a T-shirt approaches him, taking a seat across the table. A hushed exchange follows, and my suspicions are confirmed as I watch him slide an envelope across the table before leaving the scene without a second glance.

I fixate on him, my instincts screaming for caution. Is he a potential ally or a threat lurking in the shadows? We may need to take a chance, with no intel yet on Abbie and Bethanie.

Wait a few minutes. I'm about to get up and walk over to join him when Lucy grabs my arm. "Leave it to me; it will make him believe this is his lucky day."

"Hello, I'm Lucy. We saw you sitting over here by yourself, so I thought I would come over for a chat and invite you to join us," says Lucy, pulling up a chair and introducing herself.

"Hi, my name is Miguel. Are you and your friends here on the island for long?"

"We are here for the week and want to get away from the tourist trail and experience the true island life. You appear to be a local man. Can you recommend anywhere? Do you have any advice or safety tips?" replies Lucy.

"I've lived in the village most of my life, so I know the area and people very well," Miguel says, his voice hushed and cautious as if sharing a secret. He takes a sip from his bottle of beer, his gaze flickering to the shadows beyond the dimly lit bar. "As for where to go, you can visit the fishermen on the beach, but you'll have to be there about 10:00 to catch them returning with their haul of the day. There's a café across the road from the beach. Be careful of who you talk to."

"Why's that?" Lucy's voice carries a note of urgency, her eyes narrowing as she leans in, hoping for valuable intel.

Miguel hesitates, choosing his words carefully. "Let me just say there are people in there who are not as welcoming as me. They may have contacts with the gang that runs the underbelly and criminal activities on the island."

"Thanks for the info and advice," Lucy replies, her tone reflecting gratitude tinged with apprehension. "Would you like to join us for a few beers?" She gestures back to our table, attempting to lighten the heavy atmosphere.

"No, thank you," Miguel declines, his expression serious. "I'm on duty in a few hours, so I must leave in five minutes. Remember what I said. Be careful, and don't ask too many questions. The locals are wary of strangers in case they're connected with the Alex Acosta cartel, who have been known to take action against anyone who says the wrong thing."

"On duty? Are you a policeman or something?" asks Lucy.

"You could say that. Here is my business card. If you get into any trouble or want someone to show you around, I'm off for a few days after tomorrow. Call me."

"OK, thanks. We will do," says Lucy, getting up and walking over to rejoin us at the table.

In case our conversation is overheard, we keep the discussion about holidays and places to visit. Of course, we have no such plans. But for the benefit of anyone listening, we are laying a false trail in case they want to jump us.

The air, now laden with the faint aroma of Caribbean cigars and the remnants of our tropical elixirs, carries the resonance of discreet enquiries. Our mission, shrouded in the illusion of tourist whimsy, bears fruit in the strategic dance of conversation—a testament to the artistry of shadows in the world of covert operations. After a few more drinks and with nods of camaraderie and a round of laughter, we bid the bar adieu.

We ride back to the villa in tense silence, wary of the driver's ears catching even a whisper of our conversation. Not a word is exchanged except for brief instructions to guide our route and settle the fare upon arrival.

Upon reaching the villa, we conduct a thorough check of our security measures, ensuring our surroundings remain uncompromised. Satisfied that we're alone, I move to disconnect the cables from the rear door.

I join the others, who have moved into the living room and sat down in the plush leather sofas—and drinking more beer from the home bar. Derek, ever vigilant, scrutinises the room with his laptop, scanning for electronic bugs and monitoring incoming messages.

"OK, we don't have any bugs in the house, so it's okay to talk," says Derek, closing his laptop.

"So, what did we find out this evening?" I ask, plonking my arse down in one of the leather chairs.

Simon scratches his head, frustration etched on his face. "When it comes to transport, it's tricky. Locals are tight-lipped. They are too frightened to say anything. We found a few potential routes to the target area, but they're hidden. We know taxis are out of the question as they all work in some shape to Acosta's origination."

"From the information I gathered, I agree with Simon. The locals are terrified. Acosta's presence looms large," adds Lucy.

"I concur. There's an undercurrent of fear. Acosta's network runs deep, and the locals are reluctant to reveal much. Maybe they would say more if they were alone, away from anyone listening," says George.

"You're right. From the information I found out, their power isn't just about smuggling drugs and hostage-taking. It's about controlling perceptions, alliances, and fears," I reply, making a note of the information, ready to make a plan for the next stage.

"We need an insider, someone who can navigate the complexities without raising suspicion," Simon suggests.

The idea hangs in the air, a potential solution to our predicament. "We can't force the locals to help, but we can find someone disillusioned with Acosta's rule," Derek suggests.

I glance around the room, contemplating the risk involved in recruiting someone from within. "It's a gamble, but one we might have to take. Any ideas on how we identify potential candidates."

"The man I spoke to in the bar may be able to help. He is a policeman but says he has lived on the island all his life, so he must know someone who can get us in contact with an individual we can use. He gave me his phone number, said to call him if we needed anything, and offered to show us around the island. Even mentioned a café on the seafront, which might be a place to start."

"It is a starting place, Lucy. Can you call him in the morning? Pretend we want to do a tour of the island. That way, we can get a lay of the land and any potential spots of interest for the mission," I say.

After a glance at the time, "It's late, folks, so let's call it a night, as we need to start early in the morning. We will go to the café Lucy talked about for breakfast and find out who else is around. We need to set up an OP post on the roof, and I suggest we take one hour each. I'll take the first stag, which will give me time to formulate a plan for tomorrow. George, you take the last one. You need more beauty sleep, you ugly bastard."

"You looked in the mirror lately, Steve?" comes the reply from George.

As the clock strikes 23:00, the island descends into a realm of uncertainty. I ascend to the roof, peering into the abyss of darkness that envelops the villa. The night cloaks our sanctuary, its cool breath carrying echoes from the depths of the Caribbean Sea. While my team rests below, my senses remain sharp, alert to the subtle nuances of the nocturnal world.

In the distance, the flicker of passing car lights dance against the black canvas of the night. Beyond the perimeter fence, the looming forest stands as a silent guard, its secrets veiled in shadow. Who knows what dangers lurk within its depths, waiting to be let loose?

The air hums with the concerto of crickets and the distant melody of waves lapping at the shore. I scan the horizon, my gaze unwavering, on the alert for the slightest deviation in the serene landscape. In this game of shadows and silence, patience is our ally, anticipation our constant companion.

As the hour unfolds, a plan takes shape. My thoughts drift to the café on the shoreline at dawn, when the veil of night clings to the world, offering the perfect vantage point. It is a strategic move to monitor the fishermen as they land their catch at dawn, unaware they are players in this dangerous game, that could unveil the cartel's hidden movements. Perhaps, it is a risk, but the potential reward outweighs the danger.

We will enter the café for breakfast, after a quick scan of the area, our training allowing us to spot something out of the ordinary that most would overlook. No need for a lookout yet; it's early, and we should remain unnoticed.

Inside the café, we'll watch and listen for anything useful. Conversations, movements, subtle cues—everything becomes a potential lead. The main objective is clear: find someone who knows the cartel's movements, especially those holding my daughters.

The night, though calm, is alive with the unseen currents of uncertainty. I make a mental note of every rustle in the forest, every distant sound, my senses on high alert. The shadows cast by the moonlight become my allies, concealing my presence from prying eyes.

My mind turns to Abbie and Bethanie and the hell they are still going through, in whatever location is holding them. With any luck, Lucas' information is correct, and we know where to head for. I would love to rush in there now, kill anyone who gets in my way, and rescue them. But my instinct is telling me that we need to gather information and plan if they are to come out of this alive and unharmed.

Out of the darkness I detect a door open on the roof behind me. It is Simon coming to take over the sentry duty. Once he is within earshot, I brief him on events.

"Morning. All quiet so far. I have not seen any activity, apart from something moving at the edge of the woods. It might be worth keeping an eye on it if it turns out to be someone or something watching our movements."

"Will do. Did that tiny brain of yours come up with anything for the morning? We know the girls are out there. We will get them back," says Simon, taking my binoculars from me.

"Thanks, mate, and a lot of people are going to suffer before dying. As for the plan, not much. Will work it out once there," I say, as I descend from the roof.

The night on St Kitts holds its secrets close, but beneath the celestial canvas, a calculated plan unfolds. The shoreline café becomes the next stage, where the local fishermen unwittingly become our allies. The hidden threads of the cartel's web begin to unravel in the dawn light.

Chapter Eight – Café Calypso

The first rays of the St Kitts' sun filter through the villa's windows, casting a gentle glow on the bedroom walls as my alarm goes off. It is 05:00. By the side of me, Lucy clambers out of the bed and wanders off to take a shower. There is a knock at the door.

"Get your hands off each other, you perverts. It's time to get up," George shouts through the door.

"I'm fucking up, idiot," I respond.

George continues down the corridor shouting, "Up and at them, hands off cocks, on with socks."

A few minutes later, Lucy enters the room from the bathroom. "Morning, honey. Did you get any sleep?"

"Some. Spent much of the night thinking about Abbie and Bethanie and the times we all went on holiday. Such happy times. Let's hope they are coping well with the situation."

"I've said it before, and I'll say it again. These are your daughters. You have prepared them to look after themselves their entire lives. And yes, I remember the first time I ever met them. I was so nervous, but they welcomed me in a kind and warm way. Since then, we have been on many wonderful girls' days out. Plus, you will be no good if you can't stay awake. Make sure you get some sleep tonight," replies Lucy, getting dressed.

It isn't long before everyone has finished packing their kit. We may be booked here for a week, but the equipment always needs to remain packed in case we need to bug out. Once Lucy is ready, we head for the living room to join the rest. The team are all there when we arrive. Derek is already on his laptop, checking for unusual communications during the night.

Once he confirms it's clear, "We need to head for the café. It is paramount we find out information on the cartel and a way in today. We must confirm the girls' whereabouts and if they are being moved. Remember, on the last mission, the hostages weren't even in the same country. Not letting that happen again. If you can, call the local taxi firm, Derek. Use the one from last night and ask for the same driver. The fewer people who know our location, the better."

"I'll do that now," comes Derek's response.

"Simon, can you and George confirm the countermeasures are still in place on the windows, etc.? I'll reconnect the IED on the back door. So, from now on, nobody goes to the kitchen once I return."

With a tilt switch in place, I return to the front room.

"Taxi will be here in 15 minutes," shouts Derek from the hallway.

As we step into the awaiting taxi, the morning sun kisses the horizon.

"Where to?" asks the driver.

"Café Calypso, please," my voice soft but firm.

The taxi's engine hums with a sinister undertone as it weaves through the deserted streets of St Kitts. Each turn plunges us deeper into the pre-dawn darkness, a shroud of secrecy enveloping our movements, thickening with every mile we cover.

In the dim light of the vehicle, my team sits in a tense silence; their faces hidden in the shadows, their thoughts a mystery. Yet, beneath the surface, I feel their unwavering resolve, their unspoken agreement to confront any obstacles that may come our way.

As we wind through the labyrinthine streets, the only sounds are the rhythmic beat of our hearts and the steady hum of the engine. Outside, the world begins to stir, awakening to the dawn's embrace. The streets are starting to burst into life as locals begin their day. Streetlamps cast long shadows across the near-deserted roads, a silent testament to the secrets hidden within the city's alleys.

The minutes crawl by, each one stretching like an eternity as we draw nearer to our destination. The air carries the salty tang of the sea, a constant reminder of the dangers that lurk beyond the shore. The sea is whispering secrets only the waves can decipher. And then, like a spectre emerging from the mist, Café Calypso materialises before us, its weathered exterior a silent witness to the mysteries it holds within, emerging from the mist like a ghostly apparition, a testament to the passage of time and the secrets it harbours.

After carrying out a scan of the area, we step into the dimly lit interior. I'm aware of the watchful gazes that follow our every move, like predators sizing up their prey. The walls, adorned with faded maritime decor, bear silent witness to the clandestine conversations that have unfolded within these walls. As we infiltrate this unsuspecting haven, the weight of our mission hangs in the air, a silent reminder of the danger beneath the surface.

Navigating the crowded space, I sense the weight of scrutiny bearing down on me, every eye a potential threat, every whisper a possible betrayal. The fishermen huddled in the corner cast wary glances in our direction, their hushed voices tinged with suspicion. With practised precision, the team disperses, seamlessly blending into the background, their vigilant eyes scanning for any sign of danger.

Approaching the counter, I meet the gaze of the barista, her weathered features betraying nothing of the secrets she indeed holds. With a subtle nod, she acknowledges our presence, a silent agreement in our deadly game of cat and mouse.

In this innocuous café, where the aroma of freshly brewed coffee mingles with the undercurrent of danger, every interaction is fraught with peril, every word a potential trap.

As I order, "Four coffees and a tea, please," I can't shake the sensation that we are walking a tightrope, teetering on the edge of disaster with each passing moment.

Our mission takes on a new urgency in the shadows of Café Calypso, where the line between friend and foe blurs into obscurity.

I stride across the room to join the others at a weathered wooden corner table positioned to offer a panoramic view of the café. The atmosphere is charged with tension. Each team member maintains a strategic distance, ready to spring into action at a moment's notice.

With her keen interrogation skills honed to a razor's edge, Lucy positions herself near the group of fishermen, her presence casting a shadow of unease over their hushed conversations. Derek, the master of communication, blends seamlessly into the background, his ears tuned to the slightest whisper of information.

George and Simon are facing towards the entrance, vigilant for any unexpected arrivals—the dance between surveillance and blending seamlessly with the environment has begun. Each movement is calculated, and each action is deliberate.

My senses sharpen, attuned to the subtle nuances of the surroundings. The aroma of freshly brewed coffee wafts through the air, mingling with the sound of crashing waves against the shore. It's a dichotomy of calm and intensity, a stark reminder of the precarious balance we tread.

However, beneath the café's quaint façade lies a darker truth, a world of danger and intrigue. As I take in the scene before me, I prepare myself for the challenges ahead, knowing that the moment's calm is a fleeting illusion.

Sitting down next to Lucy, "You riff-raff looked at the menu yet? Could murder a full English breakfast," I say, picking up the menu.

"You're out of luck, fat boy, only eggs, bacon and fish," replies Lucy.

George leans over to the men beside us and starts a conversation. "Morning, gents. We are on holiday here. What do you recommend for breakfast? Want to try the local food, none of the tourist crap?"

After a few seconds, a man leans back, "Try the salted fish with bacon, eggs and Johnny cakes."

Keeping the conversation going, "Any places around here you can recommend for us to visit?" This time, there is silence.

The café starts to bustle with the symphony of island life as the barista sets the coffee before me. "Listen, here is a friendly warning for you. Around here, folks don't like too many questions. It is dangerous. Someone could be listening from the local gang that runs this island. People have gone missing for saying the wrong thing. Best you leave straight after your breakfast."

"Thanks for the tip. We are going with that man's advice and have five salted fish daily specials. Then we will be off," I say, lying through my teeth. I have no intention of leaving without the information we need — time is slipping by for a successful rescue.

Once she leaves, my eyes lock on a group of fishermen engaged in conversation. I overhear snippets of conversation, the local banter providing a backdrop to our surveillance.

"Storm's brewing out there," one fisherman remarks, the metaphor not lost on me.

The storm we face is not written in the clouds, but in the clandestine dealings that may unfold in this unsuspecting café.

Near the far wall, another group, a mixture of locals and fishermen, is engaged in an animated discussion that catches my attention. Their guarded glances and lowered voices betray a shared secret, a potential link to Acosta's cartel.

"Keep your eye on them," I instruct Lucy through our discreet radio devices, the tension in my voice reflecting the urgency of our mission.

The success of the task demands patience and precision. The minutes tick by, each full of anticipation of a revelation. The fishermen, unwitting pawns in our dangerous game, may hold the key to unravelling the complex web of Acosta's empire.

The morning sun continues its ascent, casting a golden hue over Café Calypso. While the team navigates the intricate dance of observation, dialogue, and anticipation, the task's success manifests in our ability to turn the mundane into a canvas for unravelling the hidden layers of St Kitts' secrets.

It isn't long before the woman returns with our food. "Here you go, five fish specials," placing them on the table in front of us.

While eating, I scan the room, looking for signs of distress or vulnerability and seeking out individuals who may hold valuable information or desire to escape their current circumstances.

My gaze settles on a young man tucked away in a small cubicle near the entrance. His hands grip a steaming mug of coffee with a white-knuckled intensity, betraying his nervous state. His eyes dart around the room, flitting from one corner to the next with a jittery urgency.

Every sudden movement sends a ripple of tension through his frame, his muscles tensing at the sound of the door slamming shut behind incoming patrons. It's clear that he's on edge, his unease unmistakable even from across the room.

Instinct tells me that he may hold the key to unlocking valuable information—time to make a move. Put my diggers on the plate and push it away from the edge of the table.

"I'm going to go and have a chat with the man by the door. Let's see what information or whatever secrets he may hold. He looks uneasy. Make sure nobody sneaks up on me."

After the short walk across the room, I'm standing in front of the table with my right arm straight out, offering to shake the man's hand.

"Hi, I'm Steve. My friends and I noticed you from over there." I point towards the team. "You look as lost as we are. Maybe we can help each other?"

"I'm Robert, and I'm OK, thanks. Just waiting for a date to show up," comes the reply.

"To be honest, you looked worried about something, and we are looking for a contact who can introduce us to Alex Acosta's cartel?" I reply, leading him to a corner he can't back out of.

"Trust me, my friend, you don't want anything to do with them. They are dangerous. If I were you, I would eat up and leave."

"Wish it was that simple. We have bosses who want to purchase his product. Can you take us to someone? I'm willing to pay."

I take out a 50-dollar bill and place it on the table in front of him. His eyes light up and open wide as if his brain is saying this is easy money.

The air in Café Calypso is tense as Robert agrees to facilitate a meeting with a member of Alex Acosta's cartel. The exchange is discreet, hushed words spoken in the shadows of a place that veils secrets beneath its quaint exterior.

"You have a deal, but you need to double that money," says Robert, tapping on the 50 dollars.

Take out another 50 and push it towards him, "You have a deal. But cross me, and I will kill you and take my money back," I say, staring straight at him, my face blank of any emotion.

"I need to make a call. Give me five minutes, exit the café, turn right, cross the road, and walk 100 metres. You will find me on the beach near several fishing boats," Robert replies, finishing his beer, standing up, and walking outside.

Back with the team, I give them the drift of the conversation and the fact, at last we have a contact that can lead us to the cartel. Things are moving forward. We have all done this many times, and not stupid enough to take the word of a man I just gave a 100 bucks. He could lead us into a trap.

As Robert leaves the café, I decide not to wait for the five minutes we agreed to before springing into action.

"George and I will head for the meeting point. Simon and Lucy cross the road and ahead towards the boats about 100 metres away to your right. Derek, stick to the shadows near the entrance," I say, the urgency echoing in my voice.

The team disperses, a calculated ballet of covert movements. Simon and Lucy, like shadows in the morning sun, stroll down the beach towards the rendezvous point. Concealed in the periphery, Derek remains vigilant for any signs of danger.

The sun hangs high in the sky, casting its warm glow over the pristine sands. The gentle breeze carries the salty scent of the sea, mingling with the crisp tang of fish and the distant hum of seagulls, as George and I follow Robert, our pace mirroring his without arousing suspicion.

Moments later, we are approaching the rendezvous point 100 metres from the café. A cluster of fishing boats rests on the beach, their nets billowing in the breeze like ghosts dancing in the sunlight.

A man emerges from the shadows, his features obscured by the sun's glare. He walks towards us with purpose, his steps measured and confident. I recognise him instantly as Robert, the man I spoke to a few minutes ago inside the café.

"Robert, where's the contact?" My voice is quiet and insistent.

"He'll be here," Robert mumbles, his eyes darting backwards and forwards from the boats to the road.

I tap the tiny earpiece radio, "Hold positions."

With that, Lucy and Simon take up a position sitting on an upturned fishing pot. One faces the rear, and the other is toward the meeting point. The minutes stretch out, the sound of waves providing an uneasy symphony to our impatience.

"Steve, we got company," Lucy's voice crackles through the radio, as several figures emerge from the shadows of a nearby sand-coloured brick building close to my position. Their intentions are dark and malevolent.

"What the fuck is this, Robert?" I snarl.

He tries to make a run, but he's caught by George, who now has him in a headlock and is squeezing the life out of him, as Robert struggles to get free. I turn to face the attackers. Five of them are led by a tall man with short, black, curly hair. In his right hand, a giant wooden bat.

"This isn't a friendly meeting, boys. You've been asking too many questions. Something our boss doesn't like," sneers the man who appears to be leading the encounter.

"Look, mate, we're not interested in a fight, so do yourself a favour and fuck off," my voice harsh and threatening.

"Try and make us, arsehole."

Moments earlier, the team was poised for diplomacy, but it soon shifts into a deadly dance of survival. The assailants close in, each holding an assortment of weapons. Unarmed combat becomes the weapon of choice. Without hesitation, the team springs into action. The beach transforms into a battleground of sand and fists as we fend off the attackers.

Simon and Lucy, now within earshot, join in the battle. Through my radio, "Steve, two more incoming from your six," Derek warns.

As one of the attackers slumps to the ground from a broken neck at my feet, I look up. A short distance away, two more locals lay on the ground. Simon's boot makes contact with one of their faces, while Lucy's size seven boot connects with the bollocks of the other.

I turn to see George being wrestled to the floor. Without hesitation, I remove the knife from my jacket—the blade glistening in the sunlight. Grab the hair of George's attacker and pull his head back at the same time, pulling the blade across his throat. Red blood shoots out across the sand. He drops, grasping at his throat as life leaves him.

For the moment, close-quarter combat becomes a deadly ballet and the line between predator and prey blurs in the scuffle. The sound of blows and grunts mingles with the rhythmic crash of waves, a discordant symphony of violence.

"You OK, George?" I reach out to help him get up.

"Fine, just a flesh wound. What about you?"

"Nope, I'm pissed off; was trying to avoid this. But that fucking man forced me into a situation where I had to kill him."

By this time, the rest of the team is at our location. Determination is etched in the seamless coordination of the team.

As the dust settles, the beach bears witness to the aftermath. Seven attackers lie defeated, their malicious intentions shattered by the team's unwavering resolve. The team's anger at the attack and the situation we found ourselves in, demanded adaptability, and the response was swift and merciless.

"Grab the bodies and chuck them in that boat. We can't afford any loose ends," I shout, the weight of our mission heavier in the aftermath of the unexpected confrontation.

With a boat loaded with bodies, we pull it into the water. Make several holes in the hull before fixing the rudder, starting the engine and pushing it out to sea. It should sink with the bodies out at sea.

By the time we finished and dusted ourselves down in the background, I detect the sound of police sirens heading in our direction.

"OK folks, we have two choices: make a run for it or sit over on the wall and act stupid. What do you all think, and quick?"

"Well, as Simon already looks stupid, I say we can stay here and see what happens. If the police run at us, we leg it," says George, looking at Simon.

"You know what you can do, arsehole," comes the reply from Simon.

"Time's run out, boys. The coppers are already here and walking in our direction," Lucy's voice cuts through the tension, her words sending a chill down my spine as I glance up towards the road.

With no escape route in sight, our only option is to face the approaching police and bluff our way out of this predicament. We move forward, the weight of uncertainty heavy in the air as we approach them.

As we reach the halfway mark and stand on the road, the law enforcement figures draw nearer. At their helm is Miguel, the same man Lucy had conversed with in the bar the previous night. Alongside him are three uniformed officers, two policemen, and a policewoman, her attire distinct in its blue shirt and black trousers adorned with a white stripe.

Before the police have a chance to address us, Lucy takes the lead, her voice cutting through the tension like a blade.

"Officer Miguel," she begins, her tone steady, despite the electric charge in the air. "We're glad you're here. We've been waiting for you."

Miguel's expression remains inscrutable, his eyes flickering with suspicion as he surveys us.

"What's the situation here?" he asks, his voice a mask for the thoughts swirling beneath the surface.

Lucy's response is swift and practised, her words a calculated dance of deception and cooperation.

"We were on our way back from the café when we stumbled upon this scene," she explains, gesturing towards the chaos behind us. "We thought it best to wait for the authorities before proceeding any further."

As Lucy speaks, doubt gnaws at me. Did they know a fight was going to happen? But I push the thought aside, focusing on the task as we stand on the precipice of discovery.

The silence hangs heavy in the air, each passing second stretching into an eternity as we await Miguel's response. My heart pounds in my chest, the weight of uncertainty pressing down on me like a leaden cloak.

"Hi, Miguel, nice to see you again," I interject, hoping to reassure the tense atmosphere and evoke a sense of familiarity.

Miguel's stern expression softens slightly, but his gaze remains sharp as he addresses us. "I thought I told you to keep out of trouble?"

"We have, unlike the group of men we saw a few minutes back fighting on the beach," Lucy counters, her voice unwavering. "From where we were standing near the road, it appeared that they wanted to kill each other."

Miguel's gaze lingers on us, searching for any sign of deception. "If by any chance I believe you, where are they now?"

"Some of them jumped into a boat and headed out to sea," Lucy responds.

"Two more ran off in that direction," I add, pointing towards a track leading into the dense undergrowth nearby. "There's a groove in the sand leading to the water," I explain, hoping to bolster our story.

But beneath my calm exterior, doubt continues to gnaw at me: how did the police arrive so quickly?

Turning to his officers, he instructs two to talk to the fishermen further down the beach to find out if they know anything and can collaborate on our story.

For a couple of minutes, the area is quiet. The only sounds are the waves crashing on the shoreline and birds squawking above the boats. They are all looking for scraps of fish that might have been dropped on the last fishing trip.

Two of Miguel's officers investigate the alleged scene of the incident and the track leading to the water's edge.

Ten minutes later, the officers return and explain that the fishermen witnessed nothing about the fight, and if they did, they wouldn't say anything due to the threat of reprisals.

However, they did recognise the two men running down the beach towards the boats as local gang members.

I scrutinise Miguel as he unbuttons the right chest pocket of his shirt and pulls out a black notebook. Flicks through it until he comes to a blank page and glances up from the pages,

"Right, give me the address of the place you are staying at, in case we need to contact you about the incident."

Not wanting to give him the villa's address, he may have links with the cartel, so give him the address of the Ramada Hotel instead. That way, if Derek picks up any radio chatter on the police radio he's been monitoring and recording on his laptop, it will give us time to vacate the area if they come looking for us.

Miguel dismisses his officers and motions for us to join him near a weathered fishing boat. The gentle lapping of the waves provides a soothing backdrop, but the air carries a tension only known to those entangled in the covert dance.

"Miguel," I acknowledge, my eyes meeting his with a measured caution.

He glances over his shoulder, ensuring his fellow officers have left the scene, before he produces a sheet of paper from his notebook, where he had written the false address I gave him and tears it up; the unspoken acknowledgement that our deception is laid bare hangs in the air.

"I know this isn't where you're staying," Miguel begins, his voice a soft murmur that only the beach and the wind bear witness to. "I've seen enough covert operations to recognise a smokescreen. As a young man, I joined the military and became a special forces soldier."

I exchange a glance with the team, the unspoken understanding that our motives are no longer veiled from the local law enforcement. Miguel, however, is not here to expose us. His intentions are woven into the fabric of a shared mission against a common enemy.

"I want to help," Miguel asserts, the gravity of his words etched on his face. "I know why you're here, and it's the same reason I can't sleep at night. Acosta's cartel has plagued this island for far too long. They took my sister a year ago. She's vanished without a trace."

"You're willing to risk everything to take down Acosta?" I enquire, gauging the depth of Miguel's commitment.

"Yes, I want to know what happened to my sister and if she is still alive," Miguel's gaze is unwavering.

"You're taking a huge risk, believing we are who you think we are. Tell me more about what makes you tick and your background." My special forces training tells me that just because someone tells you a sob story, does not always mean it is true.

"No problem, I've already lost everything. I won't let them destroy more lives. We're on the same side if your team can help me find my sister and dismantle that cartel. So sure."

For the next five minutes, Miguel explains that before he donned the uniform of the St Kitts Police Force, his journey unfolded in a different realm — the disciplined world of the military. As a young man, he ventured into the elite echelons of the special forces, where he honed his skills.

The trials of training, the camaraderie of his fellow soldiers, and the high-stakes missions were etched in his memory along with the men and women he served with. His experiences in the military prepared him for a life of service.

As a special forces soldier, he traversed landscapes far removed from the serene beaches of St Kitts. His missions were shadows in the night, covert operations that required precision and unwavering commitment. The skills acquired in those years would become the foundation upon which he'd later build his legacy.

Miguel explains that the transition from the military to law enforcement was seamless, a natural progression fuelled by an innate sense of duty. Returning to St Kitts with a wealth of experience, he joined the police force. The echoes of military precision and the bonds forged in the crucible of service became valuable assets in his new role.

Within the precinct, his leadership became defined by a quiet but commanding presence. Dedication to justice earned him a reputation as a determined defender of the island's peace. His experiences in the military remained the unspoken foundation, providing him with insights that transcended the routine of law enforcement. He now finds himself at the forefront of a battle against new shadows threatening the island.

I glance around the team, checking their expressions for signs that they believe Miguel's story or it is old cow shit.

I turn to Miguel, "Can you give us a few minutes alone?"

With him out of the way, "So, do we believe him? You're the interrogator, Lucy. You can see through people's deceptions," I say, knowing I've made my mind up.

"I couldn't detect anything that indicates he is lying, so why not? He could be the link we have been looking for," replies Lucy.

With the rest of the team agreeing, we take a chance. I call Miguel back from the water's edge, where he went to give us space.

"OK, Miguel, we believe you. However, if you cross us in any way, your last moments on earth will be painful ones."

"I wouldn't expect it any other way, Steve," comes the response from Miguel.

With him on board, I explain that the Alex Acosta's cartel has taken my daughters hostage, and we are here to rescue them. Giving only sufficient information he needs to know for now. I believe his story to a point, but I am still unsure if we can trust him. He will have to prove it with his actions rather than mere words.

After a glance at the time, it is 12:00 already. This morning has gone by fast, and we still don't have anyone who can get information on the cartel's movements. The locals are reluctant to say anything, but we have someone who might be able to locate a person who isn't afraid to talk.

Chapter Nine - Weapons Collection

With Miguel out of earshot, I turn to Simon. "Did you contact Katie and Cody about weapons? One thing the fight on the beach taught us was that we need firearms. If we had, that battle would have been over within minutes."

"Sure did, mate. Katie has organised someone to meet us at Independence Square, near an old Catholic church not far from the cruise port. Once there, we text this number. We need to be there by 15:00 today, which wouldn't be an issue if we have transport. I know you grunts like walking, but for this island, a vehicle would be handy."

"I agree with you, Simon, on this one, but where can we get one at short notice without renting?" says Lucy.

"Lucky for us, on the way here in the taxi, I noticed one for sale about one mile away. It shouldn't take us long to walk," says Simon, gesturing that we need to make a move.

"Great idea. Let's give our new friend a task to prove he is on our side." With that, I wave for Miguel to join us.

"Glad to have you with us. We have a task to complete near the cruise port."

I've told him on purpose where we are going. That way, if anyone else turns up, he would have shown us he's been lying. We still need someone inside the cartel to tell us how many people we will be dealing with, how many are guarding Abbie and Bethanie and where they are being held. We have an idea, but I want it confirmed, along with any plans to move them. Plus, an individual that can keep us updated on a regular basis?

"Do you have any informants that aren't afraid to speak up?"

"I may have just the man. Leave it with me. I need your mobile number so I can contact you once I have something," comes the reply from Miguel, as he takes out his mobile phone, ready to enter the details.

I give him my number, "Whatever happens, meet us tonight in The Siren's Call at 19:00."

Miguel jumps into his car and drives away.

The moment Miguel leaves, we start walking towards where Simon spotted the car for sale. The St Kitts beach retreats into the distance as we navigate the winding road that leads to Boyd's. An uneventful hour later, we reach the edge of the village, where a tired-looking house is set back from the road, its exterior bearing the scars of both time and weather.

The peeling paint and tired windows hint at stories untold, while a cactus fence stands as a barbed guardian. Goats tethered in the front yard add to the scene's surrealism, and their presence is an unexpected detail in this clandestine world. A towering blue water tank looms nearby, a silent lookout for the mysteries that may lay hidden within the property.

A yellow SUV, worn by the Caribbean sun, languishes on the driveway with a 'for sale' sign hanging from its rearview mirror.

"Simon, let's check this out. You three disperse yourselves into the shadows of the overgrown bushes lining the road. We have already learned that most locals are either in or have connections with the cartel," I instruct.

As we reach the front door, my pulse quickens. I rap my knuckles against the weathered wood, the sound reverberating through the stillness of the neighbourhood. Moments stretch into eternity until the door creaks open, revealing a middle-aged man whose weary gaze speaks volumes of his hidden truths. His eyes suggest a life accustomed to secrets.

"Can I help you?" His words hang in the air, a silent challenge that hints at the dangers that may lurk beneath the surface.

"On the island for a while, and hiring a vehicle will be too expensive, so we're interested in the SUV," I begin, gesturing towards the vehicle in the front garden. "We were walking past and noticed it is for sale."

The man studies us for a moment, his gaze flickering between Simon and me. "Yeah, it's for sale. Are you interested buyers or just nosy buggers?"

"As I said, we don't want to rent, so here to buy your vehicle. I have the right amount of cash on me," I say, not wanting to tell him I have any more, in case he has friends ready to pounce on us the moment we stop.

"Both," Simon interjects, his tone amiable. "This SUV caught our eye, and I love 4x4 vehicles."

The man, sensing a potential sale, opens up. "She's got some miles on her, but she's sturdy. Name's Winston, by the way."

"I'm Steve, and this is Simon," I reply, extending a hand ready to shake his.

Winston nods and leads us over to the vehicle. Simon begins a thorough examination, checking the engine, the tyres, and the vehicle's general condition.

"Does she run smooth?" Simon remarks, his experienced hands navigating the engine compartment. "Are there any issues we should be aware of, Winston?"

Winston leans against the Land Cruiser, a hint of reluctance in his eyes. "She's seen her fair share of adventures. Just needs someone who will treat her right."

As Simon continues his inspection, Winston and I engage in a subtle dialogue, a dance of haggling the price.

"If you decide to take her, I'll throw in a spare key and some advice on the best routes around the island," Winston offers, his weariness replaced by a hint of camaraderie.

Simon concludes his inspection and gives me a thumbs up, a silent indication to say the vehicle will do. I extend my hand to seal the deal.

"We will take her, Winston. Here is the $500 we agreed on," I say, offering him the money.

"Deal, take good care of her," says Winston taking the money.

Once we have the keys, Simon jumps into the driver's seat. After I'm in the passenger seat, he pulls out of the drive, turns left, and stops to allow Lucy, Derek, and George to clamber in the back, before we head for the weapon pickup at the old church.

The drive is only a short one, and we soon arrive at the edge of Basseterre. As we drive into Basseterre, the heart of St Kitts, the rhythmic hum of the SUV's engine merges with the ambient sounds of a bustling Caribbean city. The streets are alive with the ebb and flow of traffic, a chaotic dance of vehicles navigating the narrow roads.

Traffic weaves around us, a blend of colourful cars and vibrant market stalls lining the streets and the beach to our right. Adorned with Caribbean charm, the buildings display a fusion of colonial and modern architecture. People go about their daily lives, their faces a tapestry of stories hidden behind the routine of a busy city.

As Simon navigates past the bustling cruise port, a hive of activity, my senses are on high alert. Tourists swarm the streets, their excitement evident as they set out to uncover the island's hidden gems. The vibrant shops, though alluring, appear to whisper of a deeper, more sinister secret. The air crackles with anticipation, but beneath the surface, a menacing presence lurks in the shadows, ready to pounce.

Amidst the colourful chaos of souvenir shops and tourist buses, each painted in vibrant colours and displaying murals of local scenes, our SUV moves like a ghost, blending into the urban maze and navigating the city's labyrinth. But I can't shake the sensation of being watched, of unseen eyes tracking our every move.

Just past the port, we pull off onto a tarmac road leading to a large car park full of buses and cars. Fifty metres in, an older-looking woman sits sentinel at a makeshift barrier, her weathered face betraying nothing as she drops the rope, granting us passage. Taking a wild guess, this is more for the benefit of people leaving, to ensure they pay to park.

Once on the grass parking area, we approach the water's edge; Simon parks in a parking space overlooking the sea. The gentle breeze carries the scent of salt, and the distant murmur of waves becomes the backdrop to our strategic pause.

After clambering out of the vehicle, I scan the surroundings, vigilant for any signs of surveillance or unexpected threats. In the city's rhythm, our vehicle blends in.

Simon, ever the astute operative, checks the surroundings before speaking. "We'll blend in better here, among the tourists being led to their tour buses."

I gather the team around a map I've placed on the bonnet of the Land Cruiser. "I have been here a few times on one of my many cruises. Independence Square isn't far from here," I explain, tracing my finger over the map. "It is a large park with old, weathered trees, a few bushes, and manicured green lawns. Four footpaths lead to the centre from each corner. Another two leads from the two edges, one direct to the church where we will meet with our contact. In the middle is an ornamental fountain. Scattered around the park are plenty of benches, perfect for monitoring the area close to the church."

"How will we know who the person we are to meet looks like? There is bound to be a lot of people about?" asks Derek.

"Katie gave me a number. Once there, we are to text the contact. She will then give us directions to her precise location." Simon hands me a piece of paper with a number on it.

"Prior to reaching the park, we will split up, which means Derek and I will enter from the corner of West and South Independence Street; Lucy and George from the top end of the park at this point," I point to La Delicious Bar. "Which leaves Simon to enter from the corner of George Street. Once in the park, make your way to a point where you have a line of sight to the church. When you are in position and sure you have not been followed, radio it through and keep the message short. I will give it a few minutes before I text the contact."

After agreeing the emergency RV will be at the Cheers open-air bar in the middle of the port shops, due to it being easier to hide in a crowd, we set off. When we reach Bay Road, the team splits up.

Each group takes a different route to positions for the weapons collection. Not wanting to take the direct route and to ensure we are not being followed, Derek and I cross the road and head up Brumbill Street. At the end, take a left onto George Street.

Here, we pause for a few minutes, pretending to be tourists and looking in shop windows. I scan the area for signs indicating we are being followed, such as individuals we saw in the car park who may have stopped trying to blend in with the background.

I can't see anyone, so we continue down the road until we come to the next road and turn back towards Bay Road. We take another right and head back up West Independence Street, to the edge of the park and our entry point. Knowing the team as well as I do, and the fact that we have been on many missions together, they will be taking the same precautions.

As Derek and I step into Independence Square, the bustling heart of Basseterre, the atmosphere shifts. Green metal benches lining the footpaths offer respite for locals devouring their midday meals under the Caribbean sun. The square teems with life, a union of routine against the clandestine purpose that guides our every move.

I cast a wary glance around, taking note of the locals lounging on the benches. To my left, a few locals dressed in shorts and T-shirts are sitting on the grass, beer bottles in hand, indulging in the leisurely pace of island life. However, their casual demeanour contradicts the potential danger lurking in their midst.

Pigeons, opportunistic scavengers, dart around, pecking at morsels discarded by people; their constant cooing mingling with the acrid tang of pigeon droppings—a stark reminder of the city's dual nature. The square unfolds like a vibrant tapestry as we pass the central fountain, its rhythmic cascade offering a tranquil front to the casual observer. It's a meeting ground where secrets are exchanged beneath the guise of routine city life.

Everywhere you look, people take photos of anything and everything, whether it moves or not. Having done this sort of thing myself on many occasions, I would guess they are from the cruise ships that are in port.

After taking a calculated detour, Derek and I settle on a green metal bench overlooking the Church of the Immaculate Conception. Its white walls, imposing doorway, and spire stretch towards the sky, a silent witness to the life bustling around it.

"Quiet here," Derek observes, his eyes scanning the surroundings. "See why the contact picked the location."

I nod, acknowledging the strategic choice. "Keep an eye out. As we both know from experience, the person will either follow a group of people taking photos to blend in, or they will be sitting alone somewhere in the park."

Derek's gaze sweeps the area. His instincts are tuned to detect anomalies amidst the ordinary. The pigeons, oblivious to our covert intentions, continue their dance around discarded crumbs.

Minutes pass, each one charged with anticipation. Soon, my earpiece radio confirms the rest of the team are in location. I glance down at the time. It's 14:50. We have 10 more minutes before we make contact. Spend the time scanning the area for any members of the cartel that might be trailing us. I may not be able to recognise them by what they look like, having not met them. But their actions will stand out like a spare prick at a wedding to the trained eye.

I turn to Derek, "Thanks for coming on this mission to rescue my daughters. It is appreciated, and I will pay you back."

"No need for payment. I got to meet Abbie and Bethanie on many occasions when I came over from St Bethanie. I remember once when I lost my luggage. Both of them took me shopping in the local town to buy new gear. We even went for a meal."

He chuckles. A fond glint flickers in his eyes as he recalls the laughter and camaraderie they shared during that impromptu outing. The memory of Abbie's infectious enthusiasm and Bethanie's unwavering kindness warms my heart even now, years later.

"Plus, they have been communicating with my daughter, Rebecca, on a regular basis. I think they are even planning to come over for a holiday to meet up. So, as I said, you couldn't stop me from coming even if you tried."

"Cheers, Derek. I'll buy you several beers instead," I say.

"Now, that type of payment I will take," comes the reply.

Another glance at my wristwatch confirms it is time to send the text. Remove my mobile, open the text app, and type in the pre-arranged message, 'In location awaiting meet' and press send.

A few minutes go past before my phone vibrates. I read the message on the screen. 'Bench to the right of the entrance facing church, I'm sitting there under a tree. My name is Charline'.

Through my radio, "Contact made. A female is sitting on a bench close to the entrance of the church. Scan the area while Derek and I make contact. She could be connected to the cartel. When we move, watch our six, but stay out of view."

At the back of my mind, a voice is telling me the contact is safe, as Katie and Cody would have done their homework and vetted their contacts. But with this type of meeting, you always need to be prepared for something to go wrong. In this case, she might have links to Alex Acosta and his cartel.

After another quick scan of the area, Derek and I get up and wander over to where Charline is waiting. When we arrive, an attractive white lady in her mid-"Not yet," 30s, dressed in a flowery dress and a small-brimmed straw hat laced with a blue ribbon is feeding birds. I sit beside her while Derek leans against a nearby tree.

"Hi, I'm Steve. Nice to meet you, Charline. Do you have what we want?" I ask, starting the conversation.

I'm not the type of person who enjoys idle chat, so I get straight to the point.

"I have what you need. It isn't far from here. Follow me," says Charline, straightening her hat and heading for the park exit.

We walk in silence until we reach the end of East Independence Street, where Charline turns left. She walks 100 metres before turning left onto a concrete road leading to a small car park between several houses. A black pickup truck with a grey cargo box fibreglass cover is tucked away behind the first building. Charline stops and opens the back.

Inside are four green crates, metal containers, one long box, and ammo boxes. While I'm looking, Charline opens the box closest to the rear, revealing three L119A/A2 rifles.

"I've also got 20 thirty-round magazines for the rifles 3000, 5.56x45mm NATO rounds. I've also got a range of 40mm rounds for the grade launcher, including high-explosive smoke," says Charline, smiling.

"That's enough to start a small war. Did you manage to get hold of two sniper rifles?" I ask, knowing the sniper team will be a valuable asset in the rescue mission.

Charline opens the long box to reveal two L115A2 AWM special forces sniper rifles with 1000 7.62 rounds.

"Perfect, that should do us. What about payment?" I ask, remembering Katie said we could pay half now.

"Our mutual friend has sorted this, you no longer have to pay half, so no payment is required today. They said you can pay them back at a later date," comes Charline's reply.

Before we take delivery, we need to ensure the weapons haven't been tampered with and will fire when we need them. To that end, I radio the weapons expert to close in on my position. Within minutes, George arrives at my location and inspects all the weapons before giving them the all-clear.

We need our SUV to transfer them into, so radio Simon, "Simon, go get the vehicle and meet us back here."

"Already on it, should be back soon," comes the reply from Simon over the radio.

"Charline, I almost forgot. Do you have C4 explosives and detonators?"

"Yep, it's all here for you," pulling two metal boxes towards her.

It isn't long before Simon returns and backs up to the pickup truck. Once we have all the equipment loaded, we thank Charline. We clamber back in our vehicle and start making our way back to the villa, to zero the weapons to ensure rounds land where we want them to.

Back at the villa, the Caribbean sun dips below the horizon, casting long shadows over the dense foliage surrounding us. The team is always on constant vigilance, so we approach the house with caution. My eyes scan the perimeter for any signs of intrusion.

Check the defences," I instruct the team.

Simon and Lucy move to assess the exterior, ensuring that the barriers and alarms remain intact.

"Steve, defences are solid," Simon reports, his voice steady. "No signs of tampering."

I nod, acknowledging the confirmation. "Derek, how are we on surveillance?"

Derek's fingers dance across the keyboard, navigating the intricate web of electronic eyes we placed around the villa yesterday. "All systems green. No breaches detected. Our eyes are still on the perimeter."

Satisfied with the status of our defences, we unload the weapons and move inside the villa.

"Before we do anything, let's zero and check the weapons are working as they should," I say, picking one of the rifles and a couple of magazines.

Everyone does the same and follows me to the back of the house. Once we find a suitable spot facing across the open ground towards the forest in the distance, I set up a 25-metre range using a sheet of plywood I found in the shed. Place this against a fence post and mark the middle.

Pacing out 25 metres away from the target, I drop a length of timber on the floor. I go first, so I take a prone position and look through the sights before squeezing the trigger and firing my first shot. It lands left of the centre mark. I adjust my sights and fire again, this time in the centre. Once I'm zeroed in, Simon and Derek take their turns.

While doing this, our two snipers choose a different target on the edge of the forest that may conceal secrets and potential threats.

George and Lucy, a formidable pair, set up their sniper rifles with precision. Their silent communication is a testament to the unspoken bond forged through countless missions. As they calibrate their weapons, the forest becomes an ominous backdrop to our preparations.

Within minutes, the scene unfolds in the meticulous calibration of weapons and the unwavering commitment to readiness.

"George, if you do manage to hit anything alive in the woods, I'll cook it," yells Simon, as George is about to take his first shot.

"Missed," says Lucy, looking through the binoculars

George controls his breathing again, peers through the scope lining the crosshairs two feet from the ground on a tree trunk, the agreed target before squeezing the trigger. The recoil pushes into his shoulder as the round leaves the barrel, hurtling towards the target at 914 m/s. The round hits the tree, sending splinters of wood flying through the air.

"That hit the centre of the tree, but without a marker, I'm not sure if you were low or high," says Lucy.

"See the first branch coming out of the right-hand side of the tree? I'll aim there," says George, before lining himself up for the shot. Once more, a round flies through the air.

"Up two inches."

George adjusts the sights and fires again. They swap over once he is happy with where his rounds are landing. Now, Lucy follows the same procedure to zero her rifle, with George spotting for her.

In the meantime, the rest of us have zeroed, checked our weapons and gone back inside. While Derek runs through the recordings of the police radio, Simon walks towards the kitchen.

"Anyone fancy a brew?"

"Yes, please, mate," I shout.

"And me," says Derek, looking over the lid of his computer.

Fourteen minutes later, George and Lucy have finished zeroing the sniper rifles and join us in the living room. Simon pours them a brew from the flask he'd prepared a few minutes ago while making drinks for Simon, Derek and myself. At that moment, my mobile starts ringing. Once Derek confirms he is recording the call, I answer.

"Hello," I say, not giving away too much.

"Hi, Steve, this is Miguel. I have someone prepared to give us some information we require. Are we still meeting at 19:00, or have plans changed?"

I glance at the clock on the wall. It is 18:00. "Of course, I say we will be there sometime in the next hour." I hang up the phone. "For those of you who didn't hear that, Miguel has a person who will talk. You have 10 to sort yourselves out before we leave."

While the others are doing personal admin, I start to formulate a plan to return to The Siren's Call. After the attack at the beach, word will have gone around the island, including people within the cartel, of our presence. So it won't be the case as before, with us piling in at the same time.

With the team in the vehicle and heading for the bar, I outline the meeting plan, which is to arrive before the arranged meeting time. This way, we can monitor the interior and the exterior when Miguel arrives with his contact, just in case he brings someone else along. He may say he is on our side, but he's yet to prove it. Maybe tonight he will.

Simon pulls the vehicle over and parks in the dark shadows of a disused building on the edge of the road a few hundred metres from The Siren's Call.

"We need to be careful, folks. So, Derek and George, follow the road until you are at a point close to the bar. From there, check around the back before taking up a position where you can monitor people coming and going. Radio it through if you spot anything that sounds or appears out of place. That leaves you to check the beach area, Simon. Make sure you check the boats. As this is the longer route, it gives Lucy and me time to enter the bar first, once Derek has radioed through that the area is clear. If there are no questions, let's make a move."

The moment the clear message comes over the radio, Lucy and I start making our way to and entering The Siren's Call—a haven in the heart of St Kitts which beckons us back into its depths. As Lucy and I enter first, the hum of conversations and the occasional clink of glasses surround us. We move with practised care, blending seamlessly into the shadows as we navigate the bustling atmosphere.

We find a secluded corner, away from prying eyes, and take our seats. The ambient murmur of the bar is the backdrop to our wait for Miguel and his contact, an enigma yet to reveal itself. The air is thick with anticipation as we sip our drinks, eyes scanning the room.

"Any word from Miguel?" I enquire in a quiet voice, my eyes flicking to Lucy.

"Not yet," she replies, her gaze fixed on the entrance. "He said they will find us when we enter the bar."

Of course, he isn't aware we are already in situ. We sit in calculated patience, the delicate dance of clandestine meetings unfolding. I'm monitoring the room when the door opens. It's Simon. His arrival is seamless in the rhythmic cadence of the bar, his movements discreet and inconspicuous. He wanders over to the other side of the room to us. Grabbing a passing waitress, he grabs a beer and waits.

Minutes stretch into a silent vigil, each passing second heightening the tension in the air. At last, the door swings open; I check the time. It is 19:00. Two figures slip into the bar's dim light. The first one we recognise is Miguel. With him is a younger man, no more than 30 years old, shrouded in anonymity.

We scrutinise his every move as Miguel scans the room before taking a position at a table close to the stage. I allow him to sit there, pondering and looking at his phone.

I touch the radio in my ear, then in a whisper, "Did anyone follow him in?"

Derek responds, "Negative, they are alone."

We wait five minutes before we get up and wander over to join them.

"Steve, Lucy, this is a snitch of mine. He has intel that promises what you asked for," says Miguel in a hushed murmur.

Chapter Ten - Entrapment

I don't care what his name is — it could be Satan for all I care — as long as he has information on not only where Abbie and Bethanie are being held, but also the cartel numbers holding them. We take a seat at the table facing him and Miguel.

I can't be bothered with small talk, so get straight to business. "OK, what information do you have for me?"

"First, Miguel said you're willing to pay for the information," the man holds out his left hand.

I unwrap 200 dollars from my bundle of notes and slide them across the table. "My first question is, where are my daughters being held?"

"Not far from here, in a ruined plantation building near Canada Hill Estate. I can take you there."

"On to my next questions. First, how many people are guarding them, and how often do they change the guard?"

"Not sure how often they swap over, but there are five-to-ten-armed cartel members there at any one time. Alex expects you to try to rescue your daughters, so security is tight."

"When can you take us there, early in the morning?"

As a father, I want to rush in and grab my girls ASAP, but instinct and training warn me against this action, as going in without a plan could get them killed.

"Sure, meet me back here outside in the car park at 06:00 tomorrow morning. I'll make some checks for you to ensure they haven't been moved for an extra $50."

"Deal. Remember if you cross me, Miguel knows how to locate you, and you will pay the consequences." With that, they both get up and exit the building.

We wait another five minutes for them to disappear from the fence, before Lucy and I rise from our seats and walk out to join the rest of the team.

Pressing the radio transmitter, "All call signs meet at the vehicle, out."

Five minutes later, we are all back at the SUV and clamber in, where I inform the rest of the team about what had occurred inside the bar.

As Simon drives us back to the villa, I formulate a plan. One thing is for sure: I don't trust a man I've just paid for information to the extent of following him to a remote building without taking precautions.

It isn't long before the SUV rolls to a quiet stop, the engine silenced. We sit in the faint glow of the interior light, the faint hum of the night punctuating the stillness. The villa looms ahead, an imposing silhouette against the night sky. Its windows emitting sporadic glows from the upper floor cast elongated shadows on the ground as we move into action.

Though silent, the night promises both rest and potential threats. Our SOPs are not just protocols. They are the foundation of our security, the invisible shield protecting our sanctuary from uncertainties lurking in the shadows.

I glance at the team, each member catching my eye in a silent acknowledgement of the tasks ahead.

"Standard operating procedures," I murmur, the words a reminder more to myself than to them.

The team disperses, moving with the precision of a well-trained unit.

"Simon, perimeter check," I instruct, my voice quiet but commanding.

He nods and disappears into the shadows as he embarks on his reconnaissance. Derek pulls out his laptop, which he takes everywhere, and checks the electronic surveillance equipment inside.

Lucy and George split off to their assigned tasks, each disappearing into the night with purpose. The cool night air, filled with the scent of uncertainty, swirls around us as we commence our routine checks.

"Tell-tales," I mutter to myself, a reminder of the precautions we took before leaving.

I approach the first one, a small device inconspicuously placed, ready to alert us to any unauthorised entry.

It isn't long before Simon's voice crackles through the earpiece radio. "All clear on the perimeter."

"Roger that," I reply, moving on to the next tell-tale.

As we navigate the checks, the night appears to hold its breath, our collective senses heightened. The villa, our sanctuary and command centre, demands our utmost vigilance.

Derek's voice breaks the silence, "Surveillance systems online. No unusual activity."

Lucy emerges from the darkness and catches my eye. "Everything's in order here," she says, heading towards me.

George is rounding a corner of the building and joining me at the front, "All clear."

Now that the area is clear, we enter through the front door. My first task is to disarm the IED on the rear door, in case we have to bug out that way in the middle of the night.

With that out of the way, I join the others in the living room, which is time to finalise the plan for the task in the morning. From the time of meeting with Miguel and his snitch, to going with them to where the girls are being held, I take out the map of St Kitts and lay it flat on the coffee table. At the same time, Derek opens Google Maps on his laptop. This gives us a closer look at the ground of the target and the surrounding area, as well as views of the buildings from photos people have uploaded.

Combining both maps gives me a better idea of what we are up against. From the look of it, there are only a few significant buildings here. A tall stone tower that doesn't look big enough to hold people. To the right of this, is a bigger, round structure and a couple of smaller structures with missing roofs and entangled vines growing through them. One feature that stands out behind it is a high ground, perfect for the snipers to cover us.

Once I have a picture in my head, I look up. "Right folks, here is the plan. We will depart at 04:30 tomorrow morning and drive to this position on this hill overlooking the buildings." I point to the map. "Once there, George and Lucy will disembark and set up their sniper hide where you can get a clear view of the target area and cover us if anything doesn't go to plan. After you've been dropped off, the rest of us will drive to The Siren's Call and meet up with Miguel and his snitch. From there, we will follow him to the target area. Anything to add?"

"Remember, the radios we are using at the moment only have a short range, so until we arrive on-site, there will be no radio communications. Any communications will have to be made using the SIM-free phones we picked up at the airport on the way here. Which reminds me, we need better radios," says Derek, tapping the tiny radio on the table.

"Wouldn't it be better to have more boots on target and only George in the sniper position?" asks Lucy.

"According to our contact, there are only five people guarding the girls at any time, so the three of us should be able to cope. Plus, as always, we can have you two cover us from your vantage point.

141

Do you have any questions before we set up our night routine?" I reply.

"Not from me," says Simon, getting up and heading for the kitchen to make a brew.

"In that case, we better set up a sentry on the roof. We don't know what the night will hold. I'll take the first stag."

With that, everyone disperses to carry out their admin and get themselves in the mindset for the rescue in the morning. I make my way to the roof. The door hinges creak in the silence of the night. My first task: check the entire rooftop to ensure it is safe and no clever bugger has planted something up here. Something which we wouldn't have noticed when we did the perimeter checks.

Perched on the rooftop, I survey the surroundings beneath the silvery glow of a full moon. The night is a tapestry of shadows and subtle reflections, the quiet symphony of nocturnal creatures forming the backdrop to my solitary vigil. The time reads 23:00, and the air is thick with anticipation.

The next two hours or so pass without any issues. My senses are attuned to the slightest deviation from the norm. The night appears tranquil, but at the same time, it conceals the potential for unseen threats. Yet, as the minutes tick by, the peace persists.

From behind me, I detect the now-familiar sound of the door opening. I glance down at the time it's 00:01. Simon emerges from the door and walks across the rooftop, ready to relieve me from my post.

"Quiet night," Simon remarks, his eyes scanning the horizon.

"Too quiet," I reply, a hint of scepticism in my tone.

He smirks, a knowing glint in his eyes. "Maybe the universe is cutting us some slack for once."

I chuckle. The tension of the night has lifted, even if it is for only a few seconds. As we stand on the rooftop, there is a quiet camaraderie between us, a connection forged by the shared weight of our many missions.

"Out of interest, Simon, why did you come on this mission?" I enquire, curiosity lacing my words.

Simon leans against the parapet, his gaze fixed on the moonlit landscape. "Abbie and Bethanie needed someone they could trust, someone who'd watch their backs if you're not around."

The simplicity of his response strikes a chord. In the clandestine world we navigate, trust is a rare currency. Simon's commitment to my daughters echoes the unspoken bond we share as a team.

"I get that," I admit.

Simon's expression shifts, a more relaxed demeanour taking over. "You've got some strong-willed daughters, Steve. It's admirable. And hell, they even connected with my wife over video calls. She loves hearing their stories."

A genuine smile plays on my lips. Amid covert operations and clandestine missions, these moments of humanity become anchors. "Abbie and Bethanie have a way of breaking through, don't they?"

Simon nods, his gaze now fixed on the horizon. "In this line of work, it's easy to forget the human side. But knowing there's something worth fighting for, something beyond the shadows, makes a difference."

After a handover, I head back downstairs to catch some sleep for reveille at 04:00. When I arrive, Lucy is fast asleep in bed, so to not wake her, I lay down on the sofa under the window and fall asleep.

After what appears to be only minutes, the alarm goes off. I look at the bed. Lucy has gone. She either got up early or drew the last stag of the night. By the time I showered, dressed, and headed down, the rest of the team, minus Lucy, is drinking a hot brew at the kitchen table. Moments later, Lucy appears after coming down from the roof.

Once we are all ready with gear and weapons checked, we drive off into the darkness, heading for our start positions for the next phase of the rescue.

Three hundred metres away from the drop-off point, Simon turns off the vehicle lights and proceeds along the dirt track in the darkness, his expertise coming to the forefront. Simon brings the SUV to a halt behind the hill, close to the edge of Canada Hill Estate. Lucy and George disembark, their figures blending seamlessly into the shadows. Their mission: to ascend the high ground behind the ruined buildings, becoming the silent guards overseeing the unfolding operation.

Knowing we only have a short range from our radios, we stay put until we receive a message over the airwaves from Lucy, "In position."

With that, Simon pulls away, the vehicle rumbling along the track.

When we arrive at the rendezvous point at The Siren's Call, the time reads 05:00. The first light of dawn begins to touch the horizon, casting a subtle glow over the area. The only activity emanates from the diligent fishermen on the beach, preparing their boats for the day's work. The scent of salt and sea lingers in the air as we step out of the SUV. The place has become a backdrop to the clandestine mission unfolding in the serenity of the morning.

As we wait for the contacts to show up, I can't help but monitor the fishermen going about their business. Their only concern is catching enough fish to support themselves and their families.

Apart from the lights on the boats, the place is in darkness, the shadow of the bar concealing our vehicle from unwanted eyes. I glance down at the time: 05:55. Another car pulls into the car park, its headlights lighting up the place like a carnival.

Miguel emerges as a figure of discretion against the scene's backdrop. After walking over, he greets us all, his eyes holding the weight of the shared mission.

"We're ready. The contact is waiting in the car."

While Simon waits in the vehicle, Derek and I climb out and follow Miguel to where the snitch is waiting in the front seat of his car. My eyes scan the surroundings as we walk, taking in every detail.

Inside, the informant sits, his nervous demeanour belying the significance of the information he carries. The exchange unfolds like a choreographed dance, words spoken in measured tones. Miguel's gestures guide the conversation, his eyes conveying the urgency of the intelligence shared. As the dialogue unfolds, the area becomes a crucible of secrets, the information shaping our next moves. The informant, a silent actor in this covert drama, holds the key to unravelling the enemy's plans.

"What intel do you have for me?" I ask, opening the door.

"We are in luck. Your daughters are still in the same place near Canada Hill Estate. I asked around without drawing attention, and there were only the normal five to ten guards. They will swap over at 09:00. If anything, like when I was there for the last hour, people are only interested in leaving, so they spend most of their time inside packing equipment and drinking. Suggest we hit them sooner rather than later," comes the reply.

There is something about the man's answer that isn't quite right, but I brush it aside and turn to Miguel. "We will follow you in our vehicle, which means once we have Abbie and Bethanie, we can leave straight away."

"There's no need to take two vehicles. We can go in mine, as one makes less noise than two vehicles approaching," says Miguel, gesturing for us to get in his car.

"Rather take our own. You lead. We will follow," comes my reply, now turning and heading back to join Simon.

A few minutes later, we pull out of the car park, and the first rays of sunrise start to appear over the ocean's horizon. The early morning air is hushed as our vehicles navigate the narrow lanes of small villages. The villages, still cloaked in the remnants of slumber, present a tranquil exterior. The morning sun casts a gentle glow on the quiet streets as we pass through, our convoy a fleeting whisper in the serene tapestry of rural life.

On the outskirts of the village, we leave the tarmac roads behind and turn off onto deserted dirt tracks that stretch ahead, leading us into the heart of our covert mission. Dust billows in the wake of our convoy as we drive through the secluded landscape. As we approach our destination, the vehicles slow to a halt among a clump of tall trees. The hum of the engines dies down, leaving a silence hanging in the air. The team disembarks, weapons cocked, readiness etched on every face.

The sunlight comes through the trees, revealing the skeletal remains of Canada Hill Estate a few hundred metres away. The ruins stand like silent sentinels, witnessing the history and secrets woven into the fabric of their decay.

Miguel leads the way, and we follow a silent procession through the undergrowth that skirts the ruined buildings. It's now 07:00, and the daylight exposes the estate's eerie desolation. Not a single guard of the ones the snitch said were here is in sight, and the place appears frozen in time, where the only inhabitants are the remnants of what once was.

A strange stillness blankets our surroundings. An unnerving quiet amplifies the tension in the air. I scan the area, my senses heightened, and the weight of our purpose settles on my shoulders. The only movement is the sway of leaves and the occasional flutter of a bird disturbed by our presence. The distant calls of birds create a symphony, the only audible companions to our covert journey.

The group comes to a stop at the edge of the undergrowth — the ruins sprawl before us, an abandoned tapestry of decay and neglect. The informant and Miguel exchange glances as if they know what is coming next.

In this suspended moment, I find solace in knowing that Lucy and George are perched high above, guardians of the unseen, ready to release their precision if needed. I try to spot them, but Lucy and George are too good at their jobs and blend seamlessly into the shadows. Their watchful eyes will be piercing the stillness, and their scopes traversing the area, guarding our every move and providing a comforting backdrop to the uncertainty that lies ahead.

I tap the radio transmitter, hoping George and Lucy are close enough to receive my message: "All call signs, this is S3. We have a go."

Split-second later, to my relief, "S3, this is GD. All in position can see your location. Over."

"S3, Roger. Out."

With the team poised, weapons ready, and senses attuned to the heartbeat of the moment, it's time to get my girls. I signal for Derek to move to my right and cover us, while Simon and I move forward toward the bigger of the two towers.

Using all available cover, we move closer to a position from which we can launch an attack. The informant who had led us here hovers nearby. His actions give away an aura of distrust. Something is off, but this is the first lead we have had since we arrived on the island. There's no turning back now. My daughters could be inside.

As we breach the threshold, the illusion shatters. Instead of the anticipated rescue scene, we are met with the cold gaze of 12 armed men, more than we were informed were here. We've been led into a trap. The informant's betrayal hangs heavy in the air as he tries to hide from my gaze.

"Damn it!" Derek hisses over the radio as the world to our front explodes into chaos.

Bullets whizz through the air, a symphony of deadly intent, the crack and thump of every round echoing in the morning air. Simon and I dive for cover behind crumbling walls, our training kicking in. While planning my next move, my radio messages crackle in my ears. It's George from his elevated vantage point.

"Multiple hostiles, moving in from the northeast. Stay down. Lucy and I have eyes on them."

Derek, pinned down behind a toppled pillar, returns fire with precision.

He yells above the sound of gunfire, "Cover me, Steve! I'm advancing."

I squeeze off rounds, suppressing the attackers as Derek manoeuvres to a new position. The ruins have become a battleground, gunfire echoing through the skeletal remains of the estate. From the ridge, shots pierce the air, dropping assailants with lethal accuracy. Once more, our sniper team have us covered.

With the rhythm of gunfire intensifying, we inch our way through the ruins, working in separate fire teams. The pungent scent of gunpowder hangs in the air, mingling with the acrid taste of adrenaline. We move forward with calculated precision, a dance of survival in the face of overwhelming odds.

"Steve, on your six!"

Simon's warning comes just in time, and I pivot, firing at an approaching attacker. The crackling exchange of bullets continues, the ruins transforming into a deadly arena. A sniper rifle barks from above, the distinct report signalling another successful elimination.

"Three down, keep pushing forward!" I yell.

To my front, a man is running at me, determination written across his face, his AK47 firing from the hip. Even in the middle of a gunfight, the years of training and missions take over. I find time to aim, control my breathing and squeeze the trigger.

A split-second later, he joins his friend, who is face down in the dirt. I turn to see Derek in his own battle, as rounds fly past. I lay down, suppressing fire, giving him time to move forward. Bursts punctuate the relentless symphony of combat. The ruins seem to close in, a maze of peril and uncertainty.

I detect a crack of a round coming from high up, and then the thump inches away from me. Shit, I almost got hit.

"Snipers, we have a shooter high up. Think it's coming from the tall tower!" I bark into the radio.

Both George and Lucy respond with deadly precision, bullets finding their marks as the attackers fall from the tower, hitting the ground with a dull thud.

Over to my left, Simon is engaging three men firing from the shell of an old building.

"Derek, assist Simon. I'm going for the men in the round tower!" I bark into the radio, my breath now grasps for air.

I sprint across the ground, zig zagging as I go, until I reach the doorway. Drop one person who is standing just inside. The tower is dark, with very little light coming in.

My eyes scan the darkness, looking for the other man I'd seen re-enter only minutes before. I detect a sound coming from the back of the room. I aim and fire. A scream comes back, and the sound of someone hitting the deck.

Turning to leave, I receive the full force of someone trying to knock me to the ground. As I turn, my rifle is knocked out of my hands, the metal clanging as it hits the floor. Without thinking, I go for my backup weapon, the 9mm. As I do, I sense a searing pain in my left shoulder.

I've been stabbed. Instinct kicking in, I try to raise my weapon, but the man is too close. I'm thrown to the ground, where his boot comes in contact with my gut. By doing this, he's made a fatal mistake. I now have room to fire the 9mm. As he comes at me, I aim for his face and squeeze off two rounds in quick succession. His limp body falls on top of me.

Outside, the battle rages on, but in this moment of grim satisfaction, a semblance of control is regained. The attackers, disoriented and outgunned, retreat in disarray. As they run, shots ring out from the ridge.

"Excellent shooting, you two," Simon comments over the radio.

After pushing my attacker off, I dart out of the building, taking cover near a rusted boiling vessel.

The place had become silent, so I press the radio transmitter, "All call signs, sit rep. Over."

"Clear!" Derek's voice rings out, the word carrying both relief and the weight of our victory.

"Regroup in the ruins," I yell, panting, my weapons still hot from the firefight.

Within minutes, everyone checks in. We have all survived this trap. Now, it's time to look for a dead man still walking — the snitch.

Among the sounds of battle, the informant tried to seize his moment through the chaos and make a dash for freedom away from any harm that might come his way. It would appear Miguel has proven he can be trusted as he is holding him at gunpoint, preventing him from running away.

When he spots me approaching him, still nervous about reprisals, he decides he doesn't have anything to lose. Gambling that Miguel, who has known him for years, will not fire, he tries once more to make a break.

"Not so fast," I mutter.

He glances back, fear etched across his face.

As I close the distance, the snitch fumbles for a concealed weapon. In an instance, I raise my rifle and fire, hitting him in the arm and forcing him to drop his weapon.

"Now, what did I say if you double-crossed me? That was it... I would kill you."

The man begs for his life, "Please don't kill me. I have a wife and two children."

Wrong words at the wrong time, as two of my children are being held by his boss. Once more, I raise my rifle, aim and fire, the shot echoing through the ruins. He crumples to the ground, a traitor's fate sealed.

Amid the destruction, the promise of retribution hangs in the air. The battle may be won, but the war for Abbie and Bethanie is far from over.

Chapter Eleven - Alex Acosta Cartel

Alex Acosta is sitting at a large mahogany desk that looms before him. His very existence is interwoven with the shadows, a sinister figure whose name strikes fear into the hearts of even the bravest souls. As the ruthless leader of a sprawling drug cartel, he has built an empire of blood and fear from the ashes left behind by his deceased uncle, the infamous Henry.

Born into the seedy underbelly of a sprawling metropolis, Alex's childhood was steeped in chaos and violence. His parents, consumed by addiction, had left him to fend for himself in the merciless streets. It was here, amidst the rundown tenements and the vice-ridden alleys, that he learned life's most brutal and unforgiving lessons.

Unsurprisingly, Alex grew to be a man of cunning intelligence, his keen mind soaking up knowledge like a sponge. Exploiting his talents, he ascended the ranks of his uncle's cartel, outsmarting and eliminating all rivals in his path. With each calculated move, he gained respect and fear, solidifying his position as the rightful heir to the throne.

But Alex's motivations were more profound than the mere pursuit of power. Deep within him lurked an insatiable desire for retribution, a burning need to exact vengeance upon those who had wronged him. His parents, whom he blamed for his wretched upbringing until his Uncle Henry stepped in and pointed him in the right direction, were but the first targets of his unyielding rage. Their deaths, orchestrated with methodical precision, were a chilling testament to the depths of his depravity.

Alex was a master of lethal tactics. He planned and executed each move with remarkable precision. Like a skilled chess player, he manipulated his pawns and played his enemies against each other, ensuring his empire remained unchallenged. He even hired mercenaries to remove the competition if the situation warranted it. His network of spies and informants spanned far and wide, and tales of his omniscience were whispered in hushed tones among his enemies.

But behind the veneer of invincibility lay a complex, enigmatic personality. Alex's power was derived from his ruthless tactics and an uncanny ability to charm those around him, a quality that endeared him to his subordinates and commanded their utmost loyalty. Beneath his intimidating exterior, he possessed the ability to be charismatic, captivating those with whom he interacted.

Yet, behind closed doors, he grappled with inner demons that threatened to consume him. The loss of his uncle, his mentor and the only semblance of family had scarred him and haunted his every waking moment. His ruthless determination to maintain his grip on power was driven by a desire for self-preservation and a personal vendetta against those who would dare to challenge Henry's legacy.

An ominous aura surrounded Alex, an indescribable energy that made both his friends and foes uneasy. His intense stare conveyed a sense of power and an icy detachment, a gaze that could rob a person of their spirit without uttering a word. Just being in his presence instilled a sense of fear even in the most hardened criminals.

Alex's lethal combat skills complemented his unrelenting intellect and strategic thinking. There were whispers of his proficiency in hand-to-hand combat, his brutality, and his mastery of various weapons. These traits made him a formidable adversary, a man whose actions were as precise as they were deadly.

Alex thrived as a powerful force in the murky realm of crime and power, his unstoppable ascent to the zenith of the drug cartel world. Yet, deep within him, a tiny ember of humanity flickered, a remnant of the innocent child he had once been.

Whether this ember would fuel his ultimate downfall or redemption remained a mystery, shrouded in the darkness that defined his existence.

The office is an opulent sanctum that exudes an air of authority — a symbol of authority in the opulent office serving as the cartel's command centre. Deep, dark wood panelling adorns the walls, creating an ambience of wealth and power. The room is a sanctuary of luxury, reflecting the legacy that spans generations.

Towering bookshelves line the walls, housing leather-bound volumes and rare artefacts procured through connections that span the globe. A crystal chandelier hangs overhead, casting a warm glow on the mahogany furniture that befits a man of my stature.

Outside the office, the mansion itself is a testament to the might of the Acosta name. Upon entry, an expansive foyer adorned with marble floors and a sweeping staircase greets visitors. The walls are adorned with priceless artwork, whispering tales of the wealth amassed through years of cunning and calculation.

While outside, armed guards stand at the entrance, their presence an unspoken declaration of the power that resides within. Sharp and vigilant eyes survey beyond the mansion. More guards patrol the grounds, with their manicured lawns, statuesque trees, and shadows that conceal more than they reveal, on the lookout for anyone who dares to approach the house without permission.

Alex's eyes fixate on a photograph of his Uncle Henry, a man of immense influence and power. His eyes speak volumes of the wisdom he has cultivated through years of navigating the treacherous waters of the drug trade. The photograph captures him in a moment of levity, his laughter frozen in time — a picture filled with memories of his mentorship and guidance. Uncle Henry was more than just a family member, he was the linchpin holding the cartel's legacy together.

Alex mutters under his breath, "Why did they kill you, Uncle Henry? For you, I will make them suffer."

He drums his finger on the polished surface of the desk, an unconscious rhythm pulsating through his thoughts.

The cartel's legacy, woven through the fabric of time, demands a reckoning for the blood spilt. Steve and his team, those responsible for his Uncle Henry's demise, must face the consequences. The thirst for revenge courses through his veins, a relentless force driving him to the brink of an abyss.

While he stares at the photo, the telephone, bringing him out of his contemplation. Its insistent ring cuts through the heavy atmosphere of the room. He glances down at the screen. It is his eldest son, Hugo. Picking up the phone, he answers it. The connection crackles with transatlantic resonance as his son's voice comes across the airwaves.

"Hello, Father. How are you and the rest of the family? The operation in London is proceeding without any issues. The Brits remain ignorant, and the profits continue to pour in," Hugo responds with confidence in his tone, reflecting his role as the heir to the Acosta legacy.

A fleeting sense of pride flows through Alex, a rare emotion in his world of danger. His son, Hugo is not only steering the cartel's operations in international waters, but also making the cartel money and ensuring the cartel's legacy continues and isn't taken over by a rival gang.

"Well done, son, keep it that way," Alex replies, his eyes returning to the photo of his Uncle Henry while thinking the cartel's enemies, Steve and his team, must remain oblivious to the storm they're brewing. This is why he had Hugo kidnap Steve's daughters.

"Will do. After all, I've had the best mentoring a person can get with you and Henry. Plus, there's something you need to know. We've received intel about Steve and his team. They have left the UK and are hot on our trail," says Hugo, with urgency in his voice.

Alex leans back in his green leather chair, the plush cushion offering little solace as the gravity of Hugo's words sinks in.

"Thanks for the update, Hugo. We know they met with Lucas on Bonaire, who, for some reason, we can't contact. They are not a team to underestimate, and that's why we are playing this elaborate game and making them dance to our tune. I will have my contacts around St Kitts be on the lookout for them. This reminds me, I need to go and check on the hostages to ensure all security measures are in place."

"OK, is there anything you need me to do at this end?" asks Hugo.

"Not yet," replies Alex.

Alex puts down the phone, "Bring the car around the front; make sure the men are armed," his voice firm.

Ten minutes later, Alex clears all the paperwork on his desk and walks across the room to the safe, standing in an alcove at the back of the room. Places his finger on the biometric control panel. The safe unlocks. Inside are three metal shelves. The top two are full of stacks of banknotes. On the bottom shelf is a collection of expensive wristwatches. He grabs one and a stack of bank notes along with a 9mm pistol. After relocking the safe, he walks outside to meet the car.

Outside, the gravel driveway crunches beneath his boots as he approaches the black armoured SUV. Its tinted windows conceal secrets within a fortress on wheels. One of Alex's men stands watch, holding the door open as he slides inside. The interior exudes luxury, but there's an undercurrent of tension in the air, evident beneath the veneer of opulence.

Inside, Alex relaxes on the beige leather seats. One of his bodyguards occupies the other seat, and another is beside the driver in the front passenger seat. The mini fridge brims with drinks, a comfort amidst the looming danger.

Two armed guards are operating the gate at the end of the driveway. The solid metal gates swing open with ominous finality, their metallic clang a harbinger of the trials ahead.

The engine's growl reverberates through the vehicle, a steady thrum of power as they navigate the winding roads. The lush countryside unfolds as they head towards the imposing Brimstone Hill Fort. Beyond the tinted windows, the landscape teems with life, but beneath its idyllic façade lurks a darkness waiting to be unleashed.

The air inside the car is filled with the rich scent of leather, which is in stark contrast to the earthy aroma coming in from the open windows.

In the back, Alex observes the lush landscape unfolding beyond the tinted windows. The small villages they pass through appear to be frozen in time. The sun casts dappled shadows over the rustic houses, painted with the vibrant colours of tropical flowers, making for a fleeting tableau of island life.

A group of children playing by the roadside look up, their curiosity piqued by the convoy's presence. The rhythmic beats of calypso music emanating from a local establishment blend with the ambient sounds of the countryside.

"Sir, we're approaching Brimstone Hill," the front bodyguard says, his tone as composed as his vigilant gaze.

Alex nods in agreement, before gazing at the looming forest ahead. The air thickens with the scent of ancient trees and damp earth as the convoy plunges into the dense canopy.

The road narrows, twisting and turning like a serpent, each bend revealing only glimpses of the verdant wilderness beyond. The forest exudes an unsettling mix of majesty and menace, its towering trees looming over us like silent watchmen guarding ancient secrets.

As they ascend, the incline grows steeper, the vehicle's engine straining against the weight of anticipation, a metaphorical battle against the unknown. Shadows dance along the winding road, cast by the interlocking branches overhead, while beams of sunlight pierce through the dense foliage, like shards of hope in a sea of darkness.

At last, we round the final corner, and the fort comes into view, its formidable silhouette etched against the vivid blue sky. A park ranger stationed at the entrance booth recognises the convoy and raises the barrier with a knowing nod. They pass through, the weight of the fortress's history hanging heavy in the air, a silent reminder of the trials that await within.

At the top, the two vehicles, dusted with the remnants of the island's red soil emerge from a canopy of vibrant greenery and round a bend to reveal Brimstone Hill Fort's imposing silhouette against the azure sky.

The convoy parks in the shadow of the looming walls, surrounded by the remnants of a once-mighty military complex. Massive stone walls rise with defiance against the backdrop of the Caribbean Sea. Alex's bodyguards carry their weapons on slings under their jackets, ready for action. They check the area is secure before Alex steps out of the lead vehicle, the tropical breeze carrying the scent of salt and history. The fort's architectural features unfold before them.

Alex may be the head of a ruthless cartel, but he also has a keen interest in his island's history. So, he takes a rare moment of relaxation and marvels at the precision of the fort's construction. The bricks in a herringbone pattern whisper stories of skilled artisans from a bygone era.

The texture underfoot, shifting from weathered cobblestones to polished slabs, indicates the fort's evolution over time. The architecture tells tales of the soldiers who once lived within these stone walls. From the officers' quarters, with arched windows offering splendid views, to the darkened casemates, soldiers bunked in close quarters before the serious business of checking the security of the prisoners.

"Where are the two hostages being held?" asks Alex, looking over the fort and across the sea.

"They are in the old Artillery Officers' Quarters," Nico, Alex's friend and right-hand man in the organisation replies, pointing to a cluster of buildings away from the central area.

"While we are at the ticket office, have the people here been paid off to keep their mouths shut?" asks Alex.

"Yes, we don't have any concerns here," replies Nico.

"What security measures do we have in place around here for when Steve and his team turn up, and they will?"

"If you look up to the hill behind this building, we have men up there in Fort George who can see the whole site. They will spot anyone entering. They have photos of Steve. Near the officer's quarters, two men are patrolling the area. Plus, the workers have been offered a bonus if they spot and contact us if they see anyone acting suspicious."

"It sounds like you have everything covered. Let's start with the men up there," Alex says, pointing up to Fort George.

While the drivers stay with the vehicles, the remainder walk behind the stone building and the citadel and start the long climb up the worn steps leading up to Fort George — protected front and rear by his armed bodyguards.

At the top, the fort opens up, with ramparts surrounding it. Four men stand sentry, their eyes surveying the surroundings. Dressed in jeans and T-shirts, they exude an air of disciplined vigilance.

"Sir," one of the men acknowledges Alex's presence with a nod, his expression stoic.

"What's the status?" Alex enquires, his voice commanding.

"Quiet so far, Mr Acosta," another replies, his eyes never leaving the horizon.

Moving closer to his men, his boots echo against the weathered stones. The fortress, a relic of bygone eras, becomes the backdrop to their conversation. The aura of Alex Acosta's power and authority hums in the air, an unspoken force that binds everyone who works for him.

"Keep alert. We can't afford surprises," says Alex.

The men respond, confirming they understand the task they have been given. Their fear of what might happen to them resonates between them. After inspecting a small camp they have set up in one of the buildings, Alex and Nico depart and start their descent from Fort George. They walk along the pathway, their footsteps crunching on the gravel walkway.

As they reach the old Artillery Officer's Quarters, they encounter two men patrolling the area outside. Alex's gaze focuses on the entrance as they approach the weathered stone-brick building.

"Any signs of unwanted activity?" Alex enquires, his voice a murmur.

"Quiet, Mr Acosta. No movement," the other replies, his posture unwavering.

"The prisoners?" Nico asks.

"Secure, sir. We're keeping a close eye," the first man responds, his commitment unwavering.

"OK, show me where they are. I want to check them myself. The rest of you stay out here and set up a perimeter. Anyone you don't know tries approaching, shoot first, ask questions second. "

As they enter the building, tension hangs heavy in the air. Inside, several rooms reveal themselves. A small amount of natural light breaks through windows and cracks in the structure. The first serves as a makeshift dormitory, kitchen, and dining room for the guards.

The second room is empty apart from stores and rubbish, a contrast to the third room. The final room looms ahead, and as they approach, the faint sound of hushed voices becomes audible. Metal bars on the doorway reveal a makeshift cell, and through the gaps, they catch a glimpse of two figures huddled in the corner.

As Nico and Alex approach the bars, muffled voices become discernible. They are full of resolve and strength to survive anything their captures throw at them. Abbie and Bethanie sit on two wooden beds, defiance burning in their eyes. They both look up when they detect footsteps approaching the door.

"Hey, look, Beth, chief knobhead has decided to put in an appearance," Abbie lashes out, her voice a mixture of frustration and insolence.

"And he has brought his lapdog along for company," replies Bethanie.

Nico, undeterred by the verbal assault, moves closer to inspect the locks. "Shut the fuck up bitch," Nico's voice is loud and firm.

"Come in here and try to make me," says Abbie, beckoning him to come closer.

Bethanie's eyes never leave the guards. She joins in the verbal sparring. "Did you bring the cavalry, or are we still stuck with you two fucking clowns?"

Abbie and Bethanie's sharp words are a testament to their strength and their refusal to be broken by the circumstances.

In an attempt to shut the girls up, a guard steps too close to the bars. Abbie seizes the opportunity and moves as fast as a fat man seeing an unguarded burger, and thrusts her hands through the bars, grabs him by his shirt and slams his head against the cold metal. The man backs off, dazed, with blood running from his nose. Once he is composed, he brings his AK47 into the aim.

"Don't shoot her. We need them alive, for now. The bastard of a father and his mates killed my uncle. I want Steve to know what it is like to lose a loved one. When I kill the bitches, it will be in front of him," yells Alex.

Bethanie grins and points at the guard, "Next time you come that close, arsehole, you're a dead man."

With the inspection out of the way and his hostages still behind bars, Alex, Nico and his bodyguards head for the car.

On the way back, Nico turns to Alex, "So what is it with your fixation on Steve? What happened that made you want him dead so much?"

"Easy, my friend. My Uncle Henry employed them to remove a rival who'd taken over his business and property on St Halb."

"I seem to remember that," replies Nico.

"Well, after they completed the mission, they tracked him down to his office in London, where they killed him in an alleyway like a dog and left his body to rot. And as you know, we can't allow this to go unpunished."

Once back in the SUV, the convoy drives back to the mansion, arriving 45 minutes later.

Chapter Twelve - Unexpected

Back at the villa, the team gathers in the living room. The atmosphere is heavy, with exhaustion and frustration lingering in the air. The events earlier at Canada Hill Estate still hang in the air, a bitter reminder that the rescue mission didn't go as planned. Simon cleans his weapon. Derek stares into the distance, lost in thought. Both George and Lucy, though silent, exude a fierce determination.

I sink into the worn leather couch next to Simon, my mind a whirlwind of conflicting emotions of anger and frustration that Abbie and Bethanie weren't at the location. The snitch's betrayal still stings. At least Miguel stayed true and prevented the snitch from escaping. But we can't afford to dwell on it now. Our next move must be calculated and decisive, if we have any chance of rescuing my daughters.

Glance around the room at the team, their eyes a mix of exhaustion and readiness. Simon pauses in his weapon maintenance, Derek leans forward, and Lucy meets my gaze, her expression mirroring the shared resolve.

"The question is, where do we go from here?" Derek breaks the silence.

Considering all our options, "We can't trust the previous intel but can't afford to sit idle. We need a reliable lead."

Just as the weight of uncertainty threatens to overwhelm us, the shrill ring of my phone pierces the air. Katie's name flashes on the screen, and I answer with a mixture of weariness and anticipation, placing it on speaker so the team can overhear the conversation.

"Steve, I just got a call from Charline." Katie's voice carries a sense of urgency. "She claims to have reliable information about Abbie and Bethanie's whereabouts. She wants to meet with you, but discussing over the phone is too risky."

A surge of hope mixed with suspicion washes over me, due to the intel fed to us by the snitch and not wanting to trust anyone else. However, Charline has been a reliable source in the past, who supplied our weapons without any issues. But in this dangerous game, trust is a fragile commodity, but a risk we are going to have to take.

"Where and when?" I ask, trying to keep my voice steady.

"She suggested a discreet location. How about the abandoned warehouse down the cruise port? Say, in an hour?"

I glance at the team, their gaze fixed on me, waiting for a plan. An abandoned warehouse – a fittingly covert venue for a meeting. "Alright, Katie. We'll be there."

As I hang up, the room is alive with renewed energy. The team springs into action, checking weapons and preparing for the meeting that, at last, could hold the key to Abbie and Bethanie's actual location.

The drive to the docks is tense, with each passing minute amplifying the stakes. Once there, Simon parks a few hundred metres away in the shadows of a large skip full of industrial rubbish. The team exits the SUV, spreads out in a defensive formation, waits and listens for any sounds of movement. Once I'm satisfied there isn't anyone else around, I signal the team to move towards the building and the rendezvous point inside.

The abandoned warehouse, a decaying relic of industrial might, stands as a weathered sentinel on the edge of the desolate docks. Its once-majestic exterior, adorned with rusting iron girders and faded signage, tells a tale of a forgone era. The air is heavy with the scent of damp wood and aged metal, a reminder of a time when commerce thrived within.

Following our normal SOPs, George and Derek conceal themselves around the building, staying out of view but with a clear view of the entrance and exit points. Once Lucy and I have entered the warehouse, they will monitor if anyone tries to enter or leave. Simon will stay in the vehicle, ready to drive as fast as he can to collect us if things go wrong, and yet again, we have been set up.

I press against the stubborn grey door, its resistance a silent warning of what lies beyond. With a forceful shove, it yields, groaning in protest as it reveals the desolate interior. The dim light filters through broken windows, casting shadows on the neglected floor, where dust swirls in a supernatural dance.

Inside, the warehouse stands as a resting place of forgotten industry, its silence a chilling testament to its abandonment. The remnants of past commerce loom like menacing phantoms, their presence menacing in the dimness. Each step we take reverberates through the vast space, a stark reminder of our intrusion into its forgotten realm.

Amidst the stillness, the faint sounds of life — scampering rodents, the distant crash of waves — serve only to heighten the sense of isolation. We tread with caution, our senses heightened, alert to the secrets this place harbours. The air hangs thick with the weight of unseen dangers lurking in the shadows.

As we move deeper into the labyrinth, the darkness closes around us, obscuring our path and amplifying the foreboding that grips us. The walls themselves seem to whisper warnings; their secrets veiled in darkness. In this silent chamber of forgotten whispers, our meeting takes on an air of clandestine urgency, each moment fraught with unseen peril.

At the far end, a solitary figure stands in the shadows – Charline.

"Steve," she acknowledges us with a nod as we approach. Her face is a mask, revealing nothing of the turmoil within.

"Charline, as you know, the last person who said he had information led us into a trap. So if your intel is reliable, where are Abbie and Bethanie?" I ask.

Charline studies me for a moment before speaking. "They're being held at the Brimstone Hill Fortress, which the Acosta cartel is using as a temporary base."

Relief and determination surge within me. "Are you sure the information is accurate," I demand, needing to act.

Charline hands me a folded piece of paper, the details scrawled in her neat handwriting. "They're scheduled to be moved soon. My contact says in four days, as the cartel is aware you are on the island after your battle at Canada Hill Estate; plus, they were informed by someone who has met you. You don't have much time."

'The snitch must have informed them', I think to myself. The urgency in Charline's voice is mirrored in my heart.

With my PTSD reminding me not to trust anyone, "Why are you helping us, Charline?" I enquire, searching for any signs of deception.

She meets my gaze, her eyes reflecting a mix of guilt and resolve. "It's personal. The Acosta cartel has crossed a line, and I can't stand by."

"Why is that?" wanting to know more.

"As I said, it's personal. Let's leave it there."

Thankful and not wanting to push the issue, I watch Charline disappear into the shadows without another word, leaving us to digest the newfound information.

Once she disappears out of my view, I press the radio transmitter, "All call signs, RV Simon's location."

As Lucy and I leave the warehouse via the same door we went in through, I catch a glimpse of Derek emerging from the shadows.

When we get closer to the SUV, the sound of the engine ticking over reverberates off the metal skip. Once everyone is on location, we pile back into the vehicle. I can't help but wonder about the personal vendetta that drives Charline into this dangerous game.

"So, did you find out where the girls are, and what's the plan?" asks George, from the rear seat.

"According to Charline's contact, Abbie and Bethanie are being held somewhere in the Brimstone Hill Fortress. They don't know which part of the huge fort they are being held in. Before doing anything, we need to return to the villa and restock with ammo."

"Charline also confirmed that Alex Acosta's cartel was informed by someone known to us that we were on the island. An educated guess it would have been the snitch. I suggest we vacate the villa for a few nights," Lucy adds to the conversation.

"It makes sense to me. For want of a better place, as I know you grunts love living out in nature under nothing more than a tarp, why not relocate to the woods at the back of the villa until we have gathered more information?" says Simon, as we start to pull away from behind the skip.

"With you on that one, Simon. If we are lucky, we might find an old tank for you to kip in," says Derek, with a stupid grin.

"Not even going to dignify that with an answer, you green numpty," replies Simon.

By the time the SUV rumbles to a halt in front of the villa, it's 16:00, and the sun is still high, casting a warm glow across the landscape. Exiting the vehicle, I take a moment to survey our surroundings. The property, a tranquil refuge, stands against the backdrop of lush greenery. The first order of business is to ensure that our defences are intact. We move with a purpose, each team member taking a designated sector. The tell-tales and tripwires, positioned to alert us of unwanted intrusion, remain undisturbed.

Once inside, the team starts to pack everything away. Derek removes his laptop from his backpack. His fingers fly across the keys, turning off the electronic surveillance devices he configured when we arrived—first, checking to see if the villa had been compromised while we were away. It hasn't been. The room resonates with the soft hum of technology winding down. The strategic dismantling of our surveillance network is critical, ensuring we leave no trace of our presence.

Gear is packed away. All communication and electronic devices, once the eyes and ears of our operation are now silent, their screens dimmed and their designated places stored within sturdy cases.

As we move, the atmosphere is charged with a sense of urgency. Ammunition is distributed among us, ensuring we are well-prepared for whatever lies ahead. Each piece of equipment is handled with precision, a testament to the discipline instilled through years of military training.

All the equipment is loaded into the rear of the SUV. Now laden with the tools of our trade, the vehicle stands as a symbol of readiness, waiting for us to clamber aboard and depart for the woods. Once the team is ready, I sweep the house to ensure nothing has been left. The last task is to ensure the IED is in place on the back door. I found a smart plug in the kitchen yesterday, so I decided to rig up another IED for anyone who enters the kitchen.

I grab a bunch of grapes from the fridge and take seven. I cut them in half, ensuring they are still connected in the middle by their skins. I dab the open ends with tissue to remove excess moisture. Then, I placed them in the microwave with a bowl containing a mixture of petrol, lighter fluid, and some small tacks I found in one of the drawers.

Remove the plug from the mains and insert it into the smart plug. I then download the app on my phone. Now, if the need arises, I open the app and press on for the smart plug. The microwaves will cause the grapes to generate plasma, igniting the fumes of the mixture and causing an explosion, sending the tacks and glass in all directions.

With everyone ready to go and in the vehicle, Simon turns the key to the ignition and the engine roars to life. Leaving the villa behind, we navigate the familiar roads with renewed purpose, making our way to the trees behind the villa. If nothing happens tonight, we may return to the villa in the morning to regroup and plan the next stage of the rescue.

Soon, the dirt track we are driving down ends, and Simon, using all the skills he developed over many years as a recce troop commander, guides the SUV through the trees.

The dense forest on either side welcomes us. Its towering trees provide cover as we drive toward our chosen campsite. The canopy above casts a dappled pattern of sunlight on the uneven terrain. The vehicle moves with a steady hum, navigating the natural obstacles of the forest floor.

We come to a halt 300 metres from the treeline. Without saying a word, the team clamber out and move with practised efficiency, setting up camp with the precision that comes from countless missions. Camouflaged hammocks are strung between trees behind clumps of foliage to hide them from view of the villa, now in the distance. With its natural acoustics, the forest conceals our presence as we prepare for the challenges that await.

"Don't know about you lot, but I'm starving. Fancy making your world-famous chuck-in stew from the stuff we took from the fridge in the house?" George asks Simon.

"No problem, fat boy. Coming right up. Take it the rest of you are hungry as well?" replies Simon, taking out several gas cookers from the rear of the vehicle.

Without thinking, as he has done this many times, he digs a small pit to place the burner in to hide the flame from any nosey bastard looking his way.

The team sits around where Simon is cooking, discussing the recent developments and strategising our next move. The crackling fire becomes the backdrop to our collective thoughts. Fifteen minutes later, the food is cooked. After filling our mess tins with stew, Simon changes the cooking pot to a boiling water vessel to make a brew.

For the next half-hour, the team takes a break from the stresses of the mission so far, which have been relentless since first receiving the message saying the Alex Acosta cartel had taken Abbie and Bethanie. Yet again, I thank everyone for coming along on this rescue mission. Each member states they have deep connections with the girls since they first met them, and they have become like family to them. Lucy is even like a second mother to Abbie and Bethanie.

After a few minutes of silence and another swig of steaming coffee, Lucy says, "I'm still trying to understand the connection between Henry and Alex."

"I always remember when thinking about our mission on St Halb, when we met with Henry in a boozer in London, he gave us an envelope with the dreaded blue stripe down the middle. I've never seen one before that," says George.

"Me neither. But they did keep reappearing on almost every mission. They even turned up on the guy we came across in the derelict buildings in Southampton, after we beat the crap out of him," replies Simon.

"Didn't we encounter a man once who claimed Henry was his uncle? It wasn't Alex, though," I add, refilling my black mug with coffee.

"Think we did, but can't remember his name either," replies Simon.

Continuing the line of thought, "Whoever they are, they must be all part of the same family, if they believe in getting revenge on you idiots and me by kidnapping my daughters. The envelope with the blue stripe must be a family mark of some sort!"

"Well, it is going to be the mark of death for one individual — Alex."

"You're right there, Lucy," says Derek.

For the next hour, our own voices were the only sound in the forest, over the sounds of nocturnal creatures waking up and coming out to play. This moment of bliss can't last, as we need to get back on the mission. People will be looking for us, and we still need to confirm the plan for this evening and the recce of the fort tomorrow.

As the sun dips below the horizon, the last rays of light dwindling, the team returns to mission mode, and we prepare for a night in the heart of the forest. Darkness becomes our ally, and the echoing sounds of the woods offer to mask our presence.

I discuss the plan for this evening, "First, Simon, ensure the SUV is concealed. Second, we need to set up a night sentry somewhere on the forest's edge overlooking the villa. If someone spotted us going there, we have a great chance any attack will come from that direction..."

Derek interrupts me, "What about the way we came in? Do we also need someone on stag at the rear?"

"Good point, mate. If the stag post is back further enough from the treeline but we are still able to see what is going on, I can't see why we can't check the area at intervals. That way, we can all get some well-earned rest."

"Sounds good to me," adds Lucy.

"If you take the first stag, George, as you're the expert in concealing any observation post, we will then rotate every one and a half hours until first light. After Simon knocks up breakfast, if the night passes without any issues, we can take a trip to the Brimstone Hill Fort and mingle with the busloads of tourists visiting and recce the place. If there are no questions, suggest we sort ourselves out and get ready for whatever the night brings."

I crawl into my hammock and fall asleep for a few minutes, after running through the plans for tomorrow. After what appears like only minutes but must have been ages, I sense a tap on my shoulder through my hammock. It's Simon.

"Sorry, mate. You're on stag."

"Be with you in five," I say, clambering out of my maggot.

The forest is alive with the concerto of night creatures as I take over from Simon, who's now returned to the makeshift stag post watching the villa. The time on my wristwatch reads 23:59, and the full moon casts an ethereal glow over the woods and the villa. The night is creepily calm, but the tension in the air is intense.

Once Simon disappears back into the darkness, the treeline conceals my presence, providing cover as I scrutinise the landscape. I peer through my phone's night vision camera into the area surrounding the villa. The technology in my hands amplifies the ambient light, revealing the treacherous path that awaits.

The first hour of a new day is uneventful, the forest lulled into silence by the night's serenade. I scan the area, vigilant for any signs of disturbance, my senses heightened in the stillness. Then, at 01:10, the tranquillity is shattered by the distant rumble of approaching vehicles. I zoom in on the driveway leading to the villa. The headlights of two cars pierce the darkness, a convoy of ominous intent rolling toward our previous unsuspecting refuge. My heart quickens, and a cold determination settles over me as I assess the imminent threat.

'Better wake the team and get them to stand, too. Just in case they decide to come this way,' I think to myself as I tread with caution, trying not to snap any twigs under my feet that might alert the armed men at the villa to our presence. We might be a distance away, but sound travels at night. With my finger across my lips, I wake the team, whispering that people are at the villa.

By the time I return to my post, armed figures spill out from the vehicles, their silhouettes illuminated by the dim moonlight. Clad in dark attire, they move with a calculated purpose, spreading out to surround the villa. My eyes dart between the screens of the night vision camera on my phone and the people on the ground.

Once the team are in position on the ground observing the villa, apart from Derek, who is covering our rear, "Team, we've got company," I murmur into the radio, my voice hushed and urgent.

The response crackles through the earpiece, a symphony of readiness from my vigilant team members.

"Targets, seen," comes the reply from George, with Lucy to my right.

"They're armed and appear to know what they're doing," Simon's calm assessment of impending danger filters through the earpiece.

As I watch the events unfold at the villa, my mind races, formulating a plan to counteract any unexpected assault that might come our way. In silent synchronisation, the team readies itself for the impending clash. Survey the entire area as the invaders breach the villa's defences.

Wait for them to encroach deeper into the building, before I open the app for the smart plug connected to the microwave and press on. Silence erupts into chaos as my IED explodes.

Shouts and gunfire pierce the night, echoing through the trees like a symphony of conflict. The night vision camera captures the dance of shadows and flashes, a tableau of warfare played out in the digital realm.

Peering through the scope of my rifle, I lock onto the six figures advancing toward us. Are they aware of our presence, or are they playing a guessing game and clearing potential hiding spots? Either way, we can't afford to wait and find out; we can't afford not to take action.

"George, Lucy, prepare to engage," I command over the radio, my voice concealing the urgency pulsing through my veins.

In the shadows, our snipers shift position, their aim trained on the approaching threat.

For some unknown reason, gunfire erupts, shattering the stillness of the night with its deadly rhythm. Bullets whizz past, shredding trees and sending shrapnel flying. The staccato rhythm of conflict tears apart the night. As the skirmish unfolds, the air crackles with tension, the darkness now a canvas for chaos and violence.

I feel the rush of wind as a bullet misses my head, a stark reminder of the peril we face. What was once a sanctuary becomes a battlefield, the tranquil villa transformed into a battleground fraught with danger.

"Engage at will," I command, unleashing the team's expertise with calculated precision.

The forest becomes a theatre of war, and we, its silent actors, navigate the intricate dance of combat. The moon, a passive witness, casts its silvery glow on the unfolding drama.

"Simon, update on their numbers," I yell.

"Their numbers are thinning, but they're putting up a fight. We need to keep the pressure on," Simon's voice resonates through the earpiece.

As our attacker's resistance wanes, a cautious optimism permeates the air. The team, undeterred by the intensity of the conflict, moves with precision to secure the area.

"Secure the perimeter. We're not out of harm's way yet," I yell, the gravity of the situation lingering in the air.

The forest, silent witness to the clash, reclaims its serenity. The moonlight casts its ethereal glow over the clearing as the night, once fraught with danger, regains its composure. In the aftermath, the team regroups, silent understanding passing between us. As I survey the battlefield, a steely determination settles over me, and I take a deep breath.

"Simon, uncover the SUV. Lucy and Derek, dismantle the camp while George and I keep a lookout and provide cover."

With muscle memory and expertise, the team carries out the task they have done many times. It isn't long before the kit is packed, and we are in the vehicle heading out of the danger zone. The big question on my mind is how they knew to attack the villa. Were we seen there, or did someone we've met tell them?

Back on the tarmac road, Simon heads for the coast, putting as much distance between us and the villa as fast as he can. I turn around to face the people in the back.

"Anyone injured?"

I receive four 'no's. Perfect, the task now is to find another camp for the night.

Chapter Thirteen - Intel

To my right, just off the main road, I spot a dirt track heading towards the silhouette of a clump of trees.

"Simon, head down there and let's see if it is suitable for the night."

The SUV slows before turning left and driving down the bumpy track. Two hundred metres later, we find ourselves at the front of the treeline. A weathered wooden building is off to the right, close to a barbed wire fence. Its door is hanging on by one hinge.

As we come to a halt, the team clambers out and spreads out. Simon reverses the vehicle into a gap between two large trees and turns off the engine. We stay this way for the next 10 minutes to ensure no people are nearby, and nobody followed us from the villa. The only sounds are the occasional rumble of vehicles driving along the road we turned off in the distance. Even the wildlife doesn't make a noise.

Once I'm happy we are alone, I call the team to my position, "Might as well spend the rest of the night here. Set up camp. We will make plans for the way forward after first light."

The team spend the next few minutes slinging the hammocks between several trees; Simon does his best to conceal the vehicle from anyone looking from the direction of the road. After I have pitched my bed for the night, I take the first stag while the rest get a few hours of sleep. With only four hours until the first light, George and I share the sentry duties by splitting the remaining hours of darkness into two-hour stints.

It's 02:00, and the world is draped in silver and shadow, the moon's ethereal light saturating the forest with a weird hue. Every step I take reverberates through the silent expanse. No matter how hard I try not to make a noise, the crunch of boots on fallen leaves sets a rhythm in the night.

The team lies scattered within the woods, their hammocks mere shadows in the moonlight. I scan the area, my senses alert for any hint of danger lurking in the darkness. The vehicle sits in a clearing, a solitary beacon in the night, just about visible against the backdrop of the forest's edge.

After 30 minutes, my natural night vision picks out objects in the darkness, details that would evade others. The 45-litre drums near the wooden building and the fallen trees in the distance stand out against the night, enigmatic sentries in the moon's silver embrace. The forest, a repository of enigmas, whispers in the night with the rustle of leaves and the haunting call of an owl in the distance.

As I patrol the perimeter, the stillness of the night becomes a canvas for reflection. Every embrace of the night, every shadow holds a secret, every rustle a potential threat.

I find myself reflecting on the twists and turns of the mission so far, as it plays out in my mind—a reel of strategic manoeuvres, unexpected challenges, and the cartel's looming presence. The stakes are high, and every decision is a thread woven into the complex fabric of our survival. With each step, I feel the responsibility for the lives entrusted to me. I'm lucky to have them around me, who care for their safety as much as I do.

The mission has tested our mettle, pushing us to the limits of endurance. Yet, in the stillness of the night, there's an unspoken understanding among us – a silent pact to persevere, to see this mission through to its end.

A glance at the time it's 03:40 which indicates that I only have 20 minutes of my stag left, so I decide to take another patrol around the perimeter before waking George.

Tapping on the bottom of his hammock and speaking at a level only he will detect, "George, time to get up, mate. You're on stag."

Without a murmur, he unzips his sleeping bag and mosquito net and slides out.

"Anything I should know about, Steve?" asks George.

"Nope, all quiet. Just make sure everyone is awake at 06:00, I'm off to try to catch some sleep."

It is a warm night, so I don't get into my sleeping bag. Instead, I lay on top and under the mosquito net, allowing the gentle breeze to rock the hammock. Like on every mission, I don't get much sleep the night before a recce. My mind runs through every possible scenario, to ensure we find what or who we are looking for, and the team's safety.

This mission isn't about the money for them; the team are here to help me. Still, we did find a stash of cash at Lucas' place. He won't need it after taking a bullet to the head. That money should cover our expenses. Anything left over, the team can keep. I just want my girls back.

I must have dozed off, as I feel a tap and George's ugly face peering through the netting, saying, "Let's be having you." This is a phrase I've not heard since my army days.

Once I'm up and my kit is packed in the vehicle, I walk over to join the rest, sitting in a clearing just inside the woods. In a hole in the ground, Simon is boiling water, ready to make a morning brew.

"Everyone sleep well?" I ask.

"Must have been knackered, as slept like a small baby," replies Derek, handing Simon his black mug.

"What about you, Steve? Did you get any?" asks Lucy.

"Some. Have been running through the plan for later today. We need to do a reconnaissance of the Brimstone Hill Fort, which, according to a Google search, doesn't open until 09:30. And as they say, the best place to hide is in the open, so we will hide among the crowds. I'm 80% sure that the cartel members will not know what we look like and have only been given instructions to look out for anyone looking suspicious or trying to carry out a rescue attempt."

"What about the remaining 20%, if they do know what we look like?" says Lucy, after taking a drink of her coffee.

"We will have to play that one by ear. The objective of this visit is to get the layout fixed in our heads. We will come back later tonight and do a complete recce on movements, etc.; plus, if we don't find out where Abbie and Bethanie are being held, we can penetrate the buildings we couldn't get to."

"Worth a try."

"Sure is, George. I suggest we finish up here and head for a café I've found away from everything. I'm hopeful at this time of the morning, it will be free from any cartel members. From our experience, these people don't like getting up early."

Thirty minutes later, the makeshift camp is taken apart, and all equipment is packed into the SUV. With everyone onboard, we drive down the dirt track back to the road. At the end of the road, Simon makes a left and drives down the coast road, following the satnav for the next 20 minutes. At a crossroads, we turn off the highway onto a quiet, narrow street winding its way through a sleeping village.

The grey concrete houses are void of any visible life, apart from a few dogs running around and barking. To our front is a grass field where two donkeys are tethered to the floor. The road bends to the left, and we find what we have been looking for: the Island Breeze café.

The rumble of our SUV's engine fades as we pull into the dirt parking lot beside Island Breeze, a humble roadside café constructed of weathered wood and tin. The early morning sun casts long shadows on the building, and the scent of freshly brewed coffee mingles with the tropical air. A swinging sign above the entrance creaks in the breeze, like a lookout welcoming those who seek refuge and announcing the café's presence.

Though modest, the simplicity of the structure radiates a particular charm — a relic that echoes the rhythm of the island. The wooden façade may appear innocuous, but like most places on the island, it conceals a history fraught with secrets and shadows. The faded paint, a silent testament to the passage of time and the unseen battles waged within, and the relentless onslaught of the tropical elements. What may appear charming and quaint on the surface is a mere mask, concealing a deeper truth — a truth tinged with danger and intrigue.

As we step out of the SUV and into the café, the creaking floorboards echo with a foreboding melody, warning those who dare to tread its hallowed halls. A familiar song that has serenaded countless visitors over the years. The interior, bathed in soft sunlight, holds a deceptive calmness, its quaint furnishings a mask for the hidden currents that swirl beneath.

Wooden tables, worn by time and touched by unseen hands, stand as silent witnesses to the café's secrets. Vibrant flowers adorn each table, a stark contrast to the shadows that lurk in the corners, mingling with the scent of brewing coffee and the murmurs of clandestine conversation.

Despite the peaceful façade, tension hums in the air like an electric current, an unmistakable undercurrent that hints at the danger lurking beneath the surface. It is a battleground of wits and wills. At its heart, secrets thrive, and danger lurks in the shadows, waiting to pounce on the unsuspecting.

A few local patrons occupy the wooden tables, immersed in the leisurely pursuit of breakfast. The hum of quiet conversation fills the air, where every word spoken is laden with hidden meaning, and every glance holds the promise of betrayal — punctuated by the occasional clink of cutlery against ceramic plates.

I listen to the conversation for any hint of cartel activity. There isn't any. The café owner, a man weathered by the passage of time and warmed by the Caribbean sun, approaches the counter with a smile that carries the essence of the island's hidden hospitality. His lilting Caribbean accent adds a musical quality to his greeting.

"Good morning, folks. What can I get you?" he asks, his eyes reflecting the wisdom of someone familiar with the ebb and flow of island life.

"Five breakfast specials and coffee, please," I reply, my gaze sweeping over the menu painted on a wooden board behind the counter.

The simplicity of our order, a ritual of sorts, speaks to the camaraderie within the team, an unspoken language woven through our shared experiences. The cafe owner nods, acknowledging our order.

As we settle into a quiet corner, an older woman dressed in a vibrant skirt and shirt, her headscarf a burst of colour, brings over our steaming cups of coffee. Her eyes, wise and knowing, reflect a lifetime spent in this small island community.

Derek chimes in with a friendly smile, "Thank you, ma'am."

As the breakfast specials arrive, a medley of eggs, local fruits, and a hint of island spices graces our table. The flavours, a symphony of the region's culinary offerings, briefly steal our attention. However, with each bite, the team's focus shifts to the impending reconnaissance of Brimstone Hill Fort.

To ensure our conversation can't be overheard, I speak in a quiet voice, "Once we leave here, we will drive to the fort, following this route."

I point to the Splashmap I've laid on the table. To onlookers, it would appear we are tourists planning our visit to the island.

"Once we have parked the vehicle, we will split into teams to cover the ground quicker. Simon and I will cover the lower areas, while Lucy and Derek take the parts of the Hill Fort that are up here." Once more I point to the plan of the fort. "Sorry, George, you will be on your own. And cover this area."

"It's better you send George with Lucy. Not only can they spot sniper locations from up there, but there are lots of guard towers up in that part of the fort. We will never get him down until he's stood in each guard tower. I'll take that area," Derek says, chuckling to himself.

"Fuck off, you green numpty. But you are right. I will try them all after Lucy and I find possible sniper locations," comes the instant reply from George.

As we finish our breakfast, the café's owner approaches our table. "You folks are planning a hike to the fort?" he enquires, after scanning the folded map on the table, genuine curiosity in his eyes.

"Just enjoying the sights," I reply, careful not to divulge our true purpose.

With the plan solidified, we prepare to depart from the Island Breeze, leaving the locals unaware of the covert operations that unfolded in their midst. Our departure is as inconspicuous as our arrival. The rustic café becomes a fleeting memory as we step back into the island's sunlight. The hum of village life continues, oblivious to the strategic dance unfolding in the shadow of Brimstone Hill Fort.

Soon, we are navigating the winding road, ascending towards the imposing silhouette of Brimstone Hill Fort. The early morning sun casts long shadows, and the verdant hills roll beneath us like a sea of green. The SUV manoeuvres without effort as Simon negotiates each tight turn with precision.

As we approach the summit, the fortress emerges on the horizon, a keeper of history perched atop the hill. The atmosphere inside the vehicle is tense yet focused. Our mission is clear: to recce the fortress where, according to Charline's intel, the cartel might be holding Abbie and Bethanie.

We reach the parking area and the road levels, and the team disembarks, the doors close with a muted thud.

"Alright, team. You know your area to check once I have the tickets. Remember, the aim of this part of the mission is to blend in and not draw attention to ourselves. If you encounter any issues, radio it through, " my voice quiet but authoritative.

The team nods in unison, a well-oiled machine ready to execute the plan. While Simon and I move towards the entrance, the rest of the team span out, pretending to read the numerous white signs explaining the fort and its history.

A sign welcomes visitors, and we enter the first building to pay the entrance fee. The interior contrasts with the fortress's rugged exterior — a simple desk with a friendly attendant waiting. Behind her, a large clock on the wall the time reads 09:35. I approach a sense of purpose guiding my movements.

"Five tickets, please," I state, placing the necessary amount on the counter.

The attendant takes the money and hands us our tickets. "Enjoy your visit," he says, unaware of the operation unfolding within the shadows of the fortress.

As the sun beats down, we split into our designated teams, ready to uncover the secrets hidden within the weather walls of Brimstone Hill Fort. Simon and I will explore the buildings on this level. Lucy and George head towards Fort George to scout for any signs of cartel presence and potential sniper positions on the higher levels. Our plan is simple: survey and gather intel with no engagement unless necessary.

As Simon and I navigate the labyrinthine corridors, the air is thick with history and the scent of aged stone. The fortress appears to hold its breath as we move deeper into its heart. Simon's footsteps echo beside me, his gaze sharp and observant.

"Keep an eye out for any signs of recent activity," I instruct in a hushed voice. "We need to know if the cartel has set up shop here."

Simon nods, his fingers adjusting the settings on his radio. Communication is critical; in this covert dance, silence could mean the difference between success and failure. As we traverse the lower levels, the remnants of the past become our backdrop. Cannon emplacements, barracks, and storerooms are silent witnesses to the fortress' storied past. The weight of history bears down on us, but our focus is on the present.

Derek, a solitary figure on the middle ground, maintains a vigilant watch, his eyes scanning for movement. The fortress, a sprawling expanse of stone and secrets, becomes his canvas. At the same time, Lucy and George ascend the steep incline towards Fort George. The climb is arduous, but their precise movements blend with the fortress' rugged terrain. Fort George, a vantage point overlooking the entire complex, holds the promise of crucial intel.

On the higher levels, Lucy's voice crackles through the radio. "There is no visual on cartel activity yet. The place appears deserted up here."

"Keep searching," I reply. "We need to be thorough. The girls might be hidden in plain sight."

Simon and I explore the lower levels, entering buildings and alcoves. The fortress' architecture, combined with military functionality and colonial aesthetics, conceals corners that could house hidden dangers.

Once more, Lucy's voice comes over the radio. "We think we have found evidence of recent occupation in one of the rooms — discarded food wrappers and makeshift bedding."

Pressing the transmitter on my radio, "Good work. See if you can spot the cartel people who left it there. I would guess they are around somewhere. They may have eyes on you."

A few minutes later, "All call signs," Derek's voice resonates through the radio. "I've got movement down here on the far edge of the Carronade Battery green. Two armed individuals. They don't look like tourists."

"Copy that, DR," I respond. "Maintain visual, but don't engage. We need to assess their numbers and armament. LK and GD, anything on your end?"

"There are no signs of the girls or any cartel people yet," Lucy reports. "But it's eerily quiet up here. There are no tourists, no staff — just us."

With such a vantage point, anyone, never mind Alex's people, would use this to cover the whole area of the fort. They must be up there somewhere.

I press the receiver again, "Keep looking."

As the team relays information, a sense of urgency permeates the air. The fortress, once a historical relic, now harbours a hidden menace. Simon and I move towards the long building of the Infantry Officer's Quarters to the front and across the road from the ticket office, overlooking the ocean.

Places like this often hold secrets within their darkened confines. It is the first building close to the parking where two hostages could be moved at speed without being spotted.

The air grows colder as we descend, the silence broken only by the echoes of our footsteps. As we approach, our senses are heightened. The anticipation is real as we explore the rooms, our eyes scanning for any signs of recent occupation. The rooms, however, betray nothing but the echoes of past military life and the occasional rustle of guided tour groups passing through.

"I've got something," Simon murmurs, his eyes narrowing. "There are fresh marks on the floor, as if something was dragged. They go down the stairs."

As we follow the winding trail deeper into the fortress' depths, a sense of anticipation tightens its grip on my chest. The oppressive darkness envelops us, concealing our movements like a cloak of shadows. Each step takes us closer to the truth but deeper into the heart of danger.

A group of figures huddles around a woman at the entrance to a vast chamber, which offers a breathtaking view of the grassy bank and the endless expanse of sea. She gestures animatedly, her words swallowed by the cavernous corridors. She appears to be giving a guided tour of the fort.

After checking that my 9mm is well hidden, we navigate the labyrinthine halls, every shadow and every sound heightening our senses. Despite the crowds of tourists milling about, we scour every corner, every hidden alcove, but find nothing significant. The fortress' secrets remain elusive, hidden behind layers of history and tourist distractions.

Frustration gnaws at the edges of my mind as we emerge back into the blinding sunlight of the parade ground. Nothing is found, which isn't surprising with all the tourists around, as they make it impossible to conceal anything or anyone.

Even behind the few secured areas closed tight with metal bars, if anyone were inside, their voices would have attracted attention.

We head for the Prince of Wales Bastion, a secluded area away from the main thoroughfare. The mid-afternoon sun beats down as we ascend the stone steps, the fortress looming like a silent guardian against the backdrop of the sea.

We split up to cover more ground. With each step, the tension escalates, and my senses are on high alert for any sign of peril. The stone walls reverberate with our footsteps as we explore the bastion's commanding position, but there's no trace of the cartel or my missing girls.

Simon's voice crackles over the radio, "Nothing to report, Steve. No signs of hostiles or the girls."

"Roger that," I say over the radio.

My gaze sweeps the stone floor and the empty rooms, following the same search pattern, dissecting each room into search zones. I start at the far wall before moving forward along the walls and floor, looking for anything that stands out and indicates recent activity. A fresh mark will stand out against the weathered stone, like white chalk on a blackboard.

So far, the bastion appears untouched, yet the nagging worry persists. Abbie and Bethanie could be hidden anywhere, and the fortress conceals numerous nooks and crannies.

As we reach the bastion's edge, something catches my eye—a subtle scratch on the stone floor. My heart quickens as I crouch down to examine it. The letters' ABH' are etched into the hard surface. I recognise it straight away. My daughters had left their mark, a silent signal that they'd been here.

Call Simon over. "Look at this," I say, in a voice that is a mix of relief and urgency. "ABH. Abbie and Bethanie have been here."

Simon joins me, studying the scratched letters. "How do you know?"

"ABH are the initials of my kids, Abbie, Bethanie and Hadley. We know Hadley is back in the UK, so one of the girls did this to let us know they have been here."

"This changes everything. They might still be on the site," says Simon, looking for any more marks.

We move through the Prince of Wales Bastion with newfound determination. The stone walls seem to close in, hiding the secrets that Abbie and Bethanie might reveal.

At the same time, Lucy and George, perched atop Fort George, continue their surveillance.

George's voice filters through the radio, "Spotted some men heading up the steps to our location. From here, they don't look like your normal tourists. I think they are armed. Good job there are no innocent civvies up here. Plus, we can see the movement on the lower level."

"Roger that, GD, avoid contact. Observe what they do," I reply.

Derek's voice joins the chorus. "Confirmed. Two more armed individuals. They're heading your way, S3."

The fortress, once a beacon of historical significance, becomes a covert battleground. The team's convergence of efforts is crucial, as the unfolding events demand a seamless coordination of skills and precision.

"Stay vigilant, everyone," I command.

Moments later, four men appear on the wooden drawbridge, which creaks beneath their weight. Their movements are deliberate as they cross into the courtyard.

Lucy's fingers tighten around the 9mm stock, the cool metal offering reassurance that matches the resolve in her gaze. George, positioned beside her, breathes a silent breath, his eyes fixed on the approaching figures.

The sun shines through the vast open gate, casting an eerie glow on the courtyard. The four men, clad in dark clothing, move with unsettling precision, a well-coordinated unit navigating the fortress's depths.

Lucy adjusts her position for a better view. The men enter one of the rooms on the opposite side of the courtyard.

"All call signs," Steve's voice crackles through the radio. "Report."

"We've got four hostiles, armed and moving through Fort George," Lucy whispers, her eyes never leaving the courtyard.

"Stay concealed. Don't engage unless necessary," I instruct.

For the next 10 minutes, Lucy and George monitor the cartel members as they come and go from the stone doorways leading to rooms built into the fort's stone walls, one member making his way to the rampart overlooking the fort.

"We need to find out what they are saying," whispers Lucy, after tapping George on the shoulder.

Without saying anything, and after checking that nobody is observing, George darts across the courtyard to point close to the room where the men are now sitting. Through the opening that was once a window, he can hear them talking about everyday life and bitching about the cartel for making them stay up here on the lookout, for some people they don't give a flying fuck about.

George is about to rejoin Lucy when he hears, "Sick of this. Makes me want to go across the site and shoot the two bitches."

After ensuring the man at the wall is still looking the other way, George sprints back across the courtyard to where Lucy is crouched down, just inside a doorway. He explains to Lucy what he just heard. Five minutes pass without any movement, so George and Lucy seize the opportunity.

"Let's go," he says, their movements swift and calculated.

They slip out of the doorway, keeping to the shadows, and descend towards the Parade Ground.

"Something looks odd over in the distance, at the end of the Parade Ground, close to the hill. There is an old, ruined building, and behind that, a smaller one is still intact. It appears barricaded off, and two men...." Derek pauses and peers from his binoculars. "They both have rifles slung across their shoulders."

'This could be it', I think to myself, as Simon and I walk over to join Derek. We do our best not to run or walk so fast that we will stand out among the groups of tourists wandering around the sight. They all must have seen the guards protecting part of the fort. Some will see them but not register the fact that the two men are carrying weapons. Others were no doubt told they belonged to a private security company and were there on government orders.

Fifteen minutes later, the whole team have RV'd on the Parade Ground. We wander towards the brick wall at the end of the Parade Ground. It is a spot close enough to the Artillery Officer's Quarters—a concealed place where we can still see and overhear what's going on, but out of view of the guards. A group of people are standing close to the barrier, blocking the guards' view of us.

A tourist within the guards' earshot yells, "What's in there?"

"Nothing for you. This area is closed," one of the guards shouts back, carrying an AK-47 slung across his left shoulder. The tone of his voice indicates they are hiding something.

It appears we have found the right location where Abbie and Bethanie might be held. To confirm this, we need to return when it is dark to get a closer look.

Chapter Fourteen - Night Recce

With everyone back in the SUV, we head down the winding road toward an old building, off the highway we saw on the way to the Brimstone Hill Fort. It's around 16:00, and the air is tinged with the golden hues of late afternoon. Simon stops the vehicle a few hundred metres shy of the building — a strategic decision to approach our destination with caution. The team disembarks, taking up a defensive position on either side of the dirt track.

After a few minutes and seeing nobody, I signal the team to follow me, my rifle ready for any surprises. There could be innocent people loitering in or around the building. But as they say, it is better to ask forgiveness than permission, so if I shoot some harmless bystander by accident, so be it.

Raising to my feet, I head off down the track. The rest are spread out in a single file, each step calculated in the dirt-strewn earth beneath our boots. For now, Simon stays in the vehicle, where it comes to a halt, ready for a quick getaway.

To my front, I detect a noise coming from the abandoned building. A dilapidated structure standing on the edge of a small cluster of trees looms ahead, a silent witness to the passage of time. Its shattered and vacant windows stare out like hollow eyes. Once a hub of activity, the structure now stands as a skeletal frame against the backdrop of the untouched wilderness. I raise my left hand to signal everyone to stop and take cover.

Seconds later, a flock of around 10 birds fly from the rafters. We continue towards the building.

"Keep your eyes sharp. We don't know what we might find in there," I instruct, my voice a murmur that carries through the stillness of the surroundings.

As we approach the building, I signal to the team with silent gestures, each movement calculated to minimise noise and maximise stealth. Derek and George disappear into the dense woods, their presence blending with the shadows as they secure our rear. Lucy and I advance with cautious determination, our senses heightened, scanning for any hint of peril.

With the precision of a well-drilled unit, we sweep the area, each team member executing their role with practised efficiency. The tension in the air is thick, anticipation mingling with the cool breeze rustling through the trees, hinting at the mysteries ahead.

Maintaining our positions, Lucy and I wait until Derek and George reappear, their thumbs raised in silent confirmation that the rear is clear. With a nod, we converge near the entrance, the door hanging open like a silent invitation into the unknown. The scent of decay wafts towards us, a grim reminder of the building's neglected state.

Positioning ourselves in pairs, rifles at the ready, we brace ourselves for whatever lies beyond the threshold. With a silent signal, I lead the charge, bursting through the door with controlled force, my senses on high alert for any sign of movement or resistance.

Inside, the room unfolds before us, empty and devoid of life. The silence is deafening, broken only by the echo of our footsteps as we spread out, each member of the team taking up a strategic position. The space is a maze of decay, the crumbling walls and scattered debris a testament to the passage of time.

"Secure the other rooms," my command clear and loud.

As we press deeper into the building, the air grows heavier, thick with the weight of history and the secrets it holds. Dust swirls in our wake, dancing in the dim light that filters through the broken windows.

Every shadow appears to conceal a lurking threat, and every sound sets our nerves on edge as we navigate the labyrinth of forgotten corridors and abandoned rooms.

With the building secure, we emerge, the sun dipping lower on the horizon, casting long shadows across the landscape. On seeing us come out, Simon drives up to meet us, parking the SUV behind the structure, away from the sight of anyone coming down the same dirt track we came in on before joining us inside.

Back inside, the team goes about preparing themselves for a night recce. We have done this numerous times as a team, so everyone knows what to do. There is no need for instructions. I strip down my rifle into its individual parts and oil the parts that need it before reassembling it and checking it works. The last thing I need is a stoppage when I need it to work at a vital moment.

Thirty minutes later, everyone has finished what they are doing.

"Before our cordon bleu chef, aka Simon, knocks up some scran, we must go through tonight's plans. From what we saw earlier, the armed guards stopped people from getting close to the Artillery Officer's Quarters. The intel would suggest this is where they might be holding Abbie and Bethanie."

I'm interrupted, "It might be relevant: while Lucy and I were up at Fort George, I overhead some of the cartel men saying they were sick of the situation and felt like going over to the other side of the site and killing the two bitches. I'm guessing when they said this, they were referring to our objective area for tonight."

Continuing, "Cheers, George. This gives us two bits of information. First, this increases the chance the girls are where we suspect. Second, the morale among Alex Acosta's men is wavering. Better for, as we know from past experiences, people who are pissed off don't put up much of a fight."

"You're right there, Steve, remember the idiots in Puerto Rico," replies Simon.

"After concealing the vehicle at the Magazine Bastion, if the entry there is blocked by the toll booths, we will park as close as we can without going past the gate. Once the SUV is concealed, we will all make our way to the Orillion Basion, staying in the cover of the trees that run along the edge of fort. From here, we will split up. We know, from the information gathered by Lucy and George, that there are four men up on the high ground of Fort George, so this location will be out for now. Instead, if our two snipers take a position on the Prince of Wales Bastion, you should be able to cover across the open ground to the target."

Lucy nods, her sniper rifle resting on her crossed legs, ready for the task ahead. George echoes the silent affirmation.

"The close recce team will consist of Derek, Simon, and me. We will make our way from the Orillion Bastion to the target. We will use the protection of the Infantry Officer's Quarters and the grass slope to reach the solid stone wall beneath the location where we believe my daughters are being held. From here, with luck on our side, we should be able to confirm the girls' location."

"Where are the FRV and the emergency RV to be located?" asks Simon.

"The FRV will be where we conceal the SUV. The emergency RV will be at the Calvary Baptist Church across from the road we turn left on to make our way up, which isn't that far if you come straight down the hill."

"Whatever happens, do you want me to grab the vehicle, Steve?" asks Simon.

"If it is safe to do so, yes, please. It is best to keep our gear that isn't required stored in the vehicle. If all goes to plan, we should be in and out without any contact with the guards. If the opportunity arises where can we get eyes on Bethanie and Abbie, grab them. But remember, unless necessary, no engagement," I emphasise, glancing at each team member. "Our priority is to gather intel, not initiate a firefight. Saying that, if we are left with no choice, we may have to engage. Any more questions?"

"Regarding communications, the radios we have should be sufficient and work in the terrain. Sure I don't need to remind you all to keep the radio chatter to movement and mission objectives," adds Derek.

A wave of solemn nods ripples through the team—a silent affirmation of our shared commitment to the mission. The night recce is a ballet of shadows and silence, a dance where every move must be deliberate and unseen.

I glance down at the time: 19:00. "OK, we have three hours until Zulu time for the recce. Once we have dined on Simon's fine cuisine, I suggest you try to get some rest."

To clear my head, review the plans, and keep the area safe from nosey bastards, I wander outside and take up a position close to the base of a tree to the right of the building. I've been there for what seemed only minutes, but in reality, it is an hour when Lucy emerges from the building and comes across to join me.

"My stag over already?"

"Not yet. I just thought I would come out and talk to you. Knowing you, the plans will be running through your head faster than a herd of wildebeests crossing a river, making sure every aspect of the recce goes to plan."

While still watching my surroundings, "Yep, you're right there, Lucy. The sooner we get my girls back, the better."

"I miss them too," Lucy says, pulling out her phone and navigating to a photo of Abbie, Bethanie, and me at a party to celebrate my last birthday. We are all smiling, wearing stupid hats, and looking worse for the amount of alcohol consumed.

"Great evening that," I smile, as I think back to the night.

"Sure was. Now your stag is over. Go back inside. I'll take over from here," says Lucy, pushing me away from the bottom of the trees so she can get comfortable.

Back inside, Derek and George are in one corner, their heads resting on their packs, trying to catch some shut-eye. At the other end of the room, Simon puts away his cooking gear and pours boiling water into a thermos flask.

"Here you go, mate, get this down you," Simon hands me a mess tin full of stew and a black mug full of coffee.

"Cheers," taking it from him before plonking my arse down on a broken chair someone had put a board across, to stop their arse from falling through the gap where the cushion used to be. "You ready for tonight?" I say to Simon, looking up from my scran.

"Of course. Positive we have the correct location, so it will go to plan, and we are a step closer to getting our girls back."

"We just need to see them to confirm," I say, pleased; Simon said 'to get our girls back', not 'your girls'.

By the time I finish my food and drink, Simon has gone outside to relieve Lucy on stag. My body is telling me to get some rest. An old army MTO of mine used to say that if you're not eating or on sentry, you should be sleeping. Great in theory, but this brain, most of the time, will not allow me to sleep as it never shuts the fuck up.

Being the last person on stag, Simon makes his way around the team, waking up everyone. I must have dozed off as I receive a kick to the bottom of my foot. Opening my eyes, Simon is standing there.

"Come on, numpty, time to go."

With the team all awake and alert, we pack our gear into the back of the SUV in silence, ready for the night recce to begin. Within 10 minutes, the team is aboard, and Simon turns the ignition key, and the engine bursts to life. It's not long before we turn off the coast road and are driving up the steep hill back towards the Brimstone Hill Fort.

Two hundred metres from our destination, Simon flicks off the vehicle's headlights, plunging us into darkness. We inch forward, the vehicle's engine reduced to a whisper, the only sound the crunch of gravel beneath the tyres. Anticipation hangs heavy in the air as we approach the toll booth.

A dim light flickers ahead, a solitary beacon in the night. My instincts scream danger, a warning that we're not alone.

"Plan 'B', Simon," I murmur, my voice a whisper.

A few seconds pass, as Simon completes a mental recce of the ground in front of him to find the best route. Once he has it mapped out, with expertise gained over the years as a driver and then commander in the Queen's Royal Irish Hussars, he manoeuvres the SUV through the forest, the vehicle's engine humming with subdued power.

The trees, towering sentinels on either side, create a natural tunnel that guides his path. The air is thick with anticipation as we approach the FRV. The full moon, a silvery disc obscured by shifting clouds, casts intermittent beams that dance through the foliage. Emerging at the edge of a small clearing behind Brimstone Hill Fort's stone-clad structures and dormant machinery stand silent, a testament to the abandoned stillness that cloaks the night.

The engine's hum dissipates into the night's stillness. The moonlight plays upon the metal structures, crafting ghostly shadows across the clearing.

The team disperses, each member a shadow among shadows, their movements silent and purposeful. Forming an impenetrable circle, each member covers a different arc of fire. Our movements are synchronised and purposeful; our eyes scan the darkness for any sign of danger with military precision. The night holds its breath, waiting for the inevitable clash between shadows and steel.

Keeping as close to the ground as possible, I make my way to Simon. "Take George and conceal the SUV."

I was going to add to ensure it is ready for a fast withdrawal, but this would be an insult that would result in Simon slapping me around the back of the head for hinting he doesn't know his job.

"Roger that," replies Simon, creeping over to George.

Taking a prone position close to a small clump of foliage, I monitor the end of the fort's massive, weathered stone wall. Behind me, I detect the sound of the vehicle starting up. Its engine, somehow, knows it needs to be quiet as Simon reverses the vehicle deeper into the woods. The sound of snapping branches mixes with the natural sounds of the forest's nightlife.

Soon, George taps me on the shoulder, "OK, all done. Let's make a move."

After cupping my hand around my watch to confirm it's midnight and time to go, I stand up and make my way around the circle, tapping each person on the foot to indicate that we are making a move. With the team in their usual formation, we advance towards the end of the wall, a point where the fort becomes open to the landscape. The team treads with the caution and purpose of defining a well-executed operation in covert endeavours.

In the cloak of night, we advance, the darkness our ally, masking our movements in its depths. The moon, a silvered sentinel veiled by clouds, casts supernatural light upon our path. I halt at the wall's end, pressing myself against the rough stone, senses alert for any sign of danger. A quick scan reveals my team, each member hidden in the shadows, poised and vigilant—no chances taken, even in the dead of night.

Lying down, I peer around the corner, the Magazine Bastion looming like a spectre against the sky. Stones weathered by time whisper tales of centuries past, but tonight, they hold no secrets save for our own presence. Rising to my knees, I signal Simon, beckoning him to follow. A wave of nods ripple through the team, a quiet symphony of readiness as we move as one.

With stealth born of expertise, we traverse the distance to the Orillion Bastion, the foliage offering cover as we glide through the night. Moonlight filters through the canopy, painting the forest in ethereal hues as we become one with the shadows.

The air hums with the nocturnal chorus, a symphony of nature punctuated by the soft cadence of our footfalls. Each step is measured, and each movement is deliberate as we navigate the terrain with practised ease. Hand signals flicker between us, conveying our silent intentions as we flow seamlessly from one bastion to the next. It's a dance of shadows and silence, a testament to our training and unity.

At the Orillion Bastion, the team converges, each member blending into the shadows of the night's natural camouflage, each of us tucked in hard against the stone wall. I signal for George and Lucy to close in on me.

Once they reach me, I whisper, "This is where you leave us and head for your recce location up on the Prince of Wales Bastion. We will wait here until you confirm you're in situ. Stay safe and avoid contact with others."

"Roger, it shouldn't take long. It's only 50 metres away," says Lucy, before she and George head up the slope, using all available cover to hide their movements.

The rustle of leaves beneath their boots is a muted percussion, echoing the deliberate cadence of our advance. The air is charged with anticipation as we wait for a radio message, for us to move to our own recce location.

The rest of us wait in silence until, at last, Lucy's message, "S3 this is LK, in situ."

Pressing the transmit button, I reply, "LK, OK. Out."

With Derek and Simon close at hand, I murmur, "Let's make a move," my voice barely audible over the whisper of the night breeze.

Emerging from the shadow of the Orillion Bastion, we navigate the forest's maze with precision. Each step is deliberate, a silent negotiation with nature's obstacles, our footfalls swallowed by the carpet of leaves below. The earthy scent of damp soil envelops us as we press forward, the forest embracing our presence in its nocturnal symphony. The occasional hoot of an owl punctuates the stillness, a reminder of the secrecy shrouding our mission.

Ahead looms the stone-weathered barrier of the Artillery Officers' Quarters, a sentinel guarding secrets unknown. Pausing at the treeline, I assess the open ground between us and the wall, a mere 50 metres away. Above, in front of the building, a lone figure ambles with casual indifference, his rifle slung lazily over his shoulder. A cigarette glowing like a beacon in the darkness, a marker light signalling his movements — a tell-tale sign of a novice. We'll need to cross one at a time.

I wait for the man to turn away from us before I spring into action, darting across the open space with fluid grace, blending seamlessly into the shadows. The wall greets me with its weathered embrace, its ancient stones whispering tales of centuries past. Rifle at the ready, I signal for the others to follow. Soon, we're all pressed against the cool stone, hidden in the embrace of darkness. But my relief is short-lived.

The wall isn't as high as it looked from the Prince of Wales Bastion earlier today. If we have any clued-up person above, they may look down and spot us. Plus, we can only overhear conversations, and don't have eyes on Abbie and Bethanie. We may need to move from here. I rationalise the situation with the knowledge that this is one of the reasons for doing a recce.

While Derek and Simon look for a better vantage point, I radio the sniper team, "LK, this is S3. Do you have eyes on the girls?"

"S3, this is GD, nope. We can see through the open doorway into the building, but we can't see much. There is a dim light coming from a room on the right. And the guard just above you is waving his arm around, gesturing to something. Over."

"GD, Roger, we are looking for a better local. Keep us posted," I whisper into my mic.

Turning back to the others, "You spot anything, or are we moving back into the forest? At least from there, we can see above the wall."

"We might have a way in," Derek says, pointing toward a concealed entrance near the base of the wall. "We might be able to infiltrate the building and get eyes on the girls."

"Well spotted, mate. Worth a look to see if it leads inside."

For the next few minutes, I do what I do best and make a snap plan.

"Simon and I will enter via the entrance and, with any luck, make our way inside. As the comms expert, Derek, sprint back into the forest and take up a position where you can see over the wall. Get eyes on the building and have a view of the Prince of Wales Bastion.

"Ensure you have comms and inform George and Lucy what we are doing. They may not be able to see the entrance from their location. If it is a dead end, we will radio you to let you know we are coming out. Don't fancy an extra hole if you mistake us for someone else."

"No problem. Cover me while I cross back over."

With that, Derek sprints back to the woods, slipping back into the shadows of the dense treeline. He finds a concealed spot with a clear view of the Prince of Wales Bastion and the Artillery Officer's Quarters. The cartel patrols outside the quarter, his primary focus, but he can't afford to ignore the sniper's nest atop the bastion.

He settles into a tense vigil as he waits in the darkness, with his rifle gripped in one hand and the radio mic in the other. The air hangs heavy with expectation, every rustle of leaves and distant sound setting his nerves on edge.

While he waits, Derek's mind drifts back to why he chose to embark on this dangerous mission. It's not for the money — his pub provides enough financial security. No, it's the thrill of the danger and excitement that draws him back.

'This time, it's personal. The cartel's actions have touched me in a way that cuts deeper than any bullet wound. And now, as I lie in wait, my determination burns like a fire within me. They may have started this, but I'll be damned if I don't finish it', Derek thinks to himself.

Over in the hidden ominous shadows of the Prince of Wales Bastion, Lucy and George find their covert spot, peering over the exposed ground below. From this vantage point, they have a stark view of Fort George and the Officer's Quarters, their rifles poised and ready to strike any target that dares to reveal itself.

The tension is intense as they wait, the silence broken only by the distant sounds of the forest and the soft rustle of leaves in the breeze. Every second is like an eternity, their senses honed to a razor's edge as they anticipate the next move.

Then, the crackle of the radio breaks the stillness, and Derek's voice fills the air. "LK, this is DR. Change of plans: Steve and Simon will enter the Officer's Quarters from the bottom entrance. Over."

"DR, Roger that, LK. Out."

Lucy's heart races at the unexpected twist as she processes the new information. Without hesitation, she relays the message to George, their eyes meeting in silent understanding.

They shift their position just enough to cover the new entry point. A thick blanket of expectancy settles in the air. The mission has veered sharply, and they're poised to adapt to any challenge that may come their way.

"Are they in there?" Lucy's voice quivers with urgency, her eyes darting across the building for any hint of movement.

"I hope so," George replies, his gaze never leaving the target area. "Steve wouldn't risk this mission if he didn't think they were."

"They're like daughters to me," Lucy murmurs, her voice tinged with emotion. "I couldn't let them down."

George nods in agreement, recalling the bond with Abbie and Bethanie over the years. "I remember when we first met them," he says, a hint of nostalgia in his voice. "They were just teenagers. Now look at them, all grown up and fighting their own battles. Bet they are giving their captures hell."

A grin stretches across Lucy's face in a quiet laugh, "You know they are, George."

Meanwhile, Simon and I wait in the shadows, every moment stretching like an eternity. Derek's radio message to the snipers is our signal to advance, a silent cue in our clandestine dance. With unspoken understanding, we glide toward the opening in the wall.

We both slip through the entrance, passing along a 12-metre corridor before ascending stone steps in the dim light. At the top, the worn, battered, wooden door creaks. I push it open a few inches, revealing the hidden depths of the building—a labyrinth concealed within the hillside.

Inside, muffled voices drift from an open door, the glow of fire casting flickering shadows. To our right, a fortified room holds sleeping figures and a cache of weapons.

"Not our targets," Simon murmurs, his words only just audible in the silence.

Agreeing with a nod, we continue our silent exploration. The scent of burning wood mingles with the distant echoes of conversation. Each step brings us closer to the heart of the building, tension coiling with every breath.

Approaching the source of the voices, I move with utmost caution, inching closer to the door. Doing my best not to make a sound, I move within inches of the door, crouch down, and take a deep breath before peering into the room. The room is ablaze with light. Cartel members huddle around a makeshift table. Their hushed conversation is laden with cryptic references to hostages and illicit shipments. The centre is dominated by a flickering fire that casts dancing shadows on the walls.

As we explore, the secrets of the Artillery Officer's Quarters unfold beneath the dim glow of lanterns, and every discovery is a piece in the puzzle of my daughters' eventual rescue. Our exploration continues, mapping the building's internal structure. Rooms reveal themselves—some empty, others storing supplies.

"We need to investigate the room where George said he and Lucy could see from their location to the right of the entrance," I murmur. Simon raises a thumb.

Moving with caution along the corridor, I lead the way towards the front entrance, with Simon shadowing my every move. The air is thick with tension, and each step is a calculated risk in this secret operation. To our left, a doorway barricaded with solid metal bars catches my attention, its imposing presence a stark contrast to the surrounding darkness.

Curiosity piqued, we approach the barricaded door, and as I peer inside, my heart lurches at the sight of two slender figures lying motionless on wooden beds. Covered by a thin sheet, they seem strangely out of place in this desolate setting, a haunting juxtaposition to the grim reality of our mission.

Straining my eyes in the dim light, I search for any identifying features, any clue that might identify these mysterious figures. And then, amidst the shadows, I spot a familiar insignia, sending a jolt of recognition coursing through my veins.

But before we can investigate further, the tell-tale sound of approaching footsteps echoes down the corridor, the heavy thud of boots reverberating off the stone walls. Time is now of the essence — we cannot afford to be discovered.

We slip back through the doorway, the rusty hinges protesting our hasty retreat. We blend into the shadows, our breath held in anticipation as the footsteps fade into the darkness. Once they disappear into the night, we descend the stone stairs and make our way along the corridor, stopping at the end, our senses on high alert.

"DR, this is S3. We're coming out. All call signs RV at the vehicle." I wait for the reply.

"S3, Roger that."

As we make our way back to the RV, every rustle of leaves and snap of twigs sends a jolt of adrenaline coursing through my veins.

The night is our ally, embracing us as we navigate the dense foliage with practised precision.

I lead the way, my movements fluid and silent as we weave through the shadows, my eyes scanning the surroundings for any sign of danger. Simon is behind me, with Derek bringing up the rear. All our senses are on high alert, ready to react at a moment's notice.

We stop at the Orillion Bastion, its imposing silhouette looming against the night sky like a guard of the past. We watch and listen for any movements. With none seen, we start to move, when a flicker of movement catches my eye. I freeze, my heart pounding in my chest. Through the dense underbrush, I catch a glimpse of shadowy figures moving in the distance, their forms just about visible in the darkness.

"Contact," I hiss, my voice a whisper as I signal for Derek and Simon to take cover. We slip behind a cluster of trees, holding our breath as we watch the figures draw closer.

Minutes pass like hours as we wait in tense silence, every nerve on edge as we prepare for the inevitable confrontation.

And then, just as suddenly as they appeared, the figures melt back into the shadows, disappearing into the night like ghosts. We breathe a collective sigh of relief, the tension dissipating as we resume our journey back to the RV.

"Keep your eyes scanning the area," I whisper to Simon and Derek, my voice a hushed breath in the stillness of the night. "We're not out of trouble yet."

Simon nods, his gaze sweeping the area for any sign of movement. The tension is intense, hanging in the air like a shroud as we press forward, our footsteps muffled by the thick carpet of fallen moist leaves. Each step is a calculated risk in this lethal game of cat and mouse.

But as we move through the darkness, a nagging sense of foreboding gnaws at the edges of my consciousness, a silent warning that our mission is far from over.

Chapter Fifteen - The Plan

In the darkness, Simon, Derek, and I converge at the RV, our breaths held tight with anticipation. Lucy and George, already there, blend into the shadows, their presence just about discernible among the trees. Everyone is on high alert, every rustle of leaves setting our nerves on edge as we strain to detect any signs of pursuit.

Minutes stretch into eternity as we wait in silence, the night alive with the sounds of creatures of the night. I scan the surroundings — senses honed for the slightest hint of danger. But the night remains still, a shroud of uncertainty hanging heavy in the air, the sound of each breath we take a potential trigger for the lurking danger.

With a signal, I rise from my concealed position, a silent command for the team to regroup. There's no room for error, as we make our way back to the vehicle, each step a careful dance between stealth and urgency.

The drive back to the abandoned building is fraught with tension at every turn, in the dim light of dawn. Soon, Simon steers the SUV off the road, turning off the lights and plunging us once more into the darkness of the dirt track.

As we approach the RV, Simon brings the vehicle to a halt, the crunch of gravel beneath the tyres a stark reminder of our vulnerability. We disembark, rifles at the ready, taking up defensive positions along the track, our senses attuned to the slightest sign of danger.

With practised precision, I lead the team forward, each step a calculated risk in the face of unknown threats. We move with the stealth of shadows, clearing the area with systematic efficiency.

Thirty minutes later, the area has been secured, and Simon joins us inside after parking the vehicle behind the building. Once everyone has dumped their kit on the floor, I call them over for a debrief.

"Does anyone have anything to report?"

"I didn't see much for our location apart from someone walking outside the target, smoking. They were, without a doubt, armed," replies George.

After putting something away in her Bergen, Lucy looks up. "An extra light stuck out above the spotlights that are in place to illuminate the fort. I would take it, due to the intermittency of the beam as it made its way between the merlons and the crenets along the top of the wall, it was one of the cartel's people using a torch to move about."

"See anyone moving around the place?" I add, trying to build up a complete picture.

"Nope, apart from your three sorry arses moving towards the Artillery Officer's Quarters."

"Thanks, George. That's useful. This means the cartel is concentrated into two areas."

"The big questions are, what did you find inside? Were the girls there? Did you get eyes on them?" asks Derek, fiddling with his radio.

"First, the quarters are much bigger than you can see from the outside. The building extends back into the base of the hill behind it. Inside, there were more than two people whom we believed were guarding something or someone.

"From what Simon and I saw and heard, I would say there are at least six of them. They have plenty of ammo and rifles stored in a single room. As we looked at it, the room closest to the door and on our left is where they appear to spend a lot of time. We witnessed several men here eating and drinking next to an open fire.

"There are two rooms with metal bars on them. A guard was sleeping in one, so this must be the rest area/sleeping area. In the other room, I witnessed two figures sleeping under thin blankets. This is where I spotted something I recognised. A pink cashmere scarf—like the one I purchased for Abbie last year. She takes the damn thing everywhere."

I'm interrupted by Derek, "Brilliant, Steve, if you are sure it is hers."

"I'm about 90 per cent sure it's hers. Of course, I'm not stupid enough to go on the scarf alone. Some idiot could have taken it from her. But there is something about the way the bodies slept under the blankets, the long blonde hair spread out on the pillow, that makes me believe and hope it is Abbie and Bethanie."

"She always takes it with her. She even took it on our last girls' night out," adds Lucy, with a twinkle of hope that we have found the girls she has become attached to.

"It sounds like we have the right location ready for a rescue, but after a brew. Who wants one?" Simon comments, moving towards his Bergen.

"I'll have one. It's now 08:00. Give me an hour to devise the rescue plan," I reply, getting up off the floor.

While Simon adds water to a mess tin he's placed on a gas cooker, the rest of the team takes time out for some personal admin.

I start to piece together all the information collected from the day and night recce to get an overall picture. Once I have the plan sorted in my head, I focus on creating a model of the target area.

I find a couple of broken chairs and a battered wooden door, which I use to create a makeshift table. Looking around, I scavenge items from our surroundings—a few rocks representing the walls, twigs for trees, and small pieces of metal for buildings. Once it is finished, I call the team over.

As everyone settles around the crude table, looking at a rough model of the Brimstone Hill Fort using objects I've constructed, "Listen up," my voice carrying the weight of our mission. "Our objective is paramount: we must extract Abbie and Bethanie unharmed from the Brimstone Hill Fort while prioritising the safety of our team and minimising casualties. Before we proceed, we must thoroughly assess the factors at play.

"To gain supremacy, we will execute this operation with stealth, slipping in and out unnoticed. Tonight, at 23:00, under the cloak of darkness, we will make our move. In this region," I survey the room, ensuring everyone is engaged, "the weather is on our side. A full moon will illuminate the area, and if the conditions mirror last night's, the cloud cover will aid our concealment and navigation."

Pointing to the makeshift model, I highlight the varied terrain surrounding the fort.

"We know what the terrain will be like from our recces, but we need to go over it again. There are trees and a lot of vegetation surrounding the fort, so our approach should go unhindered until we reach our start RV once we have left the vehicle." I gesture towards the clearing where Simon will conceal the SUV, and trace along with a small twig I'm using as a pointer to the Orillion Bastion.

"We have several areas of open ground to deal with. But the high wall will cover us as we move from one area to another, following our standard operating procedures. Remember, at all times, there is a faint chance the people Lucy and George witnessed at Fort George could be looking over the target area from their high vantage point. Do you have any questions about what we have covered so far?"

"What are we doing about the people up in Fort George?" Lucy interjects.

"I'm about to cover potential obstacles and threats, Lucy. First, the obstacles are the guards. We know they're in the area of Fort George and in and around the main objective. We need to move undetected and be in and out before people get a sense of what is happening.

"However, if any guard becomes an issue, they will be taken out. Lucy and George, you will deal with the idiots in Fort George if the occasion arises. I'm confident in your abilities as snipers to eliminate the threat. Your sniper position is only 150 metres in a direct line from the fort." I'm confident in your abilities as snipers to eliminate the threat.

"Second, the guards inside the target area will be oblivious to our activities to start with. But once Simon and I infiltrate the building via the same route we went in last night, they may have to be dispatched without alerting others in the facility. We will need the keys to unlock the cell door to grab Abbie and Bethanie. If nobody has anything to add, let us move on to personnel roles and responsibilities." I scan each team member's face, gauging their focus.

"Our two snipers will locate themselves here," I point to the map. "You will cover the surrounding area and protect the rest of the team as we move into our start position here."

I indicate the woodline below the Artillery Officer's Quarters. "From here, Derek will initiate and coordinate the rescue..."

"Wouldn't it be better if Derek is on the high ground with us for that?" George interrupts, pointing at the Prince of Wales Bastion.

"That sounds good to me. Scratch what I just said, Derek. You will move with George and Lucy, which leaves Simon and me to make our way to the entrance to the wall. From here, we will enter and grab the girls.

"When it comes to equipment and weapons, make sure all your kit is packed in and on the SUV when we leave here; we will not be coming back. Once the briefing is over, Lucy will ensure all the ammo is distributed and the night vision scopes are working, which she will take with her and George. Derek will check all the radio equipment before departure. Everyone must carry all the necessary equipment to deal with any situation, including weapons, ammunition, and communication devices. Before I move onto procedure, does anyone want to add anything or question?"

"All sounds good so far," Simon says, shaking his head.

"In that case, we will move on to procedures. Everyone must familiarise themselves with the layout of the fort, the route in and out, the RVs at the drop-off and retrieval points, and the area surrounding the main objective. I've incorporated information from recces into the model in front of you. Please take time to study it before I destroy it."

"Preparation—Everyone should check their equipment and ensure no rattles or other sounds that might give away our position before the rescue gets underway.

"Launch – Once everyone is in the designated start positions confirmed by radio, Derek will send the following message, 'All call signs, we have a go'. Once you receive the message, Simon and I will make our way inside to retrieve the targets."

"Once we receive the message, I'll turn my attention to Fort George while Lucy covers you and Simon," George adds to the briefing.

"Good idea, mate. Next point, extraction and team deployment: our objective is to enter the building via the door, corridor, and stairs at the bottom of the wall. Our mission is to swiftly and efficiently rescue Abbie and Bethanie while minimising the risk of detection.

"Upon reaching the designated entry point, Simon and I will proceed with caution, ensuring we maintain stealth at all times. We will use hand signals to communicate, allowing us to coordinate our movements.

"Once inside the building, we will move with speed through the corridor, keeping to the shadows to avoid detection. Our primary focus will be locating Abbie and Bethanie and ensuring their safety. We will move without detection, clearing each room as we progress through the building.

"If we encounter any individuals inside the Artillery Quarters, we will incapacitate them with speed, again without drawing attention to other people inside, using hand-to-hand combat techniques or knives if necessary. Our priority is to neutralise any potential threats without raising the alarm.

"As we make our way through the building, we will communicate at all times with the rest of the team where possible, providing updates on our progress and any obstacles encountered. This will ensure we can adapt our strategy as needed and coordinate with the team for a swift and seamless evacuation."

I pause for a few moments, allowing the weight of the mission settle on everyone's shoulders.

"Alright, let's move on to retrieval. Once we have the girls, we will withdraw back the way we came in, stopping at the entrance to let you know we're coming out. From there, we'll make our way to the RV to meet up with the rest of you. It'll be a tight fit, but we'll sort something out."

"Sure I can rig up a roof rack," Simon suggests with a smirk. "Maybe we can strap Derek up there with his radio for a clearer signal."

Derek smiles, "And maybe I'll give you a tap on the head if you mess up, or just whenever I feel like it."

"Alright, Simon, I'll leave the roof rack in your capable hands," I interject, keeping the mood light despite the gravity of the situation. "Which leads me to security. In case of any complications, we'll RV back at this location. Before I move on to contingency plans, does anyone have anything to add?"

"Not from me. I'll brief us on the radio procedures at the end," Derek offers.

"Alright, let's talk contingency plans," I continue, keeping the briefing focused. "If anyone's injured, stay put unless you can walk. Derek's team will cover us if we come under attack until we have the girls back at the SUV. Our emergency RV will be the Calvary Baptist Church. Over to you, Derek, for radio protocols."

"As always, we'll keep chatter to a minimum until the rescue is underway," Derek states. "The go message will be, 'All call signs, we have a go'. I'll check the radios and set frequencies. Don't mess with them. I'll be close to George and Lucy. Lucy, it's your turn for the sniper update."

"George and I will find a concealed spot on the Prince of Wales Bastion," Lucy explains. "We'll cover Steve and Simon as they cross the open ground. Our secondary task is to monitor Fort George. Night vision scopes will help. Anything to add, George?"

"Just that Lucy and I will cover your sorry arses during the withdrawal," George chimes in with a chuckle. "Over to you, Simon."

"After this, I'll check the SUV and build a roof rack," Simon says. "For the rescue, I'll be with Steve in the Artillery Officer's Quarters."

"That's it for the brief. Apart from that, I'm not coming away without my girls. If we fail, they will be killed."

"We are with you on that one, Steve. We will bring them home," says Lucy, putting her arm around me.

"Suggest we break off and go over your individual roles. Not to teach you how to do your jobs but run through them so you can deal with any situation that arises without thinking. I'll leave my model of the target area up for the next 20 minutes. If you need to take another look, do it, before I break it up."

Following my own advice, plonk my arse down next to my Bergen and start to go over my task from the point of arriving at the RV and clambering out of the SUV. Lead the team to the Orillion Bastion, using the cover of the trees.

Once there, the sniper and Derek will split off for their location. Simon and I will move to the edge of the treeline close to the entrance in the wall, once inside the building. Follow the same route as yesterday and go where we believe Bethanie and Abbie are being held. Dispatch anyone who gets in the way. As some furry rodents say, 'simples'.

Within an hour, the whole team have finished their allotted tasks, and we are all sitting with our backs against the cold stone wall, our weapons within arm's reach. Simon starts boiling water on his stove to make a brew. Apart from the roar of the gas burner and the birds chirping outside, the room is quiet.

"Before we go and grab my girls, I would like to thank you all for helping me on this mission. I've had the privilege of knowing you all for some time. Those two idiots," I point to Simon and George, "we met at Combat Stress, where we ended up after we had seen the darkness and lived to tell the tale. As for Derek, he is a brother in arms after both of us served in the Royal Green Jackets. Then there is Lucy, who has been by my side since we met on the Isle of Wight. Even though I'm an unemotional arse sometimes."

"You are indeed, Steve. But since I've known you, your lack of empathy has worked in our favour. And you're welcome," replies George. "As for me, I left the army a few years back." His eyes are distant as memories flood back. "After the army and my time as a dog handler for the British Ministry of Defence, I felt lost—aimless, you know?

"Then, I found myself at Combat Stress. That's where I met the nutters, Steve and Simon," a hint of emotion creeping into his voice. "It was there that I realised I wasn't alone. And when the opportunity came to join this team, to fight for something bigger than myself, I knew I had to take it. So here I am. Part of this ragtag group of misfits, making a difference where we can, and here to get the two girls my wife and I have become fond of. And I wouldn't have it any other way," George concludes, a faint smile playing on his lips.

"As we are sitting around confessing, I might have something to get off my chest—something that happened in my past." Lucy takes a deep breath, "I've been meaning to tell you all something." Her gaze fixed on the flickering flame of the gas cooker. "Before I joined this team, I was a mercenary. I took jobs for anyone who could pay, no questions asked."

Derek looks at Lucy, "How deep were you in it?"

Lucy sighs, running a hand through her hair. "I didn't always know who the customer was but sometimes the customer name slipped through. It's better for everyone concerned. Jobs would come via a third party to the company I worked for, called Black Sands. Sometimes, the jobs seemed straightforward, but looking back, I realise I might have been working indirectly for Acosta and his cartel without even knowing it. His name may have been said a few times."

Simon looks at her, his expression unreadable.

"You think they might come after you?" he asks, his voice quiet but with concern for Lucy.

Lucy nods, "It's possible, but I won't let them intimidate me. I've changed since then, and I'll do whatever it takes to protect this team and get my stepdaughters back."

There's a moment of silence as we absorb Lucy's words. But then Derek speaks up, his voice firm with resolve.

"We're a team," he says, his gaze meeting each of ours in turn. "We stick together, no matter what. As for your past, Lucy, we don't have any concerns. Glad you're on our side. What about you, Simon? Got anything you want to share?"

"I'll agree with that, Derek. Like the rest of you idiots, I'd go into any battle with confidence, knowing each one of you will have my back."

Simon thinks for a few seconds, memories of battles fought, and lives lost flooded his mind.

"My time in the army ended abruptly," Simon began, his voice faint and gravelly, each word measured and deliberate. "After a particularly harrowing mission, I found myself questioning everything I thought I knew. I needed a change. That's when my doctor sent me to Combat Stress, where I met the other two.

Together, we found solace in each other's company, a shared understanding of the demons we battled every day. When the chance came to join this team, I found purpose, and I knew it was where I belonged. Now, I fight, not just for myself but for each one of you. And, of course, the girls."

"I suppose you want to hear my story. After leaving the army, I found myself adrift. It wasn't until I stumbled upon the small island of St Halb that I found a new purpose." Derek pauses as the memories of the lush tropical paradise flood his mind. "I decided to start my own bar and restaurant. It was a humble establishment, but it was mine. I spent many long hours building my business from the ground up and the camaraderie I shared with locals and tourists alike. Running the bar became my life. But deep down, I knew I was meant for something more. That's when I bumped into Steve, Simon and George in my bar on St Halb. For some reason, I kept their contact details. The meeting summoning me back into the world of covert operations, joining this team was a natural progression. A chance to put my skills to use in a new way, to fight for a cause greater than myself."

I look around at my teammates. Despite the uncertainty of the situation, I sense the solidarity among us. We may have our differences, but when it comes down to it, we're united in our determination to overcome whatever challenges lie ahead. With that thought in mind, a surge of confidence brings us together, and we can face anything that comes our way.

I glance down at the time it's 11:00 We still have plenty of time before Zulu time. With all the personal admin done and everything checked again, I'm getting hungry.

"Fancy heading back to the Island Breeze café or Simon's famous..." Before I could get all my words out, I was interrupted by Derek.

"Café, no offence, Simon, but could do with a good steak. Unless you have one in that bag of tricks of yours."

"None taken. Don't fancy cooking anyway," replies Simon, getting up off the floor and heading outside to fire up the SUV.

Simon's handiwork on the roof rack catches my eye as we exit the RV and approach the SUV. It's a makeshift contraption, cobbled together from various materials Simon found lying around the building. Despite its unconventional appearance, it appears sturdy enough to hold our gear.

"Nice rack, Simon," George quips, a wry grin playing on his lips as he gestures towards the roof. "Very... rustic."

Simon chuckles, a hint of pride in his voice. "Hey, it may not be pretty, but it gets the job done," he replies, his tone light-hearted.

I can't help but smile at the banter between them as we load our equipment into the vehicle. Despite the seriousness of our mission, moments like these serve as a reminder of the camaraderie that binds us together.

Once everything is stowed away, we climb into the vehicle, each of us settling into our seats with a sense of purpose. As Simon starts the engine and pulls away from the building, I can't shake the sensation of anticipation that courses through me. We may be heading into the unknown, but with this team by my side, I know we're ready for whatever challenges lie ahead.

Chapter Sixteen- The Rescue

We may be taking a risk going back to the Island Breeze café, but as they say, the best place to hide is in the open. Besides, the last time we were there, we didn't attract any unwanted attention.

The rumble of our SUV's engine fades as we pull into the dirt parking lot beside Island Breeze, the morning sun casting long shadows on the village.

As we step inside, the familiar creak of floorboards greets us. The cosy interior is bathed in sunlight, and the wooden tables adorned with tropical flowers bring a sense of serenity.

The café owner, a weathered man, approaches our table. "Good morning, folks. What can I get you?" he asks.

"Five specials and coffees, please," I reply.

As we settle into our corner, the same older woman who served us last time brings over our steaming cups of coffee. "You folks enjoying your visit to my island? Did you get to see what you were talking about last time you were here?" after putting the drinks on the table.

"Thank you, ma'am, and yep, saw some amazing sights," Derek says, dragging a mug towards him.

The scran arrives as we sit in the familiar confines of Island Breeze café. The clinking of cutlery against ceramic plates is the only sound amidst the quiet morning. The aroma of freshly brewed coffee swirls around us as we tuck into our breakfast, the usual patrons absent this time.

I look up as the door swings open. Out of instinct I check the time, a habit I picked up during surveillance training in my army days. It's 13:30 A familiar figure strides in — it's Miguel, his presence commanding attention. He spots us and walks over, his face etched with urgency.

"Good morning," Miguel greets us in a serious tone. "I have news."

I exchange a glance with the team, curiosity piqued.

"What's going on, Miguel? What brings you here?" I enquire, gesturing for him to join us.

After a short conversation and ordering a drink from the man behind the counter, Miguel takes a seat at our table and leans in, his voice lowered.

"I was driving past on police business, investigating a robbery, when I saw a vehicle parked outside similar to one used by the thieves. So I popped in."

"What's the news, Miguel?" I ask, still working out if he is telling the truth about the burglary or if he came in looking for us.

"Alex Acosta's son is in Southampton. He's visiting Calvin, a local dealer who sells drugs for Hugo, tomorrow at some place called the Marland's Centre, at Costa Coffee. Thought you might want to know."

"Any idea of what time, and what has Hugo to do with us?"

"I don't know what time, Steve, apart from the fact that, from what my informants tell me, Hugo always does business in the afternoons."

Lucy's brow furrows in concern. "Is it Hugo and this guy, Calvin who first took Abbie and Bethanie?"

"Yes, that's him. He took them on orders from Hugo, which no doubt came from his father, Alex. It appears like the pieces of this puzzle are starting to fall into place. I even pulled a photo of him off the police computer," replies Miguel, sliding the photo across the table.

"Thanks for the heads-up," I say, gratitude evident in my voice.

Miguel nods in agreement. "Be careful, my friends. This is dangerous territory."

With that, Miguel rises from his seat and walks towards the door.

Before leaving, he turns back and says, "If you need a way off the island when the time comes, I can arrange it. Just let me know."

"Will do, and thanks," I reply as he disappears out the door, leaving us to digest the gravity of his revelation.

After ensuring nobody could overhear what I was about to say, "Sounds like we have a job for Hadley and Gary back home. I will call him once we are back in the SUV."

"The big question is, do we trust Miguel enough to help us leave St Kitts once we have the girls?"

"We may have to, Simon. Because if the shit hits the proverbial fan later, and we don't get in and out unseen, you can almost guarantee that Acosta will have his people out in force looking for us. They may even have corrupt officials at the airport. But he will be a last resort," I say, scanning the faces of the team.

With food out of the way, we exit the Island Breeze Café at 14:00. The afternoon sun casts a harsh light, making the shadows sharper. The SUV waits, its dark windows reflecting the tropical landscape. We climb in, each of us lost in our thoughts, knowing what lies ahead.

Simon takes the wheel, his focus absolute as he drives off to our first RV. where we will go into tactical mode and lay in the forest until we drive up to the fort.

The road twists and turns, the ocean view gradually replaced by thick forest. The air grows cooler, the scent of salt replaced by the musk of foliage. The silence inside the vehicle is heavy with unspoken tension. I take the time to call Hadley.

The phone rings several times before a voice on the other end says, "Hi, Dad. Do you have my sisters yet?"

"Not yet, son, but very soon."

I never like giving too much away. You never know if your phone has been tapped and some idiot is listening to your conversation. Even though my mobile is a PAYG, I'm not taking a chance.

"Anything for me to do yet?" comes Hadley's reply.

"Yes, can you follow up on a lead for me?"

"Of course. If it helps get Abbie and Bethanie back. What is it, Dad?"

"Yes, it's connected. We need you to follow someone and take them out. Call Gary for help. I'll send you an encrypted WhatsApp message with the details. Let me know when it's done. Remember, stay safe. If you think something is wrong or out of place, abort."

"Will do. I'll contact Gary now."

By the time I finish the call, Simon is easing the SUV off the path, reversing into a dense cluster of trees. The branches close around us, concealing our presence from any passerby. We disembark quietly, each member slipping into the undergrowth, taking up positions where we can watch the road without being seen.

The forest is alive with subtle sounds—the rustle of leaves, the distant call of a bird, the occasional snap of a twig. We remain motionless, every sense heightened, attuned to the environment. Time stretches, every minute feeling like an hour. My pulse matches the rhythm of the forest, a constant reminder of the stakes.

For three hours, we watch and listen, the waiting as much a part of the mission as the action to come.

As dusk approaches, Simon signals. We regroup at the SUV, slipping back into the vehicle with practiced efficiency. The engine starts, barely a whisper, and we move out.

Soon, Simon is turning right off the winding road leading to Brimstone Hill Fort. His gaze sharpens as he navigates and scans the terrain for any signs of danger. Spotting a small, unused dirt track halfway up the hill, he makes a split-second decision, veering the SUV off the road with precision.

The vehicle jostles over uneven terrain as Simon's skilled hands guide it through the dense forest. He manoeuvres with the finesse of a seasoned recce troop driver. Every twist and turn is calculated to minimise noise and maximise concealment. Approaching a small ditch blocking our path, Simon's focus intensifies.

With a masterful flick of the wheel and a gentle press of the accelerator, he navigates over the obstacle, the vehicle's suspension absorbing the impact with ease. As the SUV glides onward, Simon's mastery of the vehicle proves why he is our transport expert. We press onward toward our objective, each movement deliberate and controlled.

On the edge of the clearing, the vehicle comes to a halt, and its engine becomes silent. The team piles out and spreads out, taking cover around the car, each covering a different arc of fire. We stay like this for the next 25 minutes, each person quiet as they lay in the foliage, ready to pounce if the situation arises.

With the rest of the team still observing, watching for anyone approaching, I make my way to Simon, lying close to the driver's door. Without saying a word, Simon and I start to conceal the SUV using the local vegetation and stuff Simon had loaded into the vehicle back at the last RV.

While I concentrate on the rear, Simon places an old sheet of canvas over the vehicle lights to prevent reflection before snapping off large branches and laying them up against the front. This way, if we need to bug out, we can do it at speed, knocking them out of the way as we depart. Once the camouflage is as good as possible, we return to our defensive positions.

We still have a few hours to wait for the rescue to start. This shouldn't be an issue for any of us, as we have all done this type of thing on many occasions. As I lie here now amidst the undergrowth, listening to the rustle of leaves and the distant calls of rainforest creatures filling the air, I can't help but draw parallels between this short OP and one I carried out in my army days. And the one we find ourselves in today.

A team of us embarked on a mission on a remote island deep in the heart of a dense rainforest. We spent seven gruelling days in that unforgiving environment, daring not to move too much in the fear we would be compromised.

Our objective was clear: observe and await the arrival of a notorious terrorist at a villa nestled within the rainforest. We lay in wait, concealed within our hide. Our eyes trained on the target, we scrutinised every movement and analysed every sound for potential threats.

The relentless rain pounded down upon us, soaking through our camouflage gear and testing our endurance with each passing hour. Yet, despite the discomfort and fatigue, we remained steadfast, knowing that the mission's success depended on our unwavering commitment. The stakes may have been different, but the essence remained the same: patience, vigilance, and an unyielding resolve to complete the mission.

I glance down at Mickey on my wrist, it's 23:00; at last, the time has come to move. With the night embracing us, we emerge from the RV, our breaths forming wisps of vapour in the chilly air. We move with purpose and determination towards the Orillion Bastion.

I take a point. My senses are alert to every rustle of leaves and snap of twigs beneath our boots. Simon follows close behind, his presence reassuring in the darkness.

"Keep it tight," I whisper over my shoulder, my voice just audible above the rustle of leaves. "We stick to the plan and stay undercover."

Simon nods in acknowledgement, his eyes scanning the surrounding area for any signs of movement. Lucy and Derek fall into position behind us, their weapons ready, while George brings his usual position at the rear, his keen eyes watching our backs.

The moon overhead hangs like a silver coin in the sky, casting an eerie glow over the forest and surrounding area. Its pale light illuminates our path, guiding us through the dense undergrowth.

We move in a tight patrol formation, using the trees as cover to conceal our movements. Each step is deliberate and calculated as we navigate our way with silent precision. The only sound is the soft crunch of leaves beneath our boots, the rhythm of our breathing as we move as one towards our first objective.

As we approach the Orillion Bastion, I raise my hand to signal the team to halt. Everyone crouches to the ground, each person facing and covering in different directions, scanning the area for any signs of activity.

"Detect anything?" I ask, my voice just above a whisper.

Simon shakes his head, "No movement yet, Steve."

We wait a few minutes in silence to ensure we haven't been followed or spotted, listening for any signs of danger. The forest is alive with the sounds of the night, but there's something else beneath the surface.

I signal to move forward, and we continue our stealthy advance towards the bastion. We stick to the shadows, using darkness to conceal our movements as we draw closer to our next RV.

To my front, the Orillion Bastion looms like a dark sentinel. Its ancient stone walls rise from the open ground, a fortress from a bygone era. We approach with caution, our senses on high alert.

As we near the perimeter of the bastion, I motion for us to split into two teams: Simon and I on one side, Lucy and Derek on the other. We move with practised precision, our footsteps silent as we hug the trees, staying close to the shadows to avoid detection.

The tension is intense as we inch towards the forward edge, overlooking the target area and our objective. Every nerve in my body tingles with anticipation. I can sense the adrenaline coursing through my body, heightening my senses and sharpening my focus.

As we reach the entrance, I gesture for Simon to cover me as I peer around the corner, scanning the area for any signs of movement. The coast appears clear, but I know better than to let my guard down.

With a single hand gesture, I signal for us to proceed, and we slip through the entrance like ghosts in the night. The interior of the bastion is dark and foreboding, the air thick with the scent of damp earth and decay.

We move with caution, our senses on high alert as we navigate the labyrinthine corridors of the bastion. Every sound echoes off the stone walls. A faint noise catches my attention, a soft shuffle of footsteps echoing down the corridor. I motion for Simon to take cover as I edge forward, my weapon ready.

Bend down and peer around the corner. To my front, a lone guard is patrolling the hallway, his eyes darting from side to side.

For our mission to go as planned, he must be taken down without any sound.

Before he has time to spot me, I launch at him, my knife in my hand, ready for action. With one swift movement, I strike him, my knife digging deep into his chest. His death cries are muffled by my other hand. In what appears to be only a nano-second, his lifeless body is eased to the ground to avoid any unnecessary noise. Simon moves forward to check the body.

"He's gone," says Simon, after checking the body.

With no one else found, we press on, meeting up with the others at the edge of the building, peering towards the Prince of Wales Bastion.

"You have any issues, Steve?" asks Lucy, without turning around.

"Just the one person who, shall we say, is taking an extra-long nap," I reply, sitting beside George.

We wait again, ensuring there is nobody else around. Once I'm sure, I give the signal to move.

Simon and I take up firing positions, our eyes scanning the darkness for movement. The night encases us like a shroud, the only illumination coming from the pale glow of the full moon overhead.

As Lucy, George, and Derek slip into the shadows, I feel a surge of tension coiling in my chest. We're on a knife's edge here, each movement, every step fraught with risk. But we've been through worse, and I trust their skill and expertise.

I watch them depart over the barrel of my rifle, my heart pounding. They're vulnerable out there, exposed in the moonlight, but also our best chance at success. We need their cover and radio control if we're going to make it through this alive.

With rehearsed precision, Lucy, George, and Derek move across the open ground, one person moving at a time while the other two cover. They inch their way toward the Prince of Wales Bastion. They move like ghosts, their footsteps silent against the soft earth, blending seamlessly into the night.

As Lucy, George, and Derek reach the Prince of Wales Bastion, I am overcome with relief. They've made it to their secure positions and are ready to provide us with the cover we might need if things don't go as planned.

But there's no time to relax. We still have a mission to complete, a rescue to carry out, and every second counts with the cartel's men lurking in the shadows. I turn my attention back to the task at hand, my senses sharpened to a razor's edge. Whatever lies in store for us tonight, we won't go down without a fight—not while there's still breath in our bodies. And I know we stand a fighting chance with Lucy, George, and Derek watching our backs from their sniper and radio positions.

As Simon and I approach the entrance of the Artillery Officer's Quarters, tension coils in my chest like a tightening spring. Every breath is a calculated measure of readiness. I grip my weapon tighter, as we make our way along the tunnel leading to the stairs.

As we reach the top of the stone staircase and approach the wooden door leading into the Artillery Officer's Quarters, a sense of urgency pulses through my body like a raging river. I turn to face Simon behind me in the tight corridor.

"You ready?" I whisper.

Simon raises his thumb. My hand grabs the metal handle and lifts the catch, and the wooden door creaks open, revealing a dimly lit corridor beyond. The flickering glow of light dances on the walls, casting eerie shadows that seem to twist and writhe with a life of their own. My senses enhance, every sound amplified in the silence of the night.

We move forward, each step deliberate, our boots making soft thuds against the stone floor. The air is filled with the scent of dust and must, mingling with the faint aroma of burning wood. As we round a corner, the muffled sound of voices reaches our ears. My heart quickens. Simon and I exchange a silent glance, communicating volumes in that single moment. It's time.

We turn around the first corner into the corridor. The scene before us is chaotic — a flurry of movement and confusion. I focus on the task at hand, filtering out the noise and distractions. Before me stands a formidable adversary, his eyes alight with malice as he brandishes a weapon with lethal intent. Without hesitation, I leap into action, my training kicking in as instinct takes over.

The building erupts into a whirlwind of motion as we clash in a fierce struggle for dominance. Each blow lands with a resounding thud, echoing through the cramped quarters. Blood pumping through my body at an increased rate sharpens my senses and heightens my awareness as I fight to gain control of the situation.

With each passing moment, the stakes grow higher, the air dense with tension as the outcome hangs in the balance. Every move is a calculated risk, and every strike is a testament to the strength of my resolve. But amidst the chaos, one thing remains clear: failure is not an option.

With a final surge of strength, I deliver a decisive blow and ram my knife into the side of his neck, sending my opponent reeling backwards in defeat. Spurts of dark red blood cover the walls in straight lines as though an artist has flicked the bristles of his brush. As the dust settles, victory hangs in the air, a small victory in the battle.

To my right, I catch a glimpse of Simon. His movements are fluid and decisive as he incapacitates another of Alex Acosta's men, rendering him unconscious before he has a chance to react.

The man crumples to the ground, his body hitting the stone floor with a dull thud.

With a deep breath, I turn my attention to the cell where, hopefully, Abbie and Bethanie are being held. We need to get to them before Acosta's men try to use them as shields in a futile attempt to get out of this place alive.

Simon and I make our way through the corridors of the building, tension hanging heavy in the air, anticipating our next move. Every step is charged with the expectancy of confrontation. We move with speed, knowing that the time for stealth is over. Each room we clear brings us closer to the cell where Abbie and Bethanie are being held captive by Acosta's men.

The sound of gunfire shatters the silence as we encounter two more of Acosta's men — a single shot racing through the air, hitting the wall behind me. With precision, we dispatch the attackers with single, well-placed shots from our 9mm pistols. There's no room for hesitation or mercy in these close-quarters engagements. It's kill or be killed. Nothing and nobody will stand in my way of rescuing Abbie and Bethanie.

As we move from room to room, every shadow becomes a potential threat, every creak of the floorboards a warning of danger. But with Simon by my side, I feel a sense of reassurance, a silent understanding that we'll do whatever it takes to complete the mission and save the girls. Each firefight is intense but brief, and our training and experience guide us through each encounter. With each enemy neutralised, we press forward. The path ahead is clear.

Deeper into the building, Abbie and Bethanie are awakened by the muffled sounds of gunfire and shouts reverberating through the thick stone walls. They exchange a glance filled with both fear and determination. The chaos outside serves as a catalyst, igniting a fire within them to reclaim control over their destiny.

Abbie's voice cuts through the tension.

"You hear that?" she yells at the guards, her tone filled with defiance. "Our dad and his friends are here, and you're all going to die!"

Bethanie's eyes blaze with intensity as she joins in, her voice carrying the weight of our shared resolve. "You think you can keep us locked up like animals? Think again. We're not going down without a fight."

Their defiance enrages the guard. With a savage growl, he lunges towards the bars of the cell, intent on hurting them and using them as human shields.

Bethanie's eyes flash with resolve as she spots the guard moving towards them. Without hesitation, she springs into action, lunging towards him before he can reach them. With a swift movement, she grabs him, smashing his face against the cell bars. Before he can act, she wraps her arm around his neck, pulling him towards her with a strength born of desperation.

The guard struggles against Bethanie's grip, his hands clawing at her arm in a futile attempt to break free. But Bethanie holds on tight, channelling every ounce of rage and desperation, her determination unwavering as she begins to squeeze his life out.

Abbie observes in awe as her sister takes control of the situation, her heart pounding. She knows she needs to act fast to help her sister and ensure they both survive.

Thinking quickly, Abbie scans the cell for anything she can use as a weapon. Her eyes land on a toothbrush she had sharpened to a point lying on the floor. One of the many lessons her dad had drummed into her and her sister while they were growing up. With a surge of adrenaline, she snatches it up, her fingers closing around the makeshift weapon.

With a fierce determination, Abbie charges towards the struggling pair at the bars. As the guard's struggles grow weaker, without hesitation, Abbie plunges the sharpened end of the toothbrush into his eye with a swift, decisive motion. Blood spurts across the cell as he lets out a guttural scream of agony.

Together, Abbie and Bethanie fight for their lives, their resolve unyielding in the face of danger. With each passing moment, they inch closer to victory, refusing to let the fear and desperation consume them.

With one last desperate gasp, the guard's struggles cease, his body going limp in Bethanie's grip. With a sense of grim satisfaction, she releases her hold, allowing his lifeless form to slump to the ground.

Exhausted and shaken, Abbie and Bethanie stand together in the dimly lit cell, their chests heaving with exertion. But amidst the chaos and uncertainty, one thing remains clear: they are fighters and will stop at nothing to secure their freedom.

Seconds later, Simon and I reach the cell door where Abbie and Bethanie are being held. With a nod to each other, we stand prepared, our weapons at the ready, to breach the room and confront whatever awaits us on the other side. At this moment, there's no room for doubt or hesitation. We're soldiers on a mission, and nothing will stand in our way.

Inside, the girls are standing close to the bars. Blood is running down a weapon Abbie is holding in her right hand, also stained a crimson red. Each drop echoes as it hits the floor in an eerie silence. A man lies motionless at their feet, close to the bars.

Their faces are pale but determined. Relief floods through me at the sight of them, but there's no time for celebration.

"Quick, search him for the keys, Simon," I say, grabbing the bars of the cell.

Seconds later, "Got them!" Simon opens the cell door.

They both understand the time for hugs would come later. We need to move them to safety as fast as we can. There could still be some diehards who want to prevent us from leaving alive.

I am right. From the room I saw earlier on the recce where the men congregated by an open fire, three men burst out firing in all directions. The room is a blur of action—shouts and gunfire mingling with the acrid scent of smoke. With the precision of a well-oiled machine, I dispatch the closest one with a single bullet to his head. Simon drops another.

As I turn to face the remaining person, a shot rings out from my right. Spin around to see Bethanie holding a pistol, her arm still recoiling from the the kickback.

With a huge grin I feel a sense of pride; both of my girls remembered my life lessons while they were growing up, and when the time came, they didn't hesitate to use the skills they learned.

Turning to face them, "We need to move back to the RV and meet up with the others. Stay between Simon and me. Simon, give Abbie your 9mm."

I head back the same way we entered the building, descend the stone staircase, and head for the exit. Stopping short, I lean against the wall. Tap the transmit button of my radio, "All call signs, this is S3, were coming out. Over."

"S3, Roger that, I've got you covered, DR. Out."

*****

Meanwhile, at the Prince of Wales Bastion, the night is alive with tension as Derek crouches beside Lucy and George, his eyes scanning the darkness for any signs of movement. They're perched in their sniper position, high up on the Bastion, their rifles trained on the ground to their front, the Citadel, Fort George, and the Parade Ground below.

"Targets spotted, two o'clock," Derek whispers, his voice just above a murmur. "Three men approaching the AOQ."

Lucy nods, her eyes focused through the scope of her rifle as she lines up her shot.

"I see them," she replies, her voice calm and steady. "George, take the one on the left. I'll take the one on the right."

George adjusts his position, his breath coming out in controlled puffs as he lines up his shot. The distance is considerable and the angle difficult, but George is a sniper of unparalleled skill. With unwavering focus, he steadies his rifle and squeezes the trigger.

The shot rings in the darkness, like a crack of thunder in the night, echoing off the fort's stone walls as George's bullet finds its mark. The man on the left crumples to the ground, his body dropping like a puppet with its strings cut.

"Nice shot, George," Derek says, his voice filled with admiration. "One down, two to go."

As Lucy and George adjust their positions, Derek, acting as the spotter, scans the area for any additional threats, his eyes darting from shadow to shadow in search of movement. The tension is thick as they wait for any remaining targets to enter their field of view.

Without warning, a rifle shot rings out from the battlement of Fort George. Derek spots a flash from a figure with a weapon sticking through the battlement, silhouetted against the night sky through his rifle scope.

"Sniper on the battlement!" Derek calls out, his voice urgent as he relays the threat to Lucy and George. "Take him out, George!"

George nods as he lines up his shot. The distance is even greater this time, and the angle more difficult, but George doesn't hesitate. With a steady hand and a calm mind, he adjusts his aim and squeezes the trigger.

The shot flies true, soaring through the night air with fatal accuracy. It appears to hang in midair, suspended in time, for a heart-stopping moment before finding its mark with brutal precision. The enemy sniper's body jerks backwards, his rifle slipping from his grasp as he falls over the wall of the fort onto the ground beneath.

"Target down," George says, his voice calm and steady.

"Nice shooting," says Lucy, looking up from her rifle.

George nods in acknowledgement, his heart pounding as the gravity of what he's just accomplished sinks in. But there's no time to dwell on success. The enemy is still out there, and our mission is far from over.

With Lucy and George covering our backs, Derek turns his attention back to the radio, ready to call in our next move, when Steve's voice comes over the air, "All call signs, this is S3, were coming out. Over."

****

I give Derek and the team a few minutes to move positions to cover us coming out before I turn to the girls, "We need to dart to the trees over there." I point to the treeline. "I'll go first. Once I'm over, you two run as fast as you can and join me. Keep as close to the ground as possible to make a smaller target. Simon will bring up the rear."

"OK, Dad, we are behind you," replies Abbie.

With everyone across the open ground, I lead off through the trees, making our way back to the RV. About halfway, I spot silhouettes of armed figures approaching our location. I wave my right arm towards the ground to tell everyone to take cover. Hand signals are one of the lessons I taught Abbie and Bethanie growing up, so they understand what my signal means.

Monitor the situation as the figures creep closer to our location through the undergrowth, the moonlight giving the occasional glimpse of their movements. I take a deep breath and bring up my rifle, ready to fire and kill anyone I don't recognise.

Moments later, I spot something that makes me lower my weapon—George's unmistakable gait due to an injury sustained a few missions back, which left him with a slight limp, especially after lying in a sniper hide for an extended time. Behind is Lucy and Derek. As we regroup in the dense cover of the treeline, a sense of relief washes over me. We've completed this part of our mission, but the danger is far from over. I glance around at the team, their faces etched with determination and resolve, ready for whatever comes next.

"Everyone okay?" I ask, my voice soft but steady.

Nods and murmured affirmations ripple through the group as we take a moment to catch our breath. But there's no time to waste; we need to return to the RV.

I take point, scanning the area for any signs of movement as we move with stealth through the trees. The team is in its usual formation, with Lucy keeping Abbie and Bethanie close to her.

Soon, we approach the clearing where we left the RV hidden. Raise my right hand and motion for the team to halt. We need to assess the situation before we make our next move.

"Stay low and quiet," I whisper, my voice just audible over the rustle of leaves. "We don't know if anyone's found the SUV yet."

With everyone taking cover, we wait in tense silence. Minutes pass like hours, each second dragging by as we listen for signs of danger. Then, a flicker of movement catches my eye. I tense, ready for action, but it's just a small animal darting through the underbrush. I release the breath I didn't realise I was holding and motion for the team to move forward.

Not wanting to fuck up at this late stage, we make our way closer to the edge of the clearing, our eyes fixed on the location where we left the RV concealed. It's still there, untouched and unnoticed by Acosta's men.

"We'll cover you while you get the vehicle ready to move," I whisper to Simon.

With a nod, Simon moves towards the SUV, his movements swift and purposeful. We monitor him from the cover as he removes the camouflage.

Moments later, we all clamber on board, "Let's get the fuck out of here," I say, my voice tense with urgency.

Simon, his hands steady on the wheel, starts the engine. With a roar, we tear through the foliage that had concealed the RV, leaving a trail of destruction in our wake.

As we speed away from the danger zone, a sense of relief washes over me. We may have faced countless obstacles and challenges along the way, but we emerged victorious, and our mission was accomplished. My daughters are safe and unharmed.

All we need to do now is get off this fucking island and head for home. But it won't be easy. Alex Acosta will have his men out looking for us, and he may even have corrupt airport officials on his payroll. We may have to think of another way off the island.

Chapter Seventeen - Escape and Evasion

Twenty minutes later, we arrive at the secluded spot just off the main road that runs along the coast. A small forest, inside a cluster of disused buildings, stands like silent guards against the backdrop of the moonlit sea. The surroundings offer us a temporary refuge from the chaos and any of Alex Acosta's people who will no doubt be doing their best to find us.

"Alright, everyone," I say in a hushed tone, my voice rising just above a whisper. "We'll hold up here until first light. Keep your eyes on the lookout for any issues and have your weapons ready. We can't afford to let our guard down."

Simon nods in agreement, scanning the perimeter for signs of trouble from the driver's seat. Even at this late stage, we can't afford to fuck up, so follow our normal standing operating procedures. While Simon stays in the vehicle in case we need to bug out, the rest of us clamber out and spread out, taking up a defensive position around the SUV.

After a few minutes, I make my way to where Derek and George have taken defensive positions, "While Lucy stays in cover with Abbie and Bethanie, we need to go and check out those buildings."

With my rifle ready for action, I stand up and walk down the track towards the first of the buildings, with the other two close behind. Continue until I'm about 20 metres away and then go to ground close to a clump of foliage. The door to the first structure is now highlighted in the moonlight. I'm about to move when George's voice cuts through the silence, his tone quiet and urgent.

"We've got company," he says, his eyes fixed on something in the distance.

I follow his gaze and see a group of shadows moving beyond the trees along the coastline. My heart quickens as I realise we're not alone.

"Stay low," my voice firm and commanding. "We don't want to draw any unnecessary attention."

We crouch down in the shadows, watching the figures pass by without incident. The tension in the air is evident, and each of us is aware of the danger that lurks just beyond the darkness. It's time to enter the building. With George in a firing position, aiming straight at the doorway, Derek and I move to either side of the door.

I give a nod to Derek. A second later, we burst through the door, each taking a different arc of fire. Apart from a collection of rubbish and empty beer cans, the room is empty. A small window high up on the wall lets in a slither of moonlight. A strong aroma of stale urine emanates from one corner of the room—a contribution from the local pissheads, looking at the number of empty beer cans.

Once we have cleared all the buildings, I radio for the rest of the team to RV in the main building. While Simon conceals the SUV by reversing among the trees, ready for a fast getaway if needed, Lucy brings the girls inside.

"This place gives me the creeps," Abbie murmurs, her voice hushed.

I offer her a reassuring smile, though I can't shake the sense of unease that gnaws at the pit of my stomach.

"It won't be long. Just until dawn breaks, then we'll move out."

There are only a few hours until morning, so while the rest of the team, Abbie and Bethanie, try to get some rest, I go on stag near the doorway. The time allows me to think of ways to get undetected off the island.

My instinct is telling me to stay away from airports. If Alex Acosta's influence runs as far as we think, he will have people covering all the roads to the airport and inside the terminal. If this is the case, he will have corrupt officials who will hand us over for a week's wages.

As the first light of dawn filters through the dilapidated buildings, casting long shadows across the floor and the area outside, I wake Simon. "Fancy making a brew, mate?"

"Sure, give me a few minutes to get my stuff from the vehicle," replies Simon, still half-asleep.

With everyone else on edge and only dozing rather than sleeping, they must have heard me waking Simon. Soon, everyone gathers around where Simon is heating water on a gas stove.

"We need to figure out how to get off this island without coming in contact with the cartel," I say, my voice low-pitched but determined. "The airport's out of the question. There will be too many of Acosta's people about. The only option left is to find a boat and head to Oranjestad, which is only 15 kilometres away across the open sea. From there, we can catch several flights back home."

"Are you sure about the flights, Steve?" asks Lucy, now sipping a drink from her black mug.

"As much as I can. I did some research on my phone while you lot were kipping."

George lets out an exasperated sigh. "Not another fucking boat! Can't we go on any mission that doesn't involve boats? Sure you idiots should have joined the fucking navy. Can't we catch a break for once?"

"Stop moaning, George. We love seeing you go green as the waves bounce us around," says Derek, chuckling.

"Do one, you green numpty," comes the reply from George.

I shoot him a sympathetic look, understanding his frustration. "I know it's not ideal, George, but it's our best shot at getting out of here in one piece."

Simon chimes in, his voice grave. "And even if we find a boat, there's no guarantee. The cartel's still out there, and they'll stop at nothing to find us."

I glance at Lucy, who's been quiet since we arrived. "What do you think, Lucy?" I ask, concern in my voice.

She hesitates for a moment before speaking, her words measured.

"We can't stay here," she says after a short pause. "We need to take the risk and find a way off this island, no matter what it takes."

"What about you girls? OK with boats?" I ask, turning to Abbie and Bethanie.

"Don't give a flying fuck as long as it gets us off this fucking Island and back home," replies Abbie.

"I'm with Abbie. I want to go home to my family," says Bethanie, after taking a drink from Simon.

"Boat it is then," I say, after putting my mug back in my Bergen.

By 08:00, all the kit is packed on Simon's earlier makeshift roof rack, everyone clambers on board; Derek, the smallest of us in the cargo compartment. Simon fires up the engine, selects first gear, and drives back towards the main road before stopping at the end.

"Where, to? And we need fuel."

"From what I can see on the map on my phone, the nearest point to Oranjestad is a place called Dieppe Day Town. With any luck, we will be able to find someone willing to take us across," I show Simon the map so he can get his bearings.

Twenty minutes later, we come across a local garage. It is a unique blend of functionality and charm, buzzing with activity as the sun pierces through the clear blue skies, casting a warm glow over the bustling scene. Nestled on the side of a main road, the garage stands with pride with its faded red and white signage, a testament to its long-standing service to travellers.

Outside, a handful of cars are parked near the building, their shiny surfaces reflect the morning light. To the left, a set of roller doors with glass windows offers a glimpse into the garage's interior, where mechanics in blue overalls scurry around with purpose, the sound of their tools clinking and clanking against metal surfaces comes from an open door.

They work on cars while the café patrons chat leisurely over their morning coffee. This was a snapshot of everyday life, where the mundane tasks of refuelling and car repairs were transformed into a vibrant and immersive experience for all who passed through its doors.

As we pull in to refuel the SUV, two rows of fuel pumps stand under a small cover, casting long shadows on the ground as they wait for the next customer. The odour of gasoline lingers in the air, mixing with the faint aroma of fried food from the café.

The hiss of air brakes and honking horns from passing vehicles adds to the symphony of sounds that fill the garage. But beneath the surface, I sense that danger lurks around every corner.

We're running out of time, and every minute counts. I exit the vehicle and scan the area for signs of trouble.

"Keep your eyes scanning the area," I murmur to the team, as Simon moves forward to refuel the vehicle. "We don't know who might be watching."

As Simon works to fill the tank, I go inside to pay. Inside, there is a hive of activity. A shop stocked with car accessories and snacks welcomes visitors. The aroma of fresh coffee from the small café tucked away in a corner adds to the inviting atmosphere.

Patrons, their conversations blending with the sound of car engines, sit at tables near the window, engaging in banter with the staff as they sip their morning brews and munch on pastries and doughnuts.

I move to the counter, where an older gentleman, wearing a smart black uniform, stands, tapping on a till. "Pump number two, please," I say, as he looks up.

"With a deep Caribbean accent, he replies, "Thirty dollars, please. Can I interest you in a bag of crisps?"

"No thanks, just the fuel."

When I return to the vehicle, the rest have climbed out and are standing by the pump. "We're starving, Dad. Is there any chance of grabbing something to eat from the café?" asks Bethanie, pointing at the window behind me.

I'm about to say, why not, the place looks secure, when a figure emerges from the shadows, his footsteps echoing off the concrete floor. Out of instinct, my hand moves to the pistol holstered at my side.

At first, I didn't recognise him. But as soon as he got closer and into the light, a familiar face came into view.

"Morning, folks," his voice tinged with a hint of nervousness. "Do you need some help with that?"

I study him, noting the way his eyes dart around the garage as if searching for something — or someone. Something about Miguel sets me on edge and a sense of unease prickles at the back of my mind.

"Morning, Miguel, how the devil are you?"

"Not too bad, Steve. I see you have your daughters. If you are looking for a way off the island, I might be able to help you find one."

The words in my mind say, 'Yes, I have managed to rescue them from Acosta', but another part of me wonders, 'How does he know what my daughters look like? He's never met them'.

"Any help getting off St Kitts would be a great help."

"Of course, Steve, anything to get back at Alex Acosta for what they might have done to my sister. I know someone with a fast fishing boat. He works out of a small village on the north of the island. If you follow me, I'll take you to him." Miguel points to a black car parked under the café's window.

Before I can respond, Bethanie lets out a sharp gasp, her eyes widening in recognition. "Miguel," she gasps, her voice becoming agitated. "I remember you. You fucking work for Acosta."

The tension in the air is intense as Miguel's face pales, and his gaze flickers between us. "I - I don't know what you're talking about," he stammers, his voice trembling.

But Bethanie isn't convinced, her eyes narrowing as she steps forward. "Don't fucking lie to me," she says, her voice cold and unyielding. "I saw you with Acosta at the fort. You stood outside the cell where we were being held. You're working for him, aren't you?"

Miguel's mask crumbles, his expression twisting with anger and fear. "Did you think you could come to our island, grab your daughters, and then just leave? You shouldn't have come here."

"So, you deceitful scum," I hiss through gritted teeth, my rage simmering beneath the surface. "You dared to deceive us with your twisted games, especially about your pathetic sister."

His response is a growl dripping with malice. "You're starting to grasp the situation at last, Steve," he sneers, his hand inching towards the hidden weapon nestled under his jacket, promising imminent danger.

Before anyone can react, the air is filled with the sound of a single gunshot echoing through the cavernous garage from over my shoulder. A nano-second later, Miguel's body recoils backwards as a round hits him in the face — a single stream of blood spurts across the grey concrete floor as his body slumps to the ground. I spin around to see Bethanie still in the aim with Lucy's 9mm. I guess he must have pissed her off, and this was revenge for being kidnapped and his part in the ordeal.

Instinct propels us into action, a symphony of action fine-tuned over many years, each heartbeat a drumbeat of survival. With everyone back onboard, Simon races away from the garage, hurtling up the road at speed until he reaches a layby.

Once out of view and concealed against the backdrop, I spin in my seat to see Bethanie, still trying to comprehend what had happened, being comforted by Abbie.

"That bastard deserved that, Beth. You just beat me to it. Remember what we were taught growing up; move on, it doesn't matter." Abbie's voice is a voice of comfort.

"Did you lot know that bastard?" Abbie asked.

"We thought we did. He helped us out a few times since we've been on the island. I guess all the time, he played us. Now, thinking about it, he seemed to know where we were and came up with a snitch far too quickly," I reply, before turning back around to tell Simon to leave.

The drive to Dieppe Bay Town doesn't take long, as Simon manoeuvres our vehicle through the winding roads. The salty breeze carries the scent of the sea as we approach the northern coast. The sun hangs high in the cloudless sky, casting a brilliant light upon the countryside.

As we crest a hill, the town unfolds before us in all its colourful splendour. The streets are alive with activity, with locals bustling about their daily routines amidst quaint shops, inviting restaurants, and busy bars. The rhythm of life here is real, a symphony of chatter and laughter filling the air.

"Looks like we've arrived," Simon remarks, as he navigates the crowded streets.

I nod in agreement, taking in the sights with a sense of awe, from the vibrant storefronts adorned with colourful awnings to the aroma of freshly cooked cuisine wafting through the air. As we drive past a row of shops, I catch glimpses of locals going about their business.

Their faces are alight with the joy of community and camaraderie, even under the constant threat of retaliation from Acosta's cartel. Some pause to exchange greetings with neighbours, while others hurry with a sense of purpose, their footsteps echoing on the cobblestone sidewalks.

"Seems like a cheerful place," Lucy comments from the back seat, her voice filled with admiration.

"Indeed," I reply, my eyes scanning the scene before us. "It's a testament to the resilience and spirit of the people here."

Ahead, a cluster of restaurants and bars beckon with their open doors and inviting ambience. Patrons spill out onto the sidewalks, their laughter mingling with the strains of Caribbean music that drift through the air.

"I could use a cold drink," Derek says with a grin, his gaze fixed on a bustling tavern ahead.

"Sounds like some sort of plan," Simon agrees, steering the vehicle toward a secluded parking spot near the beach.

"Before we leave, remember our objective is to find someone to take us to Oranjestad by boat. Acosta's people could have reached this part of the island, so don't take any unnecessary risks," the tone of my voice firm and commanding.

As we disembark from the vehicle, the warmth of the sun envelops us, the salty breeze carrying the promise of adventure. We make our way through the bustling streets, taking in the sights and sounds of the town with each step. The restaurants and bars teem with life, their outdoor seating areas filled with patrons enjoying meals and drinks in the sunshine. The aroma of grilled seafood and spicy island dishes tantalises the senses, beckoning us to indulge in the local cuisine.

After a few hours of roaming around the charming village. Lucy spots a wooden structure close to the ocean, about 300 metres from our current location — an advertisement board swings in the gentle breeze.

"Let's try that place. It might be filled with the type of person we need."

Approaching the Dieppe Bay Café, the salty tang of the ocean and the warm aroma of freshly brewed coffee create a unique sensory experience, drawing us closer to its weathered exterior.

This charming structure, crafted from driftwood and salvaged materials, is perched on the shore, offering a breathtaking view of the expansive Caribbean Sea. Its rustic exterior, adorned with colourful Caribbean flags and potted plants, invites us to enter a world of tranquillity and local charm.

A long wooden pier extends from the shore, its weathered planks bearing witness to countless tides and storms. Fishing boats bob around in the turquoise waters, their hulls adorned with bright paint and fishing nets. Seagulls circle overhead, their cries echoing against the backdrop of the crashing waves.

"Here is the plan, folks. If we encounter any nasty surprises, Lucy, Abbie, Bethanie, and I will go inside while you two," I point to George and Derek, "keep sentry on the perimeter. Simon, get the SUV and bring it closer. Don't panic, fat boy," I point to George, "once we have ordered grub and a beer, I'll send Lucy out with yours."

"So kind of you, you fucking green numpty," comes the response from George.

"You're welcome. While you are out here, try to spot a boat that might make the crossing. If we can't find anyone to take us, we may have to borrow one on a permanent basis."

Stepping into the café, a sense of unease tugs at me like a storm brewing on the horizon. Fishing nets sway gently from the ceiling, seashells pepper the shelves, and faded photographs of local fishermen proudly exhibit their bountiful catches, a large clock on the wall indicates it's 17:00.

As Lucy and the girls find a table near the window, I examine the scene around us. The sunlight filters through the windows, casting a warm glow over the worn wooden furniture. The rhythmic sound of waves crashing against the shore outside adds to the peaceful ambience, creating an almost palpable sense of serenity.

Local fishermen, their faces etched with the lines of a life at sea, sit at scattered tables. Soft light illuminates their weathered features as they exchange tales of the day's catch. Their laughter, a melodic blend of sea shanties and shared camaraderie mingles with the gentle murmur of conversation. Cold beers in hand, they embody a resilience born from a life spent battling the sea's whims.

Behind the counter, a local woman stands with a welcoming smile, radiating hospitality. She wears a vibrant sarong, a flower tucked behind her ear, her dark eyes twinkling with warmth and kindness. The scent of freshly baked pastries drifts from the kitchen, adding to the homely atmosphere.

Yet, beneath the tranquil surface, a persistent unease claws at me. The café, with its shield of familiarity, offers a brief respite from the impending chaos. The local woman behind the counter, with her welcoming smile, radiates a sense of safety. But we must remain on guard, for tranquillity can swiftly morph into chaos in our line of work.

"Welcome to Dieppe Bay Café," she says, her voice melodic with a hint of Caribbean lilt. "Sit wherever you like, and I'll be right with you."

I order the drinks before heading over to the girls and settle into a seat next to Abbie, my back to the wall. The waitress approaches with a welcoming smile, her hands balance a tray laden with drinks. She sets down glasses of ice-cold fruit punch and frosty beers, the condensation glistening in the sunlight.

"Enjoy your drinks," she says, her smile radiant with warmth. "Let me know if there's anything else I can get for you."

"Can we order seven specials, please," I ask before she leaves.

"Seven, you must be hungry. There are only four of you!"

"We have some friends outside. They wanted to admire the scenery and look for someone who rents boats or is prepared to take us out on a trip."

"Where do you want to go?" she enquires.

I've written a few stories in the past, so I'm able to come up with a load of bullshit before she can ask too many questions. "We want to go to Oranjestad on the island of Sint Eustatius. We had to get off the cruise ship because my daughter here became sick," Abbie coughs, to add validity to my story. "We would fly, but the doctor advised against it for the next week. We have family living there."

With that, she gives me one of those knowing looks; 'what a load of crap, a moment ago you wanted to go fishing', and wanders off back behind the counter and disappears into the kitchen—returning five minutes later with our food. "I've called a relative of mine. He'll be here in a few hours. His name is Desmond."

Bethanie grabs the plates of nosh for the boys and exits the café. While she is away, I engage with the woman, who I have now discovered is called Mary, for a conversation about Desmond.

"Can I buy you a drink? And is Desmond a good and reliable person? After all, I have my daughters with me and would hate for some inexperienced person to take us out to sea."

After walking over to grab herself a beer from the fridge, Mary takes a seat at the table next to me.

"What can I tell you about dear old Desmond Adolphine? He is my dear cousin and is a true son of the sea. With his weather-beaten hands and face etched with the marks of time, he bears the unmistakable signs of a life spent amidst the waves. Born and bred in our humble fishing village, Desmond has inherited the wisdom of generations past, passed down from our esteemed ancestors who forged their livelihoods upon the ocean's bounty."

"Sounds like the type of person we need," I say, before taking a swig of my beer.

"His father tutored him from a young age. His father was a revered fisherman renowned for his prowess on the water. Under his watchful eye, Desmond honed his skills and imbibed the deep-rooted respect for nature that guides his every action.

"The 'Marlin', his faithful vessel, has been his steadfast companion throughout the years, weathering storms and tumultuous seas with unwavering loyalty."

"Will the boat make it to Oranjestad?' asks Lucy.

Mary continues telling us about Desmond, who sounds better by the minute.

"Despite his gruff exterior, he's a man of deep compassion, his heart as vast and boundless as the ocean itself. His respect for nature is not just a part of him; it guides his every action. Years of experience have endowed him with a keen intuition and an innate understanding of the sea's whims. He navigates its treacherous waters with ease, relying on his instincts and the wisdom of generations past to guide him home."

As we sit at the café table talking to Mary, sipping our coffee, I casually bring up the topic of the cartel. Probing for information, trying to piece together the puzzle of Alex Acosta's influence on the island.

"So, Mary," I begin, my tone casual, "I've been hearing a lot about this cartel. It appears they've got their fingers in every pie around here."

Mary nods after taking a sip of her coffee before responding. "Yeah, they've certainly made their presence known. It's hard to escape their influence."

I lean forward, my gaze intent. "What about your relative, Desmond? Does he have any connections with them?"

Mary pauses, considering my response. "Desmond's history with the cartel is delicate, but you deserve to know the truth. Desmond had a run-in with the cartel a while back," she explains. "Let's just say he's not their biggest fan."

I raise an eyebrow, intrigued. "Really? What happened?"

She takes a deep breath, recalling the events from years ago. "Desmond crossed paths with the cartel when they tried to muscle in on his business. He didn't take to their threats and made it clear that he wouldn't be intimidated."

"Sounds like Desmond's got some backbone. Did he ever get involved in any... uh, extracurricular activities to help those in need?"

"Actually, yes. Desmond has a history of helping people who are being hunted by the cartel. He's used his resources to arrange safe passage off the island for those in danger."

I lean back in my chair, a thoughtful expression on my face. "Interesting. Sounds like Desmond could be a valuable asset to get us to where we want to go."

"Absolutely," replies Mary. "His loyalty to family and friends is unwavering, and he will go to great lengths to ensure their safety and well-being. So he will ensure you all arrive safe on Oranjestad."

"Perfect, Mary. When can we meet him?" I ask, wanting to get going as soon as possible. The more time we are on the island, the chance of us coming into contact with Acosta's people increases.

"He is on his way now and should arrive within the hour. You can wait here or on the pier," Mary says, getting up from her chair.

Once Mary has left, I turn to Lucy, Abbie, and Bethanie, who has returned from giving the boys their food.

I fill her in on the conversation we had with Mary before asking, "What do you think? Shall we trust Desmond?"

"We don't have much choice. Our options are limited and getting smaller by the hour. Let's go outside and inform the boys," says Lucy, getting up from behind the table.

Once I've exited the café, I look across towards the ocean. George and Derek are close to the pier. I find Simon sitting in the SUV nearby, so I beckon him to drive over to join us on the shoreline. Once we are all together, I inform them of the conversation with Mary, and that a bloke called Desmond may be willing to take us across.

With everybody in agreement, there is nothing to do until Desmond arrives. He is an unknown source, someone we don't know, but we have little choice but to trust him. Besides, if he turns out to be a contact for Alex Acosta, he will meet the same fate as Miguel and end up as fish food.

Chapter Eighteen - The Crossing

We are too close to the end of this mission, and we need to get over to Oranjestad alive and in one piece, so better not fuck up the meeting. With that in mind, I fill the team in on the plan.

"Derek and I will approach the contact once we are sure he came alone to the pier. I need George and Lucy to find suitable sniper positions. Lucy, if you cover the pier, leaving you, George, to cover our escape route. As to where, I will leave that in your capable hands. Which leaves you, Simon. Find a location close by to keep the SUV concealed and ready to depart if the need arises. Abbie and Bethanie stay in the vehicle with Simon. Any questions?"

"Just one. Where will yours and Derek's start locations be? So I can ensure the vehicle's location is central?" asks Simon.

"We will be hiding in the open about 300 metres away along the beach. If there are no more questions, let's get in position."

The beach lies silent, a forsaken haven far removed from the tourist throngs. Only a sparse scattering of figures drifts between the café and the shoreline, their presence mere whispers against the backdrop of the vast expanse of sand. Derek and I tread carefully towards our designated meeting spot.

The air hangs heavy with the soft hum of distant waves and the gentle rustle of palm fronds, deceptive tranquillity masking the danger that lurks beneath the surface. Birds screech overhead, their cries echoing through the stillness, while the sun casts harsh shadows across the landscape. Against this serene backdrop, we await our rendezvous with Desmond Adolphine, the enigmatic fisherman whom Mary claims can ferry us to safety to the island of Oranjestad.

A cloak of uncertainty wraps around me. I look at my watch, the ticking seconds echoing with an ominous weight. Anticipation, like a coiled serpent, tightens its grip on my chest, each passing moment intensifying the knot of apprehension. Can we truly trust Desmond Adolphine, whom we will meet for the first time? I'm hoping he is the person to take us to safety.

A distant rumble breaks the silence, signalling the arrival of our uncertain ally. My gaze narrows as a weathered vehicle grinds to a halt outside the café, its faded yellow paint a testament to years of neglect. The figure that emerges is etched with the weariness of countless journeys, his features weathered by time and experience. He disappears into the dim interior of the café, a fleeting spectre swallowed by the shadows.

Time stretches, and each minute seems like an eternity as we watch, our senses sharpened to the slightest hint of danger. I hold my breath, every nerve on edge as we await our contact's return from inside the café.

His movements are deliberate and measured when he emerges, each step a silent testament to his life as a fisherman. As he strides towards the pier, his gaze fixed on the horizon, I can't shake the sinking feeling that our destiny teeters on a knife's edge.

"This must be our man," I murmur to Derek, my voice a mere whisper against the bustling ocean backdrop.

Derek nods, his gaze locked on the figure's walking to the end of the pier. "I think you're right. Let's give him a moment to settle in and see what he does next."

At the precipice of the weathered pier, we fix our gaze on our mark. He stands solitary, a lone figure against the vast expanse of the ocean. Like twin beacons, his eyes pierce through the horizon as if he is waiting for something—or someone—to emerge from the depths below.

Every line of his weathered frame tells a story of resilience and determination. His movements are precise, honed by years of experience navigating the unpredictable tides of the sea.

Yet, beneath the calm surface, a thick and suffocating tension broils. It hangs in the air like a funeral pall, a silent harbinger of imminent danger. The rhythmic ebb and flow of the ocean's waves in the moonlight, seemingly serene, masks the urgency of our mission.

With each passing moment, the expectation swells, a tightly wound spring ready to release its pent-up energy. The distant cries of seagulls echo like a mournful chorus, breaking the silence. The rhythmic pulse of the waves against the pier serves as a reminder of the relentless march of time, ticking down to our moment of reckoning.

The moment of action draws nigh, and we teeter on the precipice, poised to plunge into the heart of the storm.

"Time to make our move," my voice quiet against the lapping waves.

"Yep, let's go and see if this is our man," says Derek, relaying the message over the radio to the others.

Before stepping onto the pier, I pause and look around, confirming in my mind that the others have us covered. Not that I have any doubt. The three people concealed in the near darkness are among the few people in the world I trust with my life.

As we approach the target, the wooden boards groan under the weight of our footsteps. Within a few feet of him, when he turns to greet us, a faint smile plays at the corners of his lips.

"Steve," he says, his voice gruff but welcoming. "I'm glad you could make it. I've been waiting for you."

We exchange greetings with Desmond, grateful for his willingness to assist us in our desperate bid for freedom, as we stand together on the weathered planks of the pier.

"I understand you're looking for passage to Oranjestad," he says, his voice low and earnest. "I can help you with that, but it won't be easy. The waters between St Kitts and Aruba are treacherous, particularly at night."

I nod in understanding, my eyes reflecting a mixture of unwavering determination and controlled apprehension. "We know the risks," I say, my voice steady. "We're committed to doing whatever it takes to get off this island."

Desmond studies us for a moment, his expression inscrutable. "Very well," he says at last. "I have a small boat moored nearby. It's nothing fancy, but it'll get us where we need to go. We'll leave at dawn, six hours from now — less chance of attracting unwanted attention."

I glance down at my watch, it's 23:00. We agree to Desmond's plan, knowing that our window of opportunity is closing fast. As we turn to leave, Desmond clasps my shoulder with a firm hand, his gaze meeting mine.

"Be ready," he says, his voice grave. "The journey ahead will be fraught with danger, but with luck and perseverance, we may just make it to Oranjestad in one piece."

With a final nod of determination, we part ways, each of us preparing for the perilous journey that lies ahead. The urgency of our situation is evident, and the weight of our decision to go by sea hangs heavy in the air.

Once Desmond is out of earshot and heading back to the café, I press the transmitter of my radio, " All call signs RV Simon's location. Out."

Five minutes later, we are all back at the SUV.

"OK, folks, there are six hours until dawn, when Desmond will be here with his boat. We can't risk going back to the café, so normal SOPs, we'll set up an RV around here. George, you take the first stag, so we don't have to hear you moaning about always getting the last one. Suggest the rest of us get some kip."

"Screw you lot, I'm not always moaning about which stag I get," comes the response from George.

Trying not to laugh, "I've seen Labour MPs that moan less than you, mate," comes the response from Simon.

It's not long before the RV is set up, and we are in our usual night routine. The dark veil of night descends upon the rustic café a short distance away, clad in the ethereal glow of the full moon. The occasional chirp of crickets punctuates the gentle rustle of the wind.

While George continues his vigil, his figure is a dark silhouette against the moonlit backdrop. His keen eyes scan the surroundings for any hint of danger. I can't help but feel a profound sense of gratitude to the team for helping me rescue my girls and get this far.

Abbie, Bethanie, and I sit huddled under the stars, the girls wrapped in my open sleeping bag, close to Lucy. From the look on their faces, the weight of their recent ordeal is still heavy on their minds.

Simon reaches into the back of the vehicle and pulls out a couple of bottles of Southern Comfort before coming over and joining the rest of us. "It may be premature, but hey, we don't know what is on the horizon. It's time for a drink to celebrate the rescue of Abbie and Bethanie."

"I can drink to that," I say, taking out my black plastic mug for Simon to fill.

After filling up everyone's mugs, including taking one to George, he sits beside me. We wouldn't touch alcohol while on stag as a rule, but it is only the one drink, and we will be departing this island soon.

"How was it, being held captive by that arsehole?" Lucy's voice, a murmur in the dark.

"Remember all those times you trained us, Dad, when we were kids?" Abbie's voice tinged with a mixture of admiration and gratitude.

I nod, a faint smile tugging at the corners of my lips as memories of our impromptu training sessions flood my mind.

"Of course I do," I reply, my voice warm with nostalgia. "I wanted you both to be prepared for anything."

Bethanie's eyes glimmer with pride and determination as she leans forward, her voice earnest. "Well, that training sure came in handy when we were held captive by the cartel," she says, a hint of defiance in her tone. "We wouldn't have made it out alive if it weren't for you, Dad."

Pride grows in my chest as I gaze at the two courageous women sitting before me. Their resilience is a testament to the strength of the human spirit, a strength that runs deep in our family.

"You both did an amazing job," I say, my voice filled with admiration. "I'm just glad I could help."

Abbie reaches across, her hand clasping mine in a gesture of solidarity. "We couldn't have asked for a better mentor," she says, her voice sincere. "You taught us how to stay calm under pressure, think on our feet, and survive."

I return her grip, the bond between us unspoken but intense. In this moment, we are family, bound together in a bond that no ordeal can break.

The conversation continues for the next 45 minutes before George comes over, taps Derek on the shoulder, and says the words we all hated to hear during our army days: "You're on stag."

The ordeal must have taken its toll on my girls, as they are soon sound asleep, Bethanie's head resting on Lucy's shoulder. As I sit in the confines of the RV, my mind races with the details of our next move. A plan starts to formulate in my head, unfolding like an orchestrated chess match.

According to a brief internet search, the journey across the open sea will be fraught with danger once we're underway. The waters surrounding St Kitts are treacherous. Hidden reefs and unpredictable currents lie in wait to thwart even the most experienced sailors. It will require all the skill, vigilance, and trust we are about to put in Desmond to navigate these dangerous waters and reach our destination unscathed.

Arriving in Oranjestad will bring its own challenges. The bustling port city will be a hive of activity, teeming with tourists and locals alike. We'll need to move without drawing unwanted attention to ourselves. Our priority will be to locate transportation to the airport without arousing suspicion — a task harder than it appears in a city brimming with potential threats. But this is why I have a team of experts around me — I'll leave this task to Simon.

Once we reach the airport, even here, amidst the hustle and bustle of departing travellers and arriving flights, our journey is far from over. We'll need to navigate the intricacies of airport security, all while keeping a watchful eye out for any sign of trouble. Alex Acosta's influence may even reach this island.

As I contemplate the daunting challenges ahead, I sense the path may be dangerous. A fierce determination envelops me like a protective shield. The odds may seem insurmountable. But with our collective resourcefulness, teamwork, and a sprinkle of good fortune, I'm certain we can conquer any obstacle that dares to cross our path, as long as we remain focused and united. We've triumphed over tougher challenges in the past, and I'm certain we'll find a way to prevail once again.

Whatever may come, I know we'll face it head-on, united in our determination to see this mission through to the end. For now, all that matters is staying one step ahead of Alex Acosta's cartel and reaching the potential safety of Oranjestad before it's too late. My mind is kicked out of this thinking malarky by Lucy telling me it is my turn to go on the last stag of the night.

I'd only been on stag for 30 minutes when the first faint streaks of dawn start to creep across the sky, casting a delicate hue of pink and gold over the isolated expanse of the ocean. It's a sight that never fails to mesmerise me, even in the midst of our dangerous and uncertain situation. I'm on high alert as I stand and watch the gentle lull of the waves providing a deceptive calm.

In the distance, a sound breaks the silence — the approach of an unseen vessel. I strain against the dim light, squinting to perceive its form against the horizon. As it emerges from behind the headland, the unmistakable outline of a fishing boat comes into view, cutting through the still waters with purposeful intent.

My pulse quickens as I recognise the figure standing at the helm — Desmond, our only hope of escape from this island. The boat itself bears the scars of countless battles with the elements, its weathered exterior a testament to its battles and to Desmond's resilience and skill.

With practised ease, Desmond guides the boat towards the pier dead on 05:00, his expert hands navigating the course through the calm waters. The soft thud of rope against wood reverberates through the morning air, as he secures the vessel to the dock.

Returning to the RV, I find the team already assembled, their readiness a silent testament to the dangers that lie ahead.

"Stay here until we're sure Desmond's alone," I instruct, my tone brooking no argument. "Lucy and I will go and meet him. Be ready for anything."

As we approach the end of the pier, our only chance of escape lies within reach, but also the possibility of betrayal or ambush. My senses are on high alert as we draw closer, every footstep echoing like a drumbeat in the stillness.

At the end of the pier stands a solitary figure, his silhouette outlined against the backdrop of the rising sun. With cautious steps, I approach, my voice cutting through the silence like a knife.

"Morning, Desmond," I call out, the tension thick in the air as we await his response.

Keeping up a pretence for any onlookers lurking somewhere out of our view, I ask, "Any luck out there today?"

Desmond turns to face me, a weary smile playing at the corners of his lips.

"Not much to speak of, I'm afraid," he replies, playing along, his voice rough from years of saltwater and sea spray. "But there's always tomorrow."

"Have you come alone, or is someone else on board?" I ask, to establish whether we are not walking into a trap.

"Just me, Steve. Go onboard and check if you like."

With Lucy stationed on the pier, I make my way onto the boat with caution, my senses on high alert. The tang of saltwater stings my nostrils, mingling with the acrid scent of diesel fuel. Every step I take is calculated; every movement deliberate as I enter the wheelhouse from the rear of the vessel. The worn wood beneath my feet offers a sense of stability, but I know better than to trust appearances alone.

As I move through the cramped passageways, my rifle ready, I scan every nook and cranny for signs of danger. The dim light filtering through the small windows casts threatening shadows, heightening my sense of unease. I check each storage compartment, my fingers poised on the trigger, ready to react at a moment's notice.

In the main cabin, I approach the simple wooden table with caution, my eyes darting around for any indication of another presence. A solitary plate with a knife and fork rests on the surface, the butter on the left side of the knife revealing the right hand that last used it. My gaze sweeps over the compact galley, checking every shadow for hidden threats.

With a racing heart, I lift the hatch leading to the engine room. The steady hum of the diesel engine drowns out any potential noise. Every sound is magnified, every creak and groan of the boat's structure setting my nerves on edge. The responsibility weighs on my shoulders as I search, knowing that the team's safety depends on my diligence.

Back on deck, I scan the canopy and fishing gear, my eyes darting from shadow to shadow. Despite the familiar surroundings, I remain vigilant, knowing that danger could be lurking around any corner. In the world of covert operations, trust is a luxury I cannot afford.

On the way back to Lucy, I pick up a small round object before getting off the boat.

"Is everyone OK? Are you ready to make a move? We need to get going," Desmond asks.

"All good, my friend, apart from I almost fell on my arse when I tripped on this, whatever it is."

I throw the object at Desmond. He catches it with his right hand. Now it is OK to leave. I tap the radio, "All call signs, this location. Over."

Seconds later, Derek's voice comes over the airwaves. "Roger, that, on our way. Out."

A few minutes pass before the rest of the team walks down the pier, with Abbie and Bethanie sandwiched in the middle and clambering aboard the boat.

I turn to Desmond, "Ready when you are."

The fishing boat pulls away from the pier, with Desmond at the helm, his hands steady on the wheel as he guides us out to sea. The rhythmic sound of the waves against the hull fills the air, accompanied by the distant cry of seagulls. I stand on the deck, my heart pounding with anticipation, watching the shore recede into the horizon.

I glance over at George, who stands on the bridge, his face pale and drawn as he battles the onset of seasickness.

"Hang on in there, George," I call out, offering him a reassuring smile. "We'll be on solid ground soon enough."

Hearing this, Simon pokes his head out of the cabin. "Anyone for a few greasy runny eggs?" laughing at George.

"Fuck off, Donkey Walloper, or I'll throw you overboard," replies George, after regurgitating some food that filled his mouth.

Bethanie and Abbie sit nearby at the stern of the boat, their faces alight with excitement as they peer out at the vast expanse of the ocean.

"This is incredible," Abbie exclaims, her voice filled with wonder. "I never thought I'd be sailing on the open sea in a small fishing boat."

Bethanie nods in agreement, her eyes sparkling with hope. "It's like something out of a movie," she says, her voice tinged with excitement.

I join them at the stern, taking in the breathtaking view of the ocean stretching out behind us. The crossing is going as planned, with no issues. Even the waves have settled to a calm ripple as though they have sensed George's discomfort.

As the fishing boat glides through the near-calm waters between St Kitts and Oranjestad, I find a moment of respite on the bridge with Desmond, the seasoned captain at the helm. The soft hum of the engines provides a steady backdrop to our conversation, punctuated by the gentle lapping of the waves against the hull.

"Desmond, I want to thank you again for helping us leave St Kitts safely," I say, breaking the comfortable silence between us. "We couldn't have made it without your assistance."

Desmond nods, his gaze fixed on the horizon ahead.

"It was my pleasure, Steve," he replies, his voice gruff but genuine. "I've seen enough trouble with those cartel scum on this island. Anything to help rid us of their presence."

I raise an eyebrow, intrigued by Desmond's disdain for the cartel. "You seem to have a personal stake in this," I say, leaning against the bridge's railing. "Care to share?" pushing for him to match up with the information that Mary had told us.

A flicker of emotion passes over Desmond's weathered features, a mixture of anger and frustration. "I've spent my whole life on these waters, Steve," he explains, his voice tinged with bitterness. "And I've watched as the cartel has corrupted everything they touch. They've brought nothing but misery to my island, and I'll be damned if I let them continue unchecked."

I nod in understanding, a newfound respect blossoming for Desmond and his unwavering dedication to his homeland. "Well, you have our gratitude, Desmond," I say, extending a hand in appreciation. "We'll do everything in our power to make sure the cartel is dealt with once and for all."

Desmond clasps my hand firmly, a determined glint in his eyes. "I'll be rooting for you, Steve," he says, his voice filled with quiet resolve. "And if there's anything else I can do to help, just let me know."

As the boat continues on its journey, I can't help but feel a sense of hope stirring within me, fuelled by the knowledge that we have allies like Desmond by our side.

Then Desmond's sharp cry jolts me from my thoughts. "Speedboat approaching fast!" he shouts, his voice tense with urgency.

I spin around, my eyes scanning the horizon for any sign of the approaching vessel. Sure enough, a sleek speedboat races toward us at breakneck speed, its engine roaring like a beast hungry for blood. My stomach twists with dread as I realise what's about to unfold.

"Get ready for incoming fire!" I bark, my voice cutting through the night air like a whip.

The team springs into action, grabbing their weapons and preparing to defend our boat against the impending attack.

As the speedboat draws nearer, I catch a glimpse of the figures onboard, their faces twisted into sneers of malice. These are no ordinary seafarers. Their weapons are pointing in our direction. At a guess, I would say they are members of the Alex Acosta cartel, sent to hunt us down and prevent us from leaving the island.

Within minutes, bullets rain down upon us like a lethal hailstorm, tearing through the air with lethal precision. Derek lets out a pained grunt as a bullet grazes his arm. But he refuses to yield, returning fire with a fierce determination that belies his injury.

Lucy and George grab their sniper rifles, go outside, and take up a firing position on the cabin's roof, returning fire and dropping the attackers one by one as they approach.

The battle rages on, each passing moment fraught with tension and uncertainty. The sound of gunfire echoes across the open sea, mingling with the roar of the waves as we fight for our lives against overwhelming odds.

Despite the chaos and carnage, we refuse to back down, our spirits unbroken as we stand united against our common foe. Derek grits his teeth against the pain of his wound, his determination burning bright as he continues to fight alongside us, his resolve unwavering in the face of adversity.

The speedboat is now alongside us. Several men are trying to board as Abbie and Bethanie join the fray, the 9mm pistols I gave them earlier blazing as they discharge a hail of gunfire upon our attackers. Bethanie's aim is true as she takes down a man attempting to board our vessel, her resolve unwavering in the face of danger.

After what appears like an eternity, the gunfire ceases, leaving behind a scene of destruction and death in its wake. The forms of our attackers lie motionless on the deck of their speedboat.

There is no time to waste. We need to sink the speedboat before we reach Oranjestad, in case the coast guard or police find it. There isn't much I can do about the bodies floating in the ocean. We can't afford the time to drag them out of the water. They have to stay where they are—a small target for any passing aircraft or boats to spot.

For the dead foes on the speedboat, I waste no time, with the help of the boys, in securing the bodies inside the cabin of the speedboat. We ensure that they will never resurface. It's a grim task but necessary to ensure our safety when we enter Oranjestad undetected.

Once the bodies are secured, I grab a boat hook from Desmond's boat and punch several holes below the waterline. As the speedboat sinks beneath the waves, I feel a sense of grim satisfaction wash over me, mingled with relief that we've emerged victorious from yet another deadly encounter.

Back on the bridge, "We need to get away from here. Did anyone see where Desmond went?" I yell, looking around for him.

"Think he dived inside once the firing started," shouts Lucy from the roof of the cabin.

After a quick search, Simon finds him hiding the bog, or as the navy types call it, the head. "It's over now; you're safe. We need to make a move." He's still shaken from the ordeal, which I can't blame him for. After all, this is not what he signed up for.

"Are you OK, mate? You look pale?" I ask, as he reappears on the outer deck.

"I'm fine, thanks, Steve; I wasn't expecting to get caught up in a gunfight. Nothing like this happened on the other crossings I made. Acosta must want you dead, " he replies, still shaking.

"Derek, you are the nearest thing we have to a sailor owning a boat in St Halb. Take the helm until Desmond brings himself back down."

"No problem, Steve. The coast isn't that far from here."

Derek makes his way up to the open bridge, presses the engine lever forward, and heads for the shoreline of Oranjestad.

"How bad is that wound? Better get Abbie to dress it for you." I point to the blood dripping from Derek's arm.

"It's just a flesh wound, but it could do with someone putting a bandage around it for me."

"Know what you mean I got stabbed at Canada Hill Estate, hurt like fucking hell, but a field dressing sorted it out," I reply showing Derek the wound.

"No problem, Dad, I'll sort it for him," says Abbie, after finding the first kit in the cabin.

We are soon on our way, but even as we continue our journey to Oranjestad, I know that our trials are far from over and that the path ahead will be fraught with danger and uncertainty.

Chapter Nineteen - Landing on Oranjestad

When we touch down in the quiet port of Oranjestad, it is around 08:00. The sky is painted in hues of pink and gold, casting a soft glow over the tranquil waters of the harbour.

The port is shrouded in near silence. The only sounds are of the waves crashing against the harbour walls, the screeching of seagulls above, and the gentle creaking of boats as they sway with the tide. The buildings along the waterfront stand like silent sentinels, their windows reflecting the soft light of the rising sun. A few locals are milling around the port while fishermen sit on the dock mending nets. It's a serene scene, but the team know better than to let their guard down.

"Stay alert," I murmur to the team, my voice hushed but firm, betraying a hint of uncertainty. "We don't know what we're walking into here, but we're prepared for anything. For the moment, keep your weapons concealed."

Lucky for us, we had found several holdalls full of fishing gear in the boat that were big enough to hold the broken-down rifles and keep them out of view from the locals.

Simon nods in agreement, his eyes scanning the empty streets for any signs of movement. Meanwhile, Derek adjusts a second radio, scanning different frequencies, ready to intercept any enemy transmissions. George takes up a position overlooking the harbour, his rifle trained on the horizon, his every muscle tense.

Lucy is close to Abbie and Bethanie, hidden behind a stone wall. Despite the calm surroundings, her expression is serious but determined.

"We can't afford to let our guard down," I say to the team over the radio, my voice filled with determination. "We stick to the plan and stay focused. And get to the airport undetected by Acosta's people who might be in the area."

After a few minutes, and I'm sure we aren't walking into a nasty surprise, we set off into the quiet streets of Oranjestad. For safety, we split into two teams, with Lucy, Abbie, Bethanie, and me in the first group and the boys in a separate group, following 100 metres behind.

The morning air is crisp as we move through the deserted port, looking for transport to the airport. The silence is deafening, broken only by our footsteps against the cobblestone streets. Every corner we turn, every alley we pass, I can't shake the sensation that we're being watched, and danger lurks just beyond my vision. Every shadow is a potential threat.

We press on, our senses on high alert as we navigate the port's maze-like layout. With each step, the tension mounts, and our nerves stretch taut like bowstrings, ready to snap at the slightest provocation.

Suddenly, a voice breaks the silence. The unmistakable sound of footsteps approaching from an alleyway to my right echoes against the empty streets.

"We've got company," I whisper to the team, my hand tightening around the grip of my 9mm in my jacket pocket.

It's times like this that our undercover training kicks in. Most people in this situation would dive for cover. The problem with that is that if this was just a local walking down the alley, you would draw attention to yourself. Instead, the team's dynamics snap into place like the pieces of a well-oiled machine, and we spread out. Each member blends into the background and vanishes as if they weren't there.

From a beige stone doorway, I take out my mobile, open the maps, and find a taxi rank at the other end of the port.

Through my radio, "We need a different route that keeps us off the primary route. As you are our recce expert, Simon, lead the way."

After a few minutes, Simon takes charge, his voice steady and authoritative as he lays out our route through the streets of Oranjestad.

"We'll take the back alleys to the taxi rank to avoid any potential traps," he says, his eyes flicking to the digital map on his phone.

"Roger that. Derek, keep an ear on communications. We need to know if there's any chatter about our presence in the area."

Derek nods in acknowledgement, his fingers twisting the frequency knob as he scans the local network.

"I'll intercept any transmissions and feed you the intel in real-time," he says, his voice confident and assured.

George stands at the ready, his eyes scanning the rooftops for signs of danger. "I'll cover our six," he says, his grip tight on his 9mm. "If anyone tries to ambush us, they'll regret it."

I watch the team spring into action, each member fulfilling their role with precision and skill. Then, with a nod, we set off into the labyrinth of alleyways, our senses on edge as we navigate the maze-like streets of Oranjestad. Every shadow and sound is a possible threat, and we move with the caution of soldiers on enemy soil.

As we wind through the narrow passages, tension mounts, and our nerves stretch taut like strings of a bow. I know that the fate of the team and my girls rests in my hands. I turn to check on Abbie and Bethanie. They are tucked between Lucy and me, each playing their part in this game of secrets and shadows. With Simon leading the way, Derek monitoring our communications, and George watching our backs, we have a fighting chance of making it out of Oranjestad alive.

As we move with caution through the intricate streets of Oranjestad, a sense of unease settles over me like a heavy fog. I still can't shake the feeling that we're being spied on, that every step we take brings us closer to danger in this world of covert operations. There's no room for fear or hesitation. It's all about trust, teamwork, and the unwavering belief that no matter what obstacles lie ahead, we'll face them head-on and emerge victorious.

Without warning, a crackle of static cuts through the silent alleyway, followed by a quiet voice speaking in rapid, broken English. Derek's eyes widen as he listens, his brow furrowing in concern.

"We've got incoming chatter," he says, his voice tense. "It sounds like they're onto us."

"How much time do we have?" my voice clipped and urgent.

Derek shakes his head. "Not much," his voice is grim. "They're closing in fast. From what I can tell, they are only a few streets away."

Without warning, footsteps echo through the stillness, getting louder by the second. I tense up, my hand instinctively moving towards my weapon. Everyone exchanges wary glances, bracing themselves for whatever may come next.

Then, they emerge from the shadows — a group of men led by a tall, slim-built, muscular man. Lucy steps forward, whispering to me, from behind me, "Steve, I think the man in front of them is someone I used to work with. If it is, his name is El Lobo Cuffy."

"Well, well, well," Cuffy sneers, his voice dripping with contempt. "Look who decided to pay us a visit."

I step forward, my resolve unyielding. "We're not here for trouble," I assert, my voice unwavering despite the surge of adrenaline. "We're just passing through."

Cuffy chuckles a deep, dark laugh, his gaze flicking over each member of our team. "Oh, I think you'll find that trouble has a way of finding you," he says, his voice like ice.

The standoff fills the air with tension. It's clear that Cuffy and his men won't let us leave unscathed. Despite the controlled fear gripping my heart, I, like the rest of the team, refuse to back down. We've faced tough challenges before and always come out on top. We stand our ground, ready to face whatever Cuffy has in store for us.

The battle may be imminent, but we won't go down without a fight. Glancing around for a moment, I can see the team concealed in doorways, reassembling their rifles, ready for what is coming next. Abbie and Bethanie are crouched on the floor of a shop entranceway behind Lucy.

Turning back to face Cuffy and his menacing crew, a flicker of something passes through Cuffy's eyes — a momentary hesitation that divulges the conflict within him. I catch it for a second, but it's enough to send a shiver down my spine and make me wonder what lies beneath the façade of ruthlessness.

I seize the moment. "Cuffy," taking a chance Lucy is right about who this man is, "you know this isn't right," I say, my voice firm. "You don't have to do this."

Cuffy's gaze hardens, but I can see the doubt lingering beneath the surface, a flicker of his humanity. "I have my orders," he replies, his voice strained. "I can't go against Acosta." His words are a plea for understanding, a cry for help.

I take a step closer, my gaze meeting Cuffy's gaze head-on. "You have a choice, Cuffy," I say, my words echoing in the stillness of the port. "You can choose to follow orders like a drone without hesitation, or you can choose to do what's right."

For a moment, Cuffy wavers, his expression caught between loyalty to Acosta and his own sense of morality. Flashbacks flood his mind – glimpses of his past, upbringing, and the events leading him down this dark path. A young Cuffy, full of hope and promise, before the allure of power and wealth drew him into the clutches of the cartel and a life of crime.

But even as Cuffy grapples with his inner turmoil, I know we can't afford to let our guard down. The threat is still real, lurking in the shadows, ready to strike. We'll need to stay vigilant and engage our senses if we want to make it out of this.

Then, with a resigned sigh, he shakes his head. "I made my choice a long time ago," he says, his voice heavy with regret. "And I'll have to live with the consequences."

Cuffy may be conflicted, but that doesn't make him any less dangerous. And as the tension mounts, I know we're about to find out how far he's willing to go to protect his loyalty to Acosta.

"Cuffy, this isn't your only option," I assert, my voice slicing through the tension like a razor blade. "You still have a choice to make."

Cuffy's gaze locks with mine, a flicker of remorse crossing his face for a second. "I wish it were that simple, Steve," he murmurs, his voice laced with resignation. "But you don't understand the situation I'm in."

I watch as Cuffy's resolve wavers, his grip on his loyalty to Acosta slipping with each passing second. And then, as if driven by some unseen force, he begins to speak – revealing glimpses of his past, his upbringing, and the events that led him to this pivotal moment.

"I was born into this life," Cuffy begins, his voice heavy with emotion. "I was raised by a father who served Acosta with unwavering loyalty. I had no choice but to follow in his footsteps."

But even as Cuffy grapples with his inner demons, I know that time is fast running out. The threat of Acosta's men looms large, and we can't afford to let Cuffy's internal conflict distract us from getting to the airport and flying home with everyone alive and unarmed, apart from the flesh wound Derek received on the boat.

Cuffy's eyes dart between each member of our team, lingering on Lucy for a moment longer than the rest. It's clear that he's wrestling with something, torn between his loyalty to Acosta and the doubts gnawing at his conscience.

Once again, I say, "You don't have to do this, Cuffy. There's another way out of this."

Cuffy's gaze fixes on mine, and I catch a glimpse of hesitation dancing in his eyes for a fleeting moment. He replies, his voice strained. "But you have no idea what Acosta is capable of."

"I think I do; seen it with my own eyes," I reply, scanning the area to ensure no one is trying to flank us as we talk.

As Cuffy speaks, his eyes flicker to Lucy, a memory flashing across his face. "Lucy... is that you?" he murmurs, his voice trailing off as memories of their past resurface.

Lucy steps forward, her eyes locked on Cuffy's. "You remember, Leroy," she says, her voice tinged with nostalgia and apprehension. "We worked together once, remember? On that mission to take out Acosta's competition."

Cuffy's gaze softens, a flicker of emotion crossing his features. "I remember," he admits, a hint of sadness in his voice. "We were a hell of a team."

"We sure were," Lucy replies, a bittersweet smile on her lips. "Took down some of the biggest players in the game."

Cuffy nods, his expression turning serious. "Yeah, they weren't going down without a fight," he recalls, his voice tinged with a hint of grim determination. "Remember that ambush near the docks?"

"Sure do. We almost got us both killed."

I lean in, intrigued by their shared history. "What happened?" I ask, eager to learn more about their past exploits.

Lucy's eyes narrow slightly as she recounts the harrowing ordeal. "We were outnumbered, outgunned," she begins, her voice steady despite the memories. "But we fought like hell, used every trick in the book to gain our advantage."

Cuffy nods in agreement. "We took them out one by one until it was just the boss left standing. Can't remember his name," he adds, a hint of satisfaction in his tone. "But he slipped away, vanished into the night."

I can see the fear in Cuffy's eyes, the weight of the consequences bearing down on him like a heavy burden. Still, doubt clouds his judgment.

At that moment, there is a shout from behind Leroy, "Less talking, boss, let's waste these fuckers and fuck off out of here." It's one of Cuffy's men.

With his sidearm at arm's length, pointing at the man who dared question his authority, Cuffy turns around, "Shut the fuck up and do as I tell you," he yells before turning back to face us.

"We'll help you, Cuffy," I say, my tone resolute. "But you have to be willing to trust us. Together, we can find a way out of this mess."

There is a few minutes of silence as Cuffy's gaze darts between us and his men, who loom with menace behind him. Their gaze tells a different story than Cuffy's—one that says they dragged themselves from the gutter and will follow orders no matter the consequences. This is the point of no return.

"You have to make a choice, Cuffy," I say, my voice soft but firm. "Are you with us, or is this going to turn nasty?"

Cuffy's jaw tightens, his eyes betraying the turmoil raging within him. I can see the conflict written across his face, the weight of his decision bearing down on him like a heavy burden.

Cuffy nods, his expression grave. "I'll do what I can," he says, his voice laced with uncertainty. "I can't do this anymore, Steve; I've killed and tortured too many innocent people just because I was following orders. I'm sick of it. I want a way out of this crap," Cuffy admits after some time, his voice just above a whisper. "I'm tired of looking over my shoulder and living in fear, being a pawn in Acosta's game. While he sits at home all the time, he doesn't have to look into people's eyes as they beg for their lives. Or hear the cries of young children as I murder their parents in front of them. You may be my only way out. But Acosta won't make it easy."

His words hang in the air, a silent plea for redemption. I know that Cuffy is on the verge of breaking, casting off the shackles of his past and embracing a new path forward.

"We're with you, Cuffy," Lucy says, her voice steady and unwavering. "Whatever it takes, we'll stand by your side."

Cuffy nods, a sense of determination settling over him like a cloak. "Then let's finish this," he says, his voice filled with resolve.

As Cuffy turns to confront his men, a wave of unease crashes over me. This is the precipice—when everything hangs in the balance, and the distinction between ally and adversary dissolves into the mist.

After a few heated words from Cuffy, his men depart, fading back into the port's alleyways. I signal for the team, along with Abbie and Bethanie, to close in on me.

"OK, there's no time to dwell on what just happened. We need to get to the airport, and fast. It's our only option now that we know Acosta's people are on the island. Simon, how far to the taxi rank?"

"About another 10 minutes' walk," replies Simon, after checking the map on his phone.

"I've got a minibus not far from here, Steve, but we need to be quick before Acosta's men get there," says Leroy.

"Take us there."

With Leroy out of earshot, I turn to the team. "He may have changed sides, but I never trust a traitor of any kind. Watch him. If he makes any movement or you think he is leading us into a trap, kill him."

Once more, as we navigate the treacherous streets of Oranjestad, Cuffy's internal struggle becomes evident. His usual stoic demeanour wavers, replaced by a haunted expression that speaks volumes of the turmoil within him.

"You seem troubled, Cuffy," Lucy remarks, studying his face for any sign of clarity amidst the chaos.

Cuffy offers a tight-lipped smile, but his eyes betray the unease lurking beneath the surface. "It's nothing," he replies, though his words lack conviction.

I glance at Lucy, acknowledging the gravity of the situation. Cuffy's inner conflict threatens to unravel our carefully laid plans, casting a shadow of doubt over our mission. The deeper we get into the town, Cuffy's demeanour grows tense. He's on edge. His senses intensify as if anticipating danger at every turn.

"Something doesn't seem right," Cuffy murmurs, his voice just about audible over the city that is starting to wake up the further we go.

I nod in agreement, the hairs on the back of my neck standing on end, a silent reminder of the dangers lurking in the shadows. The air is filled with tension as we navigate the tangled alleyways and backstreets of the port city, on high alert for any sign of danger. Acosta's men could be lurking around any corner, behind any wall or doorway, ready to spring their trap at a moment's notice.

"Stay sharp, everyone," I mutter, my voice firm but urgent. "We're walking into the lion's den."

Simon nods, his eyes scanning for any movement in the shadows. Derek keeps up a stream of updates over the comms, his voice a reassuring presence in the chaos.

"Two tangos ahead," Derek's voice crackles in my ear.

Then, without warning, gunfire erupts from the darkness of the alleyways, bullets whizzing past us with lethal intent. We dive for cover, returning fire with calculated precision as the battle erupts.

George slips ahead, his movements precise, as he takes a position on a nearby rooftop. His sniper rifle gleams in the light, a deadly promise of protection for our team.

Cuffy, our unexpected ally, emerges from the shadows with deadly precision—he returns fire. His shots find their mark, taking down his once-loyal men who have turned against him.

Abbie and Bethanie huddle behind a crumbling wall, their faces etched with determination.

Without hesitation, I charge forward, "Stay down!" I shout, my voice drowned out by the roar of gunfire. "I've got you covered!"

Bethanie's eyes meet mine, filled with gratitude and determination. "Thanks, Dad," she says, her voice steady despite the chaos around us.

I nod, my heart pounding as I return fire, each shot a calculated risk in the deadly game we find ourselves trapped in. Lucy is nearby, her movements fluid and graceful as she dispatches Acosta's men with lethal efficiency.

"Watch your six!" Derek's voice cuts through the chaos.

I spin around, searching for any sign of the enemy. Sure enough, more of Acosta's men emerge from the shadows, their weapons raining down fire as they run towards us.

"There is more coming from our left," Derek shouts through the radio, his voice a rallying cry in the darkness.

We discharge a barrage of gunfire, our weapons roaring as we fight hard to hold our ground. George's sniper rifle sings from the rooftop, picking off targets with lethal accuracy as Derek keeps us informed of the enemy's movements.

But despite our best efforts, the tide of battle turns against us. Acosta's men are relentless, their numbers endless as they press forward with ruthless resolve.

"We're outnumbered!" Lucy shouts, her voice audible over the din of battle. "We need to fall back!"

I grit my teeth, torn between the instinct to fight and the rationality of retreat. But a saying from my army days leaps out at me—those who run away live to fight another day. Before I can make a decision, a hail of bullets rains down from above, catching Acosta's men off guard and buying us a moment of respite.

"George, nice shooting!" I yell, my voice tinged with relief as I glance up at the rooftop. "Let's use this opportunity to regroup!"

We fall back, moving with trained efficiency to a narrow alley, the sound of our boots hitting the pavement echo off the walls as we regroup.

Gasping for breath before the final assault, "Alright, listen up," I bark, my voice commanding. "We need to take them out one by one, if necessary, no mistakes. Simon, you're on point. Derek and Leroy keep us covered. George, find some high ground. Lucy, stay close to Abbie and Bethanie."

The team nods in silent agreement, their faces set in grim determination as we prepare to face our enemy head-on. We move forward, our movements coordinated as we advance towards our attackers.

Once more, the silent streets erupt with gunfire from the shadows, bullets whizzing past us with deadly precision. Spotting cover near an alleyway, I charge forward, heart pounding in my chest. Almost there, a young woman launches at me, hatred in her eyes, determined to end my life.

Time slows down as seconds tick by, as we circle each other. Tension is thick in the air as we size up each other, both looking for strengths and weaknesses that will give us the advantage. Every muscle in my body is coiled tight, ready to spring into action at a moment's notice. I can feel the adrenaline surging through my body, heightening my senses and sharpening my focus.

With a sudden surge, she lunges forward, her fists a blur of motion as she aims a rapid succession of punches at my head and torso. Instinct kicks in, and I raise my arms in a defensive stance, deflecting her blows.

But she's relentless, pressing the attack with a ferocity that catches me off guard. The impact of each blow reverberating through my body, the force of her punches is like a series of thunderclaps in the stillness of the night.

I seize the opportunity to counter, launching a series of strikes in rapid succession. My fists move with practised agility, aiming for vulnerable spots in her defences as I seek to gain control of the fight.

We exchange blows with a brutal intensity, each strike a testament to the raw power and determination driving us forward. The sound of flesh meeting flesh fills the air, punctuated by the occasional grunt of exertion as we release our pent-up aggression on each other.

Despite the chaos unfolding around us, my focus remains razor-sharp, my mind clear and alert as I analyse my opponent's movements for any sign of weakness. Every feint, every dodge, every strike is a planned risk, a calculated gamble in the deadly game we find ourselves locked in.

As the battle rages on, exhaustion starts creeping into my limbs, the strain of the fight taking its toll on my body. But I push through the pain, drawing on reserves of strength and willpower I didn't know I possessed, as I continue to press the attack.

After what appears like an eternity, I see my opening. With a burst of speed and ferocity, I deliver a devastating blow that sends my opponent staggering backwards, her defences crumbling in the face of my unrelenting assault. With a final, decisive shot from my 9mm, I bring the fight to an end, my adversary collapsing to the ground in a heap. The alleyway falls silent, the echoes of our battle fading into the night as I stand victorious, my heart pounding in my chest and my breath coming in ragged gasps.

With my main focus on the intense firefight going on around me, my attention on my girls lapses for a few moments. During a short lull in enemy fire coming my way, I snatch a glance over my shoulder.

Two cartel members, armed, are sprinting towards Abbie and Bethanie, their faces twisted in malicious intent. My heart races.

"Abbie! Bethanie!" I shout, my voice lost amidst the chaos of battle.

All around them, the battle continues, the sharp cracks of rifles echoing through the air. Abbie and Bethanie hold their ground with unwavering resolve, with the rifles they have taken from the dead cartel members, all the years of training I'd taught them now coming into play.

I watch as they both hold the rifles, the butts pressing hard into their shoulders — the barrels pointing at the two approaching men. As if the sounds of the battle going on around me stand quiet, I hear the distinctive crack of bullets leaving the rifles, followed by two thuds as their shots find their marks. A nano-second later, the two bodies slump to the floor.

The battle rages on for another 10 minutes, as we fight to take down Acosta's remaining forces. Then, at last, the gunfire falls silent, the only sound the harsh rasp of our breath as we survey the aftermath of the battle. Acosta's people lay dead in the streets, their lifeless bodies a grim testament to the price of our victory.

"We better get out of this location and make our way to Cuffy's vehicle before the police show up. Thinking about it, why haven't they shown up?" I say, my voice gasping for air as I glance around at my teammates' weary faces.

"That would be my doing," says Leroy after a few seconds, "Alex Acosta is friends with the police chief. Alex has him on his payroll. The chief did something in his past that Alex blackmails him with. I don't know what, but it must have been something terrible.

"I called them before you arrived and asked them to turn the other way and not come here, no matter what happens."

"That would explain it," says George, hearing the conversation as he arrives at our location from his sniper position on the roof.

With no more issues from the cartel, we arrive at the minibus 10 minutes later. Not trusting Leroy, a man who, a few minutes ago, changed sides, we are not walking up to his vehicle and clambering in. For all we know, he could have an IED attached.

"Simon, you're the transport expert. Do you want to go and check it over?"

"You can do one, Steve. You're the mad bastard among us who loves playing with IEDs and explosives. You go and check it."

"Can't argue with that," I reply, building up my inner strength.

"Take care, Dad," Abbie shouts, with worry across her face.

As I approach the bus, the air hangs heavy with tension. My senses are on high alert for any sign of danger—my heart pounds in my chest, the weight of uncertainty bearing on me like a leaden cloak. But I steel myself against the fear, drawing on the training instilled in me by the British Army. All the times I carried out searches on suspect vehicles and packages in Northern Ireland have now come down to the next few minutes.

I approach the suspect vehicle with caution, as I prepare to confront the looming threat of an improvised explosive device (IED). With each step, I tread with care, aware that a single misstep could spell disaster.

I encircle the minibus with precise steps, scanning every inch of its exterior for any hint of an IED. My hands steady, I reach for the tools of my trade—a mirror I borrowed from Lucy attached to an extendable car aerial that I always keep in my Bergen.

Gripping the handle of the mirror tightly I examine the vehicle, every movement deliberate and calculated. The weight of obligation presses down on me like a leaden cloak, a reminder of the lives depending on my expertise.

With steady hands, I extend the mirror on its pole, peering beneath the vehicle for signs of suspicious packages or wires. My heart pounds in my chest as I inch the mirror along the undercarriage, my eyes scanning for anomalies. Each second ticks away like an eternity, as I navigate the maze of shadows and crevices, my senses heightened to the slightest hint of hidden compartments or suspicious wires that might reveal a deadly trap.

My fingers, trained to detect the slightest irregularity, trace the edges of the vehicle, searching for anything that feels it shouldn't be there. Each movement is deliberate and methodical, as I rely on muscle memory and instinct to guide my search. My breath comes in shallow bursts, adrenaline keeping my senses on a razor's edge.

I breathe a sigh of relief as I reach the end of my inspection, my pulse still racing. With a sense of cautious optimism, I step back from the vehicle, my eyes never leaving as I await my final verdict. There's no sign of tampering or danger lurking beneath the surface.

The tension that had gripped me moments before dissipates, replaced by a sense of calm and reassurance. I can't help but feel a surge of pride in my training and expertise. But even as I allow myself a moment of relief, I know there's no room for complacency in this line of work. The next threat could be lurking just around the corner, waiting to test my skills again.

"Clear!" I call out to the rest of the team, my voice ringing out in the stillness of the air. "No sign of any IEDs."

The tension begins to disperse as my teammates approach, their expressions a mix of relief and gratitude. We exchange nods of acknowledgement, the unspoken understanding binding us together in the face of danger.

But even as we exhale, I know our journey is far from over. The threat of danger still looms on the horizon, waiting to strike when we least expect it. As we continue our mission, I'll need to remain vigilant, relying on my training and instincts to keep us safe in the face of adversity.

As we are about to get in, Cuffy says, "This is where I leave you for now. I need to make some calls to friends of mine who don't have connections to Acosta's cartel, to, with any luck, ease your passage through the airport. Please park the bus in the short-stay car park and leave the keys under the seat. I'll collect it tomorrow."

"OK, Leroy, nice seeing you again, and thanks for your help with the cartel. It couldn't have been easy for you," says Lucy, hugging him.

"That's OK. Have a safe trip home."

Once we are all in and driving away, "You need to tell us more about Leroy Cuffy and your connection, Lucy," says Derek, from the back seat.

"I will, once we leave this place and are onboard an aircraft. Plus, for now, don't trust Leroy too much. He may have helped us in the fight but is as dodgy as they come. He could change sides again," replies Lucy, sitting back in her seat.

Chapter Twenty – Pursuit

Within minutes, we leave the built-up area of the port behind, the minibus hurtling down the winding roads, each turn adding to the tension coiling in my gut. The fresh air whips through the vehicle, a stark contrast to the suffocating weight of uncertainty that hangs over us like a shroud.

I'm stationed in the passenger seat, my gaze fixed ahead, scanning the road for any signs of trouble. Simon's hands grip the wheel with iron resolve, his eyes darting between the road and the rearview mirror. The team, along with Abbie and Bethanie, are in the back. Their faces are taut with anticipation as they peer out into the distance, their weapons ready.

"How far to the airport?" George's voice rings out from the rear, his words a stark reminder of the urgency of our mission.

"We're making good time," Simon replies, his tone steady despite the unease that lingers in the air. "We should reach the airport in about 30 minutes."

Despite the calm of the morning, doubts gnaw at the edges of my mind, whispering of betrayal and impending danger. Has Cuffy changed sides again, or are Acosta's men lying in wait up ahead, ready to spring their trap?

A flash of movement catches my eye in the distance. A convoy of vehicles racing towards us with alarming speed urges me to act before it's too late.

"Simon, pull off the road," I command, my voice cutting through the tension like a knife.

With precision, Simon veers the minibus onto a dirt track. The bus bounces hard as it leaves the tarmac and hits the uneven track before coming to rest among the foliage lining the road.

The abrupt motion jolts us all into action, with everybody's instinct kicking in. The team understands that if there are people looking for us, we will have a better chance in a firefight if we are out of the vehicle.

We scatter into the surrounding foliage, seeking cover as the convoy roars past, its intentions unknown and its presence a harbinger of impending danger.

I dive down behind a cluster of palm trees, Abbie and Bethanie by my side, their presence comforting amidst the chaos. Across the road, George and Derek take up firing positions, their eyes trained on the approaching convoy.

As the vehicles draw nearer, a sense of dread washes over me, each passing moment amplifying the fear that coils in my chest. Something isn't right, and my instincts scream for caution.

"Get ready," I whisper, my grip tightening on my rifle as the convoy hurtles towards us, sirens wailing in the distance.

My pulse quickens with unease, and I am ready to tackle what may come next. My breath becomes shallow as I start to control it, prepared for the attack coming our way.

I turn to my girls, "Whatever happens, stay close to me and use those weapons if you have to." I point to the rifles they have kept with them since the encounter at the port.

One minute later, the vehicles are within 30 metres of the turning. My finger confirms that the safety catch is off, and the magazine is still in place. But to my relief, I watch as the first cars speed past. Four police officers in uniforms are sitting in the first one.

Something in the second vehicle grabs my attention. As it passes, I catch a glimpse of several men, their eyes gleaming with malice.

A familiar face in the front passenger seat sends a chill down my spine, confirming my worst fears. I recognise him from the port. He stood close to Cuffy and the one who shouted out, 'Kill the fuckers'.

Their presence is a grim reminder of the dangers that still lie ahead. But as the convoy disappears, nagging questions linger in my mind.

Shit, Acosta's people must have regrouped and are now searching for us, but how did they know we are on this road? It might be the only road to the airport, and they know we must reach it to get off the island and back home. Or is it something else? Maybe the bus is being tracked. Whatever it is, we can't take any chances.

We wait 10 minutes to ensure no other vehicles follow behind, ready to catch us if we break cover too soon. Once I'm sure we are safe, I yell, "Everyone back on the bus."

As Simon fires up the engine, I turn around to face the rest. Derek is in the back. His laptop is open, and his fingers dance across the keyboard as he scans the airwaves for any sign of trouble.

As we race towards the airport, our escape hangs in the balance. Are there more of Acosta's people in the area, or worse, are they still blocking our route?

Derek's eyes widen, and he leans closer to the screen, his expression grave. "I've intercepted a communication," he says, his voice urgent. "It's from Acosta's people. They've blocked all primary routes to the airport. And Acosta is on the island."

My heart sinks at the news. We're running out of time, and Acosta's forces are closing in on us with each passing second. But we can't afford to lose our nerve now.

"Damn it," I mutter under my breath, my mind racing as I try to come up with a plan. "We need to find another way to the airport, and fast."

Derek nods, his brow furrowed in concentration as he monitors the communications. The rest of the team looks to me for guidance, their faces etched with determination despite the gravity of the situation.

"Alright, listen up. Our exit route is compromised. We need to act fast to avoid falling into Acosta's clutches. We'll have to take the back roads," I decide, my voice steady despite the fear bubbling beneath the surface. "It'll be riskier, but it's our best chance of avoiding Acosta's men."

"We could try to double back and find another way to the airport," suggests Derek.

"But that'll take us off course, and we risk getting lost in unfamiliar territory," counters Lucy, her voice edged with concern.

I weigh our options, each possibility fraught with its own set of risks and consequences. We can't afford to make a wrong move, not with Acosta's men hot on our trail.

"We stick to the back roads," I decide, my voice firm with resolve. "We must push forward but move fast and stay vigilant. We can't afford any slip-ups." Opening my phone, I search the maps for an alternative route to the airport. "OK, Simon, I've found one — take the next right."

*****

Back on the outskirts of the airport, Alex Acosta has made the trip to Oranjestad to oversee his men and ensure the only way Steve and the rest leave this island is in body bags. As his men set up roadblocks and checkpoints along the main routes to the airport, a sense of anticipation courses through him. 'This is it — the moment we've been preparing for, the chance to finally put an end to Steve and his team once and for all', Alex thinks to himself.

"Move those trucks into position," he barks, his voice cutting through the air as he issues orders to his men. "We need to make sure no one gets through."

Acosta's men move with precision, swiftness, and efficiency as they carry out his commands. Every road is covered, every possible escape route blocked off—there's no way Steve and his team will be able to slip through their grasps this time.

As the tension mounts, a rush of excitement mingles with the thrill of the chase. But as the hours pass, a sense of unease begins to gnaw at the edges of Alex Acosta's consciousness.

He turns to one of his men, "Where are they? Why haven't they shown up yet?" The man shrugs his shoulders.

Just as he starts to grow impatient, a crackle of static cuts through the air, followed by the sound of gunfire in the distance.

"You lot, head for the source of gunfire and assist. They must be heading for the airport. I'll take my bodyguards and block the road to the airport," Alex's voice is commanding and firm.

Without hesitation, Alex and his men jump into several cars and head onto the road. At a junction in the road, they split up. His men race towards the source of the gunfire, and Alex can feel the tension in the air reaching a fever pitch—this is the moment of reckoning.

*****

As we navigate the winding back roads, a palpable tension fills the air, and our senses are on high alert for any sign of danger. Ahead of us, a roadblock materialises, operated by armed figures— two men and a woman. There's nowhere to turn around, and the steep banks on either side of the road leave us trapped.

"We've got company," Simon mutters, his voice tense as he eases the minibus to a crawl, inching closer to the roadblock.

My heart pounds in my chest as we draw nearer, the figures becoming clearer in the dim light. Dread coils in my stomach as recognition dawns – these are Acosta's people.

The situation reminds me of an incident while driving alone undercover in Northern Ireland, where I came across an IRA ambush with nowhere to go. I clench my 9mm and hope for the best as I scan the surroundings for cover.

As we get closer, we have only one choice, "We need to bail," my voice is urgent as I motion for the team to prepare to disembark. "Take cover and stay low."

We spring into action, sliding out of the minibus and diving for cover behind the nearby trees and bushes. My heart is hammering in my chest as I wait for the inevitable confrontation.

Seconds tick by like hours as we lie in wait, the tension thick enough to suffocate. Then, without warning, the silence is shattered by the sound of footsteps approaching. My muscles tense, ready to spring into action at a moment's notice as I wait for the enemy to reveal themselves.

And then, they're upon us — Acosta's people, their weapons raised and their eyes gleaming with malice as they open fire. Gunshots shatter the silence, bullets whizzing past us with deadly intent. Instinct takes over as I return fire.

"Take them down!" I bark orders to the team, my voice cutting through the chaos of battle as we engage the enemy.

Bullets rain down around us, and the air is thick with the scent of gunpowder and the metallic tang of blood.

Over on the left of the road, George and Lucy have scaled the grass bank and are now picking off targets emerging from vehicles beyond the checkpoint — ones we didn't see as we approached.

The girls have taken cover by Simon close to the bus, while Derek has taken up position on the bank behind me, relaying enemy positions through the radio.

"Lucy, you have one approaching your position behind the bank. He's trying to outflank you."

With that, George slides down the other side of the bank. A few seconds later, a single shot rings out. I scan the bank, and there is no sign of George reappearing.

"You see George, Derek?" I say over the radio.

"Yeah, he's further along, close to the vehicles blocking the road."

Tension escalates as the firefight becomes a fierce battle for survival. Acosta's people fight with ruthless efficiency, and their determination is evident in every shot they fire.

But they are no match for the team, as we pick them off one by one with calculated precision until all of Acosta's people lay dead or dying on the floor. The roadblock lies in ruins, and Acosta's forces are defeated.

I take a moment to catch my breath, my heart still pounding as I survey the aftermath of the battle.

"Simon, get Abbie back in the bus and bring it down. The rest of you, help me clear the road," my voice booming out commands.

Making my way past the dead cartel members, when I look down to see a young man, no more than 20, going for his weapon. I raise my rifle, pointing at his head. For a nano-second, I think about letting him live. But then I remember what his boss had put my girls through. So, as I pass, I squeeze the trigger, his face exploding onto the tarmac, scattering blood and skull fragments in all directions.

Once the road is clear, Simon joins us with the bus, zigzagging around several vehicles on his path. The drivers are slumped over their steering wheels, caught in the crossfire, a grim reminder of the brutal reality of war.

Back on the minibus, we press on towards our objective. We know the fight is far from over — Acosta will stop at nothing to see us dead, and we must remain vigilant if we are to survive. As we make our final push towards the airport, we navigate the treacherous terrain. But our escape route is no longer a secret — Alex Acosta himself is leading the charge against us.

The airport looms in the distance like a beacon of hope. We're so close, I can almost taste the freedom awaiting us beyond its gates. But our hopes are soon dashed as a vehicle appears on the road ahead, in the distance, its presence ominous against the backdrop of the setting sun.

Simon eases the minibus to 30 mph, his eyes darting back and forth, searching for any signs of danger. Like a thunderclap, gunfire explodes from the treeline to our right, shattering the serene evening air. It's an ambush, and our world is transformed into a battlefield.

Instinct takes over, and without a moment's hesitation, I swing open the door and hurl myself from the moving vehicle, my heart hammering in my chest as I land in a crouch, rifle poised for action. Lucy, Derek, and George mirror my move, their actions a testament to our unwavering determination.

The attackers are hidden in the dense foliage, their position concealed from our view. But we're not about to let them get the drop on us.

With gunfire still echoing in the air, Lucy, George, Derek, and I sprint from the road to the trees, our hearts pounding in our chests as we move at speed through the woods. Every step is deliberate, every breath measured, as we scan the shadows for any sign of our elusive attackers.

The forest is alive with the crackle of gunfire and the rustle of leaves, a symphony of chaos that threatens to overwhelm our senses. But we press on, our training kicking in as we navigate the labyrinth of trees.

A movement ahead catches my eye. I raise a hand to signal the team to halt. We freeze in place, our senses on high alert as we scan the surrounding area. Then, like phantoms emerging from the darkness, our attackers come into view. Their forms flicker in and out of the shadows as they try to make a break for their vehicle.

"Take them down!" I shout.

We open fire, our bullets finding their marks with lethal accuracy. The air is thick with the odour of spent cases and sweat, as we engage the fleeing attackers in a fierce firefight. Our movements are fluid and precise as we navigate the treacherous terrain. Bullets whizz past us, kicking up dirt and debris as we press forward, our determination unwavering in the face of adversity.

But despite our best efforts, some of the aggressors are making ground away from us. Their movements are rapid and agile as they dart between the trees with ease. We exchange fire, our shots ringing out as we fight to protect each other in this lethal confrontation.

Amidst the chaos, I catch sight of Simon and the girls, their forms disappearing into the safety of the nearby trees. Relief washes over me for a moment before I refocus on the task at hand. Soon, the cartel has been disposed of. Some of them are lying dead among the trees while others have made a bid for freedom and are now running down the road towards their vehicle.

It's great to watch craftsmen at work, even in the heat of a battle. As I watch George taking up a kneeling firing position by the side of the road, like seconds ticking away around a clockface, you can see him controlling his breathing, ready to take the shot at two men running down the road towards a vehicle about 600 metres away. By now, they are close to their car and freedom, and you can almost sense the relief on their faces.

With each passing moment, the anticipation builds. Then, in a sudden burst of motion, George squeezes the trigger, and the rifle recoils against his shoulder. The crack of the shot reverberates through the air, breaking the stillness of the surrounding landscape. I hold my breath, my eyes fixed on the target.

In the fraction of a second that follows, the bullet spins in the rifling and leaves the barrel, a streak of metal slicing through the air with accuracy as it hurtles towards its intended mark. As the round closes the distance between itself and the target, time slows to a crawl. I watch as it impacts with devastating force, striking the man square in the back of the head. His body jerks forward, a spray of blood erupting from the wound as he crumples to the ground.

It's a moment of both triumph and terror, a reminder of the lethal power that lies within the hands of skilled marksmen like George. As the dust settles and the echoes of the gunshot fade into the distance, I can't help but feel awe at my teammate's precision and skill.

Walking in patrol formation along the edge of the road, we make our way to where Simon stashed the bus. When we arrive, I turn around to the team and asked, " Is anyone injured?"

"Fine, thanks, but getting sick of this shit." comes the reply from Derek.

"Me too. Acosta can't have that many more people on this island. We've killed most of them."

"With you on that one, Lucy, there can't be many left," walking over to check Abbie and Bethanie are OK.

"Took one in the shoulder, but I'll live. One of you lazy bastards will have to drive the rest of the way to the airport," says Simon, removing his jacket to reveal blood gushing from a wound.

"Once we are back in the vehicle, let me take care of that for you."

"Cheers, Abbie," the pain in Simon's voice indicates it is a bad injury.

"Stop moaning, you'll live. Besides, you have another shoulder," says George, taking the piss.

"That's what I love about your compassion, George, fuck all," replies Simon, as Abbie finishes applying a field dressing to his shoulder.

With me in the driving seat, we make our way once more to the airport, which is now very close, about one mile away. I allow a sense of relief to wash over me as we drive up the final stretch leading to the airport approach road. The team is in good spirits, sharing smiles and small talk as we approach our destination. But they all know beneath the surface, we must remain vigilant, knowing the danger is not yet behind us.

I glance at the rearview mirror, scanning the road behind us for any signs of pursuit. The coast appears clear, but unease gnaws at the pit of my stomach. Too many times I have seen missions unravel at the last moment, due to complacency.

"We're almost there, folks. Let's stay sharp until we're wheels up," I announce.

The tension in the air is palpable as we round the final bend in the road, the airport looming large on the horizon. Shit, as we approach the entrance, my heart sinks as I spot a familiar figure standing in our path.

"Acosta," I mutter under my breath, my grip tightening on the steering wheel.

The team falls silent, their expressions hardening as they brace themselves for another confrontation. Everyone understands that with Acosta blocking our path, we have one more obstacle to overcome before we can finally breathe easy.

"Get ready, everyone," I say, my voice steady, "We're going to have to fight our way through."

I stop the minibus in the road, and the team disembarks, rifles at the ready.

As I stand face to face with Alex Acosta, the tension between us crackles in the air like electricity. Behind him are his bodyguards; five muscular-looking men dressed in grey suits standing poised, weapons ready, their eyes glinting with fear and determination.

"Steve," Alex sneers, his voice dripping with contempt. "You think you can outsmart me? You and your little band of misfits don't stand a chance against me and my cartel."

I meet his gaze head-on, my expression stoic and unwavering. "We'll see about that," I reply, my voice firm. "I've faced worse odds than this, Acosta. And I've always come out on top."

With that, the standoff begins, each side poised for action, waiting for the other to make the first move. The tension in the air is thick, and a fog hangs over us like a shroud as we stand on the precipice of battle.

Without warning, one of Acosta's men opens fire, the sound of gunfire echoing through the air like thunder. Bullets fly, whizzing past my head as I dive for cover, my heart pounding in my chest. But even as chaos reigns around me, I remain focused, my mind sharp and alert as I assess the situation and formulate a plan of attack.

I rally the team, coordinating our movements with military-like precision. Amidst the battle, I spot Alex, his face contorted in rage and frustration as he realises victory is slipping through his fingers. With a primal roar, he charges forward, his men following closely behind, determined to crush us once and for all. But I am one step ahead. My mind is a well-honed weapon. In a calculated manoeuvre, I plan to outwit him, catch him off guard, and deliver a decisive blow to end this.

Before I can execute my plan, a single shot pierces the air, slicing through the chaos. I turn, heart pounding. Where did the shot come from? Abbie, her eyes filled with determination, lowers her smoking rifle.

A chill runs down my spine as I realise what she's done. She's taken matters into her own hands. Alex Acosta lies lifeless, and a sense of relief washes over me.

"That's for what you put me and my family through," Abbie says, her voice cold and resolute.

I nod, acknowledging her resolve. Her actions have saved our lives, but the job isn't finished. I signal the team.

"Move out," I command, my voice cutting through the tension.

Lucy and I move with precision, covering each other as we start to take down the rest of Acosta's men. Simon navigates through the wreckage, keeping us ahead. Derek's calm voice directs the chaos, his commands clear. George, always the marksman, picks off threats from the shadows.

"Clear left!" Lucy shouts, her voice steady.

"Right side secure," I respond, scanning for more threats.

The air is thick with smoke and adrenaline. Each step, each shot, feels like a lifetime. We press on, relentless.

Amidst the aftermath, I feel a wave of gratitude for our team's bravery and resolve. The nightmare is finally over.

We leave the scene at speed before anyone comes to investigate the gunfire, and head for the short-stay car park where we plan to leave the vehicle.

When we arrive, I stretch my hand out of the driver's window and grab the white ticket, from the machine. The place is full of vehicles of holidaymakers enjoying some holiday in a far-off place.

We make our way up to the top level. In my experience, this isn't used much as people are too lazy to walk and want a spot as close to the exit as possible. This always makes me smile, as they will be walking around the terminal for hours, so the extra walking distance doesn't make any difference.

Once we are all out, Simon locks the vehicle, and we abandon the minibus and our weapons in the airport car park, knowing that we'll have to depend on our wits alone from here on out. Every step we take towards the terminal is fraught with tension, our senses on high alert for signs of danger.

As we move through the busy car park, I can't shake the feeling of foreboding that hangs over us like a dark cloud. The absence of our weapons leaves us vulnerable, exposed to whatever threats may lie ahead.

"Stay close, everyone," I murmur, just above a whisper. "We don't know what we're walking into."

The team nods, their eyes scanning the surroundings for any signs of movement that appear out of place. The airport terminal looms ahead, a beacon of hope in the darkness.

But as we approach the entrance, my heart sinks as I spot several figures lurking in the shadows. "We've got company," I mutter, my hand reaching for the knife tucked into my belt. "Keep your wits about you."

Chapter Twenty-One – Journey Home

To ensure our safety, we decide to split up. The boys will take one entrance, while Lucy, Abbie, Bethanie, and I opt for another entrance located at the far end of the departure hall. As we approach the entrance, I feel a shiver of unease slither down my spine. It feels like unseen eyes are analysing our every step. To minimise risk, we decide that our group would go first, while the others check that we are not being followed. After five minutes, the others will leave and enter via the other entrance.

Lucy and I exchange a silent glance, an implied understanding passing between us as we enter the departure hall. "Stay sharp," I murmur to the girls, as we weave through the crowd of travellers. "We're not out of trouble yet."

Meanwhile, Simon, George, and Derek take the other entrance, moving with the same caution as us.

I sweep the area inside the departure hall for any signs of trouble, my senses on alert. Our standard operating procedure dictates finding the nearest café to the entrance, and I spot one nearby, its entrance beckoning like a false beacon of safety amidst the chaos.

"Let's move," I say, guiding the girls towards the café. "We'll wait there for the others to rendezvous."

The departure hall hums with activity, the air thick with passengers' chatter, and announcements echoing over the loudspeakers. But beneath the veneer of status quo, there's an eerie tension, a perception that danger lurks in every shadow.

As we reach the café, we take a seat at a table near the back. The clatter of dishes and the murmur of voices are a dissonant backdrop to our mounting apprehension. Despite the façade, I can't shake the feeling that we're walking into a trap.

The minutes crawl by as we wait. The tension coils tighter with each passing second. The perception of being watched hangs in the air, a silent reminder of the peril surrounding us.

My heart races with anticipation as I spot Simon, George, and Derek enter the café through the other entrance. We exchange subtle nods of acknowledgement as they make their way past, their movements calculated to avoid drawing attention. I watch their progress with unease, aware of the dangers lurking within the crowds of people.

After ensuring that no one is watching us, they take their seats at the opposite end of the café, their eyes scanning the room for any signs of trouble. The tension in the air is suffocating as they settle in, their vigilance a silent, nerve-wracking testament to the gravity of our situation.

Ten agonising minutes pass before we finally regroup, my voice just above a whisper as I address George. "It seems your team wasn't followed," I murmur, a wave of relief washing over me.

I keep our conversation discreet to avoid attracting unwanted attention from nearby patrons, but the tension in my voice betrays the gravity of our situation- a high-stakes mission that could change our lives.

"You neither. So what's the plan?"

"On the way to the airport, Derek booked our flights online via his laptop. We leave in three hours. But we must print off the tickets as we don't have phones. Derek and I will go to the information desk to do this while the rest of you wait here. Once we have them, we will head for the business lounge." Speaking with a normal voice is important, as whispering too much may attract attention.

"Do you want me to order you a brew while you're gone, Steve?" Lucy asks, heading for the counter.

"Yes, please, Lucy. Come on, Derek, let's get them boarding passes."

As Derek and I approach the information desk, the cacophony of the bustling airport engulfs us. Each step is burdened with the weight of an unknown peril. Maybe I am on edge because of the events leading up to this moment. I scan the crowd for any hint of impending danger or, worse, Acosta's people after revenge for the death of their boss.

A young woman in the airline's uniform greets us at the desk with a polite smile. Derek hands over the booking information, "We need to print our boarding passes, please," he says, his voice faint but firm.

The woman nods, her fingers flying over the keyboard. The printer whirrs to life, and within moments, our boarding passes slide out without a hitch.

While Derek retrieves the passes, a flicker of movement catches my attention. Two men, inconspicuously dressed yet exuding a menacing aura, loom in the corner of my gaze, their eyes fixed on us like predators stalking their prey.

"We've got company," I mutter to Derek, keeping my voice low to avoid drawing attention. "Those two haven't taken their eyes off us since we got here." I point to two men leaning against the far wall, close to a drinks machine.

Derek's jaw tightens, his expression mirroring my unease. "Keep both eyes on them," he replies, his tone terse. "Let's get the rest from the café and head for the safety of the lounge, before things escalate."

When Derek and I arrive back at the café, the rest are still sitting and drinking brews, apart from George and Simon.

"Where are the others?" I ask.

"They've gone on a perimeter check, just to be safe," replies Lucy, handing me my coffee.

Several minutes later, they return. "I think you're right about being watched. I spotted a group of people acting suspiciously near security. They might be looking for the right time to act," says Simon, sitting down.

"We need to head through security, as they will need a ticket to get past that point, but first, I need a dump. Does anyone know where the toilets are?" getting up and looking around.

Bethanie points to the far end of the hall, "Think they are over there, Dad."

"Could do with a piss myself," adds George.

George and I make our way through the bustling departures hall, keeping a careful eye on our surroundings, hyper-aware of the three men that have started to trail behind us.

We reach the entrance to the toilets, and without a word, George and I slip inside. The lights cast harsh shadows on the tiled floor, adding to the foreboding hanging in the air.

Once inside a stall, I try to focus on the task at hand, but I can sense the tension building, the hairs on my neck prickling with anticipation. And then, without warning, the attack comes.

Three shadowy figures burst into the restroom, moving with lethal precision. Before I can react, they are on us, their fists flying. However, my army training and years of mission experience kicks in, and I fight back with all my might.

The cramped confines of the stall make for a brutal battleground. Our movements are restricted as we grapple with our attackers. Every punch and kick lands with bone-crushing force, and the sound of our struggle echoes off the tiled walls.

I manage to land a solid blow on one of the attackers, sending him reeling backwards. But before I can capitalise on the opening, another attacker unleashes a flurry of punches, driving me back against the stall door. My head spins as I struggle to stay on my feet.

Meanwhile, George is locked in a fierce struggle with the third attacker, trading blows with equal ferocity. I can see the determination in his eyes, his jaw clenched with resolve as he fights to protect himself and me.

Summoning every ounce of strength I have left, with a swift move, I duck under the attacker's guard, delivering a devastating blow to his midsection. He doubles over in pain, gasping for breath as I seize the opportunity to gain control.

Across the stall, I see George land a powerful kick, sending his opponent staggering backwards. With a decisive move, he follows up with a series of precise strikes, incapacitating the attacker and leaving him crumpled on the floor.

Breathing heavily, I exchange another weary glance with George, our bodies bruised and battered from the brutal fight. But there's no time to rest. Despite the odds stacked against us, George and I refuse to go down without a fight. With a final surge of strength, we overpower our assailants, landing blow after blow until they're lying unconscious on the cold restroom floor.

With trembling hands, we drag the unconscious bodies into a nearby cubicle, stashing them out of view of anyone who comes in, before slipping out of the restroom and back into the chaos of the departure hall. Our minds already racing ahead to the next obstacle in our path.

"We need to move," I say to George, my voice hoarse with exertion. "Before anyone else shows up."

As we make our way through the crowds of travellers at a speed that doesn't draw attention to ourselves, my mind races with the implications of the attack. It's clear that Acosta's men are closing in.

As we regroup back at the café, I brief the team on our situation and what just occurred in the toilets, emphasising the need to make a swift move towards security. The threat of falling into the clutches of Alex Acosta's men looms over us like a dark cloud, urging us to act fast.

We all understand the gravity of our predicament and agree that it's our only chance to evade capture. After wiping our own knives clean of fingerprints, we discard them into the provided bins, ensuring nobody sees us and that we don't leave any trace that could lead back to us. It's a calculated risk, but one we must take to survive this ordeal.

Approaching the security entrance, the imposing gates rise before us like a formidable fortress, casting a shadow of uncertainty over our path to freedom. We exchange nods, bracing ourselves for whatever lies ahead.

As we pass through, there is a whirlwind of activity. The officers' scrutinising gaze lingers on each traveller, their suspicions detectable in the air. I can sense the weight of their scrutiny pressing down on me, every nerve on edge as we inch closer to the other side.

But as we emerge on the other side, a wave of relief washes over me, easing the tension that had gripped my chest. We've cleared the first hurdle, but the threat still looms large.

As we walk through the bustling terminal filled with an array of duty-free shops, blending into the crowd, every step is an analysed move, each glance a covert assessment of our surroundings. The terminal buzzes with activity, a chaotic symphony of voices, footsteps, and the hum of machinery, providing cover for our presence.

After a brief stop at a shop selling phones and other electronics, we make our way to the business lounge, a sanctuary amidst the airport's chaos. Inside, the atmosphere shifts, the terminal's hustle and bustle replaced by an air of quiet sophistication. Everyone finds a comfortable spot to relax and unwind while we wait for the call to go to the boarding gate.

I sink into a plush armchair, the soft leather enveloping me as I take a moment to catch my breath. The tension of the past few hours begins to melt away, replaced by a sense of calm in the familiar surroundings of the lounge.

"Is there anything I can get anyone from the buffet?" I ask.

Abbie shakes her head, a faint smile playing on her lips as she settles into a nearby couch. "I'm good, thanks, Dad," she replies, her voice betraying a hint of exhaustion.

Bethanie nods in agreement; her gaze is focused on her phone, which she purchased from the duty-free shop, and she taps away at the screen. "Abbie and I are just going to check in with our families," she says, her tone distant.

I exchange a tense glance with Lucy, who sits across from me. Her posture is relaxed.

"Stay vigilant," I say. She nods in response, her eyes darting around the room for any potential threats.

In the lounge's relative calm, we take a rare opportunity to relax, knowing that the next leg of our journey will bring its own set of challenges. But for now, we seize this moment of respite, steeling ourselves for whatever lies ahead.

It isn't long before the screen tells us to go to gate number 5.

"Come on, you lot, let's make a move."

Stepping out of the business lounge, we surge through the terminal, our strides purposeful and our presence blending with the multitude of travellers. Each action is calculated, and every glance is a silent acknowledgement of the lurking perils.

As I approach boarding gate number 5, I become acutely aware of my surroundings, scanning the crowded terminal and everyone within it for any signs of danger. We arrive at the boarding gate with an open sitting area a few minutes later. Two women in airline uniforms and a man at a desk are working to prepare everything for the passengers to board.

We keep our movements casual and inconspicuous. We take up positions within sight of the ramp entrance, tactically placing ourselves to maintain a clear line of sight while blending into the crowd.

As we wait for the call to board, I keep a vigilant watch on our surroundings, aware of the potential dangers that could emerge at any moment, even at this late stage. We may be on the final stretch of our journey, but the threat of Alex Acosta's men still looms large, a constant reminder of the dangers we face in our line of work.

With only a few minutes before boarding, Abbie heads towards the restroom. As I watch her disappear, my instincts kick in, and I scan the surroundings around the restrooms to ensure nobody follows her in.

Minutes pass like an eternity as I wait for her return. The call for our boarding group echoes through the terminal, each announcement a stark reminder of our dwindling time.

Finally, Abbie emerges from the restroom, her expression tense and grim. Before she can utter a word, I see the tell-tale signs of a struggle written on her face.

"What happened?" I ask, my voice calm but urgent as I take in her dishevelled appearance.

Abbie's gaze meets mine, her eyes flashing with intensity. "I was fucking attacked, Dad," she replies, her voice steady despite the lingering tremor of fear. "A young woman in a security uniform."

My heart lurches at her words, the gravity of the situation sinking in. Acosta does have corrupt officials on his payroll. "Are you alright?" I ask, my concern evident as I move closer to her.

Abbie nods, "I managed to subdue the bitch," she says, her voice tinged with a mixture of pride and resolve.

"Don't worry. We will be out of here before anyone finds her." Then, with perfect timing, our boarding group is being called.

The two women at the desk exchange a brief glance as we approach, their expressions neutral but watchful. I meet their gaze with a polite nod, my demeanour calm and collected despite the tension coiled up tight within me.

"Boarding pass, please," one of the women says, her voice brisk but professional as she extends her hand towards me.

I produce our boarding passes, handing them over with practised ease. "Thank you," I reply, my tone polite as I take several steps back to allow the rest of the team to pass through.

As we settle into our plush business-class seats, I'm overcome with relief. The weight of our mission lifts from my shoulders as I sink into the comfortable surroundings of the aircraft cabin.

Drained from the hardships of their ordeal, Abbie and Bethanie succumb to the allure of sleep as the air stewardess delivers the safety brief. Their steady breathing, a testament to their exhaustion, provides a comforting backdrop to the hum of the engines as we prepare for takeoff.

As the plane soars into the sky, I steal a moment to scan the cabin. Simon, always quick to seize an opportunity, wastes no time in exploring the drinks selection, his glass replenished like magic by the attentive flight crew.

I find myself drawn to the in-flight entertainment system, browsing through the selection of movies with anticipation. The prospect of a few hours of uninterrupted rest and relaxation is a welcome respite from the chaos of our recent exploits.

With a sigh of contentment, I recline my seat and settle in for the long journey ahead. The rhythmic drone of the engines lulls me into a state of drowsiness. Before I know it, I, too, succumb to the gentle embrace of sleep, the worries of the world fading into the background as I drift off into dreams.

At long last, after a connection in Miami, our second flight descends towards London Heathrow. Anticipation builds among the passengers, eager to disembark and begin the next leg of their journey. I exchange glances with Abbie and Bethanie, a silent acknowledgement passing between us as we prepare to navigate the bustling airport.

As we make our way to baggage reclaim, I pull Abbie and Bethanie aside, my voice low as I address them. "Listen, girls, I need you to stay sharp. We can't afford to let our guard down now, not after everything we've been through." They nod in understanding, their expressions serious as they grasp the gravity of the situation.

As bags emerge on the carousel, we watch our Bergens pass by several times, ensuring no one takes undue interest in our belongings. It's a standard operating procedure ingrained in us through years of training and experience. In this line of work, you can never be too careful. After the third go-around, I take charge, moving to intercept them before anyone else has a chance to lay claim. Abbie and Bethanie follow my lead.

As we approach the green lane of customs, I gather the team around me, a playful smirk tugging at the corners of my lips. "Alright, folks, listen up," I begin, my tone light but firm. "Let's try to avoid any... shall we say, 'incidents' this time. Remember what happened last year, when Derek decided to play a little prank on George?"

Lucy chuckles, remembering the incident all too well. "Oh, yeah, when he slipped that, uh, unorthodox item into George's Bergen and told the customs official about it?"

Simon stifles a laugh, shooting a knowing glance at Derek. "Poor George. I don't think he's ever quite forgiven you for that one, Derek."

George rolls his eyes, his expression mock-exasperated. "Yeah... that was very funny, Derek. I'm still plotting my revenge—just wait."

Derek grins with mischief in his eyes. "Let the fun begin, George. I'm always up for a challenge."

I chuckle, shaking my head at the banter. "Alright, enough chat. Let's get through customs, and we're on our way. No more shenanigans, got it?"

The team nods in agreement, their smiles reflecting a shared camaraderie. We proceed through customs, laughter ringing in our ears.

After ensuring that everyone passes through without any issues, we proceed to make our way through the bustling terminal. We arrive at the bus station eight minutes later and board the coach heading for Southampton.

The bus ride is quiet. All we can hear is the hum of the engine, providing a backdrop to our collective thoughts and reflections on the mission and the danger we faced. The memories are still fresh in our minds, serving as a constant reminder of the risks we take in our line of work. The coach ride lasts for two hours, a brief respite from the chaos we had just left behind.

When we arrive in Southampton, James, Bethanie's partner, and Hadley are waiting for us at the station. Their presence is a welcome sight in the midst of uncertainty.

"Welcome back, everyone," James greets us, his voice tinged with relief as he runs over to Bethanie and hugs her. "Glad to see you all in one piece."

"Thanks, James. It's good to be home," I reply.

Hadley sprints over to hug his sisters, "Glad you're both OK."

"Hadley, have you been monitoring Abbie and Bethanie's houses? Are any nosey bastards still watching the houses? Plus, are you coming back with me and the rest? We need to debrief you and Gary on Hugo. I would hate any surprises when we get back."

"Yes, Dad, Gary came back over for a few days. Together with James, we monitored both houses and didn't spot any suspicious movements or people, so I thought it was safe for them to go home. I will stay here for a few days in case Abbie and Bethanie need me. Then I'll come over, " says Hadley, still hugging his sister.

"In that case, I'll see you later, girls. Call me if you have any issues, and I'll be straight over," I say, grabbing both my girls and wrapping my arms around them.

Abbie and Bethanie hug each team member, thanking them for coming with their dad to rescue them from Alex Acosta's clutches. Once they have driven off in James' car, the rest of us walk a short distance to the ferry terminal.

As we arrive at the ferry terminal the Red Osprey Ferry is pulling into port, so purchase tickets from the ticket machine and board.

The ferry ride is a nerve-wracking experience. Each passing minute stretches into eternity, as we scan the horizon for any signs of trouble, finding it hard to come down from a mission even though we left the dangers of the cartel far behind.

For the next hour until the ferry arrives in East Cowes, I scan every person who comes close, looking for any signs they are not who they appeared to be and for signs of weakness that I could use to my advantage if the need arises.

The island is not that big, so we reach the park within 30 minutes. As the taxi pulls into the gravel car park of the caravan park, I signal to the driver to stop short of my lodge. I don't want anybody who doesn't need to know where I live, know my home's location. With a quick scan of the parked cars, we ensure no unfamiliar vehicles are lurking nearby, and there are no signs of anyone monitoring my lodge.

With the car park clear, I instruct everyone to stay put while George and I check the lodge for any disturbance.

"It looks clear," I murmur to George, tension thick in the air as we approach the lodge. Every step feels like a potential trap, every shadow holding the promise of danger.

Reaching the lodge, I say, "You take the back, and I'll go this way," pointing toward the front door.

Making my way to the first window, I check the grass for any flattening signs that someone has been standing too long in one place while trying to open a window. There aren't any.

Check the tell-tales on all the windows I left in place before our departure. Relief floods through me as I find them undisturbed, each one exactly as I left it, apart from the one on the door. I detect a sound from the back of the lodge. I turn to face it, ready for a fight.

The figure comes into view. It's George. "All clear around the back," his voice whispers, as we don't know yet if any surprises are waiting inside.

"Not here," I point to the door. "Someone has been inside," I say, grabbing the door handle. With a deep breath, I unlock the door, push it open, and step inside.

George follows behind me, his hand resting on the grip of a 9mm pistol he's removed from the stash under a bush near the door of the lodge. I keep several here for this reason. We move through the lodge, checking each room one at a time, until we are positive nobody is lying in wait.

"All clear," I call out to the team.

With cautious steps, the team enters the lodge. As the door closes behind them, a sense of calm settles over the room, and the familiar warmth of home offers a fleeting sense of sanctuary.

"Fucking made it, and with us all still alive and uninjured apart from the little hole in Simon's arm, and my shoulder," I proclaim as I slump down in my favourite chair.

"We sure did, Steve," says Lucy, sitting on the sofa. "It's all over, apart from getting a debrief from Gary about his and Hadley's task of speaking to Hugo. Suggest before we relax too much, we go straight there and get it out of the way."

"Great idea. We need a few beers; it's part of our post-mission procure," says George, getting back up.

Within 30 minutes, the team walks through the wooden door into the local pub, seeking solace in the dimly lit interior and the promise of a few cold beers. We settle into our favourite seats, the brown couches near the fire. We are in luck; Gary isn't working tonight, but he's here in the boozer.

I catch Gary's eye across the table, a silent acknowledgement passing between us. It's time to get a debrief from him on what happened during his and Hadley's mission to take down Hugo.

"So, what happened, Gary?" I say, leaning forward as I signal for another round of drinks from the person behind the bar. "How did it go?"

Gary sits down at the table; I've seen Gary in countless briefings, but the intensity in his eyes now tells me this one is different.

He begins, his voice steady but low, "Hadley and I went to Southampton to confront Hugo. Here's what happened."

Each word is deliberate, heavy with the gravity of the situation. "We parked in West Quay's underground lot, before making our way to the Marlands shopping centre, which wasn't far. We both knew what was coming."

I exchange a glance with Lucy. We understand the stakes.

"Hadley was ready," Gary continues. "More determined than I've ever seen him. We made our way to the shopping centre. As we neared the entrance, we were closing in on Hugo—the man responsible for your daughters, Steve."

He pauses, letting his words sink in. My jaw clenches at the mention of my girls and what them bastards put them through.

"We found a spot near the entrance, away from prying eyes. Hadley was firm. 'We need to make this count', he said. He knew Hugo wouldn't go down easily. I told him we couldn't let fear dictate our actions. Not now."

His voice softens, but his eyes harden with resolve. "I told Hadley we'd get his sisters back, and I meant it. We had to face Hugo, no matter what."

"We moved closer to Costa Coffee," Gary says, the memory vivid in his mind. "We saw Hugo. He was with a local dealer. The sight of him made my heart race. Hadley confirmed it was him. We couldn't lose this chance."

Gary describes the confrontation, his tone steady. "We approached Hugo. His arrogance was infuriating. Hadley and I didn't mince words. I said, 'We know what your family did. We know about Steve's daughters'. For a moment, I saw a flicker of unease in his eyes. Hadley told Hugo straight that we didn't want his help. He wanted justice for his sisters being kidnapped."

The suspense builds as Gary continues. "Hugo's lieutenant was torn. I could see it. A man caught between loyalty and ambition. He pauses, his gaze intense. "Suddenly, the lieutenant stood up, declaring his rebellion against Hugo. It was chaos. Hadley and I knew we had to move.

"We retreated, regrouping in a stairwell. But Hadley's determination was unyielding. 'We can't let them get away with this', he said. We had to stop them. Hugo was on the move. We followed him to the car park."

Gary's voice tightens with the memory. "Hugo tried to call his father. I called out, 'Asshole, we're not finished with you. Where are Abbie and Bethanie?'. Hugo turned, his arrogance cracking. Hadley didn't hesitate. He disarmed Hugo with a swift kick, his training taking over.

"Hadley's struggle with Hugo was intense." Gary's fists clench as he relives it. "Hadley's determination won out. He pinned Hugo, demanding answers. When Hugo refused, Hadley struck him down."

Gary's eyes meet mine. "I picked up Hugo's gun. The shot rang out. It was over. Hugo was done."

The team is silent, the weight of the mission settling over us. I chuckle, knowing all too well our team's resilience. "Well, I'm glad to hear it," I say, sipping my beer as I lean back in my seat. Now, let's raise a glass to a job well done." I slip Gary a brown envelope containing 10 grand, some of the money we liberated from Lucas.

We spend the next few hours drinking, eating, and laughing — the complete opposite of the past few weeks. With my glass raised, I say, "A big thank you to all of you for helping rescue my daughters. All the drinks tonight are on me."

"You fucking hear that, boys? It looks like a few moths will need new accommodation if that tight arse opens his wallet," says Derek, downing a glass of beer.

"Sure did. Make mine five pints," says George.

Not that I was expecting a 'you're welcome' from the idiots, it wouldn't be them if I received any other type of reply.

With far too much drunk, we head back to my place to settle in for the night. When we arrive back, everyone finds somewhere to crash out until the morning.

The following morning, the sun filters through the curtains, casting a soft glow over the room as I stir in my sleep, waking from a restless slumber. The tell-tale ache in my head reminds me of the previous night's indulgences, and I know that the rest of the team will be suffering the same.

With a groan, I push myself out of bed and make my way to the kitchen. I'm intent on starting breakfast before the others rise. Twenty minutes later, the smell of frying bacon fills the air. I detect the sound of footsteps approaching. Soon, the rest of the team shuffles into the room, their faces etched with the tell-tale signs of hangovers.

"Morning," I greet them, offering a sympathetic smile as I hand each of them a strong brew. "Looks like we all overdid it a bit last night."

There's a chorus of groans and nods of agreement as they accept the coffee, nursing their sore heads. As we sit down to breakfast, the conversation is subdued, punctuated by occasional complaints about the pounding headache that plagues us all.

After breakfast Simon and George head back to the mainland, their obligations calling them away from our temporary respite. Derek opts to stay behind for a few more days, his flight back to St Bethanie not scheduled until later in the week.

The morning is spent dealing with all the kit we couldn't be bothered with yesterday, before it stinks the place out. I just finish when the phone rings.

Lucy picks up the phone. "It's Simon," she says, handing me the phone.

"Hi, Simon, anything wrong?" I say.

"Nothing, Steve. Remember that job we didn't take as we went to get Abbie and Bethanie? Well, it's still on if we are interested.

Purchase the Covert-Ops box set for a great price.

Click here: https://www.green-cat.shop/steve-barker

Glossary

Army Chuckin	Stew
Bashered Up	Made Camp, Erected Shelter
Bergen	Backpack
Binos	Binoculars
Call Sign DR	Derek Radio
Call Sign GD	George Dog
Call Sign LK	Lorna Killer
Call Sign S3	Steve 3(RGJ)
Call Sign TS	Tanky Simon
Chimp	Mind / Anger Management program used in the treatment of PTSD
Click	Kilometre
Dhobi Dust	Washing Powder
Donkey Walloper	Tank Driver
Egg Banjo	Egg Sandwich
Endex	End of Mission
Escaped Librarian	A term used in the treatment of PTSD
Grunt	Ground Reconnaissance Untrainable
LZ	Landing Zone
Maggot	Sleeping Bag
Mickey	Cheap Wristwatch
OP	Observation Post
PAYG	Pay As You Go
Pit	Bed
Polo Donkey	Horse/Donkey
Range Card	A drawing or sketch used in OP's which shows potential locations and distance to targets.
Roger or Roger That	Military Speak for OK

Roger, Out	End Of Radio Message
Roger, Over	Waiting for Reply From the Radio Message
RV	Rendezvous – Meeting Point
Shanks Pony	Walking
SLR	Self Loading Rifle
Stag	Sentry Duty
Tab	Walk or Hike

ABOUT THE AUTHOR

I was born in 1962 in Farnham, Hampshire, England. I lived in several places before moving to Southampton near the south coast, where I lived before I joined the British Army.

I left School in 1979 and, within a month, joined the Royal Green Jackets in Winchester; after completing training joined 3RGJ in Cambridge. I continued to serve until 1989.

In 2017 I was diagnosed with PTSD from three life-threatening events during my service. As part of my treatment at Combat Stress, someone suggested I should begin writing.

I have always written short pieces of work which never go past the printer—writing the first two books on cruising as I love cruising.

During my last two-week stay at Combat Stress in April 2019, I wrote my first ever book on poetry called 'Poetry from the PTSD Mind,' which takes the reader on a journey from the bad times to the good.

When the world got locked down in 2020, I spent my time writing the first of the Covert-Ops series Danger in Paradise, followed a year later by Danger on the Island. Then in 2022, the third book in the series, The Golden Camel, was published, and in 2024, The Extraction.

FOR MORE INFO ABOUT OUR BOOKS AND SERVICES,
PLEASE VISIT

WWW.GREEN-CAT.SHOP

Green Cat Books

www.ingramcontent.com/pod-product-compliance
Lightning Source LLC
Chambersburg PA
CBHW060946030726
47503CB00003B/752